Diamonds in Black Sand

Ann Marston

FIVE RIVERS PUBLISHING

WWW.FIVERIVERSPUBLISHING.COM

Queen Street, P.O. Box 293, Neustadt, ON N0G 2M0, Canada.

www.fiveriverspublishing.com

Diamonds in Black Sand, Copyright © 2016 by Ann Marston.

Edited by Lorina Stephens.

Cover Copyright © 2016 by Jeff Minkevics.

Interior design and layout by Éric Desmarais.

Titles set in BlackChancery Font designed by Doug Miles. It is a calligraphic outline font based on the public domain bitmap font of the same name. It's a good looking and useful display font, lending itself well to many occasions.

Text set in Taviraj designed by by Cadson Demak. It is a serif Latin and looped Thai typeface that has a wide structure that ensures readability and legibility.

Published in Canada

Library and Archives Canada Cataloguing in Publication

Marston, Ann, author Diamonds in black sand / Ann Marston.

Issued in print and electronic formats.

ISBN 978-1-988274-19-5 (paperback).—ISBN 978-1-988274-20-1 (epub)

I. Title. PS8576.A7593D53 2017   C813'.54   C2016-906321-6 C2016-906322-4

For Laura and Dan

Contents

Prologue

THIS IS THE way the bards tell the story, the timbre of their trained voices rising and falling with the dramatic rhythm of the words while their nimble fingers skillfully stroke the harpstrings to augment the tension and drama of the saga. How much of the first part is true, and how much is bardic romance, I cannot tell you. But I can certainly attest to the truth of the rest of the story because I was there. I witnessed most of it unfolding...

Culhain mac Wellyn, King of Celyddon, fell ill in the spring of the year, just before Beltane when the young grass in the glens sprang up rich and lush, and the buds on the coretrees swelled red and bursting on the wide-reaching branches. As the life of the countryside waxed, his life waned until he was no longer able to sit his throne, and took to his bed. It was then his eldest son, Fergus mac Culhain, took the throne as Regent to rule in his father's stead until Culhain regained his health, or sooner died.

For three years, Regent Prince Fergus ruled well enough, although men said he was no Culhain. Men also said the High Priest of the Brotherhood of Uthoni, one Padreg of Nairn, might be rising rather too quickly in the Regent Prince's favour. But whether because of this, or despite it as Padreg's detractors would have it, Celyddon prospered. Her fields and herds, her flocks and forests, her towns and merchants, all provided well for the lairds and their tenants. In turn, by tax and tithe, the lairds and burghers provided well for the Regent Prince. But even as Celyddon flourished, Culhain weakened and wasted, fading more with each passing season, and no medician, no priest or sage, could say what ailment slowly sapped the life of the king, nor could they heal him.

In the spring of the fourth year of Fergus's Regency, all Celyddon was taken by surprise and watched aghast as Fergus accused his younger brother Daryn of being in league with the Feyii, that strange, almost-but-not-quite-human race of far-distant Lysandia, and conspiring with them to kill Culhain by magic.

Daryn stood accused of plotting to usurp the throne for the Feyish Queen. Although he roundly denied causing his father's illness by magic, or by any other means, and denied any but common diplomatic and trade ties with the Feyii, he could not deny that no other cause could be found for Culhain's illness.

The priests of the Brotherhood of Uthoni, who worshipped the Father God but scorned the Mother Goddess, had been long envious of the power of the Feyii, who paid special homage to the Mother. As one man, they rose under Padreg in agreement to the charge against

Daryn of murder by magic. It was, Padreg stated, only by power of the prayers and piety of the Brotherhood, and by the intervention of the Father Himself through the Brotherhood that Culhain remained alive, albeit gravely ill.

A triumvirate of Regent, Judge and High Priest condemned Daryn to death for high treason against the Crown. Guards took the young prince to the Tower of Tears in Dundregan. His cell contained one narrow window, which looked out over the courtyard.

For five days, Daryn stood calmly by the window, watching the construction of the scaffold where his life must end so abruptly. He was not yet twenty years old. He stubbornly refused to confess his crimes, scorning the absolution offered by Padreg to comfort his soul as it passed to the judgment of the Father.

On the morning of the execution, when the duly cheerless and solemn procession of guards and priests came for the prince, they found the door locked tight, but the cell empty. They found no trace of Daryn anywhere, and no clue to how he escaped.

The Tower guards, awake and alert as ever, were as dumbfounded as the execution committee. They could not explain the disappearance of their prisoner, even after Fergus in a rage had executed fully a quarter of them in Daryn's stead.

Fergus flew into a fury, raving of Feyish magic and plots. He sent every soldier, every sheriff, every sheriffman in Celyddon in search of Daryn. They combed the countryside, even to the outlaw lairs in the High Crags. They found no trace of the missing prince.

After half a year of futile searching, Fergus called off his dogs. He announced that Daryn had gone to the Feyii in Lysandia, where he continued to conspire with the Feyish Queen in a plot to take over Celyddon.

When Fergus tried to close Celyddon to the Feyii and root out all traces of magic manifest in either Feyi or human, Culhain roused himself from his sick bed only long enough to forbid it. Celyddon needed the trade with the Feyii, he said, and it needed the very few men and women who had magic. Without the trade provided by the humans and Feyii who manned the Out-ships that, through the magic of those Outsiders, plied the storm and current-wracked high seas outside the deadly barrier reefs, Celyddon would wither and die, even as he himself was withering and dying. There would be no purge while Culhain lived.

Fergus seethed with anger and frustration, but he could not gainsay his father. Culhain remained, after all, the King. And, while Celyddon prospered even as her King languished and weakened, the Council of Lairds would never agree to deposing him in favour of Fergus. In due course, as time moved in its own implacable fashion, Fergus would inherit the throne. Until then, no change would occur.

Fergus settled back to bide his time.

Chapter One

THERE WERE FOUR of them, all wearing the deep, midnight blue of a seafaring Out-ship crew, two men and two women. One of the men wore the silver insignia of a Communicator on the sleeve of his tunic. Behind them, the tall masts of the ship itself swayed against the sky in slow rhythm with the turning tide. Beside the smaller In-ships—fisher vessels and stubby coastal traders—it looked graceful and purposeful as the wing of a seagull.

The four crew members laughed together as they walked toward the gate in the perimeter fence between Portside and Cityside where I stood watching them. They wore short swords at their hips, more for ceremony, it appeared, rather than actual use. Ornate hilts of daggers protruded from the tops of their soft boots. As they came nearer, I saw that one of the women was Feyish, tall and golden-skinned, violet-eyed and very beautiful. She wore the emerald badge of a Windcaster on the shoulder of her blue tunic.

I had seldom seen an Out-ship crew before. They didn't have much call to stop at a backwater place like Caliburn. When they did come to Celyddon, they usually went to Dundregan, the Capital, twenty leagues north on the coast where trade churned the city as heat boils water in a pot. I had only seen one Feyi before, too, and that was the old man who had come to teach the Commonwealth standard trade language at the school when I was thirteen.

The other woman, dark-haired and blue-eyed like a Gael, noticed me hanging over the railed fence and smiled at me. She touched the sleeve of the Communicator's tunic and leaned slightly toward him.

"Out-port brat," she said in amusement. "There's one on every fence."

She spoke Standard, not Gael, but I understood her well enough. Thon shanMetla had done a thorough job of teaching and I had been an eager and attentive student.

The Communicator turned his head quickly to look at me. He appeared to be a Human, but he had Feyish eyes, deep violet flecked with gold, and something of the characteristic honey tones to his hair and skin. I thought he might be a Fey-Halfblood: part Feyi, part Human. I drew back respectfully from the fence as he opened the gate and came Cityside. He was young, appearing to be perhaps in his late teens, but he wore the responsibility of his position and the distinction of his uniform with the maturity of a man much older. He stopped a little more than an armslength from me.

One of the things I'd always noticed about Outsiders, the men and women who sailed the vast Wildesea of the world, was their eyes. They're not like the eyes of other people, the Insiders and the Groundsiders. They look to be larger, the colours in the irises deeper, more vivid. They seem to be somewhat blurred, almost diffused, as if Outsiders looked at things differently from other people, or saw things that nobody else could see. My father's eyes had been like that.

Meeting the Communicator's gaze was a bit like a physical shock. It was vaguely disturbing. I almost felt as if I should recognize him, but of course, I didn't. It made me uneasy, but I couldn't look away from the intense gaze that seemed to penetrate right down into me, into the depths of my spirit to my inner soul.

A chill ran down my spine. This was a man who could Communicate over the vast distances of the world, mind to mind, with other Communicators. Rumour had it they could see into men's minds, into their very hearts. Right then, transfixed by that violet and gold gaze, I almost believed it.

A memory. Vague and nebulous. Like a dream. I was very small. Someone who seemed as tall as a corewood tree crouched down, sitting on her heels, to bring her face onto a level with mine. Lustrous, clear violet eyes looked into mine. Eyes like those of the young Communicator. Eyes that inspired trust. Unsettling eyes, yet reassuring at the same time. A smile, gentle fingers touching my forehead, and a soft voice saying, "Keep an eye on this one, Drew. I think he's got all the makings."

"Did that belong to one of your parents, lad?" The Communicator's voice brought me out of my reverie with a start. His gaze had gone to the gold chain I wore around my neck and the little gold maple leaf dangling from it, the insignia of an Out-ship officer. Self-consciously, I put up my hand to grasp it.

"Yes, sir," I said a little breathlessly. "My father, sir." Someone like him, an Out-ship Communicator, taking the time to speak with me. I could hardly believe my good fortune. He fascinated me, standing there so trim and confident in his uniform. He represented everything I desperately wanted for myself—Outside beyond the barrier reefs, the chaotic, measureless sea, all the far places.

"What ship?" His voice was friendly and interested, not at all patronizing as I almost expected.

"The *Lyric*, sir." The title of respect rose automatically to my lips even though he wasn't much older than I was. The uniform demanded it. "Out of Eryndor, in the north. My father was her Third Officer." I was proud of my father, and it must have shown in my voice and in my face because the Communicator smiled.

"What was his name? Perhaps I know him."

"Drew mac Brychan clan Morgian, sir."

The Communicator shook his head regretfully. "No, I'm afraid I don't know him. Probably before my time."

"It was ten years ago, sir."

He grinned. "Then definitely before my time. What's your name, lad?"

"Iain mac Drew, sir. Born to Clan Rothsey, born for Clan Morgian."

"How old are you, Iain?"

"Thirteen, sir. Almost fourteen."

He smiled again. "You spend a lot of time here at the Outport, do you?"

The woman who looked as if she might be a Gael had referred to me as an Outport Brat. I suppose I was. I spent every moment I could watching the fisher vessel and coastal traders coming and going, hoping for a glimpse of an Out-ship. "Yes, sir. Ever since I was a child. But I've hardly ever seen an Out-ship before."

He glanced over his shoulder at the tall masts swaying against the intense blue of the sky. "Well, she's a truly beautiful ship, that one," he said. "But not so grand as some."

"She's grand enough."

Amusement glinted in his eyes, as if we were fellow conspirators. "I used to be just like you," he said. "I saw my first Out-ship when I was a little younger than you. I was twelve."

"As grand as that one?"

"The *Farseeker*? Oh, much grander." He looked at me speculatively. "You speak very good Standard, Iain."

"I had a very good teacher, sir."

"My name is Glyn shanBreyor. Can you remember that?"

"Yes, sir, I can." My curiosity got the better of the good manners my Aunt Bronwyn had drilled into me. "Sir?"

"Yes?"

I hesitated, then asked. "Are you a Fey-Halfblood?" Then I looked away, appalled and embarrassed at the effrontery of the question. What if I'd offended him?

But I hadn't. He merely inclined his head in acknowledgment. "As a matter of fact, I am."

"I've never met a Fey-Halfblood before."

Laughter danced in those strange, gold-flecked eyes. "I'm not surprised," he said gravely. "I'll admit there aren't so very many of us. We're not that thick on the ground. But we're no different from anybody else."

The Feyish woman called to him. "Glyn, we're going to be late if you don't hurry."

"I'll be only a moment," he said, glancing at her, then turning back to me. "You want to go Outside, don't you, Iain?"

"Yes, sir," I said fervently.

He became suddenly serious, his sober gaze holding

mine for a long moment. "Yes, I can tell." He reached up and unpinned one of the silver Communicator's flashes, the starburst of the Nail Star behind a small trefoil, from his sleeve. "When you turn eighteen, lad, you take this to the Outsiders Guild in Dundregan. Tell them I sent you. You'll get your chance to sail an Outship."

He held out the flash. I stepped forward hesitantly and reached for it. He took my hand, pressed the flash into my palm, and folded my fingers around it. "You'll remember my name, won't you, Iain?"

"Glyn shanBreyor," I said, clutching the flash tightly. "I'll remember. You can bet I will.

"I *will* be betting on it," he said.

He turned then and was gone with his friends. I heard the other man say something about getting the errand done quickly so they could leave this dour city in their wake as soon as possible.

The clock in the Sanctuary bell tower struck the hour. I looked up, startled. I had forgotten the time and would be left behind again if I didn't hurry.

I barely made it to the Square in time. My Uncle Durstan was just crossing the dusty street to the wagon when I fetched up against the battered oaken footboard, panting and out of breath. The sun had almost dipped below the horizon, but the rays still gilded the soaring clock tower on the Sanctuary. Durstan gave me a shrewd, penetrating glance.

"You're lucky this time, lad," he said in a mildly neutral voice. But I caught the faint glint of amusement deep in his grey eyes. Being left once to walk the three leagues home from the city had cured me of my tendency to linger overlong after the time Durstan had told me to be back by the wagon. That wasn't an easy lesson to forget.

Durstan climbed onto the creaking seat, picked up the traces and unwound them from the brake handle. I scrambled into the back with the pile of provisions my aunt Bronwyn had asked for. Durstan rattled the traces and the horses, Flicker and Fan, eager to be home and wanting the oats waiting for them, set off at a brisk pace while I wedged myself snug and comfortable, between two sacks of mealflour.

I still held the silver Communicator's flash clutched in the palm of my hand. My body heat had warmed it so that it no longer felt cold to my skin, but I could feel the distinct points of the starburst against my fingers where they held it so tightly. In memory, I saw him again, reaching up to unpin the flash, amusement and something else in those strange, Feyish eyes of his. Very slowly, I opened my hand and stared down at the silver flash.

I would not be eighteen for another four and a half years. It seemed like such a long time to wait. But then I could take this to the Outsiders Guild and apply for apprenticeship. Outside. The vast reaches of the seas beyond the barrier reefs where none but the Outsiders, aided by Windcasters and Pathfinders and Communicators and Farseers, dared to go. All the fabled lands and cities that were only names in books to me. I shut my eyes and let myself dream while Durstan guided Flicker and Fan through the narrow streets of Caliburn and out into the wide, green countryside where the land began to climb toward the immense, sheer walls of the grey crags.

Then I sighed and closed my hand again, hiding the flash.

A dream. It was only a dream, and that was all it could ever be. My uncle Durstan would never let me go Outside. He would never let me leave the Freehold croft or Glenaidyn. He had taken me in when my parents died in a landslip seven years ago. I owed him liege, one year for every year he served as guardian for me. He needed me to help him run the Freehold while his son Maelgrun attended the College in Dundregan. Maelgrun was six years older than I, and would one day be Laird of Glenaidyn. But he himself would run neither the Freehold nor the croft. He took no pleasure from the running of it and working it as Durstan did. He would become just another absentee laird who let others work his land, uncaring about the land or its people, except for what they could give him. He had political ambitions, ambitions in which Durstan encouraged him. A Freeholder laird who took up a career outside the Holding needed a younger brother, or a liege-bound to run the Freeholding in his absence. And that liege-bound was I.

My uncle Durstan and my aunt Bronwyn were kind enough to me. Durstan had been very fond of his sister, my mother, and had liked and admired my father. He and Bronwyn treated me like a younger son in the household. But like most younger sons, I would never be free unless Durstan or Maelgrun released me. And I couldn't see that happening in my foreseeable future.

In the midst of summer in these latitudes of Celyddon, the light lingered a long time after the sun went down. As we made our way along the rutted track, it faded so slowly, it surprised me to realize it was gone. I looked up to the stars that were beginning to glimmer in the deep blue velvet of the sky. Somewhere, there was a Pathfinder looking at those same stars, charting a course through the turbulence of the trackless sea toward a land I could only dream of. I wanted to be Out there. I wanted to see these stars from the deck of an Out-ship, to see lands nobody in Celyddon ever dreamed of seeing. I wanted to meet Feyii, and Dwarvenfolk, and the almost mythical Trolls of Gradchivale. I wanted to know if there really were firedrakes at the far edges of the seas where all the maps depicted the fierce and fiery beasts with the legend, Here be dragons.

I opened my hand and looked down at the silver flash. It gleamed in my palm, reflecting the ashen light of the stars.

Glyn shanBreyor. I would never forget his name. But it would do me no good. I was bound to Durstan, I was bound to the Croft, and I was bound to Glenaidyn. The far reaches of the Wildesea had to remain only a dream. I pinned the silver flash to the thin gold chain around my throat, and pulled the collar of my shirt close to hide it.

Warm, yellow light gleamed in welcome from the windows of the stone-built house as we approached the croft. My great-great-grandfather had built the house of the ancient granite taken from the crags that curved around it to hold the main yard cupped in their wide shelter. He built it big enough to raise his family and the families of succeeding generations with room enough to grow. It was a stately house, low and broad, shaded by huge coretrees and evergreens. Ivy and flowering vines climbed the rough, grey stone of the broad verandah that stretched around three sides of the house and kept it cool even in the heat of summer. I could never approach it from the road out of Caliburn without remembering the first time I had seen it, nearly asleep and curled in Bronwyn's lap. I had thought it looked like a Feyish castle from the ancient bardic songs my mother sang to me at bedtime.

Bronwyn had a meal waiting when we came in. When there were just the three of us, she saw no reason why we needed to use the elegantly polished table in the formal dining room. The kitchen was fine for family, comfortable and cozy. Durstan and Bronwyn may have been Laird and Lady Rothsey of Glenaidyn, but neither stood all too firmly on ceremony when there was no need.

Rhea and Mag, the two servant girls, rushed around under Bronwyn's direction placing jugs of milk and ale, cool from the springhouse, on the table of scoured-white corewood planks. Bronwyn smiled at me as I scrubbed my hands at the kitchen basin before seating myself at the table.

"I see you didn't lose him this time, Durstan," she said, gently teasing me.

Durstan took his place at the head of the table. "It was a near thing," he said. "Down at the Outport again, gawking at the strangers, weren't you, boy?" There was no glint of amusement in his eyes now.

I ducked my head to avoid his disapproving stare. "Aye, I was."

"Now, Durstan, go soft," Bronwyn said. She reached out from her place at the foot of the table and touched my hair lightly, smiling again as Mag set down a pot of tea before her. "He's just a lad, after all, and boys like that sort of thing."

I turned to her eagerly, still flushed with the excitement of the encounter. "There was an Out-ship there in port. And there was a Feyish woman with them. I met one of them and spoke with him—"

Durstan banged down a platter of bread slices in front of me. "I did not hold with that stranger coming to teach that foreign tongue to school children," he said. "And I certainly do not hold with boys your age maundering about Outports and imperiled by foreign ideas."

"But I met a Communicator," I said. "His name is Glyn shanBreyor. A real Communicator—"

"Foreigners and strangers," Durstan said. "It's unnatural for a man to talk with another man's mind. It smacks of witchery and you very well know it."

I also very well knew better than to argue with him. My excitement died and I dropped my gaze to my bowl which Bronwyn had filled generously with potato-leek soup. And I knew better than to let Durstan see the defiance and disagreement I knew blazed in my eyes.

"Hurry and finish eating," Durstan said more mildly now. "There's still your chores to be done before bed. And don't forget tomorrow you have to ride out and see to the mob on the west mountain. They'll be needing the foot-rot medicine."

I touched one hand to the small bulge of the flash beneath the fabric of my shirt. It wasn't witchery. It was the wondrous and necessary magic woven firmly into the weft and welt of the Outsiders Guild. Rare in the Feyii; rarer still in men, perhaps, but not unknown.

"Did you hear me, boy?" Durstan said, cocking an eyebrow at me, his spoon poised halfway between his bowl and his mouth.

"Aye, sir, I heard you. Tomorrow I'll see to the sheep on the west mountain."

I didn't mind riding out to see to the sheep. I liked working with the sturdy and crafty little animals. Celyddon had few exports, but the wool from the hardy hybrid sheep was in high demand everywhere. Woven into fabric for clothing, or spun into yarn, it was soft and warm, and very nearly indestructible. It had a unique, silky sheen that gave a soft glow to any colours used to dye it. It could be used for anything from a lady's Court gown to a protective tarpaulin. Durstan's Freeholding was one of the biggest in the realm and Glenaidyn one of the richest. His sheep produced some of the finest wool in the country. One of the reasons Maelgrun had such a good chance to succeed at Court was the fact that his father was one of the wealthiest men in Celyddon.

My evening chores done presently, I went back in to listen as Durstan read aloud from the Testaments. As usual, he chose passages that praised both the Mother and the Father. He had never said anything aloud, but I knew he had little patience with the Brotherhood of Uthoni and their campaign to denigrate the Mother and exalt only the Father.

When Durstan finished, he dismissed me, and I climbed to my second floor room. It had been a long day and I was tired. The little silver flash still hung around my neck, its small weight comforting nestled there next to my skin. I took it off and looked at it by the light of the twin moons. It fit well into the palm of my hand. Very carefully, I put it away in the carved tanglewood box on my bureau. I would keep it, along with the little maple leaf emblem, as another touchstone for dreams.

I rode out the next morning on one of the broad-footed, stocky horses we bred on the Freehold. I had raised Brindle from a colt and broken him to the saddle myself four years ago. He was ugly and perhaps ill-shaped, but he was smarter than most of the other horses, and he was deft and sure-footed as a cat among the cliffs and crags of the high country where the sheep liked to spend the hot summer season.

In the cool of the high country summer, the soft, bluish fleece grew long and fine, like silk. Before the season turned, the rangemen and their dogs would drive this mob down to the home paddock for shearing. But right now, I had to dose them against the foot-rot disease that could wipe out a mob in days if it ever got started. There were just a few more than three hundred sheep in this little mob. It might take me five or six days to complete the task. Brewing the decoction from the herbs and pouring it down the throats of the sometimes reluctant sheep, I could do no more than fifty a day, sixty if I encountered any cooperative sheep. Chancy thing, that, though.

But this was a task I enjoyed. A one-room bothy built of strong corewood stood at the edge of the high country meadow, but I seldom used it unless the weather turned wet. I preferred to sleep out where I could see the stars. That was another thing Durstan didn't hold with. I don't know how many times I'd heard him say to Bronwyn, "He'd be getting all those strange ideas from his father, I've no doubt. You'll ken I didn't hold with Meaghan marrying that foreigner."

Then Bronwyn replied, "Nonsense. You liked Drew."

And Durstan invariably said, "Aye, well, I did, at that. He wasn't like those others. He was—"

"Meaghan's husband and a good man," Bronwyn always finished the exchange with the same words, and Durstan nodded reluctantly.

My father, Drew clan Morgian, was an Outsider. He spoke Gael with the soft, slurring accent of Eyrindor in it. He was Third Officer on an Eyrindorian Out-ship that called regularly at the Outport in Dundregan. He met my mother, Meaghan mab Lludd, while she was in Dundregan attending the College. They were married before Durstan, as head of the family, Laird of Glenaidyn and Clan Rothsey, had much of a chance to say anything about it. And once they were wed, he could do little about it because it seemed that I was on the way a little earlier than convention might deem respectable.

From my father I had inherited more than just the desire to be Outside. I had his dark hair, black enough to send blue highlights back into the sun, and his deep blue eyes, and I gave promise of attaining his height. My mother had been fair with eyes like Durstan's, as grey as the sea under a mist. Bronwyn told me they were a good looking couple, and well-suited to each other.

I believe they were happy together. I can remember my mother singing to herself and to me as she worked. I remember her and my father laughing together when he was home. I lay in my bed of an evening and listened to their voices, and felt safe. I was only five when the earth tremour collapsed the building, killing them both, along with twelve others. Their bodies had protected me. Rescue workers found her curled around me, and my father holding her. He had tried and failed to save her, but together, they had saved me. All I had left of them was the delicate little gold replica of his Third Officer insignia that she had worn on a fine chain around her neck, and which I now wore about my own neck.

I didn't have many memories of him, but one was clear and vivid. I was still small enough to be carried comfortably when he took me outside one night to the top of one of the coastal watch towers and showed me the stars and the moon-silvered sea. His sense of awe and wonder was contagious. I felt it ripple through me as I followed his sweeping gesture.

"Out there, Iain," he said quietly, "out there is more beauty and wonder than a thousand Celyddons can hold. Someday, you'll be old enough to go there, too."

So now I lay wrapped in my sleepsack, cushioned by the thick grass, and looked at the stars. I dreamed of the cold, clear reaches of the Wildesea while the little, pale blue sheep slept all around me in the shelter of the Great Crags that circled Celyddon.

Dosing the sheep took me six days, working at a leisurely pace because I was in no hurry to finish and go back to the croft. I loved working out in the meadow. Only a few hundred paces up the slope from my makeshift pens, the rugged grey faces of the bare cliffs rose steeply and swiftly into the Great Central Desert that, together with the Great Crags themselves, held Celyddon protected and separate from the rest of the continent as surely as the barrier reefs separated all the lands from the wilds of the seas. Up there, nothing grew but scrub thorn bushes, flat-leaved cacti, and rusty-green lichen. But down here on the upper slopes of the glen, the patches of foxgrass grew almost thigh-high, starred with creamy pale moonflowers, red and yellow whipfern blossoms that looked like tiny pairs of folded hands, and the blue-purple hare's clover.

It was warm. The sun's heat was like a tangible weight on my bare shoulders as I worked, stripped to the waist. The heat drew the thick, sweet scent of the blaeberry bushes into the air like a haze, and the sheep drowsed lazily, unworried and placid, as I moved among them with the nozzled skin bag filled with the foot-rot decoction. The sheep struggled briefly as I trapped them between thigh and forearm and squirted the still warm liquid down their throats. I couldn't blame them for struggling. I'd tasted the foul brew once. The sheep probably found it as bitter and disagreeable as I had.

Some time during the last night I spent under the stars in the high country, Culhain mac Wellyn, King of Celyddon, died quietly and peacefully in his sleep, and Regent Prince Fergus set in motion the plans for his own coronation and rule.

Chapter Two

MAELGRUN CAME HOME a fortnight after the death of King Culhain. No one looking at Maelgrun need ask who his father was. He had Durstan's brown hair and grey eyes. But his mouth was folded small and sulky where Durstan's was level and firm.

The corners of that mouth turned down in a grimace of enmity when I came into the house to wash up after my chores. Durstan had just begun the offering before the meal as I dried my hands and slipped quietly into my chair.

I could never remember anything but antagonism from Maelgrun, ever since the day Bronwyn and Durstan had brought me home to the Freeholding from Dundregan, still stunned and numbed by the grief and confusion of the loss of my parents. He stood by, stiff and angry as

Bronwyn tried to ease my bewilderment and pain. No child of five can fully comprehend death. All I knew was that my parents had gone away and left me alone, and I couldn't understand why I had been abandoned.

After the funeral, the mourners gathered in the main hall of the house. Too many people I didn't know hugged me and murmured words of pity to disguise the morbid curiosity I felt in them, even then. Finally, overwhelmed and confused, I tried to escape by hiding in the byre, flinging myself face down into the straw, unable to stop crying.

Maelgrun found me there. Dust and bits of straw clung to my good clothes, and my face felt itchy and gritty with it. I hadn't heard him come in, but I knew he was there. I rolled over and sat up, pulling myself into a tight, defensive curl against the tightly-bound sheaves of straw. Contempt drew down the corners of his mouth.

"Miserable little cry-baby," he said. "Mewling suckling pig."

"Am not!" I tried to wipe my eyes with my sleeve.

He poked at me with the toe of his boot. I flinched away. He sneered and kicked me again, not quite hard enough to hurt. "Bleating little lamb," he said. "Only lowborns snivel like that. Sissy."

"Am not," I said again, but couldn't stop the tears running down my cheeks.

With unerring instinct, he taunted me with the one thing that could hurt most. "Your parents went away and left you because they didn't want you anymore. They're gone and mine won't ever love you because they love me."

All the pain, all the bewilderment and confusion in me suddenly coalesced into anger. It couldn't help but show on my face. I looked up at him and saw his foot twisted and lame, the way he had been born, before the Feyish

Healers had corrected the club foot. I saw the twist in his mind caused by the fear that his parents didn't want him and were ashamed of him because he had not been born perfect. And I saw his hatred of me because I had been born whole.

Spitefully, I wished his foot still twisted and deformed. I wished him far away and hopelessly lost and afraid. I wished every painful and humiliating thing I could imagine onto him. I imagined black worms crawling through his head. Silently, I called him every foul name I had ever heard. To my astonishment, he went white and staggered back a pace.

"Stop that!" he cried. "Shut up. You just shut up."

I blinked in surprise. I must have been muttering aloud without realizing it.

"You stay away from me, you little monster," he shouted. "You just stay away from me, you hear?" He turned and ran out of the byre.

Bronwyn found me there an hour later, still crying. On her knees in the straw, she folded me into her arms and rocked me gently. I tried to tell her how lost and alone I felt, but I couldn't speak through my tears even if I could have found the words. Bronwyn murmured, "I know, little love. I know." And I found I didn't have to tell her because she truly did know.

I steered clear of Maelgrun as much as I could after that. Fortunately, it wasn't difficult. Our age difference put us in separate spheres. When he wasn't in school, he was with Durstan and the rangemen in the pastures, or with the weapons master in Caliburn, learning swordwork as befit a young noble. My chores kept me close to the croft yard, helping Bronwyn and the house servants in the yard and garden. When we couldn't avoid each other, he pointedly and obviously ignored me. It wasn't until he went way to College in Dundregan that he let his animosity toward me out into the open again.

He had not been home for nearly a year, and he was brimful and bubbling over with news about the King's funeral and Regent Prince Fergus. Durstan had barely finished speaking the offering before Maelgrun plunged in with his news.

"King Fergus is going to enact a new law," he said enthusiastically.

"He's still Regent Prince until the coronation come Imbolc," Durstan said calmly. "There's another four seasons of mourning before he can be crowned."

Maelgrun's mouth turned down at the corners, but he continued with no less zeal. "Fergus is declaring Daryn wolfshead and traitor. There'll be a reward of a hundred gold weyrins on his head."

Bronwyn looked at him blankly. "Can he do that? Daryn is still Second-heir. Culhain never disinherited him."

Maelgrun dismissed her with a contemptuous wave of his hand. "Well, Fergus will be King, and he can do as he likes about Daryn. It goes with the rest of the new law."

"What law is that?" I asked, only mildly curious. Politics held little interest for me.

Maelgrun smiled grimly as he began to eat. "The law that will stop this nonsense and heresy," he said. "There will be no more truck with witchery in Celyddon."

"Do you mean Outsiders?" I put down my fork and stared at him in astonishment. "Windcasters? Pathfinders? Communi—"

"Witchery," Maelgrun said and stared at me, his grey eyes narrowed and cold. "Witchery, all of it. Feyish magic from the Abyss."

"The Abyss?" Bronwyn shook her head in protest. "Surely if it comes from anywhere, it comes from the Mother."

Maelgrun met her eyes coldly. "Padreg says it's the same thing," he said.

Bronwyn paled, but she said nothing. Her hand went to the bodice of her gown, behind which I knew hung a small golden wreath on a fine chain, a symbol of the Mother and the Unbroken Circle. Durstan glanced at her, concern tracing a line between his brows, then he turned to Maelgrun.

"That's only Padreg's opinion," he said mildly enough.

Maelgrun snorted. "It's the opinion of the whole of the Brotherhood of Uthoni," he said. "And that of King—Regent Prince Fergus, come to that."

I stirred my vegetables with my fork, my appetite suddenly gone completely. In fact, I felt almost breathless. "But banning the Outsiders." I put down my fork. "The Commonwealth—"

"The Commonwealth is riddled with witchery," Maelgrun said. "Celyddon is better off out of it."

I stared at him, nonplussed. "You mean, we'd leave the Commonwealth?"

"Aye." Maelgrun nodded smugly. "We'll have no more to do with the vile, unhuman creatures."

"But who'll buy the wool? And the planefish?" The Commonwealth of Races might well be able to get along without Celyddon's wool and planefish, but Celyddon would have a difficult time surviving without the Commonwealth as a market for those exports. I had learned that much in school, even though the facts and figures and the mechanics of trade and commerce glazed me over with boredom.

"We'll allow coastal traders in, as always," Maelgrun said. "But they'll not be allowed to leave the Outport to come cityside, and we will allow no witches to be with them."

"It will be difficult to trade with the lands across the

Wildesea without Out-ships." Bronwyn's fingers still lightly touched the bodice of her gown. She turned gracefully to take a platter of fresh bread from Mag. "There will be those who won't be happy about that."

"Others can trade with Outsiders," Maelgrun said. "We won't soil our hands by dealing with Feyish witchery."

"Aye." Durstan reached for the bread. "The Regent Prince may have the right idea there."

"He'll rid the realm of strangers and foreigners," Maelgrun said. "Celyddon will have no truck with them and their heresies. Nor with their support of Daryn's treason, either."

"We'll be well rid of the strangers and their witchery," Durstan said. He frowned at me and cut off my protest before I could begin. "And as for Daryn's treason... We'll leave that be, I think."

"The realm will be safer with Daryn dead," Maelgrun said, shooting a venomous glance at his father

Bronwyn and Durstan exchanged glances across the table. I had heard them whispering in the night when they thought me sound asleep. Neither of them had ever been convinced that Daryn was a traitor. Durstan was not one of the Lairds of the Council of Lairds who voted to hang the prince. His voice and several others had been raised against it. The Regent Prince had swayed only a little more than half the Council to his side. It had been a near thing—too near for the Regent Prince's liking, some said.

People said Fergus, urged on by the High Priest Padreg, was determined to bring about instatement of the Nine Universal Laws of Uthoni. Somewhere in there a verse that some of the more fanatical Priests of the Brotherhood interpreted to mean that witches must be burned, and that all magic was witchery. But how could even the most malevolent Brotherhood Priest, or even

Padreg himself, equate the necessary and benign magics of the Outsiders with witchery? It was the Outsiders who held together the fabric of the Commonwealth—indeed made the Commonwealth itself possible. Without them, each little country, each separate realm, would be isolated and remote from all the others. It would take a fortnight or two for even the simplest message to reach Celyddon from any other country, and seasons perhaps for a message from Lysandia to reach us.

"The Commonwealth has always accepted and relied upon the Feyish magics," I said. "Even some men have them—"

"The Commonwealth isn't always right," Durstan said. "You'd do well to remember that, lad."

"But we'll be isolated," I said. "The Outsiders—"

"Abyss spawn," Maelgrun said.

I turned to look at him. "You don't really believe that, do you?"

Maelgrun said nothing. He would believe what he chose to believe—whatever was politically advantageous for him to believe. Bronwyn looked up quickly at him, then away, but I saw the flash of sorrow in the fleeting glance.

I tried again. "Outsiders aren't witches—"

Durstan shot a warning glance at me. "There'll be no blasphemy at this table, boy," he said mildly enough. "Be quiet and eat, then tend to your chores and go to your bed. If there's more blasphemy from you, I'll have no choice but to beat the wicked thoughts out of you."

"I can't believe the Council of Lairds would let Fergus pass a law like that," I muttered.

Maelgrun shot a malicious look at me. "There are greater powers at work in Dundregan than you know," he said. "If I were you, I'd forget any grand ideas any stranger of a teacher or your foreigner of a father might have planted in your head." He returned to his meal. "And I'd not be speaking any more of that foreign tongue where the Sheriff's men could hear you. You'll be wanting them to forget you're half foreign and not pure Celyddon stock."

Durstan raised one warning finger at me. "Be quiet, lad," he said. "Eat your supper."

But I couldn't eat. I sat there, staring down at my plate, while the meal dragged on and Maelgrun spoke passionately about the coming coronation celebrations. He was in his last year at the College and had plans for making a career for himself at Court, confident he would rise high in Court circles.

Bronwyn had been sitting quietly, slender and erect, at the foot of the table, looking back and forth between her son and me. "This is folly," she whispered. But she said it so softly that neither Durstan nor Maelgrun heard her. I heard her clearly, though, and I saw the grim lengthening of her mouth and the glint of fear in her eyes.

Imbolc came eventually, marking the turn of the season from early to late winter. With it came the coronation in Dundregan, and the celebrations all over Celyddon. Durstan left his chief tacksman in charge of the croft and took his family, including me, to Dundregan to see the Regent Prince crowned as King of Celyddon.

Even in the grip of the bleakest season of the year, Dundregan was brightly decked with banners and ribbons and buntings. Snow lay thick on the ground, trampled and dirty, but the people thronged the streets in vivid colours worn in defiance of the cold. The festival mood fizzed in the air, and only here and there did I see a face marked with caution or reserve. I saw no Feyii at all in the crowd, nor anyone else who looked even remotely like an Outsider.

Within hours of the ceremony in the Central Sanctuary,

King Fergus called together the Council of Lairds. Durstan attended, leaving Bronwyn and me at the inn. Maelgrun was off somewhere with his friends from the College, celebrating the coronation.

It was late evening when Durstan returned. His mouth was a thin and bloodless line in his pale face. He and Bronwyn spoke in the privacy of their room for a long time before they joined me in the common room for the evening meal. Maelgrun did not return to the inn that night at all.

In the morning, King Fergus appeared on the balcony overlooking the Royal Plaza in the heart of Dundregan. Behind him and to one side stood a tall, thin, angular figure dressed in the grey robes of a priest of the Brotherhood of Uthoni, a rich purple shawl fringed with gold about his shoulders. Padreg, the High Priest, reminded me of nothing more than a predatory bird. He leaned on his staff, tense and fiercely watchful, his head moving slowly as he scanned the crowd. For a moment, it seemed as if he looked straight at me, and his eyes burned with an eerie, almost febrile light. I shivered and looked away. When I glanced back at him again, he had turned that raptor's gaze once again upon Fergus.

To the cheering of the people thronging the Square, Fergus declared his younger brother Daryn disinherited and outlaw, a wolfshead with a price of a hundred gold weyrins on his head. In addition, any man to bring Daryn's head, or other proof of his death, to the Lord High Sheriff in Dundregan would also receive a comfortable freeholding from the King's own lands. The cheering of the crowd drowned out the rest of his words, while Padreg leaned forward and whispered something into the King's ear.

Fergus waited until silence settled once again over the crowd. Then he held out his arms and proclaimed the new law. Celyddon had withdrawn from the Commonwealth.

No more would Feyish or Outsider magic be tolerated within the Realm. All traces of it were to be rooted out and excised like the malignant infection it was.

That pronouncement, at least, brought a grim smile to Durstan's face. But within hours, in spite of the fact the King should have called together the Council of Lairds after the proclamation, he gathered up Bronwyn and me, and left Dundregan to return to Glenaidyn. I heard later that no such meeting had been called, and I wondered if, even then, Durstan suspected what the King had planned.

A fortnight later, the first repercussions of the new law began to affect the Realm. King Fergus, his hand-picked Councilors and their priests called it The Cleansing, and by Vernal Equinox, it exploded into a reign of terror like none other in the history of Celyddon. The first victims were the Outsiders at the Outport in Dundregan, officials of the Outsiders Guild. There were ten of them, and they barely managed to escape with their lives, fleeing on the last Out-ship to leave Dundregan when the Cleansing started. In a town near the northern border, a poor, crazy old man was taken out and burned in the stocks because he claimed he was a Communicator, and that he Communicated with the spirit of dead King Culhain. If it hadn't been so horrifyingly chilling, it might almost have been funny that the Triumvirate of King, Judge and High Priest could actually believe the old man's preposterous story.

Maelgrun came home for the Vernal Equinox festival. On the day he was to go back to the College in Dundregan, Durstan was busy hiring men for the spring shearing. I drove the carriage into Caliburn where Maelgrun would catch the hackney back to Dundregan. The streets of Caliburn were nearly deserted except for sheriffmen patrolling in pairs. Many shops stood boarded up and abandoned.

"Foreigners' shops," Maelgrun said, grim satisfaction and triumph oiling his voice. "We don't need them taking Celyddonian money from us and out of the Realm. The rest of them will be gone soon, too."

I said nothing. But the silence of the streets frightened me.

After I dropped Maelgrun at the Terminal, out of habit, I went to the Outport. Unexpectedly, I found it thronged with people and baggage. Among the crowd were a few Feyii. To my surprise, I recognized Thon shanMetla, his white hair flying like a banner around his head. My old teacher stood half a head taller than any of the people around him, conspicuous for his erect posture and patient dignity. I shouldered my way carefully through the crowd to his side. He turned to look down at me, those strange violet eyes of his calm and serene in the midst of the chaos.

"Iain mac Drew, sir," I said. "Iain clan Morgian. Do you remember me, sir?"

He smiled, then stepped deftly to one side to avoid being jostled by a family group scurrying past. "Aye, I remember you well. One of my best students." He spoke Gael with lilting, Feyish overtones.

"Do you need some help, sir?" I asked. "May I help you?" A woman carrying a young child bumped into me, and I nearly stumbled into him. He reached out, steadied me, then drew me into a quieter corner of the waiting area.

"I've not much to be helped with here," he said. "The sheriffmen came last night and confiscated my home, and most of the things in it. I was allowed to take with me no more than I can carry. I'm an old man; I can't carry much."

I stared at him, aghast. "They confiscated your home?" I repeated in shock.

"Aye, lad," he said. He turned aside suddenly to pick up a small boy who had slipped and fallen, tearing his hand from his mother's hand. He set the boy on his feet, smiled at the distraught mother, then turned back to me. As if no interruption had occurred, he said, "King Fergus has proclaimed that strangers and foreigners will no longer be allowed to own property in Celyddon."

"But a man's land is his own," I said. "His property's his own. The law states that even the King can't take it from him except for treason and sedition."

"But the King can change the law, and he did." He put a hand on my arm. "Laddie, it's been happening ever since the races of this world began recording history, and probably before that, too. It's happened a few times in Lysandia. Our word for it is *dzatim*. Your word is *pogrom*. Ugly words, both of them. It will continue happening as long as the races allow themselves to be suspicious of strangers and hate people who look or believe differently than they do themselves."

"But it's not fair...."

He smiled—a smile filled with resignation and sorrow. "You'll learn that little is fair, laddie," he said softly. "I came to Celyddon twenty years ago with my wife. She was a Communicator and when she retired from the Outsiders Guild, we settled in Caliburn because we both liked it here. She worked at the Outport as an interpreter, and I taught at the school. I stayed on after she died because I had friends here. I wanted to make this my home. Now I have to return to Lysandia, and all my friends there are likely gone."

"I wish I could stop it."

"You were a good student, Iain," he said. "I tried to teach you more than a language. You were one of the ones I thought I had helped learn how to think. Let me give you some advice."

"What's that, sir?"

"If this things run true to form, Fergus and his priests will bring their Cleansing to the libraries next. You value books. You value the ideas they hold. If you wish to keep yours, take them somewhere they can't be found, somewhere they'll be safe. When this is finally over, those books will be sorely needed, I assure you."

The expression in his eyes silenced any protest I might have made. I knew he was right. "I'll take them away as soon as I get home tonight, sir."

"Good lad. Be careful, Iain. They'll try to force your mind into their mould. Once you let another man begin to do your thinking for you, you're truly lost." He put his hand on my shoulder, squeezed it gently once, then turned and vanished into the crowd.

I went home thoughtful and apprehensive. Durstan was still out in the pastures with the shearers and rangemen when I got to the Freeholding, and Bronwyn was nowhere to be seen. I found an old pair of saddlepacks in the byre in the back of the tack room. They looked roomy enough to carry all of my books. Any that wouldn't fit, I could put into a small sack.

I didn't bother to glance through the books to see if they might be on the King's approved list. I was pretty sure most of them wouldn't be, so I simply stuffed them all into the saddlepacks. Grimly, I thought that it didn't matter whether they were approved or not. I wanted no sheriffmen's grubby hands pawing over my books. Even at thirteen, I was firmly convinced that what a man thought or read was his business and his business alone. Perhaps another heritage from my father. Or even my mother.

When I had finished, I went out to the paddock, saddled Brindle and slung the saddlepacks across his broad back behind the saddle. We set out at a brisk trot for the summer pastures.

It took me only a few minutes to stow the books in a small, dry, shallow cave less than a league from the high country bothy. Later, when I had more time, I would come back and wrap them in oiled cloth to protect them from the damp of winter. Right now, during the summer, they would be safe enough from mildew. Even when it rained, the back of this cave stayed dry and secure. And I was convinced nobody would ever think of looking in here.

As I turned my back and left the cave, I felt curiously as if I were turning my back on good friends—abandoning them.

Chapter Three

THON SHANMETLA WAS right. The sheriffmen descended on the libraries and seized every book not personally judged by King Fergus or his High Priest Padreg as being non-heretical. They were burned in public squares in cities, towns and villages across the realm. For the next year, the sky was black with the smoke of their burning. When all libraries were judged Cleansed and pure, the sheriffmen went into the homesteads, the crofts and the fisherhouses, the manses of the Lairds and the cottages of the cotters, and sifted through personal libraries, and again the smoke rose in the squares.

It was barely dawn when they came to Glenaidyn. The troop of mounted men came so quietly into the croft yard, they woke neither Durstan nor Bronwyn. Nor did they waken me, although for most of the season I had been unconsciously listening for them, waiting for them to come. The thunderous banging on the door brought me out of bed all standing, my heart trying to crawl right up my throat. For an instant, I thought it was a landslip, that the massive bulk of the protective and sheltering crags was toppling onto the house and battering against the stone walls. Dressed only in my bedshirt, I flew down the stairs, taking them three and four at a time.

I arrived breathless in the front vestibule by the door at the same time as Durstan and Bronwyn. Durstan had managed to climb into a pair of breeks, and Bronwyn held her houserobe securely about her as she hastily fumbled with the belt. Mag and Rhea, themselves only half-dressed, huddled at the back of the hall by the kitchen door, bed robes clutched around them, both women held in place by Bronwyn's arresting gesture.

Durstan yanked the door open. "What in the name of Piety are you doing, man?" he roared. "No man has lawful business at this hour in the morning."

Six armed sheriffmen led by a non-commissioned officer pushed past him into the hall. All except the Squadman held small crossbows, quarrels nocked and ready. Bronwyn flattened herself against the wall as the sheriffmen streamed past her. She finished tying her houserobe belt and made shooing gestures to the two young women by the kitchen, urging them back to their quarters. Mag and Rhea slipped silently away, glancing back apprehensively over their shoulders as they went.

"We do apologize for the disturbance, Laird Glenaidyn," the non-commissioned officer said smoothly, not sounding anywhere near sorry. "We've orders to check all the crofthouses and manses in this district for forbidden books." He handed Durstan a sheet of parchment embossed with both the Royal Seal and the Holy Seal of the Brotherhood of Uthoni. "We've a royal warrant here in case you're unwilling to give us access."

"You'll find no forbidden books here," Durstan said. "This house has nothing to hide and nothing to be ashamed of."

The six sheriffmen had already fanned out to search the house while the Squadman spoke with Durstan. I heard the dull thuds of books hitting the tiled floor as the sheriffmen pulled them out of the shelves in the Hall. Durstan shoved the sheet of parchment into the pocket of his breeks and went to stand at the arched doorway, watching the sheriffmen. The skin around his mouth paled and tightened as one of the sheriffmen lifted his copy of the Testaments and dropped it to the floor with the rest of the books

That Testament had once belonged to the first Laird of Glenaidyn, founder of Clan Rothsey, and was over three hundred years old. It was beautifully bound in leather and gilt, and contained a record of all the Clan Rothsey births, deaths and marriages for the last three centuries. My parents' marriage and my own birth were recorded there in Durstan's flowing hand, immediately following the notation of Durstan and Bronwyn's marriage and the birth of their son Maelgrun. Durstan's hand, less steady there, had also recorded my parents' death. The book was Durstan's treasure and one of his most prized possessions. It was probably a good thing that the Squadman didn't see the quickly veiled fury in Durstan's eyes.

Bronwyn put out a cautionary hand to stop me as I tried to follow Durstan into the Hall. The warning was as clear and sharp as if she had spoken aloud. She motioned me back beside her where she stood against the wall and thrust her hands into the sleeves of her houserobe. The sleeves hid her hands, but from the tension in her shoulders, I guessed that they were clenched into fists. Her face was white, her mouth pinched bloodless as she pressed her lips together. It wasn't fear. Her anger flashed and crackled in her eyes like needfire.

One of the sheriffmen picked up a small book that had been sitting on the top of a cabinet. He riffled through it, then beckoned to the Squadman and handed it to him. The Squadman glanced at it and held it up so Durstan could see it.

"What's this?" he demanded.

"I don't know," Durstan said.

"It's on our list of forbidden books," the Squadman said. "*Sweet Singer to the Seas...*"

My heart made a queer little bump in my chest. "That's mine," I said.

I had recognized it as soon as the sheriffman picked it up. I had forgotten it was there when I took my books up to the high country bothy. It was the volume of verse by Campbell clan Dunshannon that Bronwyn had given me the year I turned thirteen. Campbell mac Wrochal had been born in Celyddon; he was a Communicator and became an Outsider, a ship's officer like my father. His verse was known and admired all over the Commonwealth. I had read everything he wrote, but that slim volume of verse he wrote about his experiences roaming the untamed seas of the world had always been my favourite. He was able to put my dreams into words for me and I cherished that book because of it, and because Bronwyn had given it to me out of love.

"It's mine," I repeated more firmly.

The Squadman glanced at me over his shoulder. "Yours, is it, laddie?" he asked, a cold smile stretching his lips back from his teeth. His hand closed on the title page, crumpling it and tearing it from the book. He dropped the ruined page to the floor, then opened the book and started to rip the rest of the pages from the glued and sewn spine. It wasn't just a book he was destroying; it was the sum of all my hopes and dreams.

Reckless anger boiled up in my chest. "Aye, it is." I took a step away from the wall, away from Bronwyn's protection, to confront the Squadman.

He turned to face me, still with that cruel smile on his lips. "An impressionable lad like yourself shouldn't be reading treasonous sewage like this."

"It certainly is not treasonous," I said hotly. "It's beautiful—"

"It's treasonous, and it's for the flames."

"No!" I lunged at him, trying to snatch the book from his hands. One of the sheriffmen stepped forward and swatted me down without even as much compunction as a man might kick out at a dog that worried at his ankles. His broad palm caught me on the side of the head with enough force to send me sprawling onto the polished floor half way across the room. I tasted blood as my lip split. Before I could get out of the way, the instep of the sheriffman's boot caught me in the pit of the stomach. It lifted me from the floor and sent me crashing against the panelled wall.

Gagging and gasping for breath, I only dimly heard Bronwyn's shrill cry of horror as she flung herself onto her knees beside me. My vision darkened down to a tiny point as I struggled to breathe. Bronwyn cradled my head in her lap, her hand soothing my hair back from my forehead. She made no sound except for her uneven breathing as she tried to control the blazing anger I felt in the heat of her palm. From a long way away, I heard Durstan say, low and angry, "You'd no call to do that."

"He was attacking the Squadman," the sheriffman said indifferently. "He deserved no better than what he got."

"He only wanted his book," Bronwyn said softly.

"Take the book," Durstan said, his voice strained with

barely controlled anger. "Take the book and get off my property. Any man who'd attack a boy half his size like that is a craven and a coward and has no business wearing that uniform. You're not welcome in this house."

"We have a royal warrant," the Squadman said.

"Aye, you do. And you've found what you came for. I trust you've finished your business. Take the lad's book and get out of here."

"My lord clan Rothsey, you could find yourself in deep trouble with the Priests," the Squadman said. "And the king."

"Do you dare to question my loyalty?" Durstan said coldly.

"You wouldn't be the first Laird—"

"If you've questions about me, ask the High Sheriff in Caliburn," Durstan said. "For that matter, ask the Lord High Sheriff in Dundregan. Or the King himself. My loyalty is unquestioned. The King has always counted me a trusted advisor. Take the book and get out."

The polished tile of the floor emphasized the Squadman's footfalls as he came closer. I opened my eyes to see his boots appear behind Bronwyn's arm as he stood over me. Tears of mixed pain and anger swam in my eyes and blurred my vision. When I tried to look up at him, the room reeled giddily about me and I had to close my eyes again.

"Watch this one, my lord clan Rothsey," the Squadman said dispassionately. "Any boy who reads trash like this and flies in the face of authority needs a close eye on him. You're liable to be spending bail money for him one day. We'll finish our search and be gone, as you requested."

Their heavy tread echoed through the house for a long time. It seemed an eternity until I heard the door close behind them. Durstan came back into the room and bent over me.

"Are you all right, boy?" he asked gently.

I nodded. "Aye. Just a little dizzy."

"Best you stay in bed today, I think," Bronwyn said. "Here, let me help you back to bed."

I tried and failed to get up by myself. Durstan stooped and picked me up as if I were still a small child. The movement sent a fresh burst of pain blossoming through my belly and everything went dim again.

"I've got him," Durstan said to Bronwyn as he carried me out of the room. "Keep an eye on him today. If he vomits blood, we'll get him to the medicians."

His voice came and went in surges, echoing strangely inside my head. Dizzy and sick, I clung to him, willing myself not to cry. I was just turned fifteen, nearly a man. Men were not supposed to cry.

"They could have killed him," Bronwyn murmured, following him up the stairs. "Durstan, how could they? He's but a boy."

Durstan put me down on my bed. I curled myself into a miserable fetal huddle, and Bronwyn pulled the covers up gently over my shoulder.

"Rest now, Iain," she said, her hand on my forehead. She turned to Durstan. "I'm afraid of it, Durstan," she whispered. "I'm afraid of what's happening to people."

"The worst is over now," he said.

"No," she said. "It's only begun."

I was in bed for two days, and spent another two days hobbling around like a frail little old man. By the time I was strong enough to help with the shearing again, the rumours of terror were thick everywhere. Nothing was said aloud, but everybody knew what was happening, and all men walked with their shoulders tense and hunched, as if expecting a blow from behind.

One by one, then in droves, the men and women who had been hailed as distinguished thinkers, great Healers, and prominent bards, began to disappear from the cities. First from Dundregan, then from Caliburn, then from the lesser cities and towns throughout the realm, they vanished without a trace. Where they went, none could tell. But there were rumours of prisons and work camps, and whispers of burnings of more than books.

Among the first to disappear were Durstan's good friend Bevan mac Clintlagh and his family, who owned the only printing house in Caliburn. He, his wife Ylene and their son Geordie, who was only seventeen, vanished between dusk and dawn. When the sun rose that morning, it was on a raging conflagration consuming the last of the printing house. No sign was ever found of Maister Bevan or Mistress Ylene, nor of Geordie. Durstan's anger blazed as hot and bright as the flames about the printing house. He said nothing, but the lines around his eyes deepened, and the planes and hollows of his face became more austere.

By the end of the second year, there were no more ambassadors left in Celyddon. The Outports were closed to passengers. No one was allowed in or out of Celyddon except by special permission of the Crown, and that permission was hard to come by. Trading ships still called once a month at the Outport in Caliburn to collect the wool for the textile mills of the world, and the planefish, fresh or salted or dried, for the tables of the Commonwealth, but their crews were guarded by sheriffmen and prevented from leaving the Outport compound. King Fergus and Padreg the High Priest would allow no spreading of heresies among the populace of Celyddon.

We were isolated and alone, and my dreams of escaping to the wide, wild seas were futile and barren.

Chapter Four

THE SHEARERS GUILDHALL stood on the west side of the Square in Caliburn, directly opposite the High Sanctuary with its soaring clock tower. I stood in line for nearly half an hour to register the shearers Durstan and I had hired for the summer shearing. I had come into Caliburn with Jaerl mac Neill. His father's estate was directly to the north of Durstan's, and Jaerl and I had attended school together.

I walked out into the Square, scanning the list of errands Bronwyn needed me to run, and nearly trod on Jaerl's heels. He had stopped to watch a group of sheriffmen nailing something to the public notice board in the middle of the Square. He barely acknowledged my apology, his face intent as he watched the sheriffmen.

"What are they up to now, d'ye think?" he asked as

the sheriffmen finished and marched briskly across the Square to the Law Courts on the north side of the Square, adjacent to the Guildhalls. A small group of men and women drifted toward the notice board to read what the sheriffmen had posted.

"Perhaps we should go and see," I said. It had been a long time since any good news had been posted on the notice board. I had little expectation that this would be any different.

But this wasn't a mere notice; this was a new Proclamation. With growing horror, I read through the closely printed posting. Above both the Royal Seal and the Holy Seal of the Brotherhood of Uthoni, King Fergus declared that from this day forth, no man or woman could claim adulthood or hold property in his or her own name until each attained the age of twenty-five. Property passing to minors under twenty-five would go to the Crown for stewardship, to administer as it saw fit, until the heir attained his majority. Further, boys and girls between eighteen and twenty-five of rank lower than Freehold Laird were required to report either to their own laird or directly to the Crown in Dundregan for three years' military service. Those lairds who owed military duty to the Crown could second their soldiers to the Crown for training.

Aghast, I stared at the Proclamation. In one blow, Fergus had nearly doubled the time I owed Durstan as a liege-bound. I felt as if someone had buried his fist in my belly. For a moment, I couldn't breathe as despair washed through me.

"Look at this," Jaerl said, oblivious to my stunned shock. He was a younger son, bound as I was to the land. The first part of Fergus's Proclamation affected him very little. He pointed to the last paragraph of the Proclamation. "This looks as if it might be aimed at you, Iain. Will there be trouble over it?"

I glanced at it, not really caring much. I thought nothing could be worse than what I had already read. But I was wrong. As an addendum, Fergus proclaimed that no liege-bound or bastard-born children, including acknowledged bastards of Lairds, would henceforth be allowed to attend the College in Dundregan. And the schools, formerly open to all, noble or commoner alike, were now open only to children or wards of the nobles.

The strength of the anger I felt surprised me. I had never planned to attend the College; it was not something important to me. But to be told I, and all others like me, could never attend simply because we owed liege to a man for one reason or another, was against every concept of justice King Culhain had worked so hard to achieve. It seemed as if Fergus was bent on reversing every advancement his father had ever made.

Jaerl and I rode home in silence, each of us deep in his own thoughts. When I told Durstan about the new Proclamation, he merely nodded in acknowledgement, but a muscle bulged at the corner of his jaw. He started to say something, his eyes glinting with a light that might be anger, but caught Bronwyn's eye and shook his head instead. He stamped out to the paddock to get his horse and return to the shearing stations.

Bronwyn went back to her sewing. "There'll be trouble over this," she said softly. She looked up at me, her mouth grim. "Best you're here, Iain, and not at the College." She said nothing about Maelgrun, but I saw the worry in her eyes. But I think she knew as well as I that Maelgrun would end up on the side where lay his best advantage. He always did.

We were busy for the next fortnight, fully preoccupied with the shearing. Out in the shearing stations, we heard not so much as a whisper of trouble. It wasn't until I went into Caliburn to arrange for shipment of the first bales of wool that I heard anything else.

Caliburn blazed and seethed with rumours. Fergus's latest Proclamation had produced a real grumble of dissatisfaction, mostly from young men and women who suddenly had seven more years to wait until they were recognized as adults, many of whom had already inherited property, which would now revert to the Crown for stewardship. Men whispered that the students at the College in Dundregan had protested the Proclamation. They had gathered peacefully in front of the palace in the Royal Square. There was no riot, and very little disorderliness. The Lord High Sheriff dispatched a squad of sheriffmen armed with clubs and crossbows to break up the gathering. They did it swiftly, competently and brutally.

News was slow travelling to Caliburn, and the reports were cryptic and scant. Every person I met had a different rumour. One man told me that over a hundred students had been killed. Another man said it was only thirty, but more than two hundred had been arrested and imprisoned.

I listened to the furtive, whispered comments and said as little as possible. But inside I was deep, cold scared. Thon shanMetla had outlined the course that events would take. That he was unerringly right frightened me badly.

Jaerl mac Neill and Cadal mac Lachlan were in the tavern where I usually stopped for my noon meal when I was in Caliburn on business. They beckoned to me, and quickly made room for me at the small table.

"You've heard?" Cadal asked, his voice low and intense.

"About the students at the College?" I asked. "Aye. I couldn't help but hear it. I've heard a hundred different stories. It's difficult to sort truth from rumour, though."

Cadal shot a quick glance at Jaerl. "My cousin Brady was at the College," he said. "My uncle called him home immediately after the troubles. Brady said five students were actually killed outright. Two died of injuries later. He doesn't know how many were arrested, but he thinks about twenty. Nobody knows what happened to them. The Lord High Sheriff won't even allow their families to see them."

"Seven dead then." Jaerl made a face. "There'll not be any protests here, I'm thinking."

"Aye," Cadal agreed. "I've no wish to end up dead or imprisoned." He made a wry face. "And I shall have to go for a soldier next year. My father's a merchant, not a Laird like yours."

"I'll have to go, too," I said. "My father was a ship's officer."

"But your uncle is a Laird," Cadal said. "As good as a father, I'm thinking. Besides, you're liege-bound. You can't go unless he releases you."

"He needs you at the Freehold," Jaerl said. "You're safe, Iain. You'll not be going for a soldier. Although why Fergus wants so many soldiers is beyond me. We've been at peace with Eyrindor and Thakia for a century now."

"Perhaps there's war stirring somewhere," I said. "I've heard nothing like that, though. Have you?"

Cadal shook his head. He was more likely to hear rumours than the rest of us. He lived in Caliburn while Jaerl and I were fairly isolated on our respective Freeholds. "Perhaps King Fergus is thinking of going to war with Lysandia," Cadal said.

"That's foolish," I said. "We'd stand no chance at all against Lysandia."

Cadal looked around to make sure nobody was listening. "King Fergus hasn't exactly shown himself to be wise lately, if you ask me," he muttered.

Jaerl clenched his fist and rapped him sharply on the upper arm. "Watch your tongue," he snapped. He glanced around quickly from under lowered brows. "You never know who might be listening." He looked around again.

Cadal made a stubborn face. "King Culhain would never have made those Proclamations," he said, keeping his voice well down.

"Nor would Daryn, were he king," Jaerl said softly.

"Daryn was a traitor," Cadal said. "He tried to murder King Culhain."

"No," I said. "Fergus *said* Daryn tried to murder their father. There's a world of difference there."

Cadal shot a speculative glance at me. "Do you believe Daryn was innocent?"

"You're speaking of him as if he were dead," Jaerl said, keeping his voice low, too. "He isn't. He's alive. In Lysandia."

Cadal ignored him. "Do you believe he's innocent?" he asked me again.

"He could be," I said. "But I agree that he wouldn't have made those proclamations."

Jaerl glanced around again, his shoulders hunched. Sheltering a spot on the table with his left arm, he used his right forefinger to draw the symbol of Fergus's Crown in the wet ring left by his mug of ale. Slyly, he drew a crossbow quarrel piercing it. He looked around again, a small, smug smile twitching at the corners of his mouth.

I reached out quickly and smeared my hand across the treasonous drawing, a cold knot under my heart. Bad enough we were talking about Daryn and whether or not we believed him innocent. Anyone could pass this table and glance down to see what Jaerl had drawn.

"Don't be an idiot!" I told him sharply.

Cadal paid us no attention. I doubt he even saw

what had happened. "Why does Fergus make these proclamations?" he asked almost plaintively. "Why does he want to make everyone so angry?"

"My father says he's listening to that priest Padreg too much," Jaerl said. "I heard him tell my mother that nobody knows what kind of nonsense Padreg is filling Fergus's head with, and that Padreg wants too much power."

"All priests want power," Cadal said. "They want to control the minds and souls of everyone. For the good of their souls, they say."

"The good of a man's soul should be between him and his gods," I said quietly.

Cadal shot a glance at me. "You don't pay reverence to the Father?" he asked.

"Aye, and I pay reverence to the Mother, too," I said. "But I don't believe that either of them want to own my mind and my soul."

"That's right," Cadal said thoughtfully. "Your father was from Eyrindor, wasn't he? A foreigner."

"What's that got to do with it?" I asked.

"Well, you know. He was a foreigner...."

I snorted in derision.

"Why should any man have to wait until he's twenty-five before he can inherit?" Jaerl asked. "That's nonsense."

"Perhaps not," I said. "Think of the property that Fergus has under his thumb now."

"Twenty-five," Jaerl said, not listening.

I thought of the little silver flash hidden in the tanglewood box in my room. "Nine more years to wait," I said softly.

They both nodded glumly. They thought I was referring to the nine more years before being recognized as adults. But I was thinking of the liege I owed Durstan. I had thought I could begin repaying it at the beginning of summer two springs hence when I turned eighteen. This new proclamation of Fergus's would add more than ten years onto my liege-bonding.

"There'll be no protests here in Caliburn, I'm thinking," Cadal said.

"Aye," Jaerl agreed. "None anywhere now."

Jaerl and Cadal were right. There was nothing we could do about it, and those who protested too loudly against the Proclamations or the Crown had a habit of disappearing or dying. And as we'd said, there were no protests in Caliburn, or anywhere else that we heard about.

That night, when the house was silent and dark, I lay staring up into the shadows of the ceiling beams above my head. It felt as if everything were closing in around me, suffocating and smothering, stretching infinitely into the future. I could see no end to my bondage, no chance I could ever be free of my duty to Durstan and the croft. All my dreams were dwindling and dissipating like smoke in drenching mist.

Something harsh and painful caught at my throat, wrapped cold, clawed fingers around my heart. I would never escape the domination of this thrice-cursed king.

I crept from my bed and took the small tanglewood box from its hiding place beneath the hearthstone. I slipped the chain holding the little gold maple leaf and the silver Communicator's flash around my neck and dressed quickly. The meager pile of coins in my bureau drawer seemed far less adequate than I remembered it being, but I stuffed the small leather bag into my pocket, then slipped out the window on to the roof of the verandah below.

Five minutes later, I was leading Flicker, unsaddled but

haltered, down the track to the road. I glanced up at the stars. Still a little over an hour 'til midnight.

It took me nearly two hours to ride to the outskirts of Caliburn, keeping cautiously to the shadows and not using the road itself. I dismounted and gave the horse a smack on the haunches to send him back along the road. He knew the road as well as I, and would find his way home well before dawn.

The streets of the city were quiet and deserted. Here and there, the warm, yellow glow of candlelight showed in a window of a house. Occasionally, a lamp near a doorway cast a soft pool of light onto the street. I kept to the shadows, half running, half walking, toward the Outport. My soft boots made very little sound on the cobbles of the street.

Several times, I had to duck into an alley, pressing myself flat against the stone of the walls, holding my breath as a troop of sheriffmen went past, patrolling the streets. They walked with the jingle and clatter of armaments, their boot heels clacking loudly on the pavement. I had no trouble hearing them long before they had a chance to see me, and could easily duck out of their sight.

The Outport was deserted. No lights at all showed anywhere along the waterfront. Only the gleam of starlight and the washed sliver light of the moons illuminated the area. Half a dozen fisherboats lined the long jetty, and a single coastal freighter lay snugged against the only warehouse pier still in use. I crouched in the shadow of a decaying warehouse, watching the coastal freighter. It was my only chance.

No lights showed aboard the stubby ship, and I was too far away to see if any guard stood on the deck. Between me and the pier was a sturdy railed fence, much higher than I remembered it being before Fergus made his proclamation. As I watched, a patrol of sheriffmen marched past outside the fence. A moment later, another patrol passed, this one going the opposite direction, and inside the fence.

If I could get through the fence, and past the patrols of sheriffmen, I might be able to stow away on the freighter. I hoped it was going to Eyrindor in the north, where I could go to the Outsider's Guild. If the trader ship was going to Dundregan, I'd have to try to stow away on an Out-ship. Surely showing the Communicator's flash to the captain would at least gain me a hearing. The money I carried wasn't even close to being enough to pay for passage to Lysandia, but I was young, strong, and healthy. I could work my passage.

I watched for over an hour. The sheriffmen patrolled in patterns that left only a few minutes at a time when I might be able to get to the fence, climb it, and disappear into the shadows on the other side.

Two patrols passed each other without speaking and moved off in opposite directions. If I was going to go, it would have to be now. I took a deep breath to steady my hammering heart, then ran to the fence, crouched low.

I had not done more than set my foot into the first rail when someone shouted. Something whistled through the air, then thudded into the tough corewood rail. I looked down in horror to see a quarrel from a crossbow embedded in the wood between the second and third fingers of my left hand. Someone shouted again. The sound of running feet came from the right.

I leapt down from the fence and ran to my left, dodging back across the open space to the warehouses. Another barbed steel quarrel shot sparks off the cobblestones by my heel, then went clattering and skidding away into the dark. Behind me, the shrill whistle of the alarm split the air.

Another troop of sheriffmen appeared around the corner in front of me. My feet slipped on the cobblestones as I dodged down an alleyway and around a corner. The alley opened into a street of seedy shops and taverns. I hesitated momentarily, then went right again, trying to work my way back to the City Square.

It sounded as if a whole army of sheriffmen pursued me. They shouted to each other, the thunder of their hard-soled boots loud in the night. I ran until my rasping breath tore my throat raw and my lungs burned. Sudden pain stabbed at my side, but I couldn't stop running. The sheriffmen gained on me with every step.

An arm reached out of a doorway and snagged me around the waist, yanking me off the street. A large hand came down over my mouth. The door closed quietly.

"Don't make a sound, boy," a man's voice said softly in my ear. "This way. Quickly."

It was black as the bottom of a tin mine in the house. I sensed rather than saw we were in a narrow hallway. The man pulled me up a long flight of stairs, and opened a door to his left.

"Take off your coat and shirt," he said.

"What?" I said faintly.

"Don't argue, lad. There's no time. They'll be at the door in a moment. Take off your coat and shirt."

He tore at my jacket, stripping it ungently from me. I heard fabric rip. I stepped away and took off my shirt.

A woman's voice came out of the darkness. "Over here. Quickly."

The man pushed me ahead of him. My knees bumped against a bed, and the man pushed me down onto it, reaching down to flip my feet, boots and all, under the blankets. The woman in the bed pressed herself quickly into my arms.

Only seconds after the man left the room, the loud thumping of fists on the door downstairs announced the arrival of the sheriffmen. Moments later, their heavy feet thudded on the stairs.

The bedroom door flew open. Light flooded the room. Five armed men stood in the doorway, one of them holding up a brightly flaring lantern. The woman beside me squealed in terror and buried her face against my chest. I stared up at the sheriffmen, slackjawed and blank.

In the hall, the man who had yanked me off the street spoke. "My daughter and her husband," he said, amusement in his voice. "Less than a season married."

The sheriffmen stood there for another moment or two. Then the Squadman grunted and pulled the door closed. I tried to draw away from the woman, but she held me tightly.

"Not yet," she whispered calmly, no trace of fear in her voice. She sounded very young; my age probably. "Make sure they're gone first."

It seemed like hours before the door opened again. "They're gone," the man's voice said. He was nothing but a darker shadow against the dark opening in the paler wall.

I slipped out of the bed and fumbled into my shirt. The man handed me my jacket. Moments later, I was out on the deserted street.

I never saw my rescuer's face clearly, nor that of his daughter. And I never knew their names. All things considered, all three of us were probably safer that way.

Flicker stood by the paddock, calmly cropping grass when I got back to the Freehold. I put him back into the byre and made my way back up the vines to the verandah roof, and then into my room. The sky behind the Crags was already beginning to pale toward dawn. I took off the thin gold chain, put it back into the carved box, then carefully hid the box under the hearthstone. I sat on the bed, put my head in my hands, and let despair wash through me.

I would never get away to the Outside now. I was trapped here forever.

The disappearances went on. They were not as common as they had been. Either the sheriffmen had already rounded up all the malcontents, or people had become more circumspect about whom they trusted.

Then, during one early summer night not long after I turned sixteen, the sheriffmen took away Donal mac Reilly, our neighbor and Durstan's chief tacksman.

I came down for breakfast in the morning to find Bronwyn and Durstan in the middle of an argument. Bronwyn's back was to me as I paused, startled, in the hall outside the kitchen, but I could see Durstan's face in three-quarter profile. His grey eyes were clouded and troubled.

"But they took his sheep and everything he owned," Bronwyn said, her low voice conveying anger and outrage.

"I heard it said that Donal was working actively against the Crown," Durstan said.

Bronwyn snorted derisively. "That's nonsense and you know it. In any case, I doesn't change the fact that Leita and the children need help."

"Bronwyn, no! You'll not be helping them. I forbid it. You'll have the sheriffmen down on us next."

Bronwyn stiffened. "Forbid it, do you then?" Her defiance crackled around her like subdued lightning. It was a wonder Durstan couldn't see it or feel it as clearly as I did. Or, perhaps, he saw it and simply chose to ignore it, to pretend it wasn't there.

"Aye," he said. "I forbid it. Stay out of this. It's none of our affair."

"Leita and Donal are our neighbors. Our friends.... He was your loyal tacksman. You've known him all his life. You grew up as close as brothers with his father." She didn't seem to notice that she referred to Donal as if he were already dead.

Durstan noticed. He flinched slightly, but straightened his shoulders and drew himself up straight. "Bronwyn, no."

"How can you ignore Leita and the children?" Bronwyn demanded. "Donal was outspoken and opinionated, but he was no traitor. You know that, Durstan. You know it as surely as you know your own name."

"No," he repeated. "That's flat. No." He turned on his heel and strode out the back door into the croft yard.

Bronwyn stood staring after him for a moment, her lips compressed. Mag peered timidly around the door frame, clutching a basket of eggs.

"Is it all right to come back, Mistress Bronwyn?" she asked.

Bronwyn beckoned her in impatiently. "Yes," she said. "Yes, Mag. Put those eggs on the counter and go help Rhea set the table. Go, girl. I'll fix the eggs."

"But Mistress Bronwyn—"

"Do you think I've never cooked an egg before, girl? Go on. Get out of here."

Mag sidled past me, dropping a sketchy curtsey before she scurried down the hall. Bronwyn began to crack eggs into a large, blue bowl. She looked over her shoulder as I entered the kitchen.

"I suppose you heard all that," she said.

"Aye. I couldn't help it. What happened?"

"The sheriffmen confiscated Donal mac Reilly's property last night and took Donal away. Leita and the children need help. They're turned out of the house and naught Durstan can or will do about it."

"What can we do?"

She didn't miss a beat as she whipped the eggs into a creamy yellow froth for an omelet. "The least we can do is get them into Caliburn to Leita's sister."

"Tonight, then," I said. "We'll take the carriage when Durstan's asleep."

Bronwyn looked at me again. A hint of a smile turned up the corners of her mouth. As always, we understood each other perfectly. "You'll do, Iain mac Drew," she said softly. "Aye, you'll do very well." The way she said it gave me to understand that, in her eyes, I had just attained the stature of a man. Not again would she ever treat me as a child.

Shortly after midnight, I got out of bed and dressed in the dark, not daring to light a candle. Once again, I went out the window, across the verandah roof, and down the vines outside the Hall. Only the pale Companion showed in the sky just above the Great Crags in the west. The Queen would not rise until just before dawn.

I ran to the byre, pulling my cloak around my shoulders. It was only early summer, getting close to Solstice, but the nights were still cold. And besides, the dark blue of the cloak made me more difficult to see in the night. I could more easily blend into the shadows.

Bronwyn was in the byre when I burst through the door. Dressed in a dark gown, a brown cloak thrown about her shoulders, she had already finished harnessing Flicker and Fan. I took the traces from her and led the horses around to the side of the byre where the carriage stood under a thatched canopy. Bronwyn handed me scarves to muffle the metal parts of the harnesses as I hitched the horses to the carriage. We led them down the lane to the road, each of us holding tight to a bridle, our hands at the horses' noses to keep them from snorting or whinnying.

Mistress Leita, carrying the bairn and holding the toddler by the hand, appeared out of the shadows of a coppice of hazel a furlong from where our lane joined the road. Bronwyn jumped lightly down from the carriage and took the bairn from her.

Mistress Leita's face was pale and drawn. She looked far older than when I had last seen her. She reached for Bronwyn's hand and tried to kiss it. Bronwyn gently disengaged her hand, and put her arm around Leita's shoulders, the bairn cradled in the other.

"Bless you, my lady," Leita whispered. She smiled shyly up at me. "And you, Maister Iain."

We had almost gained the bridge across the Strathflorin River, only a little less than a league from Caliburn, when Bronwyn reached out to clutch my arm. "Someone's coming," she whispered. "Get the team off the road. Hurry!"

Luck stayed with us. The verge was wide here, and the meadow dotted with shaws of holly and thickets of tanglewood. I turned the horses and urged them down into the meadow. Bronwyn jumped down and grabbed Fan's bridle, pulling him toward the shadow of a tall jumble of tanglewood. Watching the road intently, she cradled the bairn securely in one arm, holding Fan's bridle with the other hand. Leita held the sleeping toddler, her fingers pressed gently to his mouth, even as she tried to stifle her own harsh breathing.

A troop of sheriffmen clattered across the bridge, the rhythm of their horses' hooves on the wooden planking booming and hollow in the night. They were in a hurry, but not in any obvious urgency. The horses cantered at an easy pace and the men sat their saddles relaxed. I made out the dark shadows of crossbows slung across their backs.

Leita clutched at Bronwyn's arm as my aunt climbed back onto the seat beside me. "My lady, what if they're heading for Glenaidyn?" she whispered. "Oh, Sweet Mother of All, what will you do if they find you gone?"

"Leita, dear," Bronwyn said, still gently rocking the bairn in her arms, "will you hush that nonsense and sit down before you fall and hurt yourself? Iain, back on the road, please. And hurry. We've less than four hours left 'til dawn. We must be back before Durstan awakens."

Caliburn was dark and sleeping. We kept to the back streets as we made our way to the house of Leita's sister and kin-brother. The clatter of Flicker and Fan's hooves on the cobblestones echoed off the walls of the houses, and the wheels of the carriage rumbled like thunder. Bronwyn's hood hid her bright hair, and I kept my head lowered. If anyone awoke and looked out a window, they would have difficulty identifying us. I hoped.

We delivered Leita and the children safely to her waiting sister. Both tried to thank us, but Bronwyn brushed the gratitude aside, bent to hug the sleepy toddler, and then squeezed Leita's hand. "Be with the Power and the Presence and the Love," she whispered.

Three times on the way home, we had to leave the track and hide in the shadows as another troop of mounted sheriffmen rode past, two of them riding back to Caliburn. The troop we encountered just before we turned onto the road to Glenaidyn kept to the north road, heading out toward Glengarvey and the northern crags.

The first faint traces of dawn streaked the eastern sky behind the crags as we led the horses up the lane to the paddock yard. When Durstan came down the stairs, Bronwyn was in the kitchen supervising the preparation of breakfast, and I was in the byre, milking the cows.

That was the first time I had ever known Bronwyn to actively defy Durstan. It would not be the last time I did.

Chapter Five

SO THE SEASONS passed. Life settled into wary caution as Fergus and Padreg found more to displease them. I no longer wore the little golden maple leaf on its chain around my neck. It, like the silver Communicator's sleeve-flash, was tucked safely into the small tanglewood box, and the box secreted behind a loose hearthstone in my room. To display either of those symbols openly was dangerous and foolish.

There were no more wholesale round-ups of those King Fergus or Padreg branded as heretics or treason mongers. But occasionally, a laird and his family quietly disappeared. The laird's property went to the Crown, then to someone high in Fergus's favour or that of his Royal Council or Padreg. Several times, there were well-publicized trials in Dundregan of men or women accused of treason. Not once was anyone acquitted of the crime. Not once were charges dropped. The Judging Council never once returned a verdict of not guilty, and no champions were allowed to fight for the accused, even if one could be found who was willing. Evidence in all cases was overwhelmingly abundant, but too many times, the damning evidence was so thin that even a child could see through it. Any man who protested these sham trials often found himself joining the defendant in the prisoners' dock.

Maelgrun finished college in the spring and joined the Court as a clerk. It wasn't long before he was appointed to the newly-formed Royal Council and a remarkably short time later became an overseer for the many lands and estates the Crown held for young men or women who had not yet reached their majority—a powerful position. He swiftly made a name for himself as a young courtier on the rise, and rumour said the corresponding increase in his own personal fortune was nothing less than phenomenal. He was high in favour with both King Fergus and High Priest Padreg.

I turned seventeen in early spring and Durstan gradually began to leave more and more of the day-to-day running of the Freehold to me. Only during the shearing seasons did he spend most of his time at Glenaidyn. At other times, he was in Dundregan with the Council of Lairds. He may have discussed his work with Bronwyn when he was home, but in front of me, he said nothing at all about it. I heard rumours the Council of Lairds was losing more and more of its power and influence to Fergus's Royal Council, and the Lairds were worried. But Durstan never spoke to me about it. He became more dour, but oddly enough, at the same time, he became more quiet and thoughtful.

Eventually, my eighteenth birthday came. I was no longer a boy. I had reached a height of a little over six feet, and the work on the Freehold had given me a man's shape to match my height. I was a man grown, although not officially recognized as such by the new laws—not for another seven years. Had Fergus not been made King, had I not been liege-bound to Durstan, I could have gone out and made my own way in the world. I could have taken Glyn shanBreyor's silver flash to the Outsiders Guild and been given a chance for a berth on an Out-ship.

But there was no Outsiders Guild in Celyddon, not anymore. It was the most important organization in the Commonwealth, except perhaps for the Watch, but by Fergus's decree, it had no existence in this realm. Only the small coastal freighters made quick calls at the Outports now to collect wool and planefish. The rest of the Commonwealth had forgotten us, or ignored us, just as Celyddon ignored it.

I no longer went to the Outport when I went into Caliburn with the wagon for provisions. Never really busy to begin with, now that Celyddon had isolated itself, the Outport served not more than one or two In-ships a fortnight, except during shearing season when there might be four. The passenger terminal had nearly fallen to ruin, and only one of the huge freight sheds was still usable. It was a sad ghost of an Outport, peopled only by grim officials whose main task was to prevent foreign ideas from spreading first into Caliburn, and then into the rest of the realm.

Summer shearing was about to get underway when I went into Caliburn with the wagon for provisions. I was just finishing loading the last sacks into the wagon when Jaerl mac Neill crossed the dusty street to give me a hand.

He hefted a large sack of mealflour and grinned at me. "I see your cousin Maelgrun has been moving up again," he said.

"Aye." I tossed a sack of oats into the wagon. "Assistant to the Chief of Law."

Jaerl glanced at me almost slyly. "There'll soon be new laws on liege-bonding, I heard."

"Aye, so I've heard," I said sourly. Every time there were new laws, it seemed I owed more and more of my life to Durstan. I would owe Durstan the years between six and twenty-five—nineteen years. By the time I paid him back the liege I owed him, I'd be forty-four. Too old to go to sea for the first time. No captain would accept an apprentice that age.

Jaerl flung the sack into the wagon. "Would you be after coming to a prayer meeting tonight at my Holding?"

I looked at him, then shrugged and turned away to pick up a box of tea. "I'm not much for prayer meetings, Jaerl, and you know it."

"You'll like this one," he said. "Best you come. After dinner at twenty-one hour, then?"

Jaerl's sly little smile told me more than I wanted to know about the nature of this *prayer meeting*. This was probably something I'd be far better off not knowing about. "I'd sooner not, Jaerl."

"There'll be no priests of the Brotherhood of Uthoni there." He tossed me a small carton of sugar. "I think it would do you good to come. I'll expect you."

"Jaerl, no—"

"Be there, Iain," he said softly. He looked straight at me, and there was something in the depths of his eyes I couldn't quite read. He walked away, turned once to wave with a cheerful grin, and disappeared around a corner, whistling. I shook my head in exasperation and finished loading the wagon.

After dinner that night, Durstan and Bronwyn prepared

to go to the kirk for the mid-fortnight service. I had been planning to go with them, not something I usually did. But at the last moment, I begged off and told them I would be attending a prayer meeting with Jaerl Mac Neill. Durstan merely grunted, but Bronwyn gave me a quick, searching glance before she smiled and nodded.

"Be careful," she said.

Startled, I looked at her sharply. Did she sense the hesitation I felt, the misgiving I had about Jaerl's meeting?

"The shore track can be treacherous at night," she said blandly enough. She reached up to kiss my cheek, then followed Durstan out the door. I stood for a moment, thinking about the enigmatic blandness in her face, then shook my head and went out into the paddock yard.

I saddled old Brindle, who was now feeling his age and becoming cranky with it, and set out for Jaerl's Holding. Clan Gordaen's lands bordered Durstan's to the north and the main house stood on a cliff overlooking the sea. There was a road, but it was faster to take the narrow track along the shore.

Sure-footed as ever, Brindle made his way down the track at a brisk walk. He wanted to canter, but I held him down. I didn't want to risk a broken leg in the dark, and I was in no hurry in any event. I had a fairly good idea of what Jaerl was up to, and I wasn't sure I wanted any part of it. Jaerl had always been a bit of a dreamer, never firmly rooted in reality, full of ideas and plans, most of them impractical and even implausible. I had no reason to suspect anything he might be involved in now would be any different from his notions before. And remembering the sketch he had made on the table in the tavern, Fergus's crown pierced by a crossbow quarrel, I thought my doubts were justified. But I had the feeling I'd best know what he was up to, just in case it involved me or mine.

The stars burned fierce and bright in the night sky. I watched them as I rode, echoes of my dreams flickering through my mind. Out on the sea, moon-silvered by the Queen and her Companion, flashes of phosphorescence danced on the crests of the waves. For the past three or four nights, there had been a school of dolphin in the bay, playing in the glimmering plankton. The blazing and dazzling streaks of their passing etched brilliant lines in the sea. Tonight, I saw one that was larger and brighter than the rest, and idly wondered if it could be construed as an omen. And if an omen, for good or ill?

There were five or six young people already at the manse when I arrived. I knew only two of them besides Jaerl. Gwynneth mab Kinley was from Caliburn, and betrothed to Jaerl. She was at the Freehold on her betrothal visit, learning what would be expected of a kin-daughter from Jaerl's mother. I hadn't seen Cadal mac Lachlan since the time of the riot at the College, the day Jaerl had drawn that silly sketch on the tavern table. He had always been a closer friend to Jaerl than to me. We'd never had a lot in common, Cadal and I.

They were gathered in the back parlour, grouped closely around a small table. Someone found a chair for me, and I wedged myself between two young men. I seemed to be the last to arrive. Shortly after I sat down, Jaerl rose to his feet and began to speak.

"We are all of the same mind here," he said in Standard, not Gael, the intonations in his voice solemn and just a bit pompous. "All of us are pledged not to let the freedom of ideas die."

It sounded as if he were delivering a ritual opening, and I had the sudden, certain hunch that I wasn't going to like what happened at this meeting.

Jaerl reached into his pocket and pulled out a slim book. "I have here a volume of verse by Campbell mac Wrochal clan Dunshannon," he said softly.

He opened the book ceremoniously and began to read the forbidden stanzas that sang the glory of the tumultuous seas beyond the barrier reefs. Dunshannon spoke of the seas in the same manner a man might describe a woman he loved physically as well as spiritually. Padreg had banned his writings because of his voluptuous use of language and his sensual and seductive imagery as much as for the ideas of freedom and self-reliance they conveyed.

When Jaerl finished, he looked straight at me, holding my gaze self-importantly. "Will you be joining us then, Iain?" he asked.

I got to my feet, my mouth dry. This farce was even more ill-conceived than I had imagined. "I'll not," I said. "I'll certainly not betray you, but I'll not join you, either."

"You have no more reason to love Fergus and Padreg than any of us here," Gwynneth said. "In fact, you have less than most. Why will you not join us? Someone has to keep the truth alive, Iain, otherwise we will truly go down in darkness."

"Aye, someone does," I agreed. "But I'll not be doing it this way. This is foolishness. How long d'ye think you can keep these meetings secret? How long d'ye think it will take before the sheriffmen come bursting in to arrest the lot of you for treason?"

"Would it be that you agree with your Uncle Durstan, then?" Cadal asked.

"You know I do not," I said.

"Your cousin Maelgrun is high up in the Court and in the Royal Council," he said. "Might you be working with him?"

"Don't be foolish, Cadal," said the only other woman in the group. She had medium length dark hair that framed her face, and the deep blue eyes of the true Gael. I had never seen her before, and Jaerl had not bothered to make introductions. "If Jaerl thought Iain was working with his cousin, he would never have invited him to this meeting."

I smiled slightly. "My cousin and I have never seen eye to eye," I said dryly. "In this more than anything else."

"Then why d'ye refuse to join us?" Jaerl asked.

"Because it will do no good," I said. "You're begging for denouncement, meeting like this."

"Would you suggest we rush out and start an armed revolution and die gloriously as martyrs?" one of the men asked sarcastically. "That would do everyone a lot of good, wouldn't it, now?"

"It would do about as much good as this folly of meeting to read forbidden books," I said. "This changes nothing that needs changing. It's naught but romantic nonsense and certainly not worth facing imprisonment or death for. Not to my mind, anyway."

"Maybe you'd like us to join the outlaws in the Crags," Cadal said caustically.

"At least the outlaws don't have to spend their days looking fearfully over their shoulders, because the sheriffmen will never go into the Crags after them," I replied evenly. "I meant it. I'll not betray you, but I'll not join you, either." As I turned to leave the room, I noticed the dark-haired girl watching me with an expression of speculative interest in her eyes.

"You, the son of an Outsider and a foreigner, and you'll not strike a blow for freedom?" Gwynneth asked.

I stopped with my hand on the latch, and turned to look at her. "When I strike a blow, Gwynneth mab Kinley," I said with more conviction than I felt, "it will be a blow Fergus and his Royal Council will reel under."

I had not bothered to unsaddle Brindle when I arrived. He stood quietly, hipshot, cropping grass at the edge of the paddock. As I caught him and prepared to mount,

I was surprised to see the dark-haired girl come into the paddock. She caught the bridle and looked at me across the withers of the horse. She was taller than I had thought at first. She was not a pretty girl by any means, but there was an air of attractive and compelling vitality about her, and there was obviously a good mind behind that high, smooth forehead.

"You're right, Iain mac Drew," she said. "This isn't the way. When you decide on your blow, get in touch with me. I'm Holly mab Dougal. You can find me through my father, Medician Dougal mac Llyr in Caliburn."

I swung up into the saddle. "It might be a long while before I'm ready to strike my blow," I said. I used my riding crop to flip up the latch on the paddock gate.

She refastened the gate once we were through and laughed, teeth gleaming white in the faint illumination of the moons. "No matter," she said. With one hand on the bridle again, she walked beside the horse to a small two-wheel trap in the courtyard. "When you're ready, I'll be ready to help. And I have more friends than these." She tossed her hair over her shoulder, indicating the group we had left in Jaerl's back parlour. "My friends are realists and not just woolly-headed idealists like that pack back there. Be sure you keep us in mind, Iain clan Morgian. I bid you good evening." She got into the trap and moved off swiftly into the darkness.

Sure-footed and sturdy, Brindle picked his way across the pastures and down to the cliff track, better able than I to see in the dark. I let him have his head and sat thinking about what I had told Jaerl and his friends. Until I said it aloud, I hadn't realized that I intended to fight Fergus and his Royal Council, all of them backed by Padreg's fanaticism. I thought I had accepted my indenture, my servitude, given up my hope of going

Outside to the wilderness of the High Sea. Now I knew I had not.

I had not looked at the little tanglewood box which held my two treasures for over a year. But even as I thought of them now, I heard the Communicator's name echoing in my mind. Glyn shanBreyor. I hadn't thought about him for a long time, now, either—so long that I couldn't remember the last time. But his name was still fresh and clear in my memory. Glyn shanBreyor, a Fey-Halfblood Communicator who, for some reason known only to himself, had tried to befriend a young boy with a dream. It had never before occurred to me to wonder why he had done it. It was possible that he had felt sympathy for the dream he could see shining in my eyes, the dream that would never see fulfillment.

I looked up at the stars, at the familiar constellations I knew as well as I knew the map of my own country. To my right was the sea, restless and living, always moving. Both moons hung low on the western horizon, glimmering moon-paths stretching across the changeable water nearly to my feet. Somewhere out there was Lysandia, the heart of the Commonwealth. And somewhere beyond Lysandia lay the fabled Dwarvenlands and the Troll-lands of Gradichavale with their mountains of granite and gold watched over by centaurs and unicorns. Between them were vast reaches of the Wildesea, storm-wracked and tide-riven, and so treacherous that only the Pathfinders and Farseers could trace a track through the storms and whirlpools, and only the Windcasters could prevent the winds from tearing a ship to tattered shreds.

I wanted to be there. I wanted to be part of the teams that fought those dangers to bring trade and news to all the lands of the world. The need was enough to make the back of my throat ache, and tighten my chest. My father's blood singing in my veins, perhaps. Something else of his that had come to me. My chance lay hidden in a small, carved wooden box. But there was no way to use that chance. Not now.

We were traversing a narrow section of trail along the face of a sheer rock buttress jutting out over the water when old Brindle came to an abrupt stop. He tossed his head and gave a small, burbling whicker of nervousness. It brought my attention back from the sea quickly. There were wild animals out here, but most of them weren't dangerous. The horse might have smelled a foxen. They were nocturnal but dangerous only to rodents.

I urged Brindle forward. He went reluctantly. For some reason, he didn't want to move around the bend in the trail. Beyond that bend lay only a small, sheltered cove, surrounded on three sides by sheer cliffs. At high tide, it became a seething, boiling cauldron of trapped water, cutting the track completely, but the tide was well out now. The sand would be dry and safe.

I dug my heels into the horse's flanks. "It's only a foxen, you silly beast," I told him, chiding him gently. "It won't hurt you."

Brindle pranced nervously sideways on the narrow trail and nearly slipped. It was not much more than five feet down to the sand below the track, but it was enough of a fall to do a lot of damage if we went over. I dismounted, squeezed past the horse, and cautiously began to lead him down the track. Brindle was too skittish for it to be just a foxen out there in the dark. He moved forward unwillingly, allowing himself to be led, but tugging backward on the bridle.

As I approached the sharp bend, the horse whickered again, and the whites of his eyes began to show. Fearfully, he tossed his head, nearly tearing the reins out of my hands. Beginning to lose patience with him, I cursed him for a fool and yanked on the bridle.

"What is it?" I asked. "A badgercat?" Badgercats could not really harm horses, but old Brindle had always hated the scent of them. It sometimes caused him to panic. The fierce, striped little animals were all claw and fang, and wreaked havoc with the sheep, but they seldom came this far down out of the high crags.

Brindle set in his heels and flatly refused to move. I stopped tugging on the bridle and stood for a moment, wondering what the horse smelled or sensed that I couldn't. Someone or something waiting around the bend in the track? My hand went to my belt to where I usually wore my hoofing knife. But it wasn't there; it was sitting on top of my dresser at home.

A man stepped out of the shadows of the cliff beside me and put his hand up to grasp the bridle. The horse calmed down immediately, but my own heart gave a tremendous leap as if it were trying to tear itself right out of my chest. The man stood tall beside the horse, dressed in something dark and close-fitting, the dark shadow of his cloak blending with the rocks behind him. Moonlight glinted on silver against the midnight blue of his clothing. Half in shock, I recognized the uniform of the fabled Commonwealth Watch, and then I recognized the man who wore it.

"Bring him around here, Iain," the man said quietly, his hand still on the bridle. "He'll be all right now. He could smell strangers, that's all. He doesn't like it much."

Chapter Six

DOCILE NOW, OLD Brindle moved easily around the sharp
bend. I became aware of an astringent scent in the air
that I hadn't noticed before. I looped the knotted reins
over the saddlehorn, and the horse lowered its head to
nuzzle at a clump of brittle seaweed. Behind him, against
the heavy bulk of the cliff, sat a sleek and lustrous
shape. Even as I recognized it for the gig of an Out-ship,
I couldn't believe I really saw it there. The strange scent
in the air was the residue of the magic used to propel it
ashore. I turned to the man who stood in the shadows
beside me.

"I saw you come in," I said. "I thought it was just another
of the dolphins."

"It was intended to look like that." The man's teeth

gleamed in the faint light as he smiled. "Do you remember me, Iain mac Drew clan Morgian?"

"Glyn shanBreyor."

"Your memory is as good as promised." Again, the quick and lighthearted smile in the darkness.

"You shouldn't be here," I said. "It's dangerous for you here now."

"We know. I have two reasons to be here. The first is the business of the Watch."

A small kick of fear jumped in my chest. The Watch. The law enforcement agency of the Commonwealth. Almost a legend throughout the Commonwealth. All of its Membership was made up of Communicators. Rumour had it that they had more than just the gift of the Communicator, more than the simple mind magics. There were strange stories about them. Most of the stories could be dismissed as fable or exaggeration, but even if there were only a small grain of truth in them, the men and women of the Watch possessed magics that common men and women could only guess at, something that gave the Watch an aura of mystery that inspired awe and no little fear.

"What interest does the Watch have in Celyddon?" I asked.

"None until asked to intervene," he replied blandly, politely but firmly indicating the end of that subject for discussion. "My second reason for being here is you."

"Me?"

He laughed at my astonishment. "You never brought my flash back to me, Iain. I lost my bet on you."

"You know why it's dangerous for you here. You know why I couldn't take your flash to the Outsiders Guild."

"I'd have given odds you'd find a way," he said, amusement in his voice.

"I tried to get through to the Outport once when there was a freighter loading," I said bitterly. "I couldn't get past the sheriffmen. I wanted to go Outside, but I didn't want to die in the trying."

Something moved in the darkness behind him. A woman came around the sleek bulk of the gig. She, too, wore the elegantly fitted dark blue uniform of the Watch.

"We haven't much time, Glyn," she said softly.

He turned to her and they spoke for a moment, quick, musical phrases in a language I knew had to be Feyish. I watched him as they spoke. He had startled me badly when he stepped out of the shadows on the trail by the rock face. But it hadn't really surprised me to find him here in Celyddon. Now that I was over the first shock of it, I began to wonder why I hadn't been surprised. He turned back to face me.

"Because you knew I was here, Iain," he said quietly. "You were thinking of me because you knew I was here."

He had startled me again. I had forgotten what he was—a Communicator, a man who heard what was in another man's mind as easily as I listened to the murmur of the sea. My puzzlement must have been as loud as a shout to him.

He laughed. "And now you're wondering why I'd come all this way just to see you again," he said. "Iain, did it ever occur to you to wonder why you could feel my presence here? Did you ever wonder why I came over to speak to you at the Outport that day?"

"I thought perhaps you felt sorry for me," I said, remembering my awed fascination of him. He didn't look much older now in the faint starlight than he did then.

"It's true I felt your desire to be Outside," he said. "But there was more to it than that."

I said nothing, but I shivered as I waited for him to continue.

"You thought we were just an Out-crew," he said. "In a way, we were." The woman came to stand beside him. "Iain, this is Ydonda sheilVoryn. You saw her at the Outport that day. Do you remember her?"

"I remember a Feyish woman, but I don't remember what she looked like."

"Ydonda is a Member of the Watch, too. Just as I am. We came that day to talk with a man who sat as a legislator on the Council of Lairds. He wanted us to help prevent what he knew was going to happen when Fergus was crowned king. But we have no authority to step into matters of internal government, not unless there's some Commonwealth law which was violated. We found none in this case. There's no law that prevents secession from the Commonwealth."

I thought of the rows of Padreg's gibbets bearing their horrifying fruit, and of the men and women who disappeared never to be heard of again. "Are there no laws against wholesale murder?"

Ydonda sheilVoryn smiled grimly. "There are," she said. "And we're here, as you see."

Her tone invited no further comment. I turned back to Glyn. "Why did you stop and speak with me back then?"

Glyn smiled, enjoying himself. "It should be obvious," he said. "I recognized you. Just as you recognized me when you looked at me."

I couldn't speak. All I could do was stand there and stare at him.

"You have the Gift, Iain," he said simply. "It's not developed, but it's there. My flash and my name would have opened the way for you to develop it and find your way to the Wildesea."

"The Gift?" I repeated hoarsely.

"That's why you knew I was here. Even if you didn't

know you were doing it, you read me just as I can read you now."

I reached out an unsteady hand for support to the rock face of the crag beside me. "I don't believe it," I said weakly. "I've no Gift.... I've never felt it...."

"The Gift doesn't usually make itself known in men spontaneously, Iain. Aye, nor in Feyii, come to that. It has to be recognized and developed. But you must have had some inkling of it."

It all came tumbling back into my mind then. How Maelgrun had known what I was thinking that day in the byre after the funeral. The way Bronwyn and I had always seemed to understand each other without words. Even the Feyish Communicator who had been a friend of my father. Dozens of other small things I'd passed off as coincidences.

But to have the Gift.... The Gift, which would make me a Communicator....

"No," I said again, with less conviction this time.

But I knew. Glyn shanBreyor had no reason to lie to me. For an interminable time, I stood caught between wanting desperately to believe him and rigid fear that he was right.

He watched me for a moment, aware of my turmoil. After a while, he smiled. He raised his hand, fingers outstretched toward my forehead.

"May I?" he asked.

That chill, rigid fear turned me cold. I stepped away from him and shook my head, my breathing abruptly gone ragged. This was witchery. It was blasphemy and heresy.... Even as the thought flitted through my mind, I knew it was nothing but nonsense, but the fear remained.

I closed my eyes for a moment, trying to think, then looked out at the sea. Its beauty and allure would never change, and I wanted more than anything to be Out there. But if I let Glyn shanBreyor touch me, if I let him Communicate with me, I would be turning my back forever on everything here in Celyddon. Everything I had ever known. If I acknowledged the Gift he assured me was mine, I would forever be outside the law. And if I left Celyddon with him, I could never return, not while Fergus and Padreg lived and ruled. This was my home—the only home I had ever known. My mother had been born here, and her people for uncounted generations.

I wanted the sea, wanted it as I had never wanted anything in my life. The yearning had been a strong undercurrent in my life ever since my father told me how it felt to be Outside on the vast, heaving bosom of the sea. I remembered being held securely in his arms, and listening to the awe and wonder in his voice as he described the violent passion of the storms, and the colours of sunset and sunrise hundreds of leagues from the nearest land. Even then, I knew that I belonged, like him, Out there. There was no other place for me where I would really fit.

But I was still liege-bound to Durstan, lawfully bound. The law on liege-bonding was quite plain, and it dealt ruthlessly with those who defied it. Then there was Bronwyn—Bronwyn who had been a mother to me. Had I been her own child, she couldn't have treated me any better than she did, or loved me more.

Still, there was the sea, and it called me strongly and urgently. It was in my blood and I would never truly belong anywhere else.

Why was it so hard to make the choice? Glyn offered me everything I ever wanted for myself, all I had ever dreamed of having. I could have it all, now. Why was I so hesitant and fearful now that my chance had finally come after all these years of waiting and yearning?

I had not realized I would be so torn. Taking what I wanted cost more than I had bargained for, came harder to accept than I ever imagined it would be. But I knew I had made the choice.

I straightened and moved away from the rock. My thoughts were still jumbled and disorganized, but through the chaotic confusion, I knew what I had to do. I took a step toward Glyn, who stood quietly waiting, smiling faintly, his hand still outstretched.

"May I?" he asked again.

I nodded. "You may," I said, and heard the faint quiver in my voice.

He put two fingers against my forehead. I felt an odd vibration inside my head, then a warmth. Something shifted subtly deep inside me and realigned itself. Then I felt his *presence*. In my head—in my mind. I shuddered, then accepted it. And as soon as I accepted it, there was a burst of joyous seemliness to it. A sense of belonging. It was strange and different, but it was good. Breathlessly, I laughed aloud with it because it felt so right. So very perfect. As if I had been waiting my whole life just for this very thing.

Glyn withdrew his fingers and smiled. "Yes," he said. "You do have the Gift. And more, Iain."

"Glyn, remember the time." the woman said.

He nodded. He said something to her quickly, then turned to me again. "When we leave, will you come with us?" he asked.

I took a deep breath. "Yes."

"You realize what leaving means?"

"Yes," I said again.

"Be here tomorrow night at this time," he said. "We can't take you with us until we finish what we came to do." He shook his head to the question I was only just beginning to form. "No, I can't tell you what it is. We'll be back here tomorrow night, but we can't wait much past moonset."

More than a dozen horses wearing the livery of the Lord High Sheriff milled around the paddock yard when I got home. As I dismounted and led old Brindle into the paddock to unsaddle him, Durstan and a sheriffman—a Squadman by his uniform—intercepted me. The Squadman carried a crossbow and a powerful lantern. He held the light up in my face. I had to turn away and cover my eyes with my hand to prevent its brightness from blinding me. Durstan reached out and pushed down the man's arm so that the light no longer shone directly into my eyes.

"It's all right," he said. "It's but my nephew Iain. Where've you been, boy? We sent a messenger to Jaerl mac Neill, but he said you'd left his place well over two hours ago."

"I found a sheep caught in a tanglewood bush near the west meadow by the cliff track," I said. "It took a while to free it from the thorns." It was a reasonable lie, and it came so easily and naturally to my lips that it surprised me. I turned to the horse to finish unsaddling it while I tried to clear the dazzle from my eyes. "Is something wrong?"

"Ye were by the shore?" the Squadman asked.

"Aye. I was."

"Did you see anything out there?"

"Like what?" I asked, relieved their presence seemed to have no connection with the silly and distressing meeting at Jaerl's place.

"Did you see any strangers, boy?" Durstan asked.

"Strangers? There are no strangers left in Celyddon." I unbuckled the girth and threw the strap across the saddle, keeping my face turned away and hoping that neither Durstan nor the Squadman could see the surprise that jolted under my heart.

"One of their accursed ships was seen tonight," the Squadman said. "Close by the shore, outside the barrier reef just to the north of here. We aren't sure if it was coming in or going out again. Someone said they saw a gig in the water, sailing north."

"When was that?" I asked.

"Earlier this evening. Shortly after dark."

About the time I saw the bright streak of phosphorescence I mistook for a dolphin. I unbuckled the rest of the saddle straps. "I saw nothing," I said. "But I was busy with the sheep." I pulled the saddle off the horse and turned to Durstan with it in my arms. "It wasn't damaged, Uncle—"

"And you're sure you saw nothing?" the Squadman said. "You're certain?"

"Aye, I'm certain," I said. "I saw nothing. Just the sheep."

"If the gig was heading north, it might have been making for Borland's Foot," Durstan said. "You'd best check there, Squadman."

I glanced quickly at Durstan, but said nothing. Borland's Foot, ten leagues north where the high Crags came right down to the water, was a place supposedly frequented by outlaws and pirates.

"We've patrol boats out," the Squadman said. "They're armed. A gig will be no match for them."

"But what would strangers be wanting here?" I asked.

"There are the outlaws in the high Crags," Durstan said. "The dissidents and political fugitives."

"Aye," the Squadman agreed. "They might be trying to contact the outlaws. There'll be trouble to come from this night, you can be sure. We'll just finish our looking around here, my lord Rothsey, then be gone on our way."

I left them and took the saddle into the tack room in the stone-built byre. When I came out again, the Squadman was hurrying back to his horse. Most of the rest of the troop of sheriffmen were already mounted and waiting. They fell into formation and wheeled their horses together toward the road.

Durstan watched them for a moment, then turned to me. "Where did you leave the sheep, boy?" he asked as we began walking toward the house.

"I let it go," I said. "I expect it'll soon enough find its way back to the mob. It was frightened, but not hurt." Lying to the Squadman had not bothered me in the slightest, but I had never before lied to Durstan and I hated how it twisted at my gut and my heart, leaving me uncomfortable and uneasy.

"I expect you're right," Durstan replied and put his hand to my shoulder.

Bronwyn stood wrapped in a shawl at the kitchen door, pale and frightened. She glanced quickly at me as Durstan and I came in together, and I realized suddenly that she knew about the meetings at Jaerl's place. I shook my head very slightly and some of the fear left her eyes. She let the shawl droop so that it barely covered her shoulders, and closed the door behind me.

"It's late," Durstan said. "Best we all be getting to bed, I think."

"Tomorrow after dinner, I want to take my bow and go back to the cliff meadow," I said. "I think the horse smelled a badgercat out there. Something spooked it while I was freeing the sheep." It was my second lie of the night, and it came easier than the first. Becoming an expert liar was not a skill I could be even remotely proud of, especially when it came to lying to Durstan and Bronwyn.

Durstan made a wry face. "A badgercat?" he repeated. "We certainly don't need a badgercat mauling any more sheep."

"Aye. That one last winter did enough damage," I said.

"D'ye need help with it, lad?"

"No. I'll manage."

"Shall you be wanting to take some food with you?" Bronwyn asked. "In case you're out all night?"

"Aye," I said and met her eyes. They widened in sudden shock and realization. Bronwyn knew. It was for certain she knew, and she had a very good idea of why I wanted to go out tomorrow night. I had never spoken of my dreams of going Outside, but I think Bronwyn always knew of them, even if she said nothing about it. Now I realized how she knew. If I had the Gift, Bronwyn very nearly had it, too. She had enough of it to give her the uncanny intuitiveness, which had always impressed others. Bronwyn mab Dairmid clan Rothsey *knew* people.

"I'll make up a basket for you to take with you then," she said. She came forward and reached up to kiss my cheek gently. "Sleep well, Iain. And keep safe."

Chapter Seven

I SLEPT VERY little that night, but more than I expected to with the excitement and anticipation fizzing through my body like the waters of a mineral spring. In the morning, I awoke early and pulled the tanglewood box from its hiding place beneath the hearthstone. The gold of the little maple leaf shone with a soft, gleaming luster, but the silver flash had tarnished. I spent a few minutes polishing it, returning it to its original burnished luminescence, then threaded it onto the thin chain beside the maple leaf. Only these would come with me. If I didn't want to raise any suspicions, I had to leave everything else when I went out with my bow after dinner. But there was nothing I wanted, nothing I would leave behind with regret.

Except Bronwyn and Durstan....

I heard Bronwyn leave the chamber she shared with Durstan and go down the stairs. Mag and Rhea were already moving about in the kitchen, preparing breakfast. I made sure the collar of my shirt hid my father's insignia and the silver flash, then went down to the kitchen. Durstan appeared as Bronwyn supervised Mag serving the meal.

There were chores to do, and I was busy, but still the day dragged interminably. Several times, I saw troops of sheriffmen hurry past on the road, the sun flashing off their armour as they searched for signs of strangers. Occasionally, I caught a glimpse of their patrol boats when my work took me to the cliff above the shore. I hoped they would call off the search before nightfall. Armed patrol boats might easily sink even a gig propelled by the Feyish magic of a ship's commander.

Durstan came in just before dinner and announced that a forbidden book had been found in the possession of young Cadal mac Lachlan in Caliburn, and that Cadal had been arrested and taken to the Law Courts for questioning. I looked up at him, startled, from where I sat at the table mending a stirrup strap. Distracted, I managed to stab my thumb with the awl and swore softly under my breath. Durstan didn't seem to notice. He washed his hands at the sink and accepted a towel from Bronwyn to dry them.

"It doesn't surprise me overly much," he said, shaking his head in exasperation as he handed the towel back to Bronwyn. "That boy never had enough brain to rattle in a snuff box." He glanced at me. "Friend of yours, isn't he, Iain?"

"I suppose," I said. "We were in school together. He's Jaerl's friend more than mine."

"Perhaps it has something to do with why the strangers were here," Bronwyn said. "If so, perhaps they'll be gone now."

"Aye, perhaps," Durstan said as if he didn't believe it. "The sheriffmen have found no trace of the ship today. There's talk about the glens that the strangers came because the outlaws in the Crags called them."

"Outlaws?" I looked up from the stirrup strap. A few drops of blood from my thumb stained the leather, but it was hardly noticeable. "Whyever would the outlaws call the strangers here?"

"More foolish talk about starting a civil war," Durstan said. "There are rebels among the outlaws who want to oust Fergus and set up Daryn as king in his place." He shook his head and snorted derisively. "It's not Fergus they should be talking of ousting. It's Padreg who needs taking care of." He gave me a hard look. "And you'll forget you heard that from me, boy."

"Of course," I murmured. "But the strangers—or the Watch either for that matter—wouldn't help in a civil war. The Commonwealth has never yet interfered with civil matters, especially here in Celyddon. Why should it start now?"

"Why, indeed," Durstan agreed. "It's beyond me what that ship is doing here. I hope the sheriffmen either find it soon or give up and go away. It's upsetting the sheep having them bounding all anyhow around the meadows and glens."

"Will they search again tomorrow?" Bronwyn asked.

"Aye, I imagine so," Durstan replied. "They'll search until they find it, or they're sure it's gone. They'll be wanting to question the Outsiders."

Bronwyn nodded, then turned to me. "Put that away now, Iain, so we can set the table for dinner," she said, closing the discussion.

It was dark when I took my bow and went out to saddle Brindle. I took a small lantern, Bronwyn's basket, and a sleepsack on the excuse that I might have to track the badgercat late into the night, and in that case, would not return until morning. Bronwyn's idea was a good one. It would add a few more hours to the time when someone realized I was gone.

A squad of sheriffmen stopped me as I crossed the road that led to Caliburn. They recognized me and let me go with no more than a few cursory questions, and went on about their business, leaving me to go on about mine. They were armed with crossbows and daggers. Of course, they didn't know that Glyn shanBreyor and Ydonda sheilVoryn were members of the Watch. I thought perhaps the Watch might look askance at any attempt to kill or harm any of its members. Celyddon might declare itself off-limits to all strangers and foreigners, but I highly doubted even Fergus and Padreg, and their Royal Council as well, would want to take on the Watch, especially a Membership which was seriously annoyed by an attack on two of its Members. The Watch had a reputation for showing little mercy or regard for those who injured or killed Members. I thought it might make little difference whether the culprit was King, High Priest, High Sheriff, or merely an outlawed felon.

There had been some cloud early in the afternoon, but it was gone now. The sky arched high and black above me as I rode toward the cliff track. The last of the dolphins were almost gone from the sea now. I saw only one or two bright trails of phosphorescence cutting through the dark waters of the sea, moving away from land. Once, I thought I saw a dark sillhouette against the sky that might have been a sheriff's patrol boat, but I couldn't be sure.

The ebbing tide had left the rippled sand in the small cove shining in the moonlight. Seaweed lay in limp strands against the granite of the cliffs, and the air smelled strongly of its scent. I saw no sign of the Out-ship's gig, nor of Glyn and Ydonda.

Automatically, my mind already far out at sea, I unsaddled Brindle. I gave him a fond slap on the withers and left him free to wander among the clumps of seaweed, or find his way back up to the grassy meadow. Eventually, he would find his way home once I had gone. He had been a good friend these last ten years. I was going to miss him. I tried not to think of what else I would sorely miss when I left Celyddon.

I spread the sleepsack on the damp, glistening sand where I could sit on it with my back against the still-warm rock of the cliff face. A slight breeze rattled in the leaves of the tanglewood bushes high above me, and carried the warm scent of trees and pastures with it. The night air was not cold, but I shivered as I looked out to sea.

I was leaving Celyddon. After all the years of dreaming and yearning, I was going to leave, to go Outside to the open seas.

And I was going to become a Communicator.

Even in my wildest dreams, I had not dared hope for that. I drew in a deep, unsteady breath. The Communicators were the elite of the Out-ship crews, along with the Pathfinders, Farseers and Windcasters. So few people of either race had the potential to be Communicators, Humans even less so than Feyii. It was difficult to believe that Glyn shanBreyor had recognized that potential in me. But if he said it was there, it was there. All my life I had wanted this. Not once had I ever thought it would actually be mine. The Wildesea *and* becoming a Communicator. I kept thinking I was still dreaming.

Something dark moved against the scattering of stars on the horizon. I got to my feet and walked away from the shelter of the cliffs to see better. Whatever it was out there, it was big, and it came silently toward shore with most of its canvas furled. The Out-ship's gig.

The excitement I had been trying to suppress all day bubbled up in my chest and made it difficult to breathe.

The gig was still fairly far from shore when the patrol boat appeared around the curve of the cliffs. The rock behind me had masked the splash of its dozen pair of oars until it shot out from behind the tumble of broken rock on the far side of the cove.

I threw myself flat onto the wet sand, but the patrol boat wasn't looking for me. It twisted into a sharp turn, moonlight glinting on the bow wave thrown up before it. It was less than half the size of the gig, but it was fast and deft, much more maneuverable than the thirty-foot gig. The distance between the two ships closed incredibly swiftly.

Blazing streaks of flame shot away from the patrol boat. For a moment or two, I didn't realize the implications of those flaring lights. Then cold fear gripped my belly. Fire arrows, soaked with oil. Any wooden ship will burn, even an Out-ship's gig piloted by the magic of a Feyish ship's captain. I knew what those fire arrows could do if they hit their target.

There was no doubt that the two Outsiders knew it, too. I saw the gig's abrupt shift as they tried to dodge the flaming arrows.

A sudden stench filled the air, something like the odour of burning dung, but stronger, more malevolent. Perhaps a trace of sulphur in it. I had the impression of a man, arms raised to the sky, in the bow of the boat. An eerily glowing ball of pulsating, actinic green flame formed above the patrol boat. It hovered there, bobbing gently in the mild breeze. In horrified fascination, I watched it. I had never before seen anything like it.

Ball lightning?

The fiery sphere erupted into multiple bolts of fizzing and sputtering green lightning. One after another, they hit the gig, as if aimed as surely as the flaming arrows, The gig staggered in the water. Seconds later, it became an immense, searingly bright fireball in the night. Flame poured into the sky, then down onto the surface of the sea like a ghastly rain shower, sizzling and crackling and hissing in the still air. One streak of light—nearly phosphorescent—shot away horizontally from the burning horror on the sea, skittering north, approximately parallel with the shore.

I watched, stunned and impotent, frozen into immobility, unwilling and unable to believe what I saw. I think I shouted out in helpless rage and grief, and I know hopeless sobs tore at my throat. I pounded my fist into the yielding ground and shouted obscenities in my powerless anger, cursing the sheriffmen, cursing Fergus and Padreg and all the Royal Council. Cursing Celyddon.

Then I realized what that streak of greenish luminescence had to mean. I scrambled to my feet and ran to catch the horse and saddle it. I had to get to the life-slip before the sheriffmen did. It was my only chance.

And I was Glyn and Ydonda's only chance.

The life-slip had left the inferno of the gig moving north along the shore. The only point where the land thrust out into the sea far enough to catch it was nearly a league from here, not far from the foot of the crags sheltering the high country meadow where the corewood bothy stood.

I could not follow the shoreline directly. Broken rock spilling out as far as the low tide line blocked my path in too many places. Many times, I had to leave Brindle on the crest of the cliff and scramble over the tumbled boulders on hands and knees in my search, hoping I wouldn't miss the small life-slip in the dark.

Twice, I hid in the shadows to avoid detection by a troop of sheriffmen. The second time I pulled Brindle into a cleft in the rocks, the troop clattered past so close I could smell the sour scent of horse and man sweat. My heart in my throat, I held Brindle's nose so he wouldn't call out to the other horses.

I came to the road, and burst out of a shaw of hollies to cross it. I didn't notice the sheriffmen on the narrow road until the light of a lantern hit me in the eyes and a voice shouted out of the dark. I spent a couple of busy and breathless moments trying to stay on Brindle's back and calm him at the same time. He reared and pranced, startled and frightened. When he settled, I slid off and turned my head away from the glare.

"Who are you and what are you doing here?" demanded the same voice that had shouted at me.

"I'm called Iain mac Drew clan Morgian," I said. "This land belongs to my Uncle Durstan, Laird Glenaidyn of clan Rothsey." A man moved out of the glare of the light and walked cautiously toward Brindle. He pulled the bow out of its sheath on the saddle, then checked the full quiver of arrows with their iron heads.

"What are you doing out at this time of night armed like this?" the second sheriffman asked.

"There was a badgercat after our sheep," I said. "I'm trying to track it down."

"At this time of night?" Suspicion lay heavy in his voice.

"You don't know about badgercats," I said. "They're nocturnal. They hide in burrows or caves during the day. The only time you can get them is at night."

The sheriffman grunted, not satisfied. Obviously a townsman, that one. The other, who still held the light in my face, said, "He's right. You can't track a badgercat during the day."

"You can check with my Uncle Durstan if you've a mind to," I said. "I'm here on his orders."

For a moment, there was a heavy silence. Then, after a hurried consultation, they decided not to bother. They asked a few more questions before giving the bow back to me and letting me go. This was, after all, clan Rothsey land, and my uncle was The Rothsey. I was nephew to the laird, his liege-bound. The land and the sheep were my responsibility to protect from marauding animals.

An hour later I found the life-slip. It had come ashore gently enough in a tiny cove surrounded by stunted, salt-bitten blaeberry bushes. And there were no sheriffmen in sight. I couldn't stop the sob of relief that choked in my throat.

I saw no sign of movement around it as I dismounted and approached the squat, stubby cylinder. Fashioned of some smooth, hard wood I had never come across before, it was warm to the touch, almost slick. I circled it slowly, looking for some way to get into it, but I could find nothing. No seams anywhere to indicate a hatch or a door. It appeared to be all of a piece. Sealed tightly.

Finally, I tapped softly against the side and put my ear to the warm wood of the surface. No sound at all came from inside the life-slip, no sign of life. I began examining it again. There *had* to be a way into it. I used the palms of my hands, running them over every inch of the outside surface. Finally, I found a place where the smooth, polished surface seemed to be indented slightly. I pressed my hand into it and felt it yield. Silently, a section of the curved flank slid aside.

A faint incandescence that had no specific source dimly lit the interior. I had to crouch down and sit on my heels to peer into the life-slip. I heard nothing. Cautiously, stooped and still crouching almost double, I stepped through the hatch. The muted glow of radiance showed two figures held by an intricate webbing of straps in what looked like shell-cots. Neither of them moved.

The woman, Ydonda sheilVoryn, lay nearest the hatch. Her clothing was torn and bloodied, and blood matted a terrible wound in her head. She didn't appear to be breathing, and I could detect no pulse either in her wrist or at her throat. Her skin felt almost cold to the touch. Sickened and certain she was dead, I stepped quickly to the other shell-cot.

Glyn shanBreyor breathed shallowly. His glazed eyes were open, but didn't focus on me as I leaned over him. His right arm and hand were burned and blistered, but I could find no other sign of injury on him. He made no sound as I touched him, even though it must have been extremely painful when I moved him to check for other injuries. I found no indication of a head wound, nothing to explain the glassy, vacant eyes or the appearance of unconsciousness.

I didn't know what to do. If this Gift that Glyn assured me I possessed had been developed, I might have read him and discovered what to do to help. As it was, I was powerless and helpless.

Suddenly, the woman behind me took a deep, shuddering breath. I spun around and stared at her. But it wasn't repeated. She took only the one breath, then slipped back into quiescence. I watched her for a moment, then turned back to Glyn. His face was composed, but vacantly expressionless, his eyes still glazed and unfocused.

In a flash of inspiration, I reached out to touch his forehead. My Gift might not be developed and useful, but his was. Could I force a contact? Had the brief meeting of mind and mind the night before sensitized me enough so that I could get through to him?

I pressed the pads of my fingers lightly against the skin of his temple. If he was still there behind that smooth, blank facade, either I would find him, or he would find me.

Behind me, the woman took another breath, breaking my concentration with a startled wrench. I jumped, twisted around to look at her, but she lapsed back into motionless silence. I turned back to Glyn, put my fingers against his forehead again. The skin felt cool and slightly damp to the touch.

There was nothing. No faint vibrating sensation, no impression of his presence like the last time. I closed my eyes, shut out everything but the concentration, willing contact with him. I don't know how long I crouched there, bent over him, the pads of my fingers pressed gently to his forehead. I think I heard the woman take another breath, but it was only a peripheral impression.

When it happened, it happened suddenly. That same swift and shocking awareness of a subtle shifting and realignment of something deep within me....

Just as it had the other night when Glyn first made contact with me, it caught me off balance. Then *I* was in *his* mind, *in Communication* with him.

The dizzying awareness burst upon me that I was both looking down at him, and at the same time, seeing myself bent over him. The disconcerting double vision sent nausea churning through my belly. I gasped as it took all the breath from my body. It was frightening and terrifying, but at the same time, it filled me with elation and triumph.

I heard his voice, faint and preoccupied. *"...Accept it, Iain..."*

I use the term *voice* because that's how I perceived it. I could hear him, but in an entirely different sense than speaking aloud. The closest I can come to describing how it sounded would be to say that it struck me like remembering someone's voice, or hearing it in memory.

It came all of a piece, though, not really in separate words, but more in a block. Perhaps it was the auditory equivalent of looking at a word and not seeing the separate letters, only the word and its meaning. It was strange and uncanny, and it took a lot of getting used to.

"... *Accept it...*" he said again, very faintly.

It was difficult. I had to fight the unreasoning fear, struggle to overcome the disbelief and the sense of invasion that came from knowing he was in my mind just as surely as I was in his. But, as it had the night before, when the acceptance came, it came with a rush and a deep, abiding perception of joy and a sense of *belonging*. And with it came the knowledge that this was right and harmonious—a part of me I welcomed. It blended and became a completely natural and fundamental part of me.

Then I knew what was happening; I knew why Glyn lay glazed and blank. I knew what he was doing. He was holding onto Ydonda. The head injury she sustained was bad enough so that she could not help herself. He had slid deep into Communication with her. His strength, not hers, kept her heart beating just enough to move the life-giving blood around, stopped the rush of blood from the torn vessels, maintained the slow and careful breathing. If he let go, she would die. It took all of his energy, all of his concentration, to sustain the contact. He had very little left over for himself.

"*What can I do?*" I asked him.

Again, that long, preoccupied pause before he responded. "*...Medician...*"

"*Can we move her?*"

"*...No...*"

"*If the sheriffmen find you, they'll kill you. We have to get both of you out of here.*"

"*...Can't hold her...*"

"You'll have to. I'll go back to the croft and get the wagon. I think I can get it out to the meadow above the shore. Then I'll find a medician for her."

"...Hurry..." Urgency just on the edge of obvious desperation filled his projection.

"I'll be back within the hour," I promised. *"Trust me."*

I broke contact with him and paused a moment to look down at Ydonda as I hurried past, remembering what I had learned in that first instant of contact with Glyn. Her skin felt curiously cool and dry. Glyn had lowered her body temperature. Oddly enough, it seemed to lessen her requirement to breathe. He had slowed her heartbeat to one every half minute or so. If he could hold her until we could get her to a medician, provided the damage inflicted by the wound itself was not too massive, she might recover.

Brindle hesitated to gallop at night over the rocky meadow toward home. Some of my urgency must have reached through to him, though, because once I managed to overcome his reluctance, he put on a burst of speed I hadn't thought him still capable of.

I glanced at the sky as we entered the croftyard. In only an hour or two, it would be dawn. The life-slip would be easy to spot in the light of day, unless the tide carried it away. Before that, I had to have Glyn and Ydonda hidden where the sheriffmen could not find them, and I had to find a medician for Ydonda.

I swore. I had forgotten the tide. I didn't have until dawn to get Glyn and Ydonda safely away. I had less than an hour before the tide turned. Miss that, and the water would surely sweep the life-slip out to sea, and Glyn and Ydonda with it.

Brindle slowed gratefully to a quiet walk as we entered the croftyard. The sound of galloping hooves against the hard-packed ground would too easily awaken Durstan or

Bronwyn. There was no sign of movement in the dark house. I slid out of the saddle and hastily shut the horse into the paddock. It took only moments to harness Flicker and Fan to the light wagon.

As I climbed to the worn wooden seat of the wagon, Bronwyn came flying out of the kitchen door, a dark shawl wrapped around her shoulders.

"Wait, Iain," she called softly, her hand outstretched toward me.

I let the traces droop and turned on the seat. She came to the side of the wagon and reached up to grasp my arm.

"Did you find them?" she asked. "I saw the explosion and saw the life-slip get away. Durstan saw it, too. We were out on the promontory with a late-lambing ewe. Durstan sent Erid to tell the Sheriff. Did you find them?"

She saw or sensed my hesitation. Impatiently, she shook my arm. "Don't be daft, boy. I know about them. I know about you—"

"You know about me?" My heart gave a hard, startled thud in my chest. "How?"

"Your mother suspected you had a Gift," she said quickly. "She told me about it. I know. And I know about Jaerl mac Neill and his silly friends. Did you find them before the sheriffmen?"

"Aye, I found them," I said. "But the woman's hurt badly."

She took a deep breath, then nodded. "I feared they'd be hurt," she said. "Bring them back here. Both of them. We can hide them in the byre, in the loft. No one will think of looking for a pair of strangers in Durstan mac Lludd's own croft. I'll see to them while you fetch Medician Dougal mac Llyr from Caliburn. He'll help us."

"Holly mab Dougal's father?"

"Aye. Hurry, lad. There's not much time left until dawn. Will you need a hand?"

"No. You'd best stay here. If Durstan awakens and finds you gone, too, there'll be trouble."

"Then be quick, lad."

"Bronwyn...." About to ask her how long she had been involved with the rebels, I paused, then changed my mind and shook my head. It didn't matter now and there was not tine. "Never mind."

She smiled and stepped away from the wagon. I seized the traces and guided Flicker and Fan out onto the track toward the shore meadow.

I was afraid the light wagon could not negotiate the narrow track back to the shore. Several times, I heard the wheels scrape against the rocks, but the axles didn't break. Luck stayed with us. No sheriffmen crossed our path. If they were still out, they were searching far from here. I could not have hidden the wagon from them. My story about tracking a badgercat would not hold up if they caught me with the wagon.

The sky behind the ridge of crags had begun to lighten when I reached the cove where the life-slip lay. I nudged the wagon as close to the edge of the low cliff as I could, then hurried to the life-slip, slithering down the bank in a rattle of sand and small stones. I didn't have to touch Glyn this time to make contact with him.

"I've brought the wagon," I told him. *"Can we move her?"*

"...Try..."

His voice was weaker now. Weak enough to frighten me. I wondered how much strength he had left, and whether it would be enough to keep them both.

"I'll help you hold her."

"...Can't ..."

"What do you want me to do?"

"...Help me..."

"How?"

"...Join..."

"How?"

"...Join with me..."

Following his lead, I had to go deep to trace all the pathways in his brain and try to coordinate them with my own. It made for strange and exhausting work, moving two bodies. Clumsy and cumbersome and ungainly. I had to move him, and I had to move my own body. We had no time to practice. Already the incoming tide was creeping up the sand, to within a foot or two from the stranded life-slip.

Both of us moved jerkily and awkwardly, like puppets manipulated by an inexperienced and uncoordinated puppeteer. But between us, we managed to carry Ydonda's shell-cot out of the life-slip and up the bank to the wagon.

Every time Glyn moved his arm, every time even the slightest pressure tensed the muscles, the pain he ignored ripped through my own arm, and I hadn't the skill to screen it out. But together, we got Ydonda into the wagon. Glyn climbed in beside her, unsteady as a newborn lamb.

When I broke the contact and let go, he sank down onto the deck of the wagon beside Ydonda and curled his body as if he huddled around an unbearable pain. One of his hands groped blindly until he found her shoulder, then gripped tightly to it. It was a bad sign. It meant that his strength was failing so that he could not maintain the deep contact without a physical connection.

I scrambled up to the seat of the wagon and gathered up the traces. The thought of meeting more sheriffmen terrified me. If we did, all three of us were dead. Glyn and Ydonda were helpless. I could not even adequately defend myself if we were stopped. I had no illusions about my relationship to Durstan protecting me were I caught with two Outsiders, one of them a Feyi and the other a Fey-Halfblood, in the wagon.

I don't know where our luck came from. All I know is that we had more than our share that night. I heard the hoofbeats of a patrol long before they had a chance to hear us. Had we been fifty feet up or down the track, I couldn't have got off without breaking something. Right beside us stretched a smooth, grassy verge, leading into a copse of tanglewood bushes. I turned the horses, urging them behind the thick brush, then watched as the troop of sheriffmen cantered past on the track. I gave them a few minutes to get well away, then flicked the traces and guided the horses back onto the track.

Bronwyn was waiting in the croftyard when I finally guided Flicker and Fan through the gate. She helped me carry the shell-cot to the loft while Glyn stumbled along blindly behind us. It took longer than I thought, but finally we got both of them safely hidden in a space behind the heaped sheaves of straw and hay. Bronwyn found her emergency basket and quickly did what she could for Ydonda's wound and Glyn's burns.

"Fetch Medician Dougal," she said as she worked. "I'll tell Durstan I sent you to Caliburn on an errand for me. But hurry. The woman is very badly hurt. If the medician doesn't see her soon, I'm afraid she'll die." She didn't say, *I'm afraid she'll die anyway*, but the words hung in the air between us.

I stooped quickly, touched Glyn's shoulder. *"I'll be back as quickly as I can,"* I told him.

"...Don't let her die..."

"I'll try not to."

"...If she dies while I'm Holding, I die too..."

Chapter Eight

I KEPT FLICKER and Fan to a brisk trot alternating with a fast walk, but still the trip into Caliburn took nearly three hours—twice as long as normal. The highway swarmed with sheriffmen. I had not gone more than a furlong from the croft before a group of sheriffmen stopped me and demanded to know what I was about. They questioned me closely to find out if I had seen anything of an Out-ship or any strangers. I had never seen these sheriffmen before. They wore the armbands of the elite troops of the Lord High Sheriff in Dundregan. They were more suspicious and more thorough than the local sheriffmen.

I looked at them blankly as they fired question after question at me. I let my mouth hang open slightly and made the bottom half of my face go slack and loose.

"Han't seen nothin'," I muttered over and over. It convinced them I was dull and slow, and they gave up eventually. They let me go after thoroughly searching the carriage.

It worked so well with the first group of sheriffmen, I used it on the next two groups, too.

It was only seven hours thirty when I found Medician Dougal mac Llyr's house. I left the carriage at the curb and ran up the front path to the door. An ornate bell-cord hung beside the door. I pulled it several times, and heard chimes ring faintly somewhere deep within the house. It took five minutes for Holly mab Dougal to answer the door, a long houserobe belted securely around her, hair still tousled from sleep tumbling over her shoulders. Her eyes widened in surprise as she recognized me.

"Iain!" she said. "Whatever brings you here?"

"I need to see the medician," I said. "Your father. Is he here?"

"Is someone hurt? Your uncle?

"Not Durstan, but there's someone hurt. My Aunt Bronwyn says we can trust your father."

"Come in for a moment," she said. "You can't stand there in the doorway like that without attracting attention we don't need or want." She closed the door after me as I stepped into the hallway, then motioned me toward the parlour. A vague feeling of familiarity swept over me, gone in an instant as I left the hallway.

"Will you fetch your father for me?" I asked. "Will you tell him we need him?"

"Iain, I can't. He was called out by the High Sheriff a few hours ago on an emergency. He didn't give me many details, but I gather there's been a bad accident. My father won't be back for hours yet."

Black despair gripped my heart and made the backs of

my eyelids sting. Ydonda couldn't wait those hours for a medician. Even now, it might be too late.

"Is there anyone else, Holly?" I asked desperately. "Someone we can trust?"

She shook her head. "I know of no one," she said. "Who's hurt?"

A prickle of recognition trickled down my spine again. I had been here before, years ago on a night when a freighter was loading at the Outport. I was certain of it, but it was something I dared not mention. I looked at Holly, who met my gaze squarely and without that subtle recollection I felt. Then I remembered what she had said at Jaerl Neill's place, there in the darkness of the paddock, how she had talked about friends who had better ways to combat the tyranny of Fergus's Royal Council and Padreg's Inner Circle of priests than the mindless folly of merely reading forbidden books. I'd had reason to trust her twice before; it gave me cause to trust her now.

"An Outsider," I said. "A Feyish woman."

She looked at me in inquiry. "From the Out-ship gig they destroyed last night?"

"Aye. I found their life-slip."

"Is she badly hurt?"

"Aye. Without a medician, she'll die. She might die anyway."

Holly turned away and went to stand by the window. She stood there, head bowed, her arms folded tightly, hugging herself. Her concentration as she wrestled with a problem came to me strongly and clearly. Finally, she turned back to face me.

"I know someone," she said.

I went to her, gripped her arms. "Who is he?"

"Me, Iain." Then in a rush: "I've certainly not yet been

admitted to the Medician's Guild, but I entered the College autumn before last. I've not graduated, and not even started my apprenticeship but I've been helping my father since I was old enough to fetch and carry for him. I've never had a Feyish patient before, but if you trust me, I think I might be able to help. I have more medical knowledge than a lay-healer at any rate. Will you trust me then, Iain?"

I looked down at her, deep into her blue eyes. I found I could read her, just far enough below the surface to see openness and honesty and sincerity. I could detect no darkness or sinister subterfuge in her. I came to the only conclusion I could.

"Aye. I'll trust ye."

She had somehow felt me touching her mind. Her eyes went wide in shock and surprise. "You—" she stammered. "You're—"

"There's no time for that now," I said quickly, brushing aside all the unspoken questions I sensed bubbling up in her. "We've great need to hurry." I let my hands drop to my sides and stepped away from her.

She visibly pulled herself together. Her mouth firmed, and her shoulders straightened and squared. "Of course," she said too briskly. "Wait here. I'll dress and get my kit. I'll be only a moment."

She was as good as her word. She reappeared dressed in breeks, boots and a shirt, her glossy dark hair tied back out of her way with a bright ribbon, looking like any Freeholder's daughter. She carried a heavy brown leather case. I took it from her as we left the house and thrust it deep under the seat of the wagon. The space there was far too small to hide a person, and I hoped that it would be ignored if we met and were searched by more sheriffmen.

Holly sat beside me on the unpadded seat, her back

straight as she looked ahead. She pointedly and obviously did not look at me. Her curiosity fairly crackled around her like an aura of rigging lightning. It amused me, then gave me a startling kick under the heart again as I realized afresh what caused her curiosity.

Dear Mother of All, I was a *Communicator!* I laughed aloud, half with delight, half with disbelief.

"Have you never met a Communicator before then, Holly?" I asked.

She looked at me at last. "Not since Fergus and Padreg drove them out of the realm," she said. "And none of them were Celyddonians."

I smiled. "I'm really not a Communicator," I said. "I've only recently discovered I've the Gift."

"You're enough of a Communicator to make me nervous," she said. "You almost frightened me back there."

I started to reply, then stiffened. Instead, I said, "There are sheriffmen ahead."

"Stop for a moment," she said as if it didn't even occur to her to question how I knew.

I guided the horses to the side of the road. Up ahead was the bridge across the Strathflorin River. On the other side of the bridge, the road curved and dipped down into a small, thickly treed valley. The sheriffmen lay in hiding just over the crest of the hill. I had picked up their sense of purpose more than anything else. Like the faint buzzing of insects, it hummed eerily in the still morning air. I shivered. I hadn't realized I could do that, and it both startled and fascinated me.

Holly pulled a lip paint out of her pocket. She applied it quickly, then slid across the seat toward me. "Kiss me, Iain," she said with no hint of coyness or flirtatiousness.

I simply stared at her. She put her hands behind my head and pulled it down so she could reach me. She pressed her mouth to mine and rumpled my hair with her hands. Then she moved back to her side of the seat and laughed at my astonishment.

"There's nothing in the world more harmless-looking than a man with a woman's lip paint smeared all over his mouth and his hair all tousled," she said. "Or, for that matter, a woman with her lip paint kissed off. Now let's go and face down those sheriffmen."

I laughed and shook my head. She would get no argument from me on that point. I had been right about the mind that lurked behind that clear, smooth forehead.

The sheriffmen stepped out into the middle of the road as we came over the crest of the hill. They were armed and held their crossbows as if they were more than willing to use them if need be. One of them wore officer's bars on the shoulder of his tunic.

"Who are you and where are you going, boy?" the officer asked.

I saw him notice the smudge of lip paint on my mouth. It didn't take a Communicator to read his lecherous assumption or his lewd amusement.

"I'm Iain mac Drew clan Morgian," I said. "My uncle is Durstan mac Lludd clan Rothsey, Laird of Glenaidyn. We're going back to the Holding, sir."

"Who's the woman?"

I glanced at Holly and hesitated only briefly. "My betrothed. Holly mab Dougal."

She sketched a brief gesture toward her mouth, then she blushed and lowered her eyes. I wiped my hand across my own mouth. I didn't have to try to look self-conscious and embarrassed.

The officer looked at her, a trace of lewd speculation in his expression. "Are you Medician Dougal mac Llyr's daughter then, girl?" he asked.

"Aye," she said. "I am."

The officer turned his attention back to me. "And you'd be Maelgrun mac Durstan's cousin, would ye?"

"I am."

Maelgrun's name did the trick. The officer stepped back. "Be careful," he said. "There's Outsiders and strangers around somewhere. If you see anything, send immediately to the High Sheriff's office."

"Aye, we will," I said.

As I flicked the traces to start the horses moving forward, Holly let her hand trail down the back of my neck. Once we were out of sight, she moved back to her place on the far side of the seat and folded her hands quietly into her lap.

"They're very anxious to catch those Outsiders of yours," she said thoughtfully.

"Aye. As well they should be. The gig they destroyed belonged to a Watch Out-ship. I doubt very much they want word of it to reach the Watch. It would take a dim view of losing Members and ships like that."

She glanced at me, her eyes wide and startled. "The Watch?" she repeated. "Here in Celyddon? Whatever for, I wonder."

"They didn't tell me why they were here," I said. "There wasn't exactly time to ask, either, you ken."

She nodded. "Of course," she murmured, and lapsed into silence.

We met no more sheriffmen. Bronwyn was in the yard, feeding the hens, when we drove in. She dropped the grain pouch and hurried to meet us.

She glanced at Holly, frowning, betraying her anxiety. "Where's the medician?" she asked. "Where's Dougal?"

"My father couldn't come," Holly said. "I've medician

training, but I've not finished my apprenticeship yet. I think I can help. Where are they?"

Bronwyn made a rapid appraisal, then nodded once in acceptance. "In the byre," she said. "Up in the loft."

"How's Ydonda?" I asked.

"Still alive," Bronwyn said. "But barely. There's no change that I can see in her."

"Where's Durstan?"

"Out with the shearers in the west meadow," she said. "He'll not be back until late afternoon. He wasn't pleased to find that you were gone, but I told him it was an emergency. You'll have to go out there later and help him."

"Best you both come with me," Holly said. "I might need some help. Bring the kit, Iain, would you, please?"

Ydonda still lay motionless in the shell-cot. Glyn lay curled on his side beside her, eyes still open and glazed, his hand tightly gripping her shoulder. Bronwyn had covered the both of them with blankets and slipped a small pillow beneath Glyn's head. They were as comfortable as she could make them. Holly went to her knees beside Ydonda and drew back the blanket. She reached out and touched two fingers to the still throat.

"There's no pulse," she said. "I think she's dead—"

"No," I said. "He's Holding her. Wait for it."

She didn't remove her fingers. Then she nodded. "One of the Feyish healing arts," she murmured thoughtfully. "I think I see. I've read about it in my father's books, but I've never seen it before."

She turned her attention to Ydonda's wounds. Her expression became contemplative and remote as she studied them. But when she lifted the cloth covering Ydonda's forehead, she paled and made a quick exclamation of dismay.

"Iain, I don't know what I can do for her without taking her in to Caliburn to the clinic," she said. "Her skull is fractured and the bone is pressing against her brain. I can't do that sort of surgery here." She shook her head emphatically. "It's impossible."

"You'll have to," I said quietly. "We can't chance taking her into Caliburn. What do you think the sheriffmen would do if they found her in a clinic, her being both Feyish and a Communicator?"

She looked up at me, her face very pale. "But I don't have the equipment to do surgery like that. Even at the clinic, she might die. Here, she certainly will."

"We can help you," I said. "Between Glyn and me, we can help you. We can show you what you need to see."

"You can help?"

"We can tell you what you have to do. We can show you where all the bone splinters are. Anything you need. Glyn can even regulate her breathing and her heart rate. Anything at all."

She looked down at Ydonda again, and pressed her interlaced fingers against her lips, coming to a decision. She looked back at me. "What will I have to do?" she asked.

"You're going to have to cut into her scalp, through the bone—"

Holly drew back, aghast. "Cut into her *head?*"

"You have to remove the bone splinters," I insisted, knowing the words came from Glyn's mind and knowledge, not my own. "If you don't, they'll kill her."

"But, cut into her head? Through the bone? Iain, I can't! I'll kill her that way."

"She'll die if you don't. We can show you. Trust us. Please, Holly."

She took a deep breath, then wiped her hands on the thighs of her breeks. "What do I have to do?"

"It will mean deep contact, Holly," I said. "From Glyn through me to you. It's going to be very uncomfortable for you. It's going to feel like an invasion. A hundred times worse than you could ever imagine. It could be frightening if you let it."

Holly bit her lip, then looked down at Ydonda again. "She'll die if I don't, won't she?"

"Aye. And Glyn with her, I think."

"Then we'd best get started, oughtn't we?" she said, briskly, brushing her hands together. "Bronwyn, bring me clean sheets to spread out here. And the brightest lantern you have. And hurry, please." She turned to me. "Now, how do we go about this deep contact? We'd better try it once before I begin here."

"We'll show you the extent of the injuries first," I said. I reached for her hand. She hesitated, then gave it to me. "Relax and open your mind," I said. I put my other hand to Glyn's temple and made contact with him.

"I've bought the medician," I told him.

"...Hurry..." His voice sounded fainter, more preoccupied than before. He was weakening, himself, now, and afraid he couldn't maintain his hold on Ydonda much longer. Even with his hand on her shoulder, the contact was thinner, more tenuous and frail. His own injuries were virtually too painful for him to continue disregarding them much longer. His pain interfered with his concentration. He wasn't afraid of dying with her, only of not being strong enough to hold onto her, of letting her die.

"Is she worse?"

"...Yes..."

"Show me."

I took a deep breath, then made contact with Holly. At first, she resisted. For too long, Padreg's priests had preached that contact like this was practicing witchery. It was hard for her to shed that concept, even though, like me, she had never really believed it. I felt her shudder in horror and revulsion, and she drew back physically as well as mentally, trying to yank away the hand I wouldn't release. She trembled on the verge, the very brink, of panic as she fought against me. The breath went out of her in a harsh moan of protest. I didn't withdraw. Instead, I moved back closer to the surface to try again. This time, I insisted.

"Please..." I said to her. "Oh, please, Holly...."

Then I felt her relax and accept as her concern and anxiety for Ydonda overcame her fear for herself. She closed her eyes and drew in a breath that was almost a sob, then nodded. I fell deep into her in a swift rush, found her medical skills, grasped onto them. She shuddered again, then relaxed in complete acceptance.

"Show me," she whispered.

Holly mab Dougal possessed a swift, delicate and sure touch. She became so absorbed in the task of trying to repair the terrible wound in Ydonda's head that she completely forgot about being deeply and intimately linked through me to Glyn. She worked quickly and carefully, and far behind her concentration, I saw her awed fascination because she was actually able to see inside a living brain.

Myself, I think I simply drifted into a partial trance, merely letting information flow through me from Glyn to Holly, like water through a pipe. Occasionally, there would be an interrogative from Holly, then a reply from Glyn. It took all my power, all my concentration, all my strength, just to maintain the link.

It was a strange and exotic blending of three different personalities. I remember watching Holly's quick, deft initial incision from three separate viewpoints at once—my own, from hers, and very fuzzily, from Glyn's. It surprised me when the wound didn't bleed until I remembered that Glyn had Ydonda's heart rate under deep control, slowing it so the blood would not flow normally. I managed to keep my amazement from disturbing Holly, I think. In any event, she didn't hesitate in her work.

She spoke to Bronwyn, and I couldn't really be sure whether she spoke, or I spoke or Glyn did. "Swab that, please," she said.

Bronwyn leaned over Ydonda and gently wiped away the small ooze of blood that had seeped into the incision. Holly nodded her thanks, then quite literally peeled back a triangular flap of Ydonda's scalp, exposing the startlingly white bone of the skull. I remember thinking *bone white*. Of course....

Now I could see the fracture clearly. To me, it looked a little like the shell of a hard-cooked egg that had been hit with the bowl of a spoon. The depression was more or less round, dish shaped, and not more than two inches or so across. The worst part was right in the center. From Glyn, I got a picture of bone fragments pressing down into the living tissue of Ydonda's brain, piercing it cruelly in several places. It was so detailed, I could see the fine grain of the clean, white bone.

Holly leaned back to study the depression carefully, correlating what she saw with what I relayed from Glyn. She did it with remarkable ease, but I believe it was because she was so absorbed in what she was doing, she had no time to realize how strange it was. Not taking her eyes off Ydonda, with one hand, she picked up a long, slender probe with a sharp point on one end, while the other hand groped for a delicate pair of tongs.

She used the probe first, carefully inserting it under the broken bits of bone to lift them out of the way. Then she bent closer to the wound and with the tongs, gently began to pluck the bone splinters out of the delicate tissue of the brain itself. The movement of her hands was slow, deliberate, precise. She withdrew each tiny splinter with an effort to do no more damage to the affected area than absolutely necessary. With Glyn's magnified picture of what was happening, together with her own skill and dexterity, each piece came out tearing as little healthy tissue as was humanly possible.

But it was slow, arduous work. None of us had any more sense of time passing than in a dream, or perhaps in a trance. I couldn't begin to give an estimate of how long it took, even now. One by one, patiently, smoothly and coolly, Holly removed the splinters. She was calm and composed, professionally engrossed in her work.

Finally, the last splinter was gone. Holly placed the tongs neatly back onto the sheet and picked up the probe. Delicately, she realigned the broken bits of bone, bringing them together, guided by Glyn's directions.

Then I felt Glyn slip and falter. Holly felt the lapse, too. She hesitated, glanced at me in alarm. My heart pounding in my chest, I searched the link between Glyn and me. He had plunged very close to the edge of his incredible endurance and hovered on the brink of unconsciousness.

Or death....

Chapter Nine

MY HEART THUDDING painfully in my chest, I leaned forward, pressing my fingers more firmly against Glyn's forehead. Beside me, Holly caught her bottom lip between her teeth, her apprehension thrumming along the bond between us like a plucked harpstring wound around its peg to the point of snapping. I took a deep breath.

"Glyn?"

His response was delayed, very faint and weak. *"...Here..."*

"Almost finished, Glyn. Just a few more minutes. Hang on."

Again, the long pause. *"...Continue..."*

The link strengthened again and some of my fright abated. Holly looked at me in inquiry.

"It's all right," I said.

She nodded and resumed her work.

Now the last of the bone fragments had been coaxed back into its proper place. There was nothing left to cause pressure on the delicate tissue of Ydonda's brain. The shallow, bowl-shaped depression in the skull was gone. Nothing remained but the patchwork of bone Holly had pieced back together. Beneath it, the tough and durable brain had already begun to work to heal the damaged tissue.

Holly swabbed the area with a decoction to prevent wound fever, then carefully drew the flap of skin back into place. She anchored it with a few tiny stitches, then painted it with more decoction. Bronwyn handed her strips of clean linen, and Holly carefully bandaged the wound.

It was over. Holly straightened up, and moved away from Ydonda. "That's all we can do," she said. "I've relieved the pressure. The rest is up to her."

I was tired. I couldn't hold both the contact with her and with Glyn. I released her and she staggered back slightly as I let go. She pressed both hands to her eyes, then dropped her hands to her knees and stared at me. She looked like someone waking after a deep and profound sleep, momentarily disconcerted and unsure where she was. Finally, she shook her head to clear it and picked up Ydonda's pale, unresponsive hand.

"Iain, tell him to let her go now," she said. "We have to see if she'll breathe on her own and if her heart will beat."

"It's over, Glyn," I told him. *"You can let her go now. We're all finished."*

But there was no reply from him.

"Glyn?"

"What's wrong?" Holly asked.

"I don't know. I can't seem to get through to him."

"Try again. He has to let her go so we can see if she can manage on her own."

But Glyn had been holding Ydonda too hard for too long. He couldn't let her go, couldn't break the contact. I went in after him. It was like willing a cramped and clenched fist to relax and open. He had very little strength left, and what little he had, he needed for himself now. I had to pry him away from Ydonda. When he finally came away, it was like a cable snapping, flinging me away like an arrow from a bowstring. His own pain burst onto him then like a blinding white explosion, but it was I who cried out with it.

Holly gave Bronwyn a cup of something she poured from a brown leather flask. "For pain," she said. "Give it to him quickly. It's mostly poppy. It will make him sleep."

While Bronwyn gently raised Glyn's head and trickled the liquid down his throat, Holly and I looked at Ydonda. Holly put her fingers to the side of Ydonda's throat, her lower lip anxiously caught between her teeth. We both watched the still, silent chest. An eternity passed. Then Ydonda's chest rose as she took a deep, unsteady breath, let it go, took another. Holly sobbed with relief.

"Her heart's beating," she said quietly. "I think she's going to come through."

"Her other wounds?" I asked.

"They're not that serious," Holly said. "Now that the head wound is repaired, she won't have any trouble with the others."

I reached out and touched Glyn's temple. *"We did it,"* I told him. *"Ydonda's breathing on her own. Her heart's beating. Holly says she should be all right."*

This time, I received a faint pulse of relief and gratitude from him. Then the poppy took him, and he slept.

Holly reached for her treatment kit again. "I'll look after him now," she said. "Those burns must be horribly painful. Now that that head wound has been seen to, she can wait for a while."

I slumped back against a pile of straw in utter exhaustion. I hadn't slept for over thirty hours and I hadn't eaten since dinner the night before. I felt weak and dizzy, and nausea churned uneasily in my belly.

"Best you go to bed, Iain," Bronwyn said gently.

I had all but forgotten she was still there. I looked up to see her kneeling by Holly's side, calmly preparing to help her with Glyn. "I have to go out to the meadow to help Durstan," I said.

"No," Bronwyn said, not looking up from her task. "When Durstan returns, I'll tell him you caught a chill being out after the badgercat all night, and I feared a fever and put you to bed."

"But—"

"Go to bed, Iain," she said firmly.

I hardly remember stumbling out of the byre and into the house. I managed to make it to my room and fall face down on the bed, still fully dressed, before I went to sleep like tumbling down a well.

Twilight glimmered outside when I awoke. Someone— Bronwyn most likely—had removed my boots and covered me with a soft blanket. I sat up and stared fuzzily out the window, trying to decide whether it was sunset or sunrise.

Then I remembered Glyn and Ydonda, hidden in the byre loft. I got up quickly and went down to the kitchen. Bronwyn and Holly sat at the scrubbed wooden table, cups of steaming, fragrant tea before them. Durstan was nowhere to be seen.

"Glyn and Ydonda?" I asked.

"Glyn's sleeping naturally and Ydonda's doing better than I expected," Holly said. "I'll stay until I know she's out of danger. But they're both safe enough for now."

Bronwyn got up and put together a small meal for me, just bread and cheese and some cold, roasted fowl, while Holly got another cup and poured some tea. I had forgotten how hungry I was. The small meal went a long way to bring me back to feeling human again. Halfway through it, something occurred to me and I looked up at Holly, startled.

"You can't stay here," I said. "It's not seemly. What will people say?"

Bronwyn smiled, amusement glinting in her eyes. "She most certainly can stay here if it's her betrothal visit," she said mildly. "It's about time you were thinking about taking a wife anyway, young Iain."

"Betrothal visit?" I don't know what expression was on my face, but whatever it was, it caused Holly to break out into peals of laughter.

"Don't look like that, Iain mac Drew," she said lightly. "I've been told that I'm a right comely lass when I care to be. Besides, you've already told the sheriffmen I was your betrothed."

"Does your father know?"

"Bronwyn sent one of the rangemen into Caliburn to let him know where I was. He apparently thinks the betrothal visit is a good idea."

"It's a good enough story," Bronwyn said complacently. "Durstan accepted it, although he grumbled that you might have told him first."

"What in the world did you tell him?" I asked.

Bronwyn smiled. "I merely told him that if he'd spend more time paying attention to what went on at his own croft instead of hying himself off to yon Capital all the time, he might have noticed his nephew was a man grown, and it's not unknown for a young man to consider wedding a likely young lass who catches his eye."

"And what did he say?"

She laughed in pure mischief. "Not much, seeing as how there was precious little he could say."

I chose to ignore the implications of suddenly acquiring a betrothed. "Where is he?"

"In his bed," Bronwyn said. "I've no doubt but that he'll have you out of yours at dawn tomorrow to help with the shearing."

I had almost forgotten about the shearing. I had spent the whole day in bed when I should have been out in the meadow helping Durstan to supervise the shearers, or overseeing the rangemen rounding up the mobs of sheep from the high country.

"He'll also no doubt have a piece of my hide tomorrow for being such a lay-about today," I said.

Bronwyn smiled again. "It'll not be the first time he's threatened to remove a strip of hide from you," she said. "And it won't be the last, I'm thinking. I note you've got most of your skin intact, so I've reason to believe you'll survive this time, too." She got up to gather the dishes and cups from the table. "I see no reason why a young betrothed couple shouldn't take a walk in the moonlight, though, if you'd be wanting to check on your friends, Iain."

We took a lantern with us to the byre. Holly turned it down to a dim glow as we looked at Glyn and Ydonda. Ydonda's breathing was slow and even, and some colour had come back to her face. When I placed the tips of my fingers to her throat, her pulse throbbed, strong and regular, under my touch, and her skin felt warm and dry.

Holly went to her knees beside Ydonda to check the stitching under the thick padding of bandage, and make sure there was no inflammation. "No sign of wound fever," she said in satisfaction. "I can see this beginning to heal already. My father said Feyii heal quicker than we do. I'd never seen it before." She checked Ydonda's heart and her breathing, then sat back on her heels and shook her head in amazement. "I still can't believe I did this," she said. "Iain, I actually looked into her brain. It's criminal that we can't use people like you or Glyn in clinics any more. And what I wouldn't have given for a Feyish Healer this morning—"

"Witchery," I said with a bitter grimace.

She said a rude word, then blushed when I laughed. "My father told me how he used to work with Feyish Sorters and Holders before Fergus banished them from the realm. And there was a Caleddonian Healer once, too. I have no idea what happened to her. I hope she escaped to Lysandia all right. I wish—"

"Wishing won't do any good, Holly."

"No. I know that. Only actions count. But one day, Iain.... One day other medicians will be able to do again what I did this morning. Think of the lives we'll be able to save then."

"Aye. Look at the life you saved this morning. It's a start."

"Aye. A good start." She broke off and turned her attention to Glyn.

He lay on his back, a thick padding of bandage over his arm and hand. He, too, breathed slowly and regularly, his eyes closed in deep and profound slumber. A small frown of pain drew his dark gold eyebrows together above the bridge of his nose, and the colour of his irises was vaguely apparent through his eyelids, making them appear almost like bruises in his pale face.

Holly carefully lifted the bandage from Glyn's arm. "I gave him a lot of poppy," she murmured. "He should sleep for another twenty hours yet. Mostly, he was just exhausted. The burns were painful, but not that serious. The worst was on the back of his hand. But he'll regain full use of the hand and arm, I think. There doesn't seem to be any sign of wound fever here, either." She traced the small ridge of pink around the edge of the burn. "Look. He's already beginning to heal, as well. That Feyish blood must be a wondrous thing. But he's going to have some dreadful scars there."

"We'll have to move them soon," I said. "They can't stay here. We have to get them out of Celyddon somehow."

"Can he contact other Outsiders to come and pick them up?"

"I don't know. It might be a long time before he has the strength. I think he very nearly burned himself out Holding Ydonda like that. But we can't keep them here. It's far too dangerous for everyone, especially them."

"You're right," she said. "We'll have to move them. We can't take a chance on Durstan discovering them here. I know some places where they'll be safe until we can get them out of Celyddon. It will be better if we can wait until the hue and cry has died down, though. The sheriffmen will be searching every wagon and carriage in the country for a while yet, I think."

"How long before Ydonda can be moved?"

"As long as we keep her in the shell-cot and make sure she doesn't get jolted around, we could probably move her tomorrow night. But the next night would be safer."

Glyn moved restlessly and muttered something we couldn't understand. Holly put out the lantern and he became quiet again.

We left the loft in the byre and went out into the paddock. Holly climbed the fence and sat on the top rail, balanced gracefully with her elbows on her knees, chin cupped in her hands. It was quiet, the air cooling. I leaned on the fence beside her, my elbows on the rail, and tilted my head back to look up at the stars burning fiercely in the black vault of the sky above us. The Queen and her pale Companion gleamed just above the western horizon, turning the granite crags to silver.

"Can your friends get Glyn and Ydonda out of Celyddon?" I asked.

"Aye," she said. "I think it's quite possible. We've done it more than a few times in the past several years."

"Two at once will be difficult, won't it?" I wasn't quite sure what I was driving at. No, that wasn't true. I knew exactly what it was. I just didn't want to admit to the knowledge.

"Aye. More difficult than one, but perhaps not impossible." Holly didn't look at me. She, too, watched the stars.

"Three would be hopeless then." I made it a flat statement, not a question. My hand went to the chain at my throat.

She reached out and put her hand on my shoulder. I looked up at her. In the pale starlight, her eyes were deep, shadowed pools. I could not see them, but I could feel her infinite sadness as it wrapped itself gently around me.

"Aye," she said softly. "I'm afraid three would be impossible, Iain. I'm very sorry."

"No matter," I said. I looked at the stars again. In the distance, the sea pounded against the rocky shore with a sound like the beating of an eternal heart.

So close. I had come so close. Perhaps the time had come to put away childish dreams and accept a man's responsibilities. My fist closed around the little golden leaf and the silver flash. In my bleak, despairing resignation and disappointment, my grip was stronger than I intended. The chain snapped. I looked down in dismay at the pale gleam of the gold and silver in my palm, appalled and shaken. I felt foolishly close to tears at having ruined it. Then I resolutely shoved the broken chain and its small burdens into my pocket.

"It's not important," I said. "The important thing is to get Glyn and Ydonda out of here and safely away, and quickly." There was work I could do in Celyddon—work that needed doing. It wouldn't be a life on the great seas, but I could make it a life worth something that my father would have been proud of.

"It's a dangerous business, Iain," she said. "There's not many willing to undertake it. You've seen how heavily guarded the Out-port here is. It's even worse in Dundregan. And trying to get out overland is even worse."

"I know."

"It's not easy to get someone out without the sheriffmen or Padreg's Inner Circle of priests knowing. We have good friends who can do it for us if there's real need, but we can't ask them to put their lives at risk unless it's exceptionally important."

"Ydonda and Glyn are exceptionally important," I said.

"Aye. Ydonda is a Watch officer, and Glyn a squad leader."

"And I'm just a liege-bound crofter with a dream."

"Ye could join us, Iain. We have need of a Communicator."

I smiled up at her. "And who would you be Communicating with then, Holly mab Dougal?" I asked. "As far as I know, there's not another Communicator left in the whole of the realm." I stepped away from the fence, put my hands to her waist and lifted her down.

She didn't move away from me. "Iain, when we were linked this morning, I thought I could see your dreams. I know what going Outside means to you."

"I'll get another chance if it's meant to be" I said. I looked down at her. "Would it be fitting for a man to kiss his betrothed in a paddock yard?"

She considered that gravely. "Aye," she said at last. "I believe it might be fitting."

A long few moments later, Holly broke away from me and we walked back to the house where Bronwyn immediately sent us to bed, each to our separate rooms.

Chapter Ten

STRIPPED TO THE waist and sweating in the heat of the midday sun, I crouched holding the little blue sheep securely clamped between my forearm and knee as I ran the clippers swiftly over its body. The silky fleece came away in one large mass. I released the denuded yearling, gave it a slap and a push toward the dispersal paddock. The impression of outraged dignity the sheep managed to convey with its twitching tail made me laugh as it trotted quickly across the trampled grass. I tossed the fleece onto the cart. It was finally full and ready to haul to the baler. It wasn't the first cart filled this morning. Not by a long chalk. But it was nowhere being the last, either. It made for a good morning's work.

My back felt as if someone had tied knots in all my muscles. I stood up and stretched, trying to wring some of the kinks out of it, then took off my broad-brimmed hat and wiped my wrist across my forehead to get rid of the streams of sweat rolling down my face and stinging my eyes. Lammas was less than a fortnight away and late summer with it. It had been unusually warm since Beltane, and the heat was even more oppressive now. Most of the sheep scurrying past me, clipped and shorn, looked relieved to be rid of the long, heavy fleece. By the time the weather got cold, their coarser winter coats would be well enough grown to keep them warm.

Around me against the backdrop of the trees and towering crags, the crowd of men worked amid a tumult of bustle and commotion that looked chaotic. But there was an underlying pattern and purpose to it, a rhythm and flow, if you knew what to look for. The shouts and whistles of the rangemen filled the air as they worked their dogs. The anxious, confused bleating of the sheep echoed among the cliffs as the four rangemen in the holding paddock separated the ewes and lambs, and sent them down the line of shearers. At the other end, another set of rangemen herded the shorn sheep into the dispersal paddock. The reunited ewes and lambs were quieter there.

The rams in their separate paddock snorted and huffed as they waited to be shorn when the rest were done. Rams' summer wool was coarser than ewes' or lambs' wool. It had neither the fine texture nor the silky sheen, and was worth a lot less. We used it to make stout, strong rope, or tarpaulins, or coarse floor coverings. It wasn't good for much else, and it was never mixed with the rest.

Durstan walked back and forth behind the line of shearers who worked on the trampled grass, correcting some of them, praising others. He glanced at my full cart, nodded in acknowledgment, and moved on to the next shearer.

I walked over to the water bucket in the shade of a

corewood tree. I drank the first dipperful of water. The second and third, I poured over my head, then blew a long breath through my mouth upward to stir the wet hair on my forehead. Durstan came over and took the dipper from me. His shirt and the waistband of his breeks were dark with sweat. As he drank, he critically surveyed the line of shearers.

"Young Jamie mac Welland is learning fast," he said. "You did well hiring him this season."

"Aye he'll be one of the best at the winter shearing come early spring." I pushed the wet hair off my forehead and watched the balers at work for a moment. "A good lot of summer wool, this."

"Aye," he agreed in satisfaction. "It'll bring a good price, this lot. The sheriffmen will be by this evening to take the tithe."

"It's set aside by the baler," I said. I looked out at the holding paddock. A good four hundred sheep still remained, milling aimlessly about in it, and more to come out of the high country. "Is that the last of this mob, then?"

"It should be," he said. "They'll be bringing in the next lot from the high crags this evening."

Bronwyn and Holly rode into the meadow, leading another horse laden with panniers of food and kegs of the mild ale which even Padreg's Inner Circle of priests couldn't forbid to the shearing crews who worked in the blaze of the summer sun. Seeing the women, the men began to wander toward the shade of a grove of corewood trees where Bronwyn and Holly always set out the food for them on the rough, planken tables.

"You're not going to appear in front of yon lass like that, are ye?" Durstan asked severely. "Get your shirt on, lad. It's not seemly."

My shirt hung on a nail next to the water bucket.

Grinning, I reached for it and pulled it on. "Surely, Uncle, if yon lass is to be my wife, she'll soon enough see me in less than this."

"Aye," he said equably. "I've no doubt but she will at that. But not yet."

"Aye, sir. Not yet." Obediently, I fastened the laces on the shirt.

It may not have been seemly to appear in front of one's betrothed half clad, but it was acceptable to take her to a quiet and secluded corner to eat lunch with her. Holly had packed a special basket for me, an old custom I had cause to be grateful for. She spread the food on a cloth in the cool shade where we could talk without being overheard.

"Glyn awoke for a while this morning after you and Durstan left," she said. "He's still very weak, and he's worried about Ydonda, but I think he's going to recover well."

"And Ydonda?"

"Good, I think. Her colour is much better. She moved her arm this morning, so I don't think there'll be any paralysis." She reached out and plucked an eyelet daisy, twining the supple stem around her finger. "Iain...."

I looked up in inquiry.

"I think we might be able to get one person out in a few days, if we can get her to Dundregan."

"So soon?" I took the daisy and tucked it into her hair. From a distance, we would look like any other pair of lovers, doing the silly things betrothed couples do. "That certainly didn't take very long to set up, did it?"

"Sometimes, it doesn't. A friend of ours is captain of a trader ship. I got word this morning he's taking his ship with the first of the wool to Dundregan tomorrow midmorning. There's an Out-ship leaving for Eyrindor at the end of the week. The captain is another friend. She's helped us before. But I can only get one out. I think it had best be Ydonda."

"Aye, you're right," I said. "She'd do best to be seen by a Feyish Healer. You have a lot of useful friends, Holly mab Dougal."

"We do," she said and smiled. "And good friends, at that."

"Someday, I'll have to meet these good friends."

"You'll be introduced, Iain. Never fear."

I lay down, using her thigh as a pillow, and watched the shifting pattern of the leaves overhead against the sky. The firm roundness of her thigh felt good against the back of my head and neck. I decided a man could come to like the idea of having a betrothed like Holly mab Dougal.

"How do we get Ydonda to the Outport in Caliburn?" I asked.

"Tonight when Durstan and Bronwyn have gone off to meet with the wool-buyers, someone will come for her. I'll see to it that she's as ready to travel as she can be." She pushed a stray wisp of hair back from her cheek. "I hope she'll be all right, but we can't afford to wait. It might be a fortnight or two, or even a whole season before we have another chance like this. It's well worth the risks."

"How are you going to get her past all the sheriffmen prowling and skulking around out there?"

"You'll see," she said. She put up her hand to pull the daisy from her hair but I reached up and caught her hand to stop her.

"Leave it. It becomes you."

She laughed. "You'd best be getting back to work now before your Uncle Durstan thinks we're up to no good over here."

I sat up and gave her a wicked grin. "Durstan wouldn't put it past me to produce another early dividend on a wedding," I said. "He'd say I was exactly like my father."

"Early dividend...Iain mac Drew! For a remark like that, you ought to be clapped in the stocks." She spoiled the effect of all that outraged indignation by laughing. "Back to work with you. I'll see you at dinner tonight then."

We finished with the last of the mob in the holding paddock well before sundown. Durstan gave the rangemen and shearers an extra keg of ale for a job well done and sent them back to their families in their camp by the river. By tradition, these men were gypsy workers who moved from Freehold to Freehold for the shearing seasons. They tended toward a regular migration pattern, returning year after year to the same fields. The good shearers who could do thirty to forty sheep an hour made very good wages and were much in demand. Their guild was so loosely organized as to be almost non-existant, but they took pride in their work and were well aware of their own worth. Durstan had always treated his shearers fairly and with the respect they deserved. As a result, over the years had gathered the best of them for his own shearings, and they were loyal to him.

Durstan and I rode together back to the house. Bronwyn immediately packed the pair of us off to the bathhouse, declaring that we reeked of sheep and other things that had no place at a dinner table. Then she went to help Holly supervise the preparation of the evening meal. It wasn't until Durstan and Bronwyn had gone off together in the carriage to the meeting with the wool buyers that I had a chance to look in on Glyn and Ydonda. Holly gave me a covered bowl of soup to take to Glyn while she gathered what she needed to tend to their injuries.

Glyn was awake and sitting propped up against his

pillows, a thick pile of hay behind him, when I came around the sheaves of stacked hay. He looked up as I set the lantern on the floor and sat beside him.

"How do you feel?" I asked.

"A little as if I've been trampled by a large herd of rampaging horses and then left out in the rain too long. But I'm all right, I suppose. I'm not tracking too straight, and I tend to fade in and out a lot, but I'll be fine."

He didn't look all right. He couldn't have been much past his early twenties yet, not that much older than I, but he looked like an old man after his ordeal. His skin had a greyish-yellow sallowness beneath its fading golden tan, and sagged along his sunken cheeks as if with infinite weariness. Around his eyes, the skin looked bruised. He was thin enough to be gaunt, as if his great effort of holding onto Ydonda had burned the flesh from his bones. He saw what I was thinking, and gave me a ghost of his former smile.

"It can do this to you, especially if you're not used to it," he said. "It takes a while to come back, but you do come back. Don't worry about me."

"Holly sent some soup. Can you manage it?"

I helped him settle the bowl in his bandaged hand then gave him the spoon. He ate only half the soup before he tired and attempted to give the bowl back to me.

"Finish it," I said.

He shook his head. "I've had enough. Thank you."

"Finish it, or I'll pour it down your throat even if it drowns you."

"Don't get fierce with me," he said, smiling again, a trace of the old glint of lively humour in his eyes. "That would be a sinful and shocking waste of good soup." But he managed only a few more mouthfuls before he sagged back against the pillow and closed his eyes wearily. I took the bowl, set it to one side, and fixed the pillow more comfortably behind his back and head.

"How's Ydonda?" I asked.

"Better, I think. I can't seem to contact her, though. No strength there. Me, not her."

"You held on for a long time, Glyn. More than fourteen hours. I almost couldn't get you untangled."

"She's worth it."

I glanced over at Ydonda. She slept peacefully, the white of the bandage contrasting startlingly with her golden skin. "Your woman?" I asked.

One corner of Glyn's mouth quirked in amusement. "She's my superior officer. She recruited me. I think that makes me her man. Perhaps one of these days, we'll get around to sorting it out. She's the best there is to work with, Iain. We've been together for a long time. We're a very good team."

"Did Holly tell you we're getting Ydonda out tonight?" I asked.

"Yes. She said something about taking her out to Eyrindor."

"Holly's friends can get her to Dundregan, then onto an Out-ship. She says they've done it before."

"It's a good organization." He glanced up at me, almost smiling. "Are you part of it now?"

"So it would appear, after spiriting away and harbouring dangerous criminals like you."

He laughed softly. "Don't forget hardened and ruthless, too." He closed his eyes again and nodded. "Ydonda needs a proper Healer. Holly did a splendid job, though. We're in her debt. And certainly in yours, too."

Just the effort of talking had exhausted him again. He needed all his strength to recover. "You'd better rest for a while," I told him. "I'll go and see what's keeping Holly." I got him comfortably settled, then went down the ladder.

There was a light, covered carriage by the paddock fence. I hadn't heard it arrive. Holly and the driver stood talking quietly together, then she started toward the byre and he turned to open the canopy over the back deck of the carriage. As he swung the canopy up, he stepped into the spill of light from the kitchen window. He wore the uniform of a King's Guardsman, the combined insignia of the Royal Seal and the Holy Seal of Uthoni on his sleeve. One of Fergus's elite troops, known for their ruthless efficiency.

I flattened myself against the stone wall of the byre and watched as he leaned into the carriage, doing something I couldn't quite see. I didn't want him to know I was here until I discovered if he was here to help or hinder.

Holly stood by the byre, waiting just out of the light. The guardsman pulled something out of the back of the carriage and moved toward the byre, carrying it with him. He moved well, all of a piece, a powerfully built young man only a little older than I. He wore a quiver of crossbow quarrels clipped to his belt and a short sword in a plain leather scabbard, and he moved with an air of purpose about him.

"Wait here for a moment," Holly told him softly as he reached her. "I'll fetch Iain down."

"I'm right here," I said and stepped away from the shadow of the wall. Holly made a small exclamation of surprise, but the guardsman merely turned to look at me.

"Who is he?" I asked.

"It's all right," Holly assured me quickly. "This is my cousin, Alex mac Kyle. He's with us. You can trust him."

The guardsman stepped closer to me. He wore the insignia of a Unit Leader, a junior officer, on the sleeve of his tunic. "Holly tells me you're a Communicator," he said. "I'm willing that you read me if you think it will help."

His uneasiness was as clear as spring water to me. I had no need to read him to recognize the revulsion and fear that the idea of being *invaded* by a Communicator put into him. But I also understood his resolve to go through with it if there were no other way of convincing me that he meant none of us any harm. Nothing showed on his face, though. His gaze met mine, steady and level. Whatever else Alex mac Kyle was, he was a brave man.

"If Holly trusts you, I can, too," I said.

His relief was apparent in his smile. "Good, then. I've a stretcher here. Where's the woman?"

"In the loft. Holly, you'd best see to her before we move her."

Glyn watched us in silence as we carefully and gently shifted Ydonda from the shell-cot to the stretcher. When we were ready to take her out of the loft, he struggled to lift himself onto one elbow and put his hand to her forehead. He said something soft and lilting in Feyish. There may have been a slight twitch to her forehead to indicate she heard, but in the dim light, I couldn't be sure. Glyn looked up at Alex.

"Take care," he said quietly. "That's precious cargo you have there."

Alex looked quickly at Holly in inquiry, then back to Glyn.

"He doesn't speak Standard," she said.

Glyn nodded. "I see," he said, then repeated it in Gael. It shouldn't have surprised me, but it did. I hadn't realized he spoke Gael so fluently. I'd heard him speak only Standard and Feyish before. Thoughts don't need translation in Communication.

"Oh, aye," Alex said and grinned. "She'll be safe with a

Healer in Eyrindor in a week's time, and on her way to Lysandia soon after. And they tell me the *Wind Dancer* has a good medician aboard."

"The *Wind Dancer?*" Glyn said. "I know Maryesa sheilMaevid, the captain. She runs a good crew. I'd trust her with Ydonda's life, or my own. Or anyone's, come to that."

Alex grinned again and moved to the head of the stretcher. "Aye," he said. "She'll send us word when your friend here reaches Eyrindor. I'll be in touch once we've got her aboard the ship."

I went to the foot of the stretcher. Together, Alex and I took Ydonda down the steep, narrow ladder, careful not to jostle the stretcher. Holly scrambled into the back of the carriage and moved some gear to reveal a long wooden box that looked like nothing other than an oversized coffin trimmed with two fingers' width of intricate openwork carving at the edges of the lid. The box bore warning signs against tampering, and a large, official Royal Seal. It was cushioned and mounted to give as much protection as possible against the jolts and lurches of a moving carriage, and it was large enough to take the stretcher in comfort. Alex and I swung it gently up and into the box. Holly bent over and touched her fingers to the base of Ydonda's throat, then frowned thoughtfully.

"I've given her something that should keep her deep asleep for twelve hours," she said. "I don't think she'd waken and make any sound even without it, but we can't take chances." She tucked a piece of note paper under Ydonda's folded hands. "That's to tell the ship's medician what treatments I've given her and what medications I've administered. It'll be important to her. Make sure they know that, will you, Alex?"

"Aye," he said. "I'll be sure to let them know in Dundregan." He closed the lid of the box and sealed it.

We covered it with the gear again, and climbed out of the carriage.

Holly stepped forward and hugged Alex. "Take care," she said. "Oh, and let them know about Iain in Dundregan, Alex. They'll be pleased to learn we've a Communicator with us here now."

"You're going to Dundregan with her?" I asked.

"Aye. They'll be calling us off the search here soon and leaving it to the local troop. I've been summoned back. I'll be aboard the same ship."

Holly and I stood together in the paddock yard and watched the carriage move swiftly toward the road. She was close enough so I could smell the clean, delicate fragrance of her hair in the night.

"They'll never think to search a King's Guardsman carriage," she said. "And with Alex aboard the trader, they'll never think to look there, either."

"I hope not. I hadn't realized there were guardsmen amongst your friends."

"Iain, there's much you don't know," she said with quiet gravity. "There are many more of us than even Fergus or Padreg realizes, I think. They'd call us revolutionaries and call what we do treason. But we don't want to overthrow Fergus. All we're after is a return to fair and just rule. And we want to bring Celyddon back into the Commonwealth where it belongs."

"The question is, can you do that without armed revolution," I said. "I don't think Fergus will back down, not with Padreg behind him. And Padreg's had a firm grip on Fergus and on the realm for a long time now, going back to even before Culhain died. He's not about to back away, either."

"We'll find a way to convince them of the wisdom of seeing things our way," Holly said. She smiled. "We've some very persuasive and determined people with us now, and more are joining us all the time. We've people in the Council of Lairds, aye, even on the Royal Council, with us. Perhaps not enough yet, but very soon now, I think."

"And what about Daryn?" I asked.

"Daryn is innocent," she said. "It was Padreg who accused him, and falsely. We hope to be able to prove that. If we discredit Padreg, we may be able to sway Fergus."

"And if you can't sway Fergus? What then? Will it mean civil war?"

She looked at me, her mouth bleak. "I don't know," she said quietly. "We hope not. But men would follow Daryn if he came home again."

"Against his brother?"

"Aye. But Fergus will see reason once Padreg is gone. You'll see."

"It's a difficult task you've set yourselves."

"But I hope not impossible. Come with me. I'd best see to dressing Glyn's burns before Durstan and Bronwyn return. You can lend me a hand."

Chapter Eleven

SHEARING CONTINUED UNEVENTFULLY for the next six days. During the last two days, the wind had shifted and now blew from the south-east in strong, fitful gusts. That usually meant a storm in the offing. We wanted to get as much done as possible before the storm hit. Thunder and lightning and the accompanying wind made the sheep skittish, too nervous to stand still for shearing. The rain soaked the heavy fleece, making it difficult and sometimes impossible to cut through. If the storm was bad enough, the rangemen would have to watch the sheep closely to prevent panic, leaving no time for anything else. It would keep both the shearers and the rangemen busy containing the sheep and keeping them calm. A mob had gone bespelled and panicked on us last summer. We lost over twenty good sheep in the stampede, and a dozen others maimed badly enough so that I had to shoot them. It was grim, unpleasant work, and I had no wish to do it ever again. Badgercats were better targets for my bow.

The rangemen had driven another mob down from the crags. We separated the rams and put them in the far paddock, then set to work shearing the ewes and lambs. We worked quickly with one eye on the clouds building to the north of the crags. There was no time for the usual good-natured bantering.

Several times, a ragged wave of cloud spilled over the rim of the crags and spattered us with rain. The main bank of thunderheads, looking like bruises against the sky above the crags, seethed back and forth, but didn't move west into the valley. The air was hot and humid, almost preternaturally still, and by early afternoon our clothing and hair were wringing wet from sweat.

At midday on the seventh day as Bronwyn and Holly rode in as usual with food for the crews, we reckoned we were in for the grandfather of all storms. By then, the towering clouds had begun to build against the tops of the crags above us. Distant echoes of thunder shivered across the valley. The rangemen ate quickly, trying to keep one eye on the storm and the other on the agitated mob of sheep.

"I've news for you," Holly said as we sat in our secluded corner away from the rest. "The *Wind Dancer* got away yesterday morning about eleven hours with our cargo safely on board. It'll be out beyond the barrier reef by now."

"Good. How long d'ye think it'll be before we can get Glyn away."

"I honestly don't know. We can't do it often, Iain. There's so much risk involved each time. There are only a few trader ship captains we can trust, and not that many Out-ships coming to Dundregan. There aren't many ways we can get someone to Dundregan undetected to get them aboard an Out-ship. It might be a season, or even two or three, before we can attempt to get Glyn out. In the past five years, we've done it only three times. We only do it in cases of real need. Like Ydonda. Or perhaps Glyn."

"We'll have to get him away somewhere, though," I said. "It's risking too much to keep him at the Freehold here. Durstan might find him at any time. I'm surprised our luck has held this past se'nnight." I looked up as the quality of the light changed. The air had taken on that greenish glow that makes colours more vivid and intense. The storm wouldn't be long now in coming.

"We'll try to get him to a safe-house in the next day or so," Holly said. She glanced up over my shoulder at the sky behind the crags and frowned. "If it weren't for those Feyish eyes of his, it would be easy just to let him blend in with everybody else in Caliburn because he speaks Gael like a native. But those eyes stand out too plainly. There's no mistaking he's a Fey-Halfblood. He'd be spotted too quickly by any sheriffman."

"He can travel now, can't he?"

"Aye. He's still weak, but he can travel. I'd sooner he regained some strength, though, before we moved him. An invalid stands out too much, too."

I caught hold of her shoulder, drew her down to the grass beside me, and held her close against me. Then I kissed her quite thoroughly. It got a little more complicated than I had intended it to be. She laughed breathlessly into my ear.

"Keep this up, Iain mac Drew," she said, "and it's for sure you'll have to marry me."

"Durstan's coming," I told her, my lips near her ear. She smelled like spring. "I didn't want him to hear you."

Seconds later, Durstan appeared through the trees

behind her. I released Holly and we both sat up as he approached.

"There'll be none of that around here." But he smiled as he said it. "Best you go and help Bronwyn clear away, lass, before the storm hits. You'll want to be well away home before it does."

Holly scrambled up and straightened her gown. She nodded briefly to Durstan, then gathered up the remains of our meal and hurried off through the trees. I got to my feet.

Durstan frowned. "Lad, the sheriffmen said there wasn't enough wool in the tithing carts last collection. They wanted to know why."

"There was a full one part in ten," I said. "Perhaps even a bit more. I saw to it myself."

He considered that, then shook his head in disgust. "I've never yet shorted the Crown its tithe," he said. "Not like some. But their one part in ten wants to get larger each year, it seems." He made an impatient sound with teeth and tongue. "That isn't right." He shook his head again. "Time to get back to work. We've need of hurry if we want to finish before the storm hits. Come."

Late that afternoon the pounding of hooves announced the arrival of a horse at a frantic gallop. I looked up from my shearing to see Holly bring her horse to a sliding halt and slither from its back to the ground in one smooth movement. She was pale as a moonflower, and even from where I stood, I felt her agitation.

"Iain," she shouted. "Iain, I must speak with ye."

Fearing something was wrong with Glyn, I dropped the shears and ran across the meadow to her, dodging through the sheep. She was breathless, biting back tears, her eyes wide with fear and worry. She seized my hand, drew me further into the grove of corewood trees, and threw herself into my arms.

"Is it Glyn?" I asked quickly.

"No," she gasped. "It's Cadal mac Lachlan. They sent an Inquisitor out from Dundregan, Iain. They questioned Cadal this morning. He held out as long as he could, but he broke. They killed him...he's dead."

"Dead?" The blood drained out of my face. Cadal mac Lachlan had never been a good friend, but.... "Dead?" I repeated stupidly.

"That's not the worst," she said, clinging to me. "Before he died, he gave your name to the Inquisitor. Oh, Iain, he's betrayed you. They're coming for you."

I had to still the thrust of panic that kicked in my belly before I spoke. "Did he give them the names of the others?" I asked. "Did he give them your name, Holly?"

"No. Just yours. They asked specifically about you. Why would they do that, Iain?"

I shook my head, baffled. "I don't know. I've done nothing—"

"I was told he died before he could give them any more. Iain, you must get away. They'll be here soon. Athan nearly killed his horse to get the message to me. He said they'd be no more than an hour or so behind him."

"You'll have to get Glyn away, too," I said. "They'll search the croft from top to bottom if they don't find me here. They'll not miss Glyn there if they search. Go back to the house and get him away as quickly as you can. And yourself, too."

"Where will you go?"

"I don't know." I clenched a fist, trying to think. "Perhaps to the crags, to the outlaws. I'll send word to you."

Something moved in the trees behind me. Both Holly

and I jerked around to stare as Durstan moved out of the shadow of a corewood tree.

For several long seconds, Holly and I stood frozen in dismay and simply stared at Durstan. He looked back and forth between the two of us, his face grim and set. The sun was behind him. I couldn't read the expression in his eyes.

It seemed very quiet there under the trees. I was no longer conscious of the tumult of the shearers and rangemen shouting or of sheep bleating. All I knew was the despairing certainty that I could not harm Durstan even if it meant my loss of freedom.

He finally broke the long, uneasy silence.

"I feared as much," he said, his voice quiet and calm. He came forward until he was close enough to reach out and touch my shoulder. "Cadal mac Lachlan gave your name to the Inquisitor, did he, Iain?"

"Aye," I said hoarsely. "It appears he did."

"Are you part of his foolish little group?"

I could look my uncle straight in the eye and answer that question quite truthfully. "No, sir. I am not."

He nodded. "I thought you had more sense than that bunch of addle-headed dreamers," he said. "How did young Cadal get your name to give to the Inquisitor?"

"I went once to a meeting. I told them then I wouldn't join them."

"But you didn't betray them, either."

"Some of them are my friends."

He turned his head to look up at the storm clouds building behind the crest of the crags. For the first time, I saw what he would look like as an old man. His gaze came back to me, the grey of his eyes calm and clear.

Although I couldn't discern what it was, I knew he had come to a decision, and the tension knotted tighter in my belly.

"Aye," he said softly. "An honest man can't betray his friends. A man without loyalty is a man without honour. Whatever else you have, Iain mac Drew, you have honour. I believe you got it from your father, who was an honourable man. But I hope you took some of it from me, too, these last dozen years. A man cannot betray his own flesh and blood, either. You've been a good son to me, lad. A son a man can take pride in. I'll not see you taken by the sheriffmen over such nonsense as this from the likes of Cadal mac Lachlan."

Holly stepped forward and touched his arm. "Durstan—"

"Hush, lass." He smiled gently at her. I saw in that smile how he had grown truly fond of her. "Iain, take your young woman here and go back to the house. Take the carriage from the byre. It's faster than the wagon. I've no doubt you can find somewhere to disappear in the city. I believe you've friends there."

"Aye, we do," I said, and Holly nodded.

"Good. I'll not see you gone to the crags with those forsaken outlaws, either. I release you, lad. You're no longer liege-bound, neither to me nor to the Freeholding. Holly mab Dougal, you're my witness."

Tears stood in Holly's eyes as she replied. "I'm your witness, my lord clan Rothsey. And bless you."

I grasped his hand. "Bless you, Uncle Durstan."

"I'll miss you grievously, lad. I'll tell the sheriffmen you've gone to fetch a mob of sheep from the north pasture. Best you go now. There's not much time. There's a bad storm coming and you'll not be wanting to be caught out in that."

Holly and I turned to leave.

"Iain...."

"Yes, Uncle?"

"I trust the sheriffmen will find no trace of any strangers or foreigners if they come to search my croft. I have no wish to try to explain something embarrassing like that. It wouldn't be seemly for a man in my position." His tone was entirely casual and conversational, but his grey gaze drove straight into me like a blade.

I caught my breath. "There'll be no trace."

"Aye. I thought as much. Go now."

It was a wild ride Holly and I had back to the crofthouse. The storm that had been brewing for the past half fortnight boiled up into heaving, surging towers of black and green, and came tumbling over the crest of the crags. The first savage gusts of wind caught us out in the open only half way back to the house. Both of us bent double over the shoulders of the horses to prevent ourselves from being blown off their backs. Wild slashes of lightning split the seething cauldron of the sky, and the thunder cracked and rattled as it rebounded back and forth among the cliffs and crags. When the rain hit, it slanted out of the sky sharp as needles against our faces, driven by the fierce gale. We were wet to the skin in seconds, gasping for air as the rain and wind tore the breath from our bodies. The horses slowed to a walk, hunching themselves against the storm, ears flat against their heads.

A summer storm like this can go on for days at a time. This one gave every indicating of lasting. The only good thing about it was that it would slow down the sheriffmen looking for me and give us more time to get away.

We reached the croftyard, wet and chilled, and put the horses into the shelter of the byre. I had to put my arm about Holly's shoulders as we ran to the house so the wind wouldn't tumble her backwards into the mud.

We found Glyn in the kitchen, seated at the table,

fingers tapping on the table top in an impatient, staccato rhythm, his eyebrows drawn together in a thoughtful frown. He looked up as Holly and I quite literally blew into the room. He wore a pair of my breeks and one of my shirts. The breeks were too short in the leg by several inches, but a pair of high boots would mask that.

I pushed the soaked hair out of my eyes. "Where's Bronwyn?"

"She's in the byre," he said. "Tidying up my mess. She wouldn't let me help."

"You'd end up being blown into the sea," I said. "That storm is straight out of the Abyss. You're ready to go. That's good."

He smiled faintly and switched to Gael. "Meet your Cousin Glyn from Alcolmvale, Iain. I've had a terrible accident and come north to recuperate."

He had the accent down perfectly. It wasn't the Gael of this area, but it was certainly the Gael of the south province of Alcolmvale. It struck me that he looked different. Too different for it be just the clothing. It took me a long while to grasp exactly what the difference was. It was his eyes. They were no longer that distinctive and unmistakable gold-flecked violet. They were as blue as my own. He saw me notice it and grinned again.

"I've enough magic left for a small illusion like this," he said. "Blue suits me better than brown would, d'ye not agree?"

"It suits you very well indeed," I said.

Holly laughed breathlessly. "Well, that certainly solves one of our problems. Iain, gather up what you need, but keep it sparse. I'll go help Bronwyn in the byre. What did she do with your uniform, Glyn? D'ye know?"

"She said she was going to burn it."

"Good. I'll be back in a few minutes. Be quick, Iain. We've not much time."

I caught her arm as she started for the door. "You'll be blown away out there," I said. "I'll go help Bronwyn. Stay here with Glyn."

As I was helping Glyn into the carriage, Bronwyn came running out into the yard, her clothing soaking wet. Her hair, draggled and disarrayed, blew wildly about her head in the wind and rain.

"Iain, you've forgotten something," she cried.

She took my hand and dropped the little gold maple leaf and the silver flash into it, then closed my fingers tightly over them. It was the same gesture Glyn had used all those years ago when he gave me the flash. Bronwyn had strung the flash and the leaf on a longer, more sturdy chain.

"You can return the chain to me later," she said. "Yours wants mending. I'll see to it and keep it until you come back for it someday."

I slipped the chain around my neck, then stood looking down at her for a moment. I didn't know what to say to her, and the lump in my throat wouldn't let the words past anyway. She smiled up at me, and I knew that, as always, she understood exactly what I wanted her to. Finally, I took her into my arms and hugged her fiercely. We stood together, ignoring the ferocity of the storm. She felt thin and frail against me.

"All these years," I said unsteadily. "All these years and I've never said how much I love you, Bronwyn. I've never told you that before. It's well past time I did."

"Ah, Iain," she said softly. "I always knew it, even if you didn't say it. I love you, too, lad. As if you were my own son. Go with the Power and the Presence and the Love, and come back to me one day if you can. Hurry now. You'll have need of this." She thrust a small, heavy leather bag into my hands, then turned and hugged Holly.

"Be careful, lass. The road will be full of sheriffmen. And be careful of the storm. You don't need an accident."

I tied the small bag, heavy with coins, to my belt. Something tugged at my heart as I looked around the croftyard. This place had been my home—the only home I could really remember. I had been happy here. It occurred to me then that I might never see it again. The sharp hook of loss that caught at my throat hurt and brought a sudden, stinging tears to my eyes.

Glyn and I got into the back of the carriage. Holly and Bronwyn handed us a pile of empty mealflour sacks to cover ourselves with. It wasn't much of a disguise, but the sheriffmen would be expecting to find me out in the meadow with the shearing crew, and the storm might even keep them in Caliburn until it was over. If Durstan's misdirection worked, by the time the sheriffmen began searching the roads, we'd be in Caliburn and hidden somewhere safe.

Holly climbed onto the seat. She gathered up the traces and called softly to the horses. They were reluctant, but they began to move slowly toward the road. The wind caught the carriage and rocked it for a moment. Holly negotiated the lane to the road carefully, and turned onto it. She kept the horses to a slow walk, her foot against the brake lever in case a gust caught the carriage and made it swerve. It wouldn't do to have the carriage swing around beside the horses and panic them.

I squirmed around, trying to get more comfortable against the hard, ridged deck. We hadn't much room. Glyn's knee pressed into my side, and my own knee was hard up against his calf. It would be a long and uncomfortable trip. The rain drummed hollowly against the canopy, almost as loud as the explosions of thunder outside. We couldn't talk to each other and be heard over the din, but we could Communicate. I had to initiate the contact, though. He still hadn't the strength to do it.

"You speak Gael like a native," I said.

"I am a native, Iain. I was born in Alcolmvale. My father was a planefisher. He owned three fisherboats. My mother was with the Lysandian Embassy in Alcolmvale."

"Does your father still live there?" I knew his mother wouldn't. There were no Feyii left in Celyddon now. He used the Feyish form of his name—shanBreyor, meaning son of the house of Breyor as Ydonda's name shielVor meant daughter of the house of Vor. Feyish families belonged to the maternal house. If his father was in Lysandia, he likely called himself shanBreyor, too.

"He died when I was fifteen. His fisherboat was lost in a storm. Pretty much like this one, I expect, by the looks of it. My mother and I went to Lysandia after that. She's still there."

I told him of my own parents, then. I had never spoken about them much. The pain and helplessness I felt at their loss was still too bright and clear in my mind. But I found I wanted Glyn to know about them, and as I told him, perhaps some of the pain diminished in the sharing.

"You might have inherited your Gift through your father," he said. *"It tends to show up more often in the children and grandchildren of Outsiders more than Groundsiders or even Insiders. But there's no hard and fast rule."* He shifted to a more comfortable position. *"You activated your own Gift. That's the first time I've heard of that in a Human. It usually takes another Communicator to activate it."*

"You activated it," I said. *"That first night when I met you by the track. I couldn't have done it if you hadn't shown me how to use it."*

He was quiet for a while. We moved about, trying to find a more comfortable position. I sensed something troubling him, something he hadn't chosen to speak with me about. Finally, I asked what was bothering him.

He gave me a quick grin in the gloom. *"I keep forgetting I can't shield from you,"* he said. *"I was just thinking about the sheriff's patrol boat that attacked the gig."*

"And the ball of green flame that produced those lightning bolts and burned it?"

"Yes, that. It was magic, Iain. Strong magic. I'm wondering about the man or woman who worked it."

"Magic? Fergus has banned all magic here."

There was a hard grimness in Glyn's mind. *"Yes. Exactly. He has indeed, hasn't he?"*

The carriage rocked to a stop. A man's voice came faintly through the uproar from outside. I sent out a thin thread of awareness to Holly to see what was happening.

A troop of sheriffmen blocked the road. Three sheriffmen, fully armed and armoured, stood before the mounted troop, leaning into the brutal wind. A fourth approached the side of the carriage, hunched against the rain. He demanded to know who Holly was and where she was going. She had to shout over the howl of the wind as she told him she had been visiting friends and now had to get home before nightfall. He took only a cursory look into the back of the carriage, then waved her on. The sheriffmen on the road ahead moved their horses aside to let her negotiate the narrow opening between them and the deep ditch.

We had passed the first hurdle. But the storm was getting worse.

The carriage rocked violently on its wheels, slipped sideways. Holly caught it, holding the horses steady. We were coming to the bridge across the Strathflorin, only a little more than half a league from the outskirts of Caliburn. Once we were into the city, the buildings would absorb some of the force of the wind and offer some protection.

The sound of the wheels changed to a hollow rumble

as the carriage rolled over the wooden planking of the bridge instead of the slippery mud of the road. Another vicious gust of wind slapped against the side of the carriage like a clenched fist. It slithered sideways. Holly had no time to catch it before another burst hit. The carriage skidded, came up hard against the low rail of the bridge. It hesitated there for a moment, tilting with the force of the gale. Holly shouted at the horses, urging them against the wind. For a moment, I thought she might be able to catch it and recover. Then I knew she couldn't.

The horses screamed, and the carriage lurched as they plunged sideways, trying to regain their balance. The tongue of the carriage snapped. I had barely time to shout a warning to Glyn before the carriage tipped onto its side and fell off the bridge into the river.

Chapter Twelve

THE FALL THREW us hard up against the side of the carriage, tangled together. My elbow rapped painfully into the iron seat support. Glyn grunted in pain as the carriage rolled.

The bridge was a low one, near to the water. It wasn't far to fall and we weren't hurled around enough to knock us unconscious. That was probably all that saved our lives. The canopy tore as we hit. Icy water cascaded into the back, swirling and boiling around us, tumbling us about like beads in a child's rattle. I grabbed hold of the back of Glyn's shirt and dragged him with me as I struggled to find a way out of the carriage.

The river helped. We hit against a submerged rock, swinging violently around. The whiplash movement threw the carriage onto its back. It flung Glyn and me out into the torrent like seeds spit from a roasting ironwood nut.

I surfaced, gasping for air, still holding tightly to Glyn's shirt. The current bore us swiftly downstream. I looked around frantically for Holly, but saw no sign of her. I could not even see the carriage now. It had disappeared below the turbulent water.

A frothy eddy slapped against my face and I swallowed silt. Beside me, Glyn coughed and spewed as he tried to keep his head above the surface. It seemed we were also likely to disappear like the vanished carriage if I didn't do something in a hurry.

Glyn had the good sense to relax and not struggle. He rolled onto his back to keep his face out of the water as much as possible. I got my arm under his, and across his chest, for a firmer grip as the current swept us around a broad curve and into a wide pool. I tried to speak, swallowed another pint of water, and made contact instead. His collected composure at first surprised me, then steadied me.

"All right?" he asked.

"Yes. You?"

"Wet. Very wet." A brief bubble of quiet laughter. Then: *"Can we make the bank?"*

"Yes. Now we can."

The water was calmer here in the pool formed by the curve of the embankment. I found it not so difficult to keep my face out of the water. Because I didn't have to struggle to breathe, I could look around. The driving rain blurred the riverbanks, but I knew where we were. I took several deep breaths. The last of my panic drained away. Under control now, able to think more clearly, I struck out for the shore, kicking strongly with my feet, pulling with my free arm. Our clothing dragged at us, but I didn't dare try to stop to get rid of it. Besides, we would need it later. I made better progress once I stopped struggling against the current and let it help carry us toward the bank.

The current swept us at least two furlongs downstream of the bridge before my knee scraped hard against the rocky bottom. I staggered to my feet and stumbled onto the bank, dragging Glyn with me. The rain pelting onto my head and shoulders felt warmer than the river. We crawled to the shelter of a tumbled pile of rocks on the steep ridge overgrown with maiden willow and foxgrass, and found a hollow large enough to hold us. It was almost dry inside.

I collapsed onto the damp sand and pushed the streaming wet hair from my eyes, too tired even to feel uncomfortable. It took a long time to catch my breath again. For those few moments, all I could do was lie sodden and exhausted on the sand beside Glyn, gasping and coughing. I was chilled to the marrow, so numb I couldn't think. But I was alive. And so was Glyn.

And Holly?

Renewed panic gripped my belly. I scrabbled to my hands and knees, and darted for the gravel bank. Glyn caught my ankle and dragged me back into the shelter of the rocks.

"Let me go," I cried, struggling against him. "Let me go. I have to find Holly."

He didn't release my ankle. "Iain, calm down," he shouted over the lashing storm. "Make use of your Gift, man."

I eeled around and stared at him. "How?"

"Look for her—"

"How? For Piety's sake, show me how!"

His grip tightened on my leg. "You know how...." He shook his head in exasperation. At himself, though. Not me. He drew in a deep breath. "Forgive me, Iain," he said.

"You've used your Gift so well, I forgot you haven't been trained. Make contact. I'll show you. It's called Casting."

I made contact and he showed me. It was so simple and obvious, I couldn't understand why I hadn't already known how to do it. I broke contact and looked out at the grey sheets of rain slashing at the rocks in the driving wind.

"If she's alive, you'll find her," Glyn said quietly.

I concentrated. For a long time, I couldn't make it work properly. I needed to calm myself, to get rid of the apprehension and fear. I closed my eyes, took several deep breaths and Cast again.

I sent a thin haze of awareness out into the slanting rain, searching along the riverbank for that pulse of life that was uniquely Holly. I was only vaguely conscious of Glyn's quiet breathing beside me, his own distinctive rhythm of thought patterns.

This time, it worked.

"I found her!" I cried. "She's alive. She's all right." Relief hollowed out my belly and I sagged against the broken, irregular rocks behind me. Glyn's relief, sharp as my own, washed against me.

The sheriffmen had seen the carriage go off the bridge. Two of them had plunged in after it and pulled Holly out of it even as it was filling with water. Helped by the others, they managed to get her onto shore. Right now, she stood between Flicker and Fan, calming them as best she could. One of the sheriffmen had found a thick cloak and put it around her shoulders. She huddled in it, holding it close around her, wet, miserably cold and worried sick about Glyn and me. She didn't dare tell the sheriffmen about us, and had no way of knowing we had survived.

"She's all right," I told Glyn breathlessly. "The sheriffmen got her out. Can I make contact with her?"

"I doubt it," he said. "She doesn't have the Gift. You can receive her, but she can't receive you without physical contact. There's nothing you can do."

I nodded. "We'll have to make our way into the city when this storm lets up. We'll get in touch with her at her father's house." I looked at him and burst out laughing in the sudden relief and release of tension. "Glyn, you're a stranger again. You've one blue eye and one violet one. You've let the spell slip. And you're a wreck, my friend."

"You're no prize yourself," he said. He closed his eyes, his face going blank with the effort of his concentration. When he opened his eyes, he had two blue eyes again. "How's that?" he asked.

"Better. How's your arm?"

"It's well." He flexed it, then made a small grimace of pain. "It hurts a little, but not too badly. I'll be all right."

"We're stuck here until the storm lets up," I said. "Will you be able to walk tomorrow?"

"I'll have to, won't I?"

Eventually, spent and exhausted, we slept, huddled together for warmth in the little hollow. I didn't awaken until the heat of the sun slanting through the opening in the rocks onto my back thawed the ice in my bones.

Glyn still slept, his burned arm held carefully across his chest. I left him there and crawled out into the strong sunlight. Its heat was like a blessed energizing tonic. In moments, I was warm again and, I found, ravenous. I went to wake up Glyn. The sun's heat would do him the world of good, too.

He came out onto the bank yawning, and spread his arms to the warmth. When he turned to me, I saw he had let the spell slip again. He was violet-eyed.

"Your eyes," I said, smiling.

He grimaced, then put his hand up to his forehead. When he lowered his hand, he was a blue-eyed Celyddonian once more. It didn't seem to take as long this morning as it had yesterday.

He looked much better than he had when we brought him to the Holding, despite the dirty and wrinkled clothing. His skin was beginning to fit his face again, and his colour was almost back to its natural tone.

My clothing wasn't in any better shape than his, all of it wrinkled and stained. I was uncomfortably aware my boots were still unpleasantly damp. We hardly looked civilized. We weren't going to be able to walk into Caliburn unremarked, looking like this.

"We're both sadly in need of a hot bath and a good barber," he said. "But first things first." He took a flint sparker from his pocket and flipped it to me. "See if you can get a fire going. Hungry?"

"Starving."

"I'll see about breakfast, then."

He sat down and took off his boots, then crawled out and lay flat, belly down, on a spike of rock that thrust out into the pool. He lay there, utterly still, peering intently down into the water. I gathered maiden willow and driftwood for a fire, glancing at him occasionally. He might have been carved out of the rock itself, so still did he lie. He looked as if he'd become a part of the spur.

I managed to find some dry, dead grass near the back of our small hollow and built a fire, coaxing the small spark in the tinder to life. When I finally had it going, I looked at Glyn. He still hadn't moved.

Suddenly, his left arm flashed down into the river. He gave a gleeful whoop as a brief commotion thrashed and churned the water. He brought up a ling-trout nearly as long as his forearm, his fingers hooked firmly through its gill. It flapped and twisted frantically, trying to escape.

He tossed it up on to the bank beside me, then crawled backwards from the narrow spit of rock.

"It's called gilly-whomping," he said, grinning broadly. "I haven't done it since I was a child."

I was impressed and said so. "You wouldn't want to do that with a planefish," I said, thinking of the double row of razor-like teeth and the sharply spined fins.

"Not bluidy likely, chum," he said with the broad accent of Alcolmvale. "Got a knife? Breakfast in ten minutes."

I handed him the hoofing knife from my belt sheath. It's slender blade wasn't designed for carving fish, but it would have to do. The fish made a decent breakfast when roasted in thick layers of wet foxgrass and leaves, and we were both hungry enough to wish it was twice as big. We made short work of it.

"We'd better wash these shirts out," I said. "If we let them dry in the wind, they'll be a lot less wrinkled, and at least they'll be clean. We won't look quite so much like a pair of outlaws wandering around the city. Are the boots dry yet?"

He poked experimentally at one. "Nearly."

Bronwyn's little leather bag had survived the wild ride down the river, still tied securely to my belt. I set it aside by the fire as I took our shirts to the river and did the best I could with them. Bronwyn would have been horrified at the results of my efforts, but I got most of the mud out before I spread the shirts on bushes to dry. Enough of a breeze still rippled the maiden willow to blow out most of the wrinkles. We might not look too much like complete outcasts when we got to Caliburn.

"Are you strong enough to walk to the city?" I asked Glyn as I sat down beside him again.

He grinned. "You won't have to carry me," he said. "I told you it takes a while to come back, but you do come back. I've had half a fortnight. I'm a lot stronger than I was. It won't be long now, I think, before my brain kicks back in, too."

I tilted my head back, closing my eyes to catch the heat of the sun on my face. Memory flashed a picture of him, glazed and blank, gripping Ydonda's shoulder. Again, I felt his grim determination not to let her die.

"How did you do that?" I asked, curious and intrigued. "Hold onto Ydonda like that, I mean."

He rolled onto his stomach and chewed a piece of foxgrass. "It's a Gift, Iain. My Gift isn't very strong, so I haven't been trained to use it as well as some of the Gifted who work with Healers. That's why it took so much out of me when I used it. And it went on a lot longer than I've ever tried to Hold before. Not all of us have it, just as not all of us have the Talents."

"What's a Talent?"

"It's sort of hard to explain. I suppose you could say that the Gifts are more or less passive. Like Communicating, or Holding, or Tracing. Aye, and Casting. The Talents are active. If you have the Talents, you can make things move. For instance, you could use Shifting to take that rock and put it over there, or half way around the world, if you wanted. Ydonda used Shifting to bring the gig ashore. There are even some who can Travel, make themselves move like that. But that's a rare Talent."

"You mean, magic themselves somewhere?"

"That's it. Then there's Manipulation."

"What's that?"

He grinned. "I've been told a Manipulator never needs to worry about getting locked out of—or into—anything. There are a few more Talents that don't even really have names." He looked at me. Even the spell couldn't disguise the penetrating gaze of the Outsider. "I think you have some of the Talents, Iain. I'm not sure which ones, because I haven't got any of them myself so I wouldn't recognize them. There are only a few Members who have more than Two Gifts and Talents. I think you could have at least two Gifts, and as many as two Talents, perhaps three."

"Two Gifts?"

He shook his head. "I don't know what the second one is. Whatever it is, I don't have it."

I paused, trying to frame the question properly. "Tell me something. If you can't identify the other Gift I have, how can you tell it's there?"

He laughed. "They show up like diamonds in the sand," he said. "Look at me. Can you see my Gift for Holding?"

I made deep contact with him and concentrated. And felt it, or rather, saw it. His Gift for Communication was bright and obvious. I had no trouble identifying it. When I searched myself, I saw my own Gift for Communication, identical to his and equally obvious.

It took me a moment of intense effort once I discovered how to look, but I thought I saw his other Gift, his Gift for Holding, shining there like silver in moonlight. But if he hadn't told me what it was, I could not have said it was the Gift for Holding. But behind it, something else, glimmering softly, deep and hidden. Faint and nebulous. Something I couldn't identify. Another Gift? A Talent?

"Glyn? Look." And I showed it to him.

His astonishment was a bright spark dancing between us.

"What is it?" I said aloud.

"Blessed if I know. I never realized it was there. Nobody ever saw it before." He frowned, his face both thoughtful and perplexed, as he examined that glimmer I showed him. Finally, he shook his head in resignation, no more able to identify it than I. "That will certainly bear investigation if we ever get out of here."

"I see what you mean," I said. "I can't tell what they are, but I can see they're there. Why did nobody ever see that one before? I would have thought someone would have found it during your training."

"Sometimes deep Talents develop late." He rubbed his ear and shrugged. "I just didn't ever think I'd be one of the lucky ones. Commander sheilDatya in Lighthaven will know what yours are. And she'll very likely sort out this extra one of mine, too. You'll have to go to Lighthaven for training." He smiled. "I'm assuming you'll join the Watch. You'll be my first recruit."

"As you say, we have to get out of Celyddon first. That's not going to be easy."

"It would certainly be a lot easier if I could contact someone to come and get us. Whistle up a hack, so to speak."

"Could I do it?"

"I don't think so. The Gift is odd that way. You can contact another Communicator almost anywhere in the world, but you have to know where they are. It's almost instantaneous when you do know. It's as if you think of somewhere, and your thoughts are already there. But if you don't know where *there* is, you don't get through. For instance, Ydonda could find me because she knows where I am. I couldn't find her, though, because I don't know where she is. But I'd know if she found me and I could contact her again after that. Clear?" He looked at me, one eyebrow raised. I stared back blankly. "Well, no. I can see that it isn't. I can't explain it any plainer than that. You found Holly last night because you knew she was somewhere along the bank of this river, and you know the bank of the river. But suppose she was in Caliburn, and you were looking for her along the bank of the river."

I shook my head, confused. "I have an idea I have a lot to learn."

"Yes, you do. It's a rigorous training course. But it's worth it."

"How long is the training?"

"Two years." He grinned. "You pack a lot of learning into that two years, believe me."

"I think the shirts are dry now," I said. "It's almost midmorning. We'd better get started for the city. Maybe if we stay off the main roads, we might not have any problem meeting any sheriffmen."

He glanced at me, one eyebrow cocked. "You're changing the subject, Iain. Why?"

I shook my head.

"What I'm asking is, will you join the Watch?"

I hesitated, then looked away. "I'm sorry, Glyn. I wanted an Out-ship. New lands. New people...."

He looked at me, perplexed. "Why would you want to settle for just an Out-ship? Iain, my friend, I'm offering you the whole world. New lands, new seas. Everything. All of it. All wrapped up in a big, happy package and tied with a red ribbon. You'll have so many new things, it'll make your blood sing. Only an Out-ship? I thought you wanted more than that."

"I do."

He laughed in delight. "You've been recruited, Iain mac Drew clan Morgian. You're mine now." He sat up and reached for his boots. "Let's start that hike to town."

The streets of Caliburn ran with thick, muddy brown water that swirled in the gutters and lapped sullenly against the wooden planks of the sidewalks. People thronged the Square, intent on business or pleasure, most of them in a hurry, all of them carefully negotiating the small rivers in the streets. They paid little or no attention to Glyn and me. We looked like half a hundred other semi-disreputable, grimy gypsy shearers looking for a crofter or a freehold laird to hire us for the remainder of the shearing season.

We stood on the perimeter of the Square adjacent to the Law Courts, an ugly, black brick structure with thick walls and narrow windows. A steady stream of sheriffmen flowed in and out of the huge, ornate doors. Occasionally, a merchant or a businessman entered or left, most of them well-dressed and prosperous-looking, all of them moving briskly with an air of purpose. Once, a pair of sheriffmen hauling a manacled, draggled-looking man between them got out of a wagon and went into the building.

On the other side of the Square, opposite the Law Courts, stood the old stone Sanctuary of the High Temple, its doors flung wide to the late summer sunshine. Once dedicated to both the Mother and the Father, now only the Father was worshipped there, and only by the rites of Uthoni. Atop the slender, graceful bell tower that rose regally to the sky, the old brass bell, reputed to be the oldest in the realm, chimed the hour.

A smartly turned out carriage pulled before the Law Courts. The Royal banner flapped from a standard by the driver. Directly below the banner fluttered the bright gold four-pointed star of Uthoni's Inner Circle of priests.

Two men alighted from the carriage. I immediately recognized the tall, emaciated figure of Padreg in his grey and purple robes. A hard thud of shock went through my chest as I realized the other man was my cousin Maelgrun. I drew back into the shadows as they mounted the steps to the Law Courts building and disappeared inside. I turned to leave the Square, but Glyn touched my arm.

"Wait a moment," he whispered. "Something's happening. I want to see what's going on."

Gradually, the Square filled with men and women. An

air of sullen expectation hung in the air. The crowd was silent, waiting. Sheriffmen patrolled the edges of the crowd and kept it back from the raised platform near the foot of the steps to the Law Courts.

The elaborately carved double doors opened and two sheriffmen came out, dragging between them a man dressed in the tattered remnants of what had once been a laird's council robe. As they hauled him to the dais, Padreg and Maelgrun appeared at the head of the steps.

I didn't recognize the man on the dais. He shook off the hands of the sheriffmen and straightened his shoulders, facing Padreg and Maelgrun squarely.

"You may kill me," he cried, "but you'll not silence my voice—"

"Treason and blasphemy," Padreg shouted, and thrust his hands into the air. A ball of sizzling, acid green appeared in above the head of the prisoner. "See how Uthoni strikes down and destroys evil! The wrath of Uthoni be upon you and consume you!"

He gestured toward the prisoner. The ball of light began to expand almost gently. Then, like the one I had seen in the cove, it erupted a shower of lightning bolts. The man had time only for one long, bubbling scream of agony as the horrifying green spears engulfed him and hid him from sight completely. Seconds later, the glare vanished. Gleaming white bones clattered into an untidy pile on the stone dais. An instant later, nothing was left but a pile of fine, grey ash. A visible shudder rippled through the crowd, and a soft, anquished sound like the moan of the wind in the trees rose from half a thousand lips.

Cold, jagged fear grew in my belly. I looked up at Padreg, standing with his arms outstretched at the head of the steps. His lips were drawn back from his teeth in a wild grin of exultation, and his eyes gleamed with the same actinic glow as the foul, green magic flame. Still shivering, I looked at Maelgrun. His eyes, too, seemed to radiate a faint glimmer of that green glare in dimming light of the twilit sky.

Chapter Thirteen

GLYN GRABBED MY arm and pulled me into the mouth
of an alley. His face was ashen pale in the dim shadows,
his mouth pressed into a thin, bloodless line. His fingers
moved in the sign against evil. I had never seen him so
shaken, and it frightened me badly.

"The Light be with us," he whispered. "*Chausey magic.*"

"*Chausey magic?*" I repeated weakly. "What—?"

"We have to get out of here." He slipped deeper into
the alley. "I'll tell you about it when we find somewhere
we can rest for the night. Hurry. We can't let them see
us."

We found an inn near the old Out-port. The area was
run-down and dispirited, smelling of decay. Once this
inn had been busy and prosperous with the brisk traffic

of In-ships trading along the Inside passage of the barrier reefs. But those In-ships had brought Caliburn goods to the Out-ships in Dundregan and those Out-ships were now few and far between. The inns in the Outport area suffered the loss severely.

The inn was untidy, but reasonably clean. For a few coins, we were given a place in the corner of the common dormitory in the loft above the main room. Glyn wrapped himself in his cloak and settled onto his pallet with his back against the rough wall, legs drawn up, forearms resting on his knees.

I spread my cloak and sat cross-legged on it beside him. "Tell me about *chausey magic*," I said. I really didn't want to hear, but I was sure I had to know about it.

He glanced quickly at me. He was still pale, and his eyes appeared to be a dark, turbulent indigo. A strangely haunted expression tightened the skin around them, making him look far older than he was.

"It's ancient magic, Iain," he said softly. "The ones who used it were a sept of Feyii who broke away from the Lady's Court so long ago the stories about them are almost dismissed as myth. It's said they found a way to draw dark magic straight from the Abyss. Ancient evil, based on blood letting, blood drawn by suffering and pain. *Chausey* is an old Feyii word meaning suffering, pain, bloody wounds or agony. Horror and fear mixed in. Not anything like the Feyish mind magics, or the elemental magic of earth, fire, wind and water that the Watch or the Outsiders use."

I shook my head. "I've never heard of it."

His smile was more like a rictus. "No, you wouldn't. It was before Celyddonians even began to learn civilization. The bright Feyii and the Dwarvenfolk of Gradchavale fought the dark Feyii of the Unseleighe Court from the far south. Feyish legends say thousands died, but eventually the bright Feyii and their allies triumphed and destroyed the dark Feyii. King Canlaugh shanGallyer and the Selieghe Court banished the *chausey magic*. Everyone thought they had erased all traces of it. Legends said that the *chausey magic* could reach out and possess any man or Feyii who called it up deliberately— or even accidentally. But no Feyii would dare to call it, and no Human knew of it. Or so the Court thought. Until now."

"But Padreg knows," I said.

Glyn nodded wearily. "Aye, so it would seem." He made a fist and pounded it softly against the floor. "I *must* find some way of letting the Watch know of this. If this evil spreads..."

I shuddered again as I remembered the seared bones clattering to the stone. That kind of power loose in the world... It was enough to turn me cold with abject terror. As it had the last time I saw it used. I looked up and met his eyes, my lip caught thoughtfully between my teeth.

"It was a lightning shower just like that one that destroyed the gig when you and Ydonda were coming ashore to pick me up. I didn't know what it was then, but I saw it come from the sheriff's patrol boat and hit the gig."

He looked at me, his mouth twisted into a rueful and bitter grimace. "I know. I didn't want to say anything, though. I had hoped I was mistaken."

"You weren't." I hesitated for a moment. "I think Maelgrun has some of it, too. Not much yet. But I saw it in his eyes."

He shot a sharp glance at me. "Did you, now?"

"Yes. As if he were just waking to it. I don't mind admitting that it frightened me."

"Aye, as well it might. Well, you told me he was a man who looked for power where he could find it."

I nodded. "And he's been close to both Fergus and

Padreg since he finished his education at the college and went to work at the Court."

"Tomorrow we must get in touch with Holly," he said. "We have to get away from here and back to Lysandia. If I can't warn the Watch that *chausey magic* is loose in the world again, it might destroy us all."

It was raining again, but lightly, when we left the inn late the next morning and made our way toward the Square. In one of the side streets, we found a messenger shop tucked between a chandler and a wine merchant's shop. A young messenger presented himself to us as available, and we dispatched him to Holly, asking her to meet us at the Sanctuary at thirteen hours if she could get away. If she couldn't, the messenger was to ask for an appropriate time, and bring the return message back to us. The boy nodded, repeated the message twice to make sure he had it right, then set off bare-headed despite the rain, moving at a brisk trot along the wet wooden sidewalk.

We waited outside under the brightly striped awning, letting the swirling crowd flow past us. Neither of us were comfortable this close to the Law Courts and the High Sheriff's office, but there weren't many messenger businesses left in Caliburn, and most of them were centered around the main Square. We had little choice, but we hoped it would not occur to any sheriffmen that a pair of fugitives would be loitering on the sidewalk kitty-corner across the Square from the Law Courts—within spitting distance, so to speak. If Durstan's misdirection had worked, the sheriffmen might think we had not yet made it into the city and were still out near the crags.

The merchants and crofters moving around us didn't worry us overly much. It was a good bet the sheriffmen had not advertised the fact they were looking for me.

I had learned over the years they preferred to do their work in secret, not taking any chances friends of their quarry might give a warning.

The messenger came back presently. He snapped the wet hair out of his eyes with a toss of his head, and stared blankly at a place just over Glyn's shoulder while he recited, "The lady says she'll be at the Sanctuary at thirteen hours. She says to tell you that she was happy to hear from you." The glazed expression left his eyes and he looked straight at Glyn, then me. "Is that all right?"

Glyn flipped him a silver coin. "Just fine," he said.

The boy snatched the coin from the air while it was still spinning and flashing. Grinning, he made it disappear into a pouch hanging from his neck. "Thank ye kindly, my lord," he said, then turned and darted back into the dark office.

Glyn snorted. "My lord, indeed," he said. "That lad has a lot to learn about proper flattery." He dug into his pockets and came up with a handful of coins. He counted them quickly and put them away. "Enough for some food, I think. And even a quick visit to the barber. How much money do you have?"

"Enough," I said. The stay at the inn hadn't depleted my store of Bronwyn's coins by much.

"I shouldn't think the sheriffmen have a description of me," he said. "But they're sure to have one of you. We should perhaps take ourselves out of their way quickly now we've got our message."

"Aye. But even if the sheriffmen knew about you, they'd be looking for a Fey-Halfblood. You look and sound enough like Gael now, as long as you're holding that illusion spell. Where shall we go?"

He grinned at me. "From the look of you, Iain my friend, you belong in an Outport gin-mill dive, as probably so do I," he said. "But there's precious few of those left in Caliburn left to hide you in now."

I ran my hand over the coarse, bristly stubble on my cheeks and chin. After two days without shaving, I usually looked as if I'd been sweeping chimneys with my face. Glyn's beard, reddish and softer than mine, wasn't quite as apparent, but neither of us looked even remotely respectable. His suggestion about a barber wasn't a bad one. Neither, I realized, was his suggestion about food. There had been little at the inn to break our fast this morning, and I was hungry again.

"First a barber and a fuller, I think," Glyn said. "Then food. With luck after that, it should be time to meet Holly."

Two hours later, washed, combed and clean-shaven, our clothing cleaned and pressed, and our boots polished until they gleamed, we looked like productive members of the community again. We were also much less conspicuous. We found a modest tavern and took a small table in a corner. Businessmen, crofters and town merchants discussing the price of wool—as well as everything else that crossed their minds, I suppose—filled the tavern to overflowing. Glyn and I blended in reasonably well. It was almost time to meet Holly when I paid the tavern keeper and we left.

Glyn looked around as we walked out onto the street. The rain had stopped and the sun shone tentatively through the broken clouds. "It occurs to me that the sheriffmen might be watching Holly," he said. "They know she's your betrothed. They might be expecting you to try to see her. Let me go ahead. When we get to the Sanctuary, if she's there, I'll talk to her. You wait somewhere inconspicuous until I see if she's come yet. If she is, I'll call you."

"Can you?"

He smiled. Then he made contact with me. It was only a thin, tenuous thread of contact, but it was there and it was unmistakable. "Not much strength or range yet," he said, pleased with it. "But give me a day or so and I'll be nearly back to normal."

"What if Holly's being watched?"

He gave me a look of incredibly boyish innocence. "Why, then surely what I'll do is take her for a stroll through this fair city, Cousin Iain, and have her show me all the sights and landmarks a poor fisherlad from Alcomvale would want to see."

"Can you lose the sheriffmen?"

He merely raised an eyebrow. "Iain, the day has yet to dawn when even the most tanglefooted member of the Watch can't lose a Celyddonian sheriffman. And take my word for it, laddie, I'm no tanglefoot."

I believed him.

Glyn began walking briskly toward the Sanctuary. I followed more slowly. When I reached the Sanctuary, he was already inside. I slipped into the cool shadows of the nave and looked in. I saw Holly first, sitting near the outside of an ornately carved pew, halfway down one of the side aisles. She wore a veil that obscured her face and frosted her shining black hair with filmy white. Glyn sat two rows behind her, and to her left. I took a seat near the back and made contact. Glyn acknowledged my presence and got to his feet. His boots made no sound on the thickly carpeted floor as he walked to Holly's pew.

"Excuse me, my lady," he said softly, his voice rustling and hissing among the stone pillars and beams of the vaulted chamber. "You'd be Holly mab Dougal, wouldn't you?"

Holly looked up at him, her expression carefully blank. Glyn might have been a perfect stranger.

"Glyn mac Tavish," he said. Tavish had been his father's name. "Remember me? From Alcolmvale?"

Holly smiled and moved over to give him room to sit beside her. She held out her hand and he sketched a polite bow over it. "Glyn mac Tavish," she said. "Of course I remember. It's good to see you again. Is your cousin with you?"

"Aye, he's around somewhere."

"And you're both all right?"

"We're fine," Glyn said cheerfully. "We got a wee bit wet in the rainstorm the other day, but I suppose we were both born to hang, not drown."

"We'll have to get together, all three of us," Holly said. "Somewhere that we can talk without disturbing people." She glanced at two men sitting across the aisle from her.

Glyn looked briefly over his shoulder at me, one eyebrow raised eloquently. I understood. Holly *was* being watched, ostensibly by the two nondescript men who were studiously ignoring both her and Glyn.

"You could show me the city," Glyn said. "I've never been to Caliburn before."

"I'd love to show you around," she said. "Call for me at my father's house in about an hour. That will give me time to finish my errands and get ready."

"I'll make arrangements to meet my cousin, then," Glyn said. "He'd be pleased to see you again, too."

"Keep an eye on him," she said. "You don't want him getting into any trouble."

"Oh, aye," Glyn agreed. "I'll keep him out of bad company, Mistress Holly. Never fear."

"And have him keep you out of bad company, too, Maister Glyn. I have to leave now." She rose to her feet. "Good bye," she said formally and held out her hand again. "It's very good to see you again." Glyn took her

hand and bowed briefly over it before she rose to her feet
and slipped out of the Sanctuary. Her glance fell on me
as she passed, but she gave no indication of recognition
and walked by me with no hesitation. Moments later, the
two men across the aisle got up and walked out after her.

Glyn waited until they were gone. *"We'll meet back at
the tavern where we ate,"* he told me. *"It won't take me
more than an hour to shake any sheriffmen following us."*

I left the Sanctuary and walked back out into the
strong sunshine. For a moment, I stood blinking as my
eyes adjusted to the glare after the cool dimness of the
Sanctuary. Then I turned to make my way out of the
Square. I didn't hurry, but I didn't dawdle either. I was a
crofter in the city on business and moved accordingly.
If I didn't act as if I had something to hide, the chances
were no passing person would look askance at me. I
passed a man I knew and exchanged greetings with him.
He gave no indication that he might have reasons to
suspect I was in trouble.

Several streets radiated out from the Square, branching
like the rays of a star through the city. Without
hesitation, I chose the street that went past the side of
the Law Courts rather than the front where I might be
seen and recognized. Blocks of shops selling all sorts of
goods lined the street, interspersed with taverns and
coffee houses. Hurrying people intent on their own
business hastened along the board sidewalks, paying
little attention to anything but their own thoughts and
errands.

A carriage went by, splashing foul muck onto the planks
of the walk. I sidestepped the filthy spray automatically,
without looking up, my mind on the meeting with Holly
and Glyn two hours from now.

The carriage pulled up by the curb ahead of me. A
man got out and picked his way delicately through the
puddles toward the walk. He was watching his feet and I

was thinking of Holly. We nearly collided as he stepped up onto the walk. I looked at him then, and recognized my cousin Maelgrun only an instant before he recognized me. He took a step backward, surprise and shock on his face.

"Iain!" he exclaimed.

I met his gaze levelly. "Good day to you, Maelgrun."

Maelgrun mac Durstan was no Durstan mac Lludd. He wasn't half the man his father was, nor would he ever be. Still looking at me, he signaled to the pair of sheriffmen in the carriage. They leapt down and stepped forward smartly. One of them put a hand to the sword hilt at his belt.

"This man is Iain mac Drew," Maelgrun told the sheriffmen, still watching me. His mouth bent into a malicious little half-smile. "He's wanted for treason against the Crown."

Glyn brushed past us then, giving a remarkable imitation of a man sidling hastily away from a confrontation he had no wish to become involved in. He made contact as he moved quickly down the sidewalk away from us.

"Iain?"

"My cousin Maelgrun."

"That's torn it."

"Tell Holly."

"Right away." The contact broke.

There was no use in running or trying to fight. The sheriffmen both carried crossbows across their backs and a full quiver of quarrels clipped to their belts. I knew they would not be averse to shooting into a crowd after a fugitive, and I wanted no innocent blood spilled on my account. I had enough burdens to carry without that. I held out my hands in front of me, wrists crossed. One of the sheriffmen clamped a pair of manacles around them tightly enough to cut into the skin where it was thin across the wristbone. I didn't look at him. I watched Maelgrun steadily.

"You'd see your own cousin arrested then, Maelgrun?" I asked softly. I wanted to make this as difficult as I could for him. I hoped it was the first glimmer of an idea and not just sheer obstinacy and dislike for my cousin on my part.

"Aye, I'll see a treasonous bastard arrested no matter who he is," Maelgrun replied harshly. "My cousin or not. It makes no difference under the Laws."

I lifted one eyebrow. "You'd admit before all these men that your blood kin committed such a crime, then?" I raised my voice to attract even more attention than the manacles and the sheriffmen had already garnered. I wanted overt attention from the small crowd that had gathered. I smiled coldly. It cost me an effort, but I believe it was a creditable smile. "You'll not be doing your own career a great deal of service, Cousin Maelgrun, d'ye think? Treason runs in families, if we can believe what Padreg and the Royal Council have been telling us all these years. Will Padreg next be accusing Fergus himself? After all, Fergus's own brother committed treason, too, didn't he?"

"That's enough," Maelgrun snarled, his fists bunching at his sides. "Keep quiet!"

"Will you also arrest your own father and confiscate his land because a man you accuse of treachery and treason lived there?" I asked, raising my voice again.

He winced. I had struck a nerve. I thought for a moment that he looked frightened. But it turned soon enough to anger.

"Enough," he shouted. "That's enough!"

He looked around as he realized a crowd had collected. On the fringe of it, I saw Holly standing close to Glyn, his arm protectively around her shoulders. There were a few other faces I recognized, men who knew me and who knew Maelgrun. Right now, their expressions were guarded, carefully held blank, giving nothing away.

"No, it's not enough," I replied, pitching my voice so that it carried. "Will I die like Cadal mac Lachlan died? Die for the great crime of reading Campbell Dunshannon's poetry? 'Tis a shame indeed to die for reading the writings of one of Celyddon's finest and most famous men." A murmur of agreement rippled through the small crowd. I bit my lip to hide my relieved smile. As I had hoped, I had sympathizers among these people. More than Fergus and his lot would be comfortable with.

Maelgrun glanced nervously at the sheriffmen. "Silence him," he said shortly.

One of the sheriffmen hit me. The blow caught me just below the cheekbone. My teeth cut into the side of my mouth and I tasted blood. I spat a mouthful at Maelgrun's feet, but he moved his boot and I missed.

"You'll be a long time silencing my voice, Maelgrun mac Durstan," I told him. My words sounded a lot braver than I felt right then.

The next blow caught me across the back of the head. I went to my knees on the dirty sidewalk. The sheriffmen, the crowd, Maelgrun—all seemed to recede from me into a misty distance, and I fell deep, deep inside myself. I was only vaguely aware of the sheriffmen dragging me off the walk. Bright light turned to shade, then light again, and finally to deep shadow.

When I returned to myself, I was in a cell. I lay curled on my side in a corner, my bleeding wrists raised to protect my cheek from the rough stone of the wall. Cold from the stone floor seeped into my body through my clothes and I shivered.

But I knew now. I knew part of the secret that lay within

me. Submerged as I had been deep in unconsciousness, I thought I had seen what Glyn had seen in me.

But he was wrong.

In my dazed stupour, I caught glimpses of three other Gifts besides Communication. Only one of them made any sense to me. I had seen it so clearly, so lucidly, that its purpose was strikingly apparent. It shone, as Glyn had told me, like a diamond in black sand.

I thought now that I could see what was there, I might be able to activate it, as I had activated my Gift for Communication once Glyn had shown me what it was. I'd done that through dire need. I had just as much need now for the second Gift. With that Gift and the Talent that now lay crystal clear in my mind, a plan began to come together in more coherent form. I desperately hoped I could make it work.

I looked up. The cell had no windows, but I knew it was evening. I began Casting and found him quickly, Casting for me.

"Glyn?"

"Iain! I've been trying to reach you."

"Is Holly all right?"

"Yes. She's here with me. What about you? Are you all right?"

"I'm still alive."

"They're going to take you to Dundregan in the morning for trial. Your cousin Maelgrun will take you himself. That crowd began to get ugly after the sheriffmen knocked you down."

"Is your range improving?"

"Yes. Better each day."

"Good. Will you be able to reach your people?"

"I hope so."

"Do it as soon as you can. Tomorrow, when they take me out of here to transfer me to Dundregan, can Holly gather a large crowd?"

"Hang on. I'll ask." Moments later, he was back. *"Iain?"*

"Still here."

"She says she can have a hundred people there. Perhaps more. And the crowd itself will attract more people."

"Good. I want as big a crowd as we can get."

"Why?"

I smiled grimly to myself. *"Tell Holly I'm about to strike my blow. She'll understand."*

Chapter Fourteen

THE NIGHT PASSED. Part of the time, I lay awake, my mind churning feverishly. Other times, I think I must have slept, but restlessly. The pain in my tightly manacled wrists woke me several times, and often I came out of a fitful doze when heavy footsteps passed the door of my cell. Once, someone was dragged down the long corridor, sobbing in grief or pain. The sound of a heavy door thudding shut cut off the sobbing. I shivered in the clammy darkness of my own cell, feeling stifled and more alone than I had ever been in my life.

Toward dawn, the first misgivings gnawed at me. I began to doubt what I had found buried deep in my spirit. I began to doubt my understanding of it, my ability to use it, even to doubt it was really there. When I tried to go back and examine it, I found the pain in my wrists and the chill discomfort of the cell distracted me too much and I couldn't concentrate. I began to be afraid.

I knew what lay in store for me when the sheriffmen delivered me to Dundregan. A quick travesty of a trial. A sham and a mockery, in reality. Then, if I was lucky, a life sentence at hard labor in a work camp. If I wasn't lucky, the gallows in the public square in front of Fergus's palace. I didn't know which I feared more.

Or I might end up as a pile of white, gleaming bone-ash on the charred stones of a dais. I shuddered.

Exhaustion and fear are powerful agents for draining strength and resolve. My brave words to Maelgrun now sounded hollow and empty as I lay waiting in the dank cell for them to come for me. Childish braggadocio. Boasting in a schoolyard. The universally human conviction that nothing as terrible as death by execution could ever overtake one's own self. But I was no hero from the ballads and sagas the bards sang. It was monstrous stupidity to think I could take on Fergus, Padreg and the whole of the Royal Council, or even my cousin Maelgrun, and believe I could actually win.

Holly's people needed someone to rally behind. Prince Daryn would have been perfect, were he here. But no word of Daryn had been heard since he disappeared all those years ago. If he were in Lysandia, there was nothing but rumour to substantiate it. He could well be dead. It might have suited Padreg to have him strangled and disposed of the day before Fergus sent the sheriffmen to execute him. There was no one else who could rule in Fergus's stead.

I moved restlessly on the cold floor, trying to find a way to ease the aches and pains in my body, but I could find no comfortable position. My head ached abominably. A sharp, stabbing pain wracked my side every time I breathed. The cold ate into my flesh, down to the marrow of my bones, stiffening my muscles. No matter how I shifted, the uneven stones dug cruelly into my flesh.

I remembered hearing somewhere, a long time ago, that a man's will to live, his courage to go on, is weakest in that bleak hour just before dawn. Sourly, I reflected that it was small comfort to know that I was no different from any other man in that regard.

Finally, spent and exhausted, and full of fear, I slept again.

They came for me just as the clock in the bell tower struck nine hours, two sheriffmen armed with daggers and short swords. One of them was a squadman. Neither of them looked directly at me as they yanked me to my feet and propelled me out of the cell and down the corridor. They were as impersonal about handling me as they would be about handling a side of meat. They casually discussed the duty roster, as if I weren't there. Or worse, as if I were not even worth thinking about. It was humiliating and dehumanizing, and even though I knew it was supposed to make me feel less than human and fought against it, it couldn't help but work as efficiently as it was calculated to.

They dragged me to a small, bare room and thrust me onto a wooden chair. One of the sheriffmen manacled my ankle to the chair leg, then they left the room, still arguing about who was going to take which duty slots. They had not spoken one word to me.

The room contained a single window. Not a large one; it was barely big enough to let in the morning light. I turned my head stiffly and painfully to look at it. Through it, I could see a small square of the sky and part of the bell tower of the Sanctuary. A small cloud edged slowly from behind the bell tower, serene and beautiful against the clear blue of the sky. Watching it, I began to relax. Some of my confidence returned, and with it, my courage.

"Iain?"

It was Glyn, strong and clear, and close by.

"Here."

"We're outside the building. Nearly three hundred of us and more coming each minute."

"Good."

"Not many of Holly's people yet, but the word has been spread that something important is going to happen down here today."

"I hope it will, anyway."

"Someone's painted Cadal mac Lachlan's name on the wall out here. We saw several other instances on our way here. Someone's been very busy. The sheriffmen don't like it much at all. They're trying to remove it now."

"Good. Let them worry."

"They're more than just worried. They're spooked." His little bubble of quiet laughter sounded as clearly as if he were in the same room with me. *"It would appear they don't much like the idea of martyrs."*

Cadal mac Lachlan was an unlikely candidate for a martyr's shroud, but he would serve my purpose. I only hoped I wouldn't be another before this day was through. I was an even less likely candidate than Cadal. But if they were painting his name on walls, perhaps the time was right. Perhaps my plan would work, after all. I began to believe again that I had been right.

"Iain?"

"Still here. Thinking."

"Your cousin just showed up."

"So soon? Is Padreg with him?"

"No. He's alone. He doesn't like the crowd, either."

"Is it orderly?" I wanted no more breaking up of demonstrations such as the one at the College in Dundregan all those years ago.

"Very orderly. But there are sheriffmen with clubs and spears out here. No trouble yet."

"Good."

"Your cousin just entered the building."

I broke off Communication and stared out the window again. The cloud behind the bell tower was gone.

Maelgrun entered the room a few moments later. He was impeccably dressed, neatly groomed—a perfect example of a member of the Royal Council. He stood back against the door, as far from me as he could get in the small room, smiling maliciously at me.

"I trust you spent a pleasant night, Iain," he said.

"I've been more comfortable."

"You'll be a lot less before this thing is done." He beckoned to the two sheriffmen who waited in the corridor. They came in stiffly and he motioned them to loose my ankles. He made an expression of distaste as I creaked to my feet.

"Ye might have thought to clean him up a bit before you brought him here for me," he said to the squadman. There was still blood caked on my face, on my wrists and arms, and my shirt was stiff and stained with it. The cell had been none too clean, and the evidence showed plainly on my clothing.

The squadman came to attention and stared woodenly at the wall just above Maelgrun's left shoulder. "We had no orders for that, my lord."

Maelgrun made a disgusted noise with teeth and tongue. "No matter. Bring him along. I've a carriage waiting outside."

We came through the doors out onto the wide stone steps above the Square. To my left, in letters almost as high as a man, was Cadal mac Lachlan's name scrawled in glaring white against the black brick. Two men worked doggedly trying to remove the limed words, but it was slow going. They seemed painfully conscious of the crowd in the Square watching them intently.

The two sheriffmen to either side of me held tightly to my arms. They were taking no chances. The crowd made them nervous. Their wariness surrounded them in a palpable haze. Maelgrun strode ahead, obviously trying to ignore the crowd that had congregated in the Square.

Glyn was right. It was an orderly assembly. The people merely stood quietly, waiting with an air of patient expectancy. Somehow, the very orderliness of the crowd made it more ominous and dangerous than if it had been angry, shouting and gesticulating. There had been a low murmur like the ebb and flow of the sea, but it ceased as we walked out onto the steps.

I scanned the crowd quickly. Many of the faces I saw out there were familiar. Some I knew well. Cadal mac Lachlan's father and two younger brothers were there. So were Caerl mac Neill, his father and his older brother.

I found Holly and Glyn standing together near the edge of the crowd not far from the Sanctuary. Holly was pale. She watched me with an expression of both puzzlement and apprehension. But she was curious, too. Glyn was calm, almost amused. I thought he may have had an idea of what I was going to try.

I took a deep breath, reached deep down to where I knew the Gift lay. I was calm now, almost relaxed. I knew it would work. What little remained of my fear left. No longer aware of the pain in my wrists, I touched the Gift, examined it again.

Yes. It was exactly as I thought it was. A wave of serene confidence washed over me, calming my wildly beating heart. At least this part would work as I had planned. I smiled, then *Stilled* the two sheriffmen.

They dropped their hands from my arms and froze into

glazed immobility. I stepped away from them and took another deep breath.

"Maelgrun mac Durstan," I called. "Listen to me. Listen to me, your cousin."

He paused for a startled second, one foot already on the first step down, then spun to stare at me. He saw the two unmoving sheriffmen, and went white. Rage and fear flickered in his eyes. I was still on the top step. He had to look up at me, a small advantage in my favour.

"Before you take me to Dundregan to be tried for treason and treachery, Maelgrun mac Durstan, let these people try you, along with Fergus and Padreg's Inner Circle of priests, for the same crimes." My voice carried around the Square, echoing from the stone Sanctuary walls.

For a moment, Maelgrun was too startled to try to interrupt. But he found his voice soon enough. "Silence him," he cried to the motionless sheriffmen.

"They can't hear you," I said. I raised my voice again. "It used to be that a man accused of a crime in Celyddon had a right to speak. I claim that right now."

A ripple of sound came from the crowd. An assent.

"You have no rights," Maelgrun cried hoarsely.

"Aye, I have. I have the rights of any free man in this realm."

Someone in the crowd shouted, "Let him speak!" A chorus of agreement went up, and the crowd surged forward a step or two.

Maelgrun looked at the two Stilled sheriffmen. "Shoot him," he shouted. "Shoot him, now!"

"They'll not answer you, for they can't hear you," I said softly.

The beginning of a harsh green flicker showed briefly in his eyes. I sensed his uncertainty. He was not yet fully trained in use of Padreg's *Chausey* magic. And he was frightened. I touched his mind, felt his fear grow. The glimmer faded and died.

"Listen to me, Maelgrun mac Durstan," I cried. "You say all Celyddon must now live by the Nine Testamentary Laws of Uthoni. Those laws are good and just laws. Yet how many good men like Cadal mac Lachlan now lie dead because of the likes of you, Maelgrun mac Durstan, even though the Laws state ye shalt not kill? How many shops and crofts, how many freeholdings and fisherboats, has the Crown seized and given to the likes of you and others of the Royal Council, even though the Laws state ye shalt not steal and ye shalt not covet your neighbour's goods? How many good men lie wasting in prisons or mouldering in graveyards because of the false or manufactured evidence given at trials by the likes of you and your Royal Council, or Padreg's Inner Circle, when the Laws state ye shalt not bear false witness?"

Maelgrun looked around himself frantically. He found a sheriffman in the crowd below the steps. "Shoot him," he shouted. "Shoot him now."

I looked at the sheriffman. He froze for an instant, like a block of sandstone, then took a quick step backward. "He'll not move against me," I said.

The crowd surged forward. The sheriffmen with their clubs and spears and crossbows fell back before it. Helpless and without direction, they had no idea what to do. Nothing like this had ever happened before, but they seemed to realize if they fired either on the crowd or on me, the crowd would surely tear them to pieces or trample them underfoot.

"Listen to me, Maelgrun mac Durstan," I said. "Listen well to me. How many of the Royal Council, including yourself, have broken Padreg's own First Law? How many worship the false gods of the power of their position? If you can find none, then take me to Dundregan and put me on trial. But if you're going to try me, then do it for something you can prove without perjuring yourself or others. Try me for the crime of possessing the Gift of a Communicator. Try me for having the Gift of Stilling. Try me for this." I raised my manacled hands above my head. The movement opened the raw places on my wrists and fresh blood trickled down my arms.

Still holding his gaze riveted to mine, I concentrated on the manacles. For a moment, I was afraid I couldn't find the trigger. But then I felt the now familiar flowing and realignment. *Shifting*, Glyn had called it. Making something move by mind-magic alone. The tiny tumblers in the locks of the manacles moved as I triggered the Talent. I smiled and the manacles opened, dropped to the stone at my feet. The metallic clank they made hitting the stone rang loud in the sudden silence. I lowered my arms.

"Try me for witchery, then," I said. I lowered my voice until only he could hear me. "Try me for having what you, yourself, possess. Only my magic isn't *Chausey* magic from the Abyss."

A feeble ball of greenish flame began to waver in the air above his head. But he was no Padreg to hurl the wrath of Uthoni. He had neither the strength nor the power. The faint glow disappeared, but the green light flared briefly in his eyes. He flushed crimson with anger and frustration.

"Trickery," he shouted. "The sheriffmen helped you."

"No. They didn't help me, Maelgrun. It's not trickery, as well you know. These are the Gifts and Talents of the Outsiders. Only that. Earth, air, fire and water magics. Gentle magics. Only that. And now you've lost. You'll never hold these people again."

I walked past him and down the steps. A path opened for me in the crowd, closed behind me. It was unnaturally quiet in the Square. I felt their eyes on me as I passed them, but not one of them made a move to stop me. Even the sheriffmen stood unmoving. I felt unreal, ethereal even, as if I only dreamed and would soon waken in my own room at the Freehold, with Bronwyn supervising the making of breakfast in the kitchen below me. And I felt an unholy urge to howl with hysterical laughter. I managed to keep my face composed.

Holly had disappeared, but Glyn came forward to meet me. We walked out of the Square to the street behind the Sanctuary, out of sight of the square. There was a carriage waiting there. Glyn got up onto the seat and picked up the traces.

Holly stepped out of the alleyway and ran to me. She threw her arms around my neck and held me as tightly as I held her.

"I have to go," she said. "I can't let them see me with you. But I'll come to you later. Be careful, Iain." She glanced up at Glyn. "You, too, Glyn. Both of you be very careful." She hugged me once more, then broke away and hurried through the alleyway to the back entrance of the Sanctuary.

I climbed up beside Glyn, still feeling hollow and unreal.

"Ready?" Glyn asked.

"I suppose so."

"Very effective," Glyn said quietly as he flicked the traces to start the horses moving. "I'd say you certainly gave them something to think about, Iain mac Drew clan Morgian." He laughed. "That's not something every Watch Member can do in a day. The story will be all over the realm by the end of the fortnight."

Glyn was right. By the middle of the fortnight, the story had spread clear across the realm, and was on its

way to Eyrindor. Cadal mac Lachlan's name began to
appear on walls in Dundregan. My name stayed off the
walls, because a dead martyr makes a far better symbol
than a live fugitive. But I didn't find out about that until
much later.

We left the carriage a short distance from the Sanctuary
among a cluster of waiting carriages and horses. A silent,
dour man with a stern, solemn face picked us up in a
dray pulled by four of the biggest horses I'd ever seen.
He took us to a large house on the outskirts of the city.

Holly had told me of this place. The house belonged
to another friend, a man who was highly placed in the
Royal Council in Dundregan. He spent half of each year
in the Capital, his wife and children with him. While he
was gone, a housekeeper looked after the house. Several
times, it had been used as a safe-house. Because of the
owner's high status, it was a good place to hide people
like Glyn and me. The sheriffmen dared not offend the
Councillor.

The housekeeper, a spry, alert woman with a face
etched deep with lines like a dried apple, met us at the
door. She could have been any age between sixty and
ninety. She and the driver of the wagon had a hurried,
whispered conversation before he climbed back onto the
heavy dray and left us at the door.

No one made any introductions. Glyn and I never did
learn the name of the housekeeper. Somehow, it seemed
a lot safer that way.

The housekeeper took us to a comfortable room high
up near the back of the house. She made clucking,
dismayed noises about the state of my wrists and insisted
on cleaning and bandaging them. I tried listlessly to tell
her they were all right, but she wasn't about to listen
to me. In the end, I gave in because it was easier than

arguing. When she finished, she left us alone in the room, and went back to work.

Glyn sat in one of the comfortable chairs by the window, fingers tented against his chin, uncharacteristically quiet, a thoughtful frown on his face. I lay down on one of the beds, feeling logy and oddly disconnected. My head felt as if it were stuffed with wool. If fifty sheriffmen had burst into the room just then, all of them carrying swords and crossbows at the ready, I doubt I could have worked up the energy to care. All I wanted to do was sleep.

It was dark when I awoke, and Glyn was gone. I went downstairs and found the housekeeper. She was sitting in the kitchen, knitting, with a large, nondescript black dog curled at her feet. The dog got to his feet warily as I entered. The woman spoke a sharp word, and the dog came forward to sniff at my hand, ears pricked forward. Finally, satisfied, it went back to its place beside her chair. She reached down to tousle his ears.

"Black's a good companion," she said fondly. "Aye, and good protection for an old woman alone."

"He looks fierce enough."

She laughed. "It's more than just looks, young man. Had I not told him you were a friend, you'd certainly be lacking a hand now." The dog looked up, tongue hanging in a doggy grin, and I knew she told the truth.

"Where did my friend go?"

"Out for a while. He said to tell you he'd be back presently." She squinted at me searchingly. "You look hungry. When did you last eat?"

I had to think about that. "I don't remember."

"Aye, I thought so."

She made me a light meal, then shooed me back upstairs when I had finished. I came to the conclusion I needn't worry about Glyn. Nobody was looking for him in particular, and he knew well enough how to take care of himself. I felt strangely remote and detached, as if I wasn't connected to my body any more. It had to be exhaustion, I decided. My whole body ached, and my mind felt choked and clogged. It made it difficult to think, difficult to worry about anything. I lay on the bed again, listless and apathetic, my eyes squeezed shut, and merely waited for Glyn to return.

Chapter Fifteen

IT WAS ALMOST midnight when Glyn slipped wraithlike into the room. He appeared highly pleased with himself.

"Where have you been?" I asked.

"Listening, mostly." He laughed softly. "The High Sheriff had to put down a minor mutiny. None of the sheriffmen showed much enthusiasm for searching for a man who could freeze them into statues for several hours at a time."

"Did it last that long?" It was useful information, knowing how long the effects of Stilling lasted, but I really didn't care right now. But I probably would later,

"Aye, it did. You've a powerful Gift there."

"What happened to the crowd? Was there a riot? Did the sheriffmen arrest or kill anyone?"

"The crowd broke up quietly and went home as soon as we left.". He looked at me narrowly. "You're still feeling the aftereffects, are you, Iain?"

"Aftereffects?"

"Tired? No energy?"

"A little. I keep feeling as if I should be doing something, but I can't for the life of me think what, and I really don't care anymore, either."

"I'm not surprised," he said, shaking his head. "Using a Gift and a Talent for the first time, and with no training at that, I'm surprised you're still awake and making any sort of sense at all."

I raised myself on my elbow and looked at him. "Does it always do this to you? Using these Gifts or Talents?"

He smiled sympathetically. "It takes a lot of energy to use them. If you're not used to it, it can be more than a bit overwhelming. Look what Holding did to me."

"Aye, and you're trained." I fell back onto the bed and put my arm over my eyes. "I ache all over. If this is what it does to you, I'd sooner not have anything to do with these Gifts and Talents."

"You'll feel better soon," he said.

I wasn't sure I believed him. I wanted to. "Where have you been?" I asked, not sure whether I had already asked him that or not. If he had answered, I had forgotten what he said.

"Out listening to the rumours and gossip. To hear tell now, you disappeared from the steps of the Law Courts in a flash of fire and brimstone." He laughed softly. "You'll be a long time living that down, my friend. The flash gets brighter and the brimstone smell stronger with each telling. One man swore he saw Daryn come out of the crowd to help you get away."

I had to smile at that. "Daryn himself, was it?"

"Aye. There are rumours about he's back in the country and soon will be raising an army."

"You've been busy."

"Aye, I have. A man who knows how to be a good listener can pick up a lot of information." He grinned. "Aye, and plant a rumour or three here and there. But you're about the only topic of conversation in the whole city right now. People weren't quite sure how to react when you Stilled those sheriffmen. Or that little trick with the manacles." He smiled grimly. "But everyone I spoke with agrees that you made good sense when you spoke. It was a brilliant performance, Iain."

"Sheer desperation," I said. "Besides, I was reasonably certain getting rid of the manacles would be all right. Most of those people know me and I know them. It's hard for most people to associate something like real witchery with a man they've watched grow up."

"Still, you took a chance."

"Yes, I suppose so. But it seemed worth it. What about Padreg?"

"Gone, it seems."

"Did you hear anything about Maelgrun? What's happening with him? What are they saying about him?"

"Your cousin Maelgrun was rushed back to Dundregan this morning. No one seems to know quite what's happening with him. I heard they clapped him into prison—not because he was guilty of what you accused him but for letting you get away. But I heard, too, he's been placed in charge of the picked troops who are going to try to track you down. Myself, I'm more inclined to believe the second rather than the first." He laughed again with mild satisfaction. "He's a much chagrined man right now, is your cousin. And he hates you mightily."

"He always has," I said. "Ever since Durstan and Bronwyn took me in. Glyn, I really believe he's got that same magic you were talking about. The *chausey magic.* I'm certain I saw it this morning."

Glyn eeled around in his chair and stared at me. *"Has* he now. That's interesting. I know you said it before, but you weren't sure. I thought he might have some, but I wasn't sure, either."

"Have you heard anything about Holly?"

"You needn't worry about her. She's all right. They were watching her, but she went straight home. She's safe there with her father."

As he spoke, my mind wandered off on a tangent. It occurred to me I had never met Holly's father. I wondered now if I ever would. It struck me as odd that I could be officially betrothed to his daughter and not even know what the man looked like.

"Iain?"

Glyn's voice brought me back with a start. "Sorry. I was wool-gathering. What were you saying?"

"I said Holly told me she'll try to come here to see you tomorrow night, probably around two or three hours."

"You've spoken with her?"

"Yes, but only for a moment or two. She's worried about you. I told her you were going to be fine once you got some rest."

"What about Durstan?"

"For certain the sheriffmen'll not be bothering Durstan. He's a popular and powerful man hereabouts. The feeling in the city is still too high about Cadal mac Lachlan. If they try to move against Durstan, they'll assuredly be chancing an all-out rebellion, and that's a risk they can't well take right now."

"Which leaves me."

"Exactly. Yes. Which leaves you. This realm will hardly be big enough to hide you soon, my friend. In three or four days, sheriffmen from Dundregan will be arriving here in droves to look for you. If they have to, they'll take this city apart, brick by stone by board to find you."

I nodded. "I need to leave the city then."

"Yes, we do. But not yet. You need rest first, and there's time. Holly's arranged to get us out tomorrow night. She'll come here just before the wagon comes to pick us up."

"Where are they taking us?" I didn't really care, but I felt I should show some interest.

"To the crags—"

"The crags?" I, sat up and stared at him. "To the outlaws?"

He shook his head. "No, not to the outlaws. We'll be heading out overland for Eyrindor. It shouldn't take more than a se'ennight to get there. I contacted my Section Commander today. An Out-ship is coming for us. Ydonda arranged for it when she regained consciousness aboard *Wind Dancer*. It will meet us in Eyrindor in about a fortnight." He laughed. "Even if they wouldn't risk one for me, they're not about to let you get away from them, Iain. A man with two Gifts and at least one Talent, and self-activated at that. They're anxious to make your acquaintance."

"The sheriffmen—"

"The sheriffmen won't touch this Out-ship, Iain. This one is going to Eyrindor, and it's going to be official. It will declare its intentions to recover a couple of errant Members of the Watch, and it will announce it's prepared to destroy anything that attempts to stop it. I doubt any sheriff's patrol boat is going to put itself in the way of an alert and belligerent Watch ship."

"What about the *chausey magic*?"

He smiled grimly. "There are ways of countering *chausey magic*." His tone made me shiver.

"How soon will the Out-ship be there?"

"It's already underway. They started a day or two ago. They'll be almost half-way from Lysandia now."

I closed my eyes and lay back on the bed. A few more days. A few more days and my dream of going Outside would be a reality. I reached up to touch the little golden maple leaf on Bronwyn's chain at my throat. But I was too tired to feel excitement or anticipation. Too much had happened over the last few days. All I felt was confusion and numb weariness.

Holly came shortly after two hours the next night. I was asleep and didn't hear her when she came in. I didn't know she was there until she bent over me and touched my shoulder. I sat up, startled, then relaxed as I recognized her. Glyn was not in the room. Holly sat on the edge of the bed. I reached for her hand.

"You're looking much better, Iain," she said softly. "You looked like death itself when we left the Square the other day."

"I felt a little as if I'd been whacked across the back of the head with a fencing post," I said, smiling. "But I'm not quite so groggy now."

"Glyn tells me there'll be an Out-ship coming in a fortnight to take you two out."

"Aye. Even Fergus wouldn't dare attack an Out-ship declaring its intention to pick up a Member of the Watch."

"You'll be going with him?"

"Aye."

She nodded. "Well, you surely can't stay here. You'll get to the Wildesea after all."

"Will you come with me then, Holly?"

She looked at me, lips parted. For a moment, her face was radiant and her eyes shone. Then her eyes clouded, and she shook her head slowly. "I can't," she said quietly.

"Why not?"

"I just can't. I belong here, in Celyddon, not out there on the high seas like you."

"I want you with me."

"I know. And I want to be with you. But sometimes what we want and what we must do are two different things." She put her other hand over mine so that my hand was cradled gently between both of hers. "Iain, you started something back there that Fergus and Padreg and the whole of the Royal Council and Inner Circle of Priests will never be able to stop. The time was ripe and you provided the push to start it. It won't happen overnight, but Fergus will topple, and Padreg with him. When they go, we're going to need people here to rebuild. Someone will have to find Daryn and ask him to come home and take his place as king. My place is here, in Celyddon, in Caliburn, working for that, not out on the seas or in some foreign land somewhere."

"Then I'll stay here with you."

She smiled and shook her head. "No, you can't stay here, Iain, and you know it. My place may be here, but yours is Out there. I saw what you did back in the Square. Glyn told me a little about the Gifts and Talents. You can no more stay here than I could go Out there."

"You won't change your mind?" Even as I spoke the question, I knew her answer. She was adamant and I knew I could not persuade her. This wasn't the way it was supposed to be. Not once since we had fled the Holding had I imagined that Holly would refuse to accompany me when I left for Lysandia. I had not realized until just now how much I depended on having her with me, how much I wanted and needed it.

"No, I won't change my mind," she said. "No more than you can change yours. Iain, you've spent your whole life wanting the Outside. Now you can have it. If you don't go, you'll never be happy. You've done your part here. There's nothing to hold you here now."

I sat up and put my hands to either side of her face. "There's everything to hold me here. There's you. You know I love you, don't you?"

She smiled. "Yes, I do know." She reached up to undo the fastenings on the bodice of her gown. "I can't go with you, Iain," she murmured, watching her hands and not me. "But we can at least have this. We can give each other this."

I caught her wrists gently in my hands. "You don't have to...."

She smiled again and looked straight into my eyes. What I saw there made the breath catch in my throat and the backs of my eyelids sting. "We're betrothed," she said. "I've had my betrothal visit with your family. My father has settled my dowry with your Uncle Durstan. We've done everything but say the words before the priest and sign the registry. It's all right." She laughed softly. "I believe it's even expected."

"Holly...."

She bent forward and put her lips to mine. It was as sweet and as wonderful as I knew it would be. I reached up and pulled her down beside me on the bed.

I had never known that a joining between a man and a woman could be like that. It was a physical and spiritual union, a joining more powerful and sweet than I believed possible. When finally everything had been given and taken joyously and without reserve, and we lay in each other's arms, I knew that this woman was my love, no matter what distances might separate us. No matter how long it might be until I could come back to her. And I *would* come back to her—and *for* her—if I had to move sky, crags and Wildesea to do it.

After a long time, she stirred in my arms. "Iain?"

"Yes, love?"

"If there's a child, I'll call him Drew."

I raised myself on one elbow and looked down at her, startled. She was smiling. "Might there be a child?" I asked.

She laughed. "It has been known to happen."

"Then you must go to Durstan and Bronwyn," I said. "They'll look after you and keep both you and the child safe."

"If there's a child, I will. It certainly won't be the first time one was born to a betrothed couple. It likely wouldn't be the last, either." She reached up and traced one finger down the center of my brow, down my nose, across my lips. "I'd cherish your child, Iain."

I could find no words. I bent and pressed my face into her soft, fragrant hair. I put my spread fingers on her flat belly, as if I could almost feel our child growing there already.

Finally, I said, "Drew?"

"It's a good name, don't you think?"

"A very good name," I told her gently. "I'd like that. If a name is needed, that is."

"Oh, of course," she said with great gravity, then laughed and kissed me. "Roddy mac Gowan will be here soon to take you and Glyn out of the city. The sheriffmen are already looking for you. They'll search even this house. Their orders are to miss nothing. I must go now."

"I wish you'd change your mind."

"You know I can't." She got out of the bed and dressed quickly. "Someday, you'll be able to return here without a pack of sheriffmen after you like hound to a foxen. I'll still be here."

I dressed and went with her down to where she had left her light, two-wheeled trap. She turned to me in the darkness.

"Ah, Iain, I'll miss you so...." she whispered.

I took her into my arms and kissed her. "I'll miss you, Holly." I took the chain from around my neck and slipped it over her head. She put up her hand to touch the little emblems. "I'll come back for that someday," I promised her. "And I swear I'll be back for you."

"I know you will." She broke away and got into the trap. "Good bye, Iain. Be ready for Roddy."

I stepped away from the trap as she picked up the traces. She raised her hand in farewell as she drove off, but she didn't look back. I returned to the house and climbed the stairs wearily. Glyn stood at the window, watching the trap disappear down the street.

"She'll not come?" he asked without turning.

"No."

"I thought as much. I'm sorry, Iain."

I went to stand beside him. This high up, I could see the sea and the silvered moon-paths leading from the Queen and the Companion to the city. "It's as she said," I murmured. "It won't be forever."

"Aye. Not forever."

Holly's trap had barely turned the corner and moved out of sight down the street when an ancient dray pulled by four immense horses entered the yard and pulled up in front of the house. I recognized the horses before I recognized the man who slid out of the driver's seat. He was the same dour, taciturn man who had brought us to the safe-house.

Roddy mac Gowan was in a rush. He ran up the steps

to the front door of the house and hammered his fists on the polished wood. Glyn and I turned away from the window to hurry downstairs as the housekeeper, wrapped in a thick sleep-robe, opened the door to Roddy's frantic pounding.

She met us on the first landing of the stairs. "Quick," she gasped. "Roddy said the sheriffmen were just behind him as he came down the street. It could be they're coming here to search. Come with me. Quickly now. Don't dawdle." She grasped my arm and pulled me toward the parlour, beckoning Glyn to follow. "Ah, I hope they didn't stop the wee lassie out there. Perhaps they missed seeing her."

The housekeeper led us to a corner behind a heavy sofa that stood away from the wall, and reached behind a picture. A small section of the wall slid away to reveal a cubbyhole not more than four feet deep, and scarcely two feet wide. It was barely high enough for a grown man to stand within without crouching. She pushed Glyn and me inside.

"A bolt-hole," she said, smiling grimly. "The Maister built it with his own two hands six years ago, bless him. We've hidden more than a few of the Mother's priestesses here. You'll be safe here. The sheriffmen will never find this place. They haven't yet. Don't move—and say nothing until I come for you again."

The section of wall slid shut as she reached up behind the picture again. Darkness closed around us like a shroud. I didn't have to ask what Glyn was doing. He was doing the same thing I was—sending out a thread of awareness to the housekeeper. We had to know what was going on out there.

The sheriffmen's horses surrounded Roddy mac Gowan's dray. As the sheriffmen dismounted and approached the steps, Roddy mac Gowan cowered on the step, twisting his cloth cap in his hands while the housekeeper stood on the verandah in front of him, her hands on her hips, thoroughly upbraiding him. Beside her, elaborately unconcerned, Black searched his flank with his teeth, hunting fleas.

"...And furthermore, Roddy mac Gowan," she said severely, "when I say I want something delivered as soon as possible, you can be sure I mean at a decent hour of the day. What d'ye mean, getting a respectable woman out of her bed at this hour—" She broke off as six armed sheriffmen led by a Squadman came up the steps. "And what would you be wanting at this hour, young man?" she demanded of the Squadman. "I don't know what this world's coming to, truly I don't. Can't an old woman even get a decent night's sleep without all this to-ing and fro-ing going on at all hours of the night? It's not proper, that's what."

The Squadman sketched a polite gesture toward the brim of his helmet. "We've orders to search every house in the city, mistress," he said. "We're looking for an escaped felon, a man accused of treason and treachery."

"Treason and treachery, is it?" the housekeeper said acidly. "Well, it's for sure you won't find any man like that in this house, young man."

I glanced at Glyn. We both fervently hoped she was right.

"You'll forgive us if we look anyway, mistress," the Squadman said. "We have our orders."

"Orders." She snorted derisively. "This is the house of Magister Innis mac Forgal. You'll not be finding any criminals here."

"Our orders, mistress—"

"Search if you must." She stepped aside. "But I'll be watching the silver, mind."

The Squadman stiffened with indignation. "I can assure you, mistress, that my men will touch nothing."

She waved away his protest impatiently. "Well, see that they don't, young man. Just get on with your searching so I can return to my bed. And see you wipe your muddy boots before entering. I spent all day scrubbing these floors. I want no mud and dust tracked in."

"Thank you, mistress." The Squadman turned to Roddy mac Gowan. There may have been a touch of something akin to sympathy in his glance for a fellow victim of the blade-sharp tongue of the housekeeper. "You'll stay right there and wait until we're finished," he said. "We'll be wanting to search that dray of yours, too." He detailed one man to stand watch over the decrepit wagon. Roddy mac Gowan made an expression of disgust and hoisted himself up to sit patiently on the tailgate to wait until the Squadman came back.

Magister's house or not, the sheriffmen did a thorough job of searching from cellar to attic. When they came to the room Glyn and I had been in, I suddenly remembered the rumpled bed. I had meant to make it up before we left, but I had completely forgotten it in the rush. A bad mistake. The housekeeper was supposed to be alone in the house. What reason could she give for the bed being so obviously slept in? I cursed myself for the carelessness.

Stricken, I felt my thread of awareness waver. Glyn's hand came down lightly on my shoulder. "Wait," he whispered.

The Squadman stood at the door of the small bedroom, staring at the untidy bed. Holly had straightened it up before we left the room, but it didn't look crisp and fresh as the other bed did, and the pillow still carried the faint impression of my head. It had obviously been used, and recently. The young Squadman stood looking thoughtfully at it for a moment, then called to the housekeeper.

"Who's living in this house with you?" he asked, still looking at the rumpled bed, frowning.

"No one," the housekeeper said shortly. "The Maister and his family are all in Dundregan conducting the business of the Royal Council, as well you know."

"Then who was sleeping in this bed?"

"What d'ye mean?" she demanded crossly.

The Squadman pointed to the bed. "Someone slept here recently."

Chapter Sixteen

THE HOUSEKEEPER LOOKED at the bed, then at the Squadman. For a moment, her lips thinned and her face paled. Then she threw up her hands and made an exclamation of annoyance.

"That wretched dog again. I can't keep him off the beds. Look at that. Dog hair all over my good coverlet. I must have left the door open after I dusted this morning." She went to the bed, twitched the coverlet and the pillow straight, and quickly smoothed out the remaining wrinkles. "I'll be making stew for the cat out of that dog one of these days," she muttered darkly. "You just see if I don't."

The Squadman stood, still thoughtful, staring back and forth between the bed, the housekeeper and Black for a long time, regarding the woman in speculation and assessment. She met his appraisal stiffly, her whole posture that of outraged indignation.

Finally, he nodded, satisfied, and beckoned his men out of the room. They continued their search and finished up in the parlour. Glyn and I, only scant inches away behind the thin wall, held our breath. The Squadman's voice sounded preternaturally loud as he thanked the housekeeper for her cooperation. Moments later, we heard the sound of their booted feet as they left, and the housekeeper's voice berating them for barging in on an innocent old woman in the middle of the night.

Glyn's laughter fizzed along the Communication thread between us. *"That woman should have been a Thespian,"* he said. *"She definitely missed her calling, she did."*

"She's a tongue like a rusty razor," I agreed, having trouble controlling my own amusement which was more than three parts nervousness and sheer relief. *"He'll be smarting from that tongue-lashing for days."*

"I almost found it in my heart to pity him."

In the yard, they searched Roddy mac Gowan's dray while he glowered at them, but found nothing more than bags of fresh fruits and vegetables and sacks of grain. Both his relief and the housekeeper's were palpable when all seven sheriffmen mounted their horses and disappeared down the street toward the next house.

The housekeeper waited a long time to make sure they would not return, then fetched Glyn and me out of the tiny bolt-hole.

Roddy mac Gowan's old-fashioned dray was much larger and clumsier than a carriage or an ordinary wagon. It had a false deck in the back with a space beneath it just barely large enough to hold two grown men. He shut Glyn and me into it, and set out for the crags with much clattering of traces and tack and the thumping rumble of iron-bound wheels on the cobblestones.

It was stuffy and cramped in the tiny space, and it was dark as the heart of a storm cloud. Road dust filtered in through every seam. It wasn't long before my skin felt gritty as emery. If I lay on my back, the dust sifted down into my eyes. If I lay on my side, my shoulder scraped the rough planking of the wagon bed above me. I could find no way to get comfortable.

"Join the Watch and see the world, they told me," Glyn muttered as he tried to find room for his legs. "See the unlimited vistas of the Wildesea. Room for a man to breathe, they told me. Your elbow is in my eye."

I wriggled around a bit. "How's that?"

"Better. Now it's poking into my throat."

I moved again. There wasn't a lot of space. "That's the best I can do."

"I'm going to request sea duty from now on," he said. "Believe me, I've had more than enough of being stuffed into small, dark places."

Sheriffmen stopped the rattling old dray twice on the way out of the city, and searched it thoroughly each time while Roddy mac Gowan grumbled and growled about being late on his deliveries. Glyn and I could do nothing but hold ourselves completely motionless and pray the sheriffmen didn't find the false bottom.

Our very helplessness made it worse, harder to bear the tension. After the second time, I was positive every nerve in my body was outside my skin and scraped raw on the rough surface of the floor of our hidden compartment. From what I could read of Glyn's state of mind, he wasn't in any better shape. Both of us were going to be much happier when this journey was over and we could breathe clean, fresh air again, and stretch our cramped muscles.

When Roddy finally stopped the dray and opened the trap door in the decking, Glyn and I crawled out, dirty, stiff and sore, to find ourselves on the edge of the wild country at the foot of the crags. We had been almost three hours in the cramped little space, because dawn had just begun to brighten the eastern sky behind the grim, jagged towers of the crests. It was yet barely light enough to see, not yet light enough to distinguish any colour definition in the forbidding landscape.

Roddy pulled two travel-packs out from a cubbyhole under the decking in the rear of the dray, and tossed one to Glyn, the other to me. "The lass sent these along for you," he said. "There's food and a sleepsack each. I'll leave you here. I can't take the dray much further. I wish you both luck."

We watched the ancient dray lurch off down the track, horses straining to pull it over the rutted and broken ground. Then we turned and began climbing the low, sparsely wooded hills to the foot of the first ridge of crags. It was an easy walk even without much light. The ground was smooth enough with few rocky outcroppings and the bushes thin and wispy below the widely spaced trees.

In half an hour, it was full light and we were well into the rough country, accessible only on foot or on horseback. The walking was more difficult here, the slope steeper, the ground littered with loose rocks and stones. We found a sheltered place amid a tumble of rock and sat down to eat some of the bread, cheese and fruit Holly had sent.

"Where's the Out-ship now?" I asked.

Glyn glanced up and I sensed his flash of Communication even though I couldn't pick up what he was saying. He frowned and bit his lip.

"They're still four days out from the barrier reef," he said. "They'll negotiate the passage through the reef just north of the border with Celyddon on the morning of the sixth day, they tell me. Then another two or three days to bring them in close enough to launch the gig. I've told them we can be back down on the coast close to the border of Eyrindor by then."

I looked up to the high crags above us. "That's a long trek on foot along the ridges," I said. "It will be a close thing."

"Where do we go from here?"

I pointed to a narrow pass through the crags. "That way, I think. There are caves up there, and a stream. It's rough, but it's not desert."

"I should have known." He sighed and shook his head in weary resignation, then grinned as he studied the valley. "You had to pick the tallest and meanest looking crag around here to climb over, didn't you?" He got up and slung his travel pack resolutely over his shoulder. "Lead on, then."

We climbed steadily throughout the afternoon, stopping only once to eat again and drink some water. By early evening, we were almost through the pass. The country had flattened out a little and the walking was a bit easier. We were now moving quickly along the grassy floor of the twisting valley that led through the soaring crags. Huge boulders, jagged and raw, that had tumbled from the high cliffs, littered the ground. Many of them were twice as high as a man, and as broad as they were high. To our right rose a sheer cliff. It towered well over three hundred feet straight up, bulging forward and leaning ominously out over the valley. To our left, the river ran swift and turbulent as it plunged down the steep slope between the walls of a narrow gorge. Ahead of us, a fall of rock cluttered the valley, treacherously loose and slippery. Only a few hundred feet before the rockfall, the canyon where the river ran narrowed to some fifteen feet or so, constricting the river to a leaping, frenzied maelstrom. Too far for a man to jump, perhaps, but in his youth Brindle could have leapt it easily enough.

Fortunately, we wanted to keep to the south side of the river. We had no need to cross it. The valley on the other side of the chasm appeared far rougher than this side. Good footing for neither man nor beast.

"We might as well camp here," Glyn said as we stopped to catch our breath. "We're going to have to stop for the night soon anyway. I don't know about you, but I don't feel like risking a broken leg or ankle climbing over that scree in the dark."

Even as he spoke, a small section of the flat slabs of slate slipped from its precarious perch at the top of the fall and rattled down the steep slope, raising a cloud of dust and bouncing echoes off the walls of the pass. Some of the slabs had enough momentum to send them plunging and plummeting over the cliff into the tumbling river. Only a few stones had fallen, but it was enough to convince me of the wisdom of making camp here on this side of the landslip and waiting for morning and full light to traverse it. I, too, had no desire to go slipping and slithering down the fall and over the steep bank into the river.

We turned aside and made our way to the shelter of the overhanging promontory behind a low ridge of rock which had fallen from the crest of the cliff. We were well above the tree-line, so there was no wood available to build a fire. But we couldn't risk a fire in any case. It was going to get cold at this altitude once the sun went down, but we had our sleepsacks, and the dark granite of the cliff reflected the heat it had been absorbing throughout the day. We would be warm enough without a fire.

We made ourselves as comfortable as possible. In the last of the light, Glyn rolled up the right sleeve of his shirt and looked at his arm. The skin was red and shiny, but it appeared to have nearly healed. He nodded in satisfaction and rolled the sleeve down again.

"It's a bit stiff yet," he said, fastening the sleeve cuff

around his wrist. "But I can get it fixed once we get out of here. A visit to a Healer in Lighthaven, and you won't even be able to see the scar anymore."

"Lighthaven is where Watch Headquarters is, isn't it?" I asked.

"Yes. And the Academy. You'll be two years in classes, Iain, with two full seasons out of each year at sea."

I started to reply, but he suddenly held up his hand for silence.

"There's somebody out there, and they know we're here."

I stiffened. *"Sheriffmen?"*

"I don't think so. They don't feel like sheriffmen. There are three of them."

"Outlaws, perhaps?"

"I don't know. I think so."

We sat up as two men and a woman came around the spur of rock in a rush, hoping to take us by surprise. The two men carried swords and daggers, and the woman held a short bow, an arrow nocked in the string. Glyn lit a small lantern and smiled at them.

"Good evening," he said pleasantly. "What can we do for you?"

I had grown up knowing there were outlaws living in the Crags, but I had never seen any. Their numbers were made up of those who had fled to the crags to escape punishment for some crime against the Crown—theft, fraud, assault and murder, for the most part. Some of them were liege-bounds who had run away from their lawful masters for one reason or another. And some of them, undoubtedly, were simply those who found living within the restrictions of civilization too much to bear. Except for the occasional foray down to the freeholdings or crofts to steal a lamb or two, or fruit from an orchard, they seldom really bothered anyone. It was said they had crofts and villages of their own hidden on the edge of the Central Desert, but no one I had ever spoken with had ever seen them.

The country they chose—or were forced—to live in was rough and inhospitable. In the winter, snow clogged the mountain passes and it was bitterly cold. Even in the middle of summer, the land was not welcoming. The sheriffmen very seldom ventured into the Great Crags. Unless an outlaw had committed some monstrous crime, he was usually left to survive as best he could on his own and take what comfort and fellowship he could from the other outlaws, providing they accepted him into their company.

Undoubtedly, now there were political fugitives among the outlaws. It occurred to me suddenly to wonder if they had set up their own enclaves.

The three who stood over Glyn and me with weapons ready were a fierce-looking trio. The men wore beards, untrimmed and tangled, their clothing patched and worn, and none too clean. The woman was cleaner, her clothing a little neater, her hair not quite so unkempt. But she didn't look to be much gentler or kindly disposed toward intruders than did the two men. They studied us closely in the light of the small lantern, their suspicion and wariness as strong in the air as the scent of impending lightning before a storm.

"We've nothing of value, if you've come to steal," Glyn said mildly, his voice quiet and calm. He smiled at them, apparently completely unruffled.

"We didn't come to steal," the woman said scornfully. "We certainly are not thieves."

"Who are you and why have you come this way?" one of the men demanded. He held his sword easily and loosely, but it would take him the space of less than two heartbeats to raise it and swing it if Glyn or I made a wrong move.

"We mean you no harm," Glyn said. "We're not sheriffmen."

"Aye, I can see that. You'd be a stranger, by your eyes."

Glyn inclined his head in acknowledgment. "I'm a Fey-Halfblood," he said. "My name is Glyn shanBreyor. From Lighthaven in Lysandia."

"Iain mac Drew," I said. "From just outside Caliburn. We're on the run from the sheriffmen."

The outlaw turned his attention to me. He had a broad, unlined brow, and clear, intelligent dark eyes under the shaggy eyebrows which nearly met over the bridge of his nose. That nose had been broken a time or two and improperly set. "Iain mac Drew," he repeated thoughtfully. "You'd be the man who escaped the sheriffmen in Caliburn the other day then, would you?"

"Aye, I would," I said. "They were going to take me to Dundregan and try me for treason and treachery."

"Those are harsh words," he said. "The penalty is always death."

"Aye, it is. I've no wish to die on the scaffold because of the likes of my Cousin Maelgrun."

"Nor do any of us," the second man said. He had been standing back out of the light while the other man spoke. All I could see of him was that he was older than the first man, his beard shot with white. He stepped forward now into the gentle glow of the lantern. With a shock, I realized I knew him. He was Bevan mac Clintlagh. He had been a good friend to Bronwyn and Durstan when he owned the only printing house in Caliburn before Padreg's Inner Circle had burned it. He and his family had simply disappeared between dusk and dawn with no word as to what happened to them. We had thought them dead or in a work camp like too many other people who had disappeared since Fergus took his crown. I wondered again how many like him had taken refuge in these High Crags.

He laughed softly as he saw my recognition. "I see you remember me now, Iain."

"Aye, sir, I do," I replied. "Have you been up here all this time then, Maister Bevan?"

"Yes. All these years," he replied. "Do you remember my wife Ylene and my son Geordie?"

"Aye," I said, turning to nod to her. "I remember Mistress Ylene well, but Geordie only vaguely."

Geordie sheathed his sword and thrust his dagger through his belt. He went down on one knee and held his hand out to me. "We heard of what you did in the city," he said. "We're in touch with certain people in Caliburn—the Cymry. They're saying what you did the other morning will mean the beginning of the end for Fergus, for all Padreg and his cursed Inner Circle may rant and rave. You're welcome to come with us until you can return to Caliburn a free man."

Glyn glanced at me. *"Stay if you want. It's your decision, Iain."*

But I had made my decision when I let Holly leave the safe-house in Caliburn without me. I smiled and shook my head.

"That won't be necessary," I said. "There should be an Out-ship coming to pick us up within the next fortnight."

Bevan looked at Glyn. "You'd be one of the Outsiders off the Out-ship gig the sheriffmen sank a while ago," he said. "You speak very good Gael for a stranger."

"I'm a Celyddonian, too," Glyn said. "I was born in Alcolmvale."

"There'll be more trouble if another Out-ship tries to enter Celyddonian waters," Mistress Ylene said.

"This will be an official Watch Out-ship," Glyn said grimly. "And they'll be picking us up across the Eryndorian border. Mind, they'll be in no mood to take any nonsense from a pack of sheriffmen who might take it into their heads to try to stop them. I believe they'll have the authority to carry it through." He looked up at them speculatively. "I think it was your people that Ydonda sheilVoryn and I were speaking with? You'd be with Keagan mac Brys's group, would you then?"

"Aye, we are," Geordie said.

"Keagan mac Brys?" I glanced quickly at Bevan, then back to Glyn. "He's here?" Keagan mac Brys had been Chamberlain to King Culhain, and a great man in his own right. He was one of the first to vanish. Even before Fergus took the crown, Keagan mac Brys had disappeared as mysteriously as Daryn had. "He's still alive? He's here in the Crags?"

"Aye," Bevan said. He laughed softly. "There's quite a number of us here, laddie. A lot of us saw the way it was going and came up here to wait until Fergus's regime collapsed under its own corrupt weight."

Glyn nodded, then turned to me. "There are a lot of good people here, Iain."

Bevan laughed again. "Aye, and we're tough enough and stubborn enough to wait them out."

"But who would be King if Fergus was ousted?" I asked.

"That's something you'll not have to worry about," Bevan said. "I take it you'll not be wanting our help right now, then?"

"No, thank you," I said. "It would be best, though, if you stayed away from us and under cover in case the sheriffmen come into the Crags to search for us. You don't need them finding you."

Geordie made a soft sound of contempt. "They haven't found us yet. And not for lack of trying."

Bevan and Mistress Ylene drew aside and had a quick, whispered conversation. Then Bevan stepped back into the circle of light cast by the small lantern.

"I don't like the idea of leaving you out here like this," he said. "I think it best if you come with us." He looked at Glyn. "I'll take it you'll have no trouble letting the Out-ship know where you are?"

"No trouble," Glyn said. He began rolling his sleepsack to stow it back into his travelpack, motioning me to do the same. It took only a few minutes to get ready to go.

We fell into single file, Bevan leading. Glyn and I followed Ylene. Geordie, his sword still held ready in his hand, brought up the rear. It occurred to me that perhaps they didn't quite trust Glyn and me quite as much as they implied they did.

The stars cast very little light on the barren landscape, but Bevan must have had the eyes of a cat. He led us toward the tumble of scree, then took a sharp turn to the right and disappeared into what looked to me to be a wall of solid rock. But when I followed Ylene to it, I saw it was a narrow slit between the solid slabs of the cliff that might look like little more than a dark shadow against the rocks in daylight. I had to turn sideways to get past several places without collecting some painful scrapes to my shoulders and arms. I was certain that Geordie barely made it through, broad-shouldered and big as he was.

The path twisted and turned tortuously for a long way. The rock walls had a presence and a solidity that was oppressive and all-pervading. Occasionally, I caught glimpses overhead of the stars, but that only served to emphasize the constriction of the passage. The walls seemed to hover over me, closing in inexorably, and I shivered.

But eventually, we came out the other side into a narrow valley. The Queen's upper rim appeared above the crags to our left as we did, and I oriented myself quickly. This was not the valley the pass would have led us into. I had no idea where we were.

But Bevan mac Clintlagh knew. He turned unhesitatingly to follow a slender path down the side of the crag, sure-footed in the dark as any nocturnal animal. Glyn and I slipped and slithered down the steep trail behind him. Once, Geordie had to grab my arm as my foot skidded on a loose rock, or I would have plunged helplessly down the steep slope off the side of the track.

We descended a long way before we entered the trees and the night darkened as the thick canopy of leaves above us shut out the faint light cast by the Queen and the Companion. Still Bevan didn't falter. He moved decisively down the path, obviously completely familiar with it even without light.

Presently we entered a small clearing and Bevan stopped. The figure of a man materialized out of the shadows.

"You brought them along, did you?" the man asked.

"Aye," Bevan replied. "They're best with us."

The man nodded in the direction of the sheer crag behind him. "Then bring them along here."

"Is Keagan back yet?"

"Not yet," the man said. "Tomorrow morning, perhaps. Or early afternoon." He stepped aside at a huge slab of rock that stood leaning against the side of the cliff. Bevan slipped behind the slab, Ylene following him. When I followed her, I stopped so suddenly on the other side that Glyn nearly trod on my heel.

We were in a vast cavern, lit by lanterns and torches. The interior of the cavern was dry, the temperature cool, but more than comfortable. We stood at the end of a long hall. The whole area inside the cavern had been partitioned off by rough plank walls into roomy alcoves, and gave the impression of a small village. In the center, surrounded by the dividing walls, lay what looked like a common gathering area. Tables and benches were scattered around a large central hearth. No fire burned there. It wouldn't be needed for warmth at this time of year. The furniture looked solid and comfortable.

Several people, among them a young woman nursing a baby, sat at the tables, or on benches around the hearth. They looked up, only mildly interested, as Glyn and I followed Bevan and Ylene down the long hall into the open area. Geordie crossed the room quickly to the woman with the baby. He bent to kiss her, then tickled the baby's feet, grinning as the baby gurgled in delight.

"If all the outlaw enclaves are like this, it's no wonder the sheriffmen haven't ever found them," I said to Glyn. He gave me a quick grin in reply.

The man who had led the way into the cavern beckoned Glyn and me to follow. He showed us to a small alcove containing two narrow cots covered with thin straw mattresses.

"You can sleep here," he said. "Please stay in here and don't come into the common area. It's best if you see as few of us as possible."

Glyn shrugged out of his travelpack and dropped it onto one of the cots. "We understand."

I spread my sleepsack on the other cot, then lay down on it. I ached all over and I was more tired than I had believed possible. I looked up at Glyn, a question forming in my mind. He grinned.

"No, I wasn't afraid of them," he said.

"That's not what I was going to ask."

"I know." He laughed softly. "It would have been your next question, though. Remember, you could have Stilled the lot of them any time they started to look dangerous."

Startled, I stared at him.

His eyebrows rose in surprise, then quirked thoughtfully. He shook his head. "Some Watch Member you're going to make, Iain mac Drew, if you go around forgetting your Gifts all the time."

He was right. I had completely forgotten. I had no excuse but weariness. "Aye," I said at last, grinning ruefully. "I suppose I could have. If I'd thought of it in time."

He settled himself comfortably into his sleepsack. "In answer to your other question," he said. "I told you it was Watch business we were on when we met you in the cove that first night. The Commonwealth wants Celyddon back safely in the fold, but it can't overtly interfere." A quick grin turned up the corners of his mouth. "The Watch has never been above dabbling in a little subterfuge now and again, mind you. It keeps us from going stale merely chasing freebooters and pirates around inside the barrier reefs." He pulled the sleepsack up around his shoulders. "Go to sleep now. It's been a long day."

"But—"

"Go to sleep."

I wanted to know more about his and Ydonda's discussions with these outlaws who had banded together under Keagan mac Brys. But I knew I wasn't going to get any more information out of Glyn. Not then, at any rate. I went to sleep.

Chapter Seventeen

I **AWOKE KNOWING** I had dreamed of Holly. I lay on my back in the dark, fingers laced behind my head, and remembered how she had looked as she reached up to unfasten the lacings of her gown there in the safe-house in Caliburn. Her face was beautiful, her eyes full of love. The memory set my heart beating faster.

I should have insisted she come with me. No matter if she protested. I should have insisted. I had no way of ensuring her safety if she wasn't with me, no way of knowing what happened to her. Surely I needed her more than the organization of rebels—the Cymry as Geordie mac Bevan named it—needed her.

Her voice was there with me in the cool dark, whispering softly. *"Sometimes, what we want and what we must do are two different things."*

I moved restlessly on the narrow cot. I could have insisted she come with me. And if I had persisted, she might well have given in and come. But leaving what she saw as her duty would have killed something in her, something that made her uniquely Holly. It would have destroyed any joy she might have taken in our future together.

Or I could have stayed with her, knowing that the sea would call me even more irresistibly than ever it had before, because I would know I'd thrown away my chance to be Out there on its limitless reaches. Eventually, that would kill something just as essential in me, and Holly had known that.

She was, perhaps, far wiser than I. And far stronger.

I heard movement in the corridor outside the alcove. It must be close to dawn, perhaps even full daylight. It was impossible to tell in the gloom of the cavern. Glyn stirred on his cot, then stretched lazily and sat up.

"What time is it?" he asked, yawning widely.

"It's a bit difficult to tell. Quite some time after dawn, I expect."

He rumpled his hair, then scrubbed both hands over his face. "I certainly hope it's breakfast time," he said. "I could use a bit more than cheese and fruit."

"Where's the Out-ship?"

Again, I sensed his flash of Communication, but could get no impression of the message.

"They're still seven days out from the barrier reef," he said. "Perhaps eight, if the winds don't come." He paused, then frowned. "The Windcaster reports difficulty raising the wind. Something seems to be holding it back."

"Could it be some kind of *chausey magic*?" I asked. "Do they know about it?"

The flicker of Communication was slightly longer

this time. Finally, Glyn nodded. "They know. Their Communicator has been in touch with Lysandia. Ydonda told them about the *chausey magic* that sank the gig. The Windcaster thinks it's possible it's *chausey magic*, or some kind of unfamiliar magic."

The curtain at the entrance parted to admit Geordie, carrying a tray loaded with food. He sat on a low stool as Glyn and I ate.

"We'll take you out of the valley later today," he said. "There's a faster way down to the coast at Borland's Foot than the way you were headed. It's narrow and perilous, but it'll see you there a full day sooner."

Glyn raised his head, listening. Beyond our small alcove, the buzz of conversation in the common area sounded suddenly louder. Moments later, Bevan pushed aside the curtain and entered the tiny room.

"Keagan's back," he said to Geordie. "Bring them outside now."

Glyn and I followed them down the long hall. The common area was empty of people when we passed through it, but I heard the quiet murmur of voices beyond some of the thin partitions, and the cry of a small, hungry child, quickly muffled against a breast.

When we came out from behind the leaning slab of rock protecting the entrance of the cavern, the sun was only just above the crags on the opposite side of the valley. The valley itself was little more than a narrow cleft in the fabric of the crags. It was barely five furlongs wide, and not more than half a league long. It would be very difficult to find if one didn't know exactly where it was.

We stood about halfway up the side. A short distance above us, the trees thinned to the sharp demarcation of the tree-line. Below, the cleft narrowed until it was wide enough only for the small stream that rushed and tumbled at the bottom, the water white and turbulent enough to send a fine spray of mist purling up into the morning light. Around us, the tall corewood trees with their slender leaves, the delicate mountain laurel and thickly spreading rock maples formed a canopy through which the light filtered with a fresh, green glow. Near the edges of the small clearing, irregular patches and rows of vegetables ripened neatly toward harvest.

Two men, cowled and cloaked, stepped out of the trees, emerging from the same path I thought we had followed to get here. One was tall and slender, but stooped with age, and walked with the aid of a staff. The other was not so tall but more powerfully built, obviously much younger. They saw us standing by the entrance with Bevan and Geordie, and paused for a moment, then the elder man came forward to meet us. He shook back the hood of his cloak to bare his head and reveal his face. The other man remained in the shadow of the trees, watching us.

Keagan mac Brys had not been young when Fergus ascended the throne of Celyddon all those years ago. Now he looked older than he should have. Deep lines and furrows etched his face, and his beard had gone completely white. Only the brilliant blue eyes remained bright and youthful, alert and direct.

Bevan stepped forward. "Did you have any trouble getting back?" he asked.

Keagan mac Brys put his hand to Bevan's shoulder. "None of particular note," he said. He turned to Glyn and me. "How good to see you again, Glyn shanBreyor," he said, the timbre of his voice rich and powerful still. "I was sorry to hear your friend had been hurt."

"She's recovering well in Lighthaven, I'm told," Glyn said.

"So I've heard, too." Keagan turned to me. "You'd be Iain mac Drew, nephew to Durstan mac Lludd," he said, smiling. "Most of our news concerns you, my young friend. You've truly turned them upside down and shaken them in Caliburn, and in Dundregan, too. Quite the kerfuffle you've caused."

"Aye, well, it was something I'd rather not needed to do," I said.

A glint of amusement sparked in his blue eyes. "I can see how you'd feel that way," he said. "I'm afraid, though, you can't leave here for a while. There are sheriffmen and soldiers hunting through the Crags, thick on the ground as ants to spilled honey. You can't take the chance of them finding you."

Glyn glanced at the man still standing beneath the trees at the edge of the clearing. "I trust they're looking for us and not for someone else," he said.

White teeth flashed in a grin under the shadow of the hood as the man came forward. "You needn't worry, Glyn, my friend," he said. "They assuredly don't know I'm here."

"Well, you certainly look different from when I last saw you," Glyn said. "Suitably disreputable and scruffy. Your own mother wouldn't know you."

I stared at the young man, a nagging suspicion growing in my mind. He laughed at Glyn's remark and threw back the hood of his cloak. His bright red-gold hair caught the morning sun and flared like a corona about his head. Ginger-red stubble covered his jaw and cheeks, and dirt smudged his forehead. There were lines furrowing down from his nose to bracket his mouth, lines that shouldn't be there yet, but I recognized him. And suddenly I knew what Glyn and Ydonda's mission had been the night I met them in the cove on my way home from Jaerl mac Neill's absurd meeting.

I dropped to one knee. "Your Highness," I said, my voice sounding hoarse in my own ears.

Prince Daryn raised me quickly. "Just Daryn," he said. "A wolfshead and traitor doesn't rate the title of Highness. Nor the honour of a bent knee, come to that." His voice carried a trace of bitterness, but his smile was bright against the stubble of his beard.

"There are those in Celyddon who never believed that of you," I said.

"Yourself among them?" he asked, amusement glinting in his green eyes.

"Aye. And my uncle and aunt."

"But not your cousin."

I shrugged. "I've given up trying to sort out what Maelgrun actually believes from what he professes to believe. Have you come home to lead the revolution against Fergus, then?"

His expression hardened. "I'll not lead any revolution against my own brother," he said. "I'll not become a kin-slayer. Nor would I ask it of any man. But I'll lead the fight against that Abyss-spawned Padreg and his pack of jackals in priest's robes. It was they who killed my father. Degree by slow degree, they poisoned him, as they poisoned my brother's heart and spirit."

"That hardly surprises me," I said. "But I wonder why you didn't denounce them."

"I told a few trusted friends," Daryn said grimly. "Except for Keagan, all of them were found dead in their beds the next morning. Fortunately, he was warned in time to flee here. That night found me in the Tower of Tears, watching them build my scaffold."

"How did you escape?"

He grinned. "A small matter of a member of the Watch with magic to cast an illusion, and the Talent of a Manipulator. We walked past nearly two dozen guards, and all they saw was their own shadows moving along the walls of the Tower. We were beyond the Barrier on our way to Lysandia before they knew I was gone."

"And now you're home again," I said.

"And now I'm home again," he agreed. "And it seems I owe you a debt of gratitude for stirring up the people of Caliburn to the point where an attack on Padreg might be feasible."

Glyn cleared his throat. "Before you talk about storming Dundregan and taking Padreg," he said, "there are a few important matters we need to discuss. One of them is about how this spirit-poisoning of Padreg's comes about."

We kept ourselves busy with chores during the rest of the day. Geordie remained with us, cheerfully repeating Keagan's news, hiding very well the fact that he was there to make sure we stayed where we were supposed to and didn't wander where we weren't wanted. There was a Council of War in the common area. Glyn and I weren't invited until after the evening meal.

Glyn and Daryn spent most of the evening in the common room, arguing. Daryn wanted to call the Watch in to help him against Padreg, and Glyn insisted that the Watch couldn't interfere in any internal problems unless specifically asked by the ruler of the country.

"That's ridiculous!" Daryn exploded. "Preposterous!"

"It's the law," Glyn said. "I didn't make the rules. I only keep them and try to enforce them."

"But we need help."

"You're not king, Daryn. We can't interfere."

"Not even against *chausey magic*?" Daryn demanded.

Glyn made a fist on the scarred oak table in frustration. "Not even against *chausey magic*," he said. "Daryn, I'm sorry. You know how the Watch works. You lived all those years in Lighthaven."

"Aye, I did. But for all of those years, *chausey magic* was just an ancient legend to frighten children into good behaviour. Now it's a reality, and a mortal danger to Lysandia—to the rest of the world!—as well as to Celyddon."

"If it were up to me, I'd go after Padreg myself." The muscle of Glyn's arm bulged as he pounded his fist softly on the table. "I was born here, Daryn. My father was Celyddonian. This is my home. But I can't go against the Watch. Even if I had the magic to fight Padreg, I can't go against the Law of the Watch."

Daryn looked at me, his eyes like green stones in his haggard face. "And you?" he said. "You're not a member of the Watch."

"Not yet, no," I said. "If I thought it would help, I'd go. But except for an untrained Gift and a Talent, I've not the magic."

"Aye," Daryn agreed heavily. "You're not Feyish, or even a Fey-Halfblood." He put the heels of both hands over his eyes and drew in a long, shuddering breath. "Never mind that it's an untenable situation to set neighbour against neighbour, and brother against brother. The realm would bleed to death. And against *chausey magic*?" He shook his head. "I refuse to send any man to certain death for no purpose." He looked around the table at the men of the Enclave. "I know you men would follow me on such a campaign. But we could do nothing against that accursed magic. It would cut us down before we could get close enough to fight."

"You could return to Lysandia with us, and go before the Watch Council," Glyn said. "You're still Second-Heir here."

The ghost of a wry smile twitched at the corner of

Daryn's mouth. "I'm a wolfshead and traitor here. Declared so by the King."

An answering curl quirked at the corner of Glyn's mouth. "Culhain never disinherited you. Fergus has that power only over his own sons, were there any."

Keagan mac Brys cleared his throat. "Is there no way we can fight the *chausey magic*?"

I remembered the fiery sphere spewing green lightning that destroyed the Out-ship gig. The clatter of polished bones falling to a stone dais echoed in my ears. I shuddered.

"Not without magic more powerful," Glyn said. "I haven't got it. I wish I did, but I haven't. Very few in Lysandia have that kind of power.

"How many priests besides Padreg have it?" Daryn asked.

"I don't know," Glyn said. "I've seen it used twice. Once by Padreg himself. It couldn't have been Padreg in the Sheriff's Launch that sank our gig. So at least two. I'd say likely at least five or six, but probably less than a dozen."

"Not just priests have it," I said. "There's Maelgrun, even if his ability isn't fully developed yet. And if he has it, have any other members of the Royal Council got it, as well?"

Glyn shot a startled glance at me. "I hadn't thought about that."

Daryn gave me a bleak, speculative look "We'd better think hard on it," he said grimly.

"It's said it takes kin-blood to bring it to full power," Glyn said. "That's likely why he wanted you, Iain."

"Kin-blood?" A sudden knot of fear clutched my belly. "Bronwyn and Durstan—" I said softly.

Glyn's head came up and his eyes widened in shock.

"Sweet piety, do you think he might— But surely he wouldn't harm his own parents, would he?"

I shook my head, not in denial but out of lack of knowledge. "I don't know. I honestly don't know." But I remembered his burning ambition, his thirst for power, his willingness to betray me.

"We can send someone to bring them here on the morrow," Keagan said, rising. "But it's late. We'd best get some rest tonight."

I slept poorly, my dreams filled with confused images of men and women fleeing blindly through the dark, pursued by robed figures whose eyes flared angry green. Again and again, I found myself back in the filthy cell in the Law Courts, struggling to find my Gifts while my cousin Maelgrun stood over me laughing, his eyes glinting baleful green like poisonous mushrooms in a dank cave. Holly and Bronwyn fled from the robed figures, then stood clinging to each other, trapped on a stone dais. On wide stone stairs, a tall, thin man robed in grey and purple raised his hands to conjure a ball hazy green mist in the air above them. Molten lightning flared briefly in the night, and two piles of polished bones clattered onto the dais.

I came out of sleep in a gasping spasm, tangled in my sleepsack, sweat pouring in streams down my face. An instant later, light flared as Glyn lit a lantern, calling the spark from the air. In the soft glow, his eyes were haggard and sunken, his face pale.

"You, too?" he asked.

My heart hammered in my chest and my breath came in painful rasps. "Nightmares?"

"The worst." He swung his feet to the floor and scrubbed his hands across his face. "Something's wrong somewhere. What was in your dreams?"

"Holly and Bronwyn in trouble." I shuddered. "And *chausey magic*. That nasty green horror Padreg threw."

He looked at me for a long time, his expression bleak. He didn't have to speak. His face said it all.

"He's used it again, then," I said. "Padreg's used that unspeakable abhorrence again."

"It upsets the balance when it's used," Glyn said hoarsely. "I don't have a lot of magic, not nearly so much as Ydonda, but I can feel it. It's like a sudden cold draft in a warm room."

"And Bronwyn and Holly?"

He shook his head. "I had no glimpse of them. Just Padreg's *chausey magic*."

I closed my eyes, composing myself. Glyn reached out and caught my arm. "If you're Casting, you may not be able to find either of them," he said quietly. "You still haven't got all your strength back. You might be better off to save what strength you have."

I glanced at him, eyes narrowed. "Did you try?"

He nodded. "And found no trace." He gave me a wry, rueful grin. "But I'm not exactly at the peak of my strength, either, ye ken. I'm just saying you mustn't jump to the wrong conclusions if you can't find them."

I nodded, then settled myself on the cot. But I could find no trace of either Holly or Bronwyn, no matter how hard I tried. Sweat rolled down my face, stung my eyes. Shards of pain lanced through my head. Panting, I slumped back against the wall to rest for a moment. Then I tried looking for Durstan, but couldn't find him, either.

Glyn touched my arm again. "Don't, Iain," he said. "You'll exhaust yourself, and you're going to need all the strength you've got soon."

"I can't find anyone," I said rather querulously. "Not Holly, not Bronwyn, or Durstan."

"It's because you haven't got the range back yet."

I hoped so. I fervently hoped so. "What shall we do?"

"What *can* we do? We wait."

The messenger arrived shortly after dawn. The sound of running feet echoed softly through the cavern. Before Glyn or I could rise and move out into the corridor, Bevan swept aside the curtain.

"There's need," he said breathlessly. "Come quickly."

The urgency in Bevan's voice brought me to my feet even before he finished speaking, and I was in the corridor, running, my mouth dry, my heart pounding above the knot of cold fear in my belly. I was barely conscious of the thud of Glyn's feet behind me.

I burst out into the open area of the gathering hall and paused, uncertain where to go. Geordie caught my arm and, without a word, led me to a smaller cavern walled off by a plank screen. Daryn and Keagan stood just inside the door, watching a medician who worked over a man on the bed against the far wall.

Blood, black and crusty, stained the clenched fist lying on the thick wool coverlet. I couldn't see the man's face, hidden by the medician's back, but I knew who it was.

"Durstan!" I cried, and took a quick step toward the bed.

Daryn held me back. "No, Iain," he said. "Let Malachi help him."

"What happened?" Glyn asked.

"We're not certain," Daryn replied. "One of the scouts found him in the pass. He'd fallen from his horse. He said he was looking for Iain. How he managed to elude all the sheriffmen and soldiers out there, we don't know. He's taken a crossbow quarrel in the chest, and he's lost a lot of blood. Malachi thinks he should recover, given time and proper treatment. I can't think how he ever made it here in that condition." He shook his head in wonder.

I went to the bed and stood behind the medician. Durstan lay unconscious, his face grimed and ravaged. A deep vertical furrow in his forehead drew his thick eyebrows together over his closed eyes. Malachi had cut away his bloodstained shirt. It lay in tatters on the blanket.

"He's a strong man," I said softly. "He's one of the strongest men I've ever known. And a good one."

"I've stunned him with poppy." Malachi didn't pause in his work. "As soon as I get this quarrel out of him, I can assess the damage."

"May I help?" Glyn asked.

Malachi glanced at him over his shoulder. "Feyish?" he asked.

"Fey-Halfblood," Glyn said. "With a Gift for Holding."

Malachi nodded. "I'd appreciate the help," he said. "The rest of you, leave us. We'll call you when we're finished."

Daryn took my arm again and led me back out to the common area. We found seats, and we waited.

The wait stretched out over an interminable length of time. Nearly an eternity. I sat with my elbows on my knees, my head cradled in my hands. No coherency joined the jumbled thoughts tumbling through my mind. Disjointed flashes of Durstan's presence as I grew up kept tangling with images of my nightmare of green balefire and clattering bones.

Presently, Glyn came to sit beside me. He slumped onto the bench, his head tilted back against the wall, eyes closed. "Malachi believes he'll live," he said, not opening his eyes. "We got the quarrel out without opening any large vessels, and he has some of the Healer's Gift. Durstan wants to see you."

Relief made me dizzy. I said nothing because words didn't seem adequate. My knees were strangely reluctant to bear my weight as I hurried across the large cavern. Glyn's mind touched mine in a gentle interrogative. With no hesitation, I let him in.

Malachi was washing his hands when I entered the room. Durstan lay on the bed, a white bandage around his chest. Bruises turned the flesh of his shoulder and throat ugly blue and purple, and his face had been battered so that his lip was split and one eye swollen nearly shut. His hands lay across his belly, fingers gently curled. With a shock, I realized it was the first time I had ever seen his hands completely still.

He turned his head as I crossed the room, his one good eye clouded with pain. I went to my knees beside the bed and took one of his hands in both of mine.

"So, I found you." His voice sounded rusty and hoarse, as if he hadn't used it for too long, or his throat was raw from shouting.

"Aye, you did," I said. "You've been ill-used, Durstan. Who did this to you?"

His mouth twisted into a bitter grimace. "They left me for dead," he said. "They took Bronwyn and the lass. I fought them, but it was no use. I couldn't help them. There were too many of them."

"They took Holly and Bronwyn?" *Dear Mother of All... Green balefire and crumbling bones...* I shuddered.

"Aye." He moved restlessly on the thin mattress. A coughing spasm wracked his body. Two splotches of hectic colour appeared in his cheeks. "I couldn't stop them, Iain. I tried."

Malachi stepped forward and bent over the bed, holding a horn cup to Durstan's lips. In a moment or two, the paroxysm quieted, and Durstan lay back on the bed, his eyes closed. Flecks of blood stained his lips.

I glanced up in question at Malachi. He nodded reassuringly. "I've not the strong Gift of a Feyish Healer," he said. "But I've enough to start the healing. The draught will help."

I nodded, then turned back to my uncle. "Who took them, Durstan?" I asked. "Was it sheriffmen? Or was it Padreg's priests?"

"Aye. Sheriffmen." Pain that had nothing to do with the wound in his chest contorted his face. "They had a priest with them. And Maelgrun...."

My heart gave a startled kick against my chest. "Maelgrun?"

Durstan looked up at me. His eye glittered fever-bright. "My own son," he said softly. "Iain, lad, I'd always meant that you have the land. Maelgrun would become laird and have half the living of the Freehold, but he never loved the land the way you do. He's never shown any interest in the running of the holding. I kent he wasn't happy about the way I dictated my bequest, but I didn't realize he hated both of us so much because of it. My own son...." The puzzled expression in his eyes was painful to watch.

"Durstan," I said gently. "What happened?"

He shuddered. "He washed his hands in my blood," he whispered. "He purposely opened the quarrel wound wider, and he washed his hands in my blood. Then he cupped his hands against the wound and drank— Sweet piety, he drank my blood."

I bent my head and pressed my forehead against our clasped hands. Nausea clenched hard against the muscles of my belly. Glyn's shocked revulsion echoed my own. I couldn't speak, couldn't risk looking at Durstan for fear I'd lose control of my belly.

Maelgrun had spilled kin-blood. He had gained strength.

"He said a curious thing."

I couldn't raise my head, but forced myself to speak. "What did he say?"

"He said if he couldn't have your blood, mine would do." His other hand touched my head. It trembled against my hair. "Whatever did he mean by that?" he asked, his tone baffled.

I took a deep breath and raised my head. He was watching me, frowning.

"Durstan, Maelgrun's not your son anymore," I said. "Something's taken possession of him, something horrifying, and he's not Maelgrun now. It wasn't him did that terrible thing. It was the thing within him."

He accepted that without comment. He merely nodded.

"Do you know where they took Bronwyn and Holly?" I asked.

"To Dundregan," he said. "The sheriffmen and priests accused them of High Treason and took them to Dundregan."

"I'll get them back, Durstan. I promise you, I'll get them back."

"I promise, too."

Daryn's voice behind me startled me badly. I jumped and spun around. Daryn approached the bed.

"D'ye recognize me, my lord Rothsey?"

Durstan looked up. One corner of his mouth twitched with the ghost of a smile. "Your Highness," he murmured. "So the rumours are true."

"They're true," Daryn said. "I swear to you, we'll do everything we can to rescue Lady Rothsey."

Durstan nodded. Malachi stepped forward and held the cup to Durstan's lips again. Slowly, Durstan's eyes closed and he drifted into sleep.

Chapter Eighteen

HAD I BEEN allowed my own way, only moments after Durstan finished speaking, I would have been scrambling up the narrow trail toward the defile leading to the pass in full cry for rescue and revenge. And, no doubt, I would have run smack into a patrol of sheriffmen or soldiers combing the area in search of me, and ended my days rather sooner than I wished to. Cooler heads than mine prevailed, however. Glyn calmly pointed out that I could do nothing to help Holly and Bronwyn if I were slung in chains into a cell next to theirs, or hanged from the nearest gibbet. Daryn and Geordie were less subtle than Glyn; both offered to bounce something large and heavy off my skull, if need be, to dissuade me from doing something incredibly stupid.

They were all three of them right, of course. We

needed to plan carefully if we were to have a chance at succeeding. Daryn motioned us to a small table near the hearth. With the urge to storm off to do something— *anything*—thundering in my chest, I followed reluctantly and sat down.

"I can understand how you feel, Iain," Daryn said. "Your cousin's head begs breaking, but this smells too strongly of a trap. You'll do no head-breaking if you walk directly into an ambush, and you'll certainly do no good for Lady Bronwyn and Mistress Holly." He glanced at Glyn. "How well do you know Dundregan?"

"Not well," Glyn admitted.

Daryn turned to me. "How about you?" he asked.

I shook my head. "I've only been there three or four times in my life."

Daryn grinned. "Then you'll simply have to take me with you." Keagan started to protest, but Daryn cut him off with a sharp hand gesture. "No, Keagan. Someone has to guide them, and you're still too well-known there."

"You're just as well-known, Highness," Keagan said drily. "Perhaps even more so than I."

"I would doubt that," Daryn said. "It's been several years since I left for Lysandia, and I was not much more than a boy then. I've grown and if we stain my hair and beard with walnut juice, even my own brother won't recognize me. Besides, I know Dundregan as well as I know the palace. In my misspent youth I had cause to do a lot of exploring. Not all of it sanctioned." He turned to Glyn again. "I'll assume your sword-work is still as good as ever was."

Glyn didn't bother to reply, but his slow grin reminded me of the lethal claws of a badgercat.

"Iain?"

I shook my head. "I've trained, but it's been years

since I practiced regularly. I can use a bow well enough, though."

Daryn nodded. "We three by ourselves will have a better chance of getting through to Dundregan than a whole troop of men, I think." He clenched his fist and thumped it softly onto the scarred planking of the table top. He glanced around the table, his brows drawn together in a thoughtful frown. "And I think this is the best way. If I can take care of Padreg while we're at it, it may break his influence on my brother. Even without considering that appalling *chausey magic*, this realm can't afford a civil war, not after all these years of oppression. Setting neighbours against each other; brother against brother; rending families down the middle. No. We need to avoid that at all costs. It would take centuries for the wounds to heal, if ever." He glanced at me, grinning crookedly. "But first things first. The Lady Bronwyn and your own lady need to be taken out of Dundregan. And quickly, I'm thinking. We should have time to deal with Padreg after that."

"The best time to leave would be shortly after sunset, I think," Glyn said. "With luck, the patrols will be camped by then and easier to avoid."

"Good idea," Geordie said. "I'll guide you out myself, and come with you, if you'll have me. And there'd be others who'd want to come."

Daryn shook his head, then put his hand on Geordie's shoulder. "You're a good man and true, Geordie, and I appreciate your offer. But I think three of us will be best. Too many men riding into Dundregan might attract more attention than we want to deal with."

Darkness wrapped itself around us as we climbed the steep path toward the narrow defile at the top of the valley. Geordie's eyes seemed to be as sharp as his father's as he led us unerringly up the side of the cleft. In the deep shadow below the trees, I could not clearly see Daryn, who walked immediately in front of me. Geordie, ahead of Daryn, was completely invisible in the gloom. Behind me, Glyn walked so softly I could not discern his footsteps in the dense silence of the night. I might have been alone in the murky night.

Trees crowded closely along the track, filling the air with the resinous scent of pine and the rich perfume of corewood sap. Their branches swept low over the trail, forcing me to bend and dodge constantly to prevent tangling the bow slung across my back. Daryn and Glyn had muffled the swords they carried with scarves so that no jingle of metal against metal might betray our presence to any sheriffmen beyond the cleft in the rock.

Presently, the track ascended beyond the tree line. Scudding clouds raced across the sky, obscuring the Queen and the Companion. Alternating patterns of pale light and black shadow danced across the rock face of the cliffs above us as the light ebbed and flowed. A sudden patch of moonlight illuminated Geordie just as he vanished into the cleft of the rock. Then Daryn disappeared as if he had been swallowed up by the stone itself. I hesitated, then plunged into the defile behind them.

I managed to bruise my elbow on the rock in the narrow passageway as I threaded my way behind Geordie and Daryn. I swore softly, and my voice echoed and re-echoed off the cliff around us, hissing and rasping, startling me. The next time I scraped my shoulder, I rubbed the bruise and gritted my teeth, simply swallowing the curse. Sound carried all too well in the stillness.

I came out of the defile below the cliff with little warning. The Queen appeared from behind a scudding cloud, flooding the rocks and grass with silver. Ahead, Geordie and Daryn stood like shadows in the dark. As

Glyn joined us, Geordie pointed to the gently sloping space below the ridge of rock where Glyn and I were camped when Geordie, Bevan and Ylene found us.

A campfire blazed in the dark, illuminating the pale fabric of four large tents. Each one of those tents might hold eight to ten men. A good sized troop. Beyond the tents, ridges of rock as tall as a man braided themselves along the rim of the canyon between the river and the camp. And between the rock and the camp, a long line of picketed horses stood wakeful and snuffling in the dark.

"They've picked a good spot," Geordie whispered.

Glyn swore softly. "That's a whole company down there," he said. "Are they sheriffmen or King's Guards? Can you tell?"

"Sheriffmen, I think." Daryn stepped ahead of Geordie and squinted down into the darkness. "I can't see the King's banner flying anywhere."

"Well, sheriffmen or King's Guard, they're not doing us much good down there," I said.

Geordie grinned at me in the fitful moonlight. "They'll do you much good indeed," he said. "You'll need horses to get to Dundregan, won't you?" He pointed. "There must be at least four dozen horses down there. The sheriffmen'll hardly miss three of them. And you might as well borrow some uniforms, too." He glanced at Daryn and rubbed his chin thoughtfully. "One of them should perhaps be an officer's uniform."

"If that camp runs true to form, the tack will be stacked behind the picket lines where the horses are staked," Daryn said. "Getting the uniforms may not be as easy as borrowing the horses."

"Well, you'll notice the horses are a bit restive," Geordie said. "On a bewitched night like tonight with the Queen and the Companion flitting among the clouds like ghosts, they might well break away and stampede, no?"

Daryn laughed softly. "And of course, the sheriffmen will become very busy rounding them up again."

"Aye, they might," Geordie said. "And they might leave some uniforms lying around, too. Or you might come across someone who could be persuaded to give you the loan of one." He pointed to the rocky outcrop that marked the beginning of the ridge Glyn and I had camped behind. "I'll meet you there with three horses when they all start running around like ants in a smashed ant-hill. You should have no trouble nipping in to get the tack and the uniforms." He started to slip away into the darkness, but Daryn caught his arm and pulled him back.

"You'll be careful, Geordie. I need men like you." Then he grinned. "I shall be quite cross with you if you get yourself killed."

"Oh, aye," Geordie replied gravely. "And young Aislinn needs her father, no? Start for the camp when you hear a thrush singing its evensong."

The Queen soared out from behind a cloud as Geordie turned to go. In the faint silver wash of light, he vanished into the shadows like a ghost. I strained my eyes trying to see some sign of him on the open meadow between the rocks and the camp. But I saw nothing. It was as if the ground had opened and swallowed him.

Time dragged. We waited tensely. The guards around the camp paced off their measured sectors with clockwork regularity. No one raised a cry of alarm.

I almost missed the exchange of significant glances between Glyn and Daryn. Glyn spoke before I could ask what they were doing.

"It would be best, I think, if you gathered up three saddles and bridles from the tack pile, Iain," he said softly, mindful of the propensity of sound to carry. "Let Daryn and me go into the camp for the uniforms."

The bitter anger that boiled up through my chest surprised me. "I'm not a child—"

"No," Daryn said. "You certainly are not. But at the same time, neither have you ever trained to kill a man if you had to do it."

"I've trained with a sword." Even to myself, I sounded sullen and sulky. I knew they were trying to protect me, and I resented it more fiercely than I'd ever resented anything before.

"More as a sport than as a killing weapon," Daryn said. "Believe me, Iain, we mean you no insult. Glyn and I have trained as soldiers and you've not. It's as simple or as complicated as that. Once you've begun your training in Lysandia, you'll understand."

How often had I heard those words as a child. *"You'll understand when you get older."* I stiffened and stared hard at him, but he only smiled. There was no mockery in the expression, no insult. Only friendship. And wry understanding. Finally, I dropped my gaze.

I capitulated, of course, but not with the best of grace. "Yes, Your Highness," I muttered.

The sweet song of a thrush sounded clearly in the quiet of the night. Daryn put his hand to my shoulder and gripped it for a moment, then he and Glyn turned and melted into the night as swiftly and silently as Geordie had done. Seconds later, I could see no sign of them. I had to admit to myself that I could not move so stealthily even on ground I knew well, let alone on unknown terrain. They had been right, as much as I hated to admit it.

The darkness intensified as clouds covered the moons. I set out to my right, circling wide around the campsite, using the scattered boulders as cover. The small stones my feet disturbed made scraping and clattering sounds that surely had to be loud enough to wake every sheriffman in the camp, and alert every sentry posted around the perimeter. But no outcry of alarm came from the pacing guards. Once, a horse whickered loudly, but subsided back into silence a moment later.

Eventually, I found myself in the shelter of one of the huge boulders slightly above the picket lines where the horses were tethered. There was no sign of Geordie, nor of Glyn and Daryn. I settled back against the stone to wait.

The shrieking cry of a badgercat split the night, and a horse screamed in panic. In moments, the picket line was a confused mass of plunging, rearing horses. Then, as if on signal, they all wheeled as one and stampeded up the pass toward the rock fall and the place where the chasm cut by the river narrowed to a mere fifteen feet or so. I caught a glimpse of Geordie on the back of one of the horses, crouched low, clinging like a limpet to its back and neck.

A sentry went down beneath the flying hooves as the horses swept past him. Seconds later, pandemonium erupted in the camp. Shouting men spilled from the tents, scrambling for weapons left stacked near the entrance flaps. The plunging horses flowed like a living river past the tents. One of the tents collapsed as a few horses tangled themselves in the ropes holding the fabric taut.

Still yelling, most of the men ran after the horses. Only a few had the presence of mind to grab for their weapons. Countrymen, I thought. Aware of what the claws and teeth of a badgercat could do.

I broke cover and ran for the empty picket lines. The tack had been stacked in neat piles in the shelter of a rocky outcrop exactly as Daryn had said it should be. I grabbed the first two saddles I came to and ran back to the jagged tooth of rock where we had agreed to meet. As I turned to go back for another saddle and three bridles, the clouds parted for a moment and the Queen and the Companion shone full down on the pass.

The horses all galloped straight at the rock fall. At the last second, it seemed, they turned away from the tumble of broken scree toward the lip of the canyon. Two of the lead horses sailed into the air, crossing the gap easily and gracefully. Geordie showed plainly on the back of one of the horses in the center of the herd.

Something metallic glinted in the moonlight. Moments later, the unmistakable, almost musical, *twang* of a crossbow loosing a quarrel carried back to me on the still air. Then another, and another. Geordie ducked low across the neck of the horse. Three or four sheriffmen knelt for a steadier aim as the horse bearing Geordie sped for the rim of the chasm.

They couldn't go on missing forever. Sooner or later, one of them would get a clear shot. Desperately, I gathered my strength and searched for the trigger. The now-familiar shifting and realignment stirred subtly in my chest, sending the Stilling impulse out toward the sheriffmen far below me.

But nothing happened. One of the kneeling sheriffmen sighted along the shaft and loosed the quarrel. Again, I triggered the impulse. Energy drained from me like water from a broken bowl. It had no effect on the sheriffmen. None at all. Either the distance was too great, or I had not enough strength back.

A crossbow thrummed once more. Just as the horse gathered itself to leap the chasm, Geordie threw up his arms and toppled off its back. Thrown off balance, the horse stumbled and plunged over the lip of the canyon. Geordie fell with it.

My heart made a hard, shocking leap in my chest, then tried to choke me as I stumbled to my knees. But I had no time for sickness or grief. I scrambled to my feet and ran back to the empty picket lines. I seized a saddle, grabbed what I hoped were three bridles, and ran back to the needle of rock. Only when I had my back again to the solid rock did I allow myself to give in to the gnawing grief and anger.

Tears stung the backs of my eyelidss and I closed them tightly, trying to banish the sight of Geordie tumbling into the canyon. Even if the crossbow quarrel had not killed him, he stood no chance in the violent turbulence of the water in the bottom of the gorge. His body would be battered to a bloody pulp on the rocks.

In that moment, hate of Fergus and Padreg, and all of their Royal Council and Inner Circle of Priests, solidified into a stony lump in my chest. What had been done to Durstan—what had been done to Bronwyn and Holly— had angered and horrified me, but it had not produced this implacable hatred. Glyn and Daryn had been right when they said I hadn't been trained to kill. When they said it, I could not have killed a sheriffman in cold blood, and I knew it. But at that moment I could. With my bare hands. Too easily. I shivered with the knowledge that I was, after all, fully capable of murder. It wasn't a comfortable discovery to make about oneself, but it was a needed attribute in time of war. And that this was war I now had no doubt at all.

But what use had these Gifts and Talents of mine been when I needed them so desperately to help Geordie? I couldn't use my Gift for Stilling to save him. It was absolutely useless. The range was too limited, the strength not nearly powerful enough. It was no help at all.

I became aware of Glyn trying to contact me. I huddled down against the rock, refused to let him in. He tried again, his probe tinged with anxiety and concern, then with insistence. I let him in.

"Geordie's dead," I told him bluntly, and sent him an image of that tumbled plunge into the chasm. His

shocked response gave me some satisfaction. He wasn't quite the hardened warrior he pretended to be at times. Moments later, he and Daryn appeared around the rock, carrying three large bundles between them.

"What happened?" Daryn demanded.

I told him what I had seen. "Someone will have to go back," I said. "We have to tell Bevan and Ylene."

"Tell Bevan and Ylene what?" Geordie asked cheerfully, appearing around the shoulder of the outcropping. He looked little the worse for wear after his tumble.

I stared at him in shock. "But I saw the quarrel hit you," I said. "I saw you fall into the canyon..."

"I wasn't hit. Just shamming." He grinned at me. "Take a lesson from the foxen," he said. "Never go to earth unless you have a back door. There's a small ledge an armslength or two below the lip there. I jumped down onto it. If you thought I was dead, so do the sheriffmen. They won't be looking for me." He bent to pick up a saddle and a handful of bridle. "Hurry. We've not got a lot of time. Those sheriffmen won't be much longer rounding up the horses still on this side of the river. They'll not know how many crossed to the other side, or how many fell into the river, so they won't be coming after you. I hid three horses down among the rocks a little way from here before I stampeded the rest. Let's get them saddled and get you on your way before that kerfuffle down there is sorted out."

Chapter Nineteen

LATE IN THE afternoon of the third day, we left the mountains and rode out onto the vast, rolling coastal plain to the north of Borland's Foot. To either side of the track, grain crops grew belly-high to the horses in fields edged by low green hedges and dry stone walls. An orchard, the trees set out in neat rows, lay to our right. The boughs of the trees hung low, laden with fruit ripening to harvest. In the distance, men laboured to bring in a crop of hay.

This was the Royal Estate, King Fergus's own lands, rich and bountiful. Part of it by rights should have been Daryn's.

Daryn reined in and shaded his eyes. "Down there," he said, pointing. "There's Dundregan. We should reach it by dusk, I think."

The city gleamed in the late afternoon sun. Beyond it, the sea shone blue and green, traced with streaks of lacy white. The palace, built of white stone on a promontory near the sea, flared like a beacon. Below it, huddled against the rock, stood the somber grey prison overlooking the main public square. Its one tower, the walls broken only by narrow slits of unglazed windows, thrust upward like a broken tooth at the near corner. The Tower of Tears.

Holly and Bronwyn might be in that tower now. Or in the dungeon cells below the palace.

I refused to think about the notion they might already be dead.

The horses were tired. The best they could manage was a brisk walk. By the time we reached the massive city gates, the sun had dipped to the horizon, painting the palace blood red.

We had to stop behind a clumsy dray blocking the gate. Its load of wooden beer kegs swayed alarmingly as the restive horses fidgeted, halfway through the gates. The driver, perched high on the seat, fumbled in his pouch for his pass, then leaned far over to hand it to the guard below him. The guard gave the pass only a cursory glance, then waved the dray through. The driver gathered the traces in one hand and cracked his whip with the other. The six huge horses threw their weight into the harness and the dray inched forward.

The guard turned to us. Daryn rode forward to meet him. The guard took the pass Daryn handed him, and grunted.

"You made it back just in time," he said. "We'll be closing the gates once you're through."

Daryn grinned at the guard, his teeth flashing white against the darkened walnut of his beard. "It's a good thing we hurried that last league or so, then. I wouldn't want to explain to the wife why I wasn't home tonight. She'd have my ears, thinking I was with a tavern wench."

The guard laughed. "Wives." He shook his head. "All alike, they are. Mine would have more than my ears, she would, if you get my meaning. Kiss the tavern wench for me."

He waved us through, then turned to supervise the other guards as they strained to swing the gates closed.

Just inside, a dark figure stood in the shadows of the guard house, grey-robed and silent, his head shrouded by his cowl. Beneath the drooping fabric, the man's eyes glinted like green sparks in the dusk. A cold chill rippled down my spine and I shivered. Instinctively, I ducked my head and looked away, but I was conscious of the intense gaze of the priest of Uthoni on my back. A small spot between my shoulder blades itched furiously, waiting for the quarrel from the crossbow of one of the guards.

But nothing happened. We turned into a side street and left the guards and the priest behind.

"They're expecting trouble," Glyn said softly. "Did you notice the priest's eyes, Daryn?"

"No." Daryn smiled crookedly. "I was too busy not looking at him. That was Bors of Lederhill. He knows me well."

"His eyes glowed greenish," Glyn said. "He has it, too."

"*Chausey magic*," I said. "Are they looking for us?"

"Perhaps not us, exactly," Daryn said. "But the temper of the city is tense. They're looking for anyone who might foment trouble."

We made our way through the city to the Cauldron, a narrow strip of dilapidated shops and seedy taverns and inns lining the waterfront within the shadow of the Tower of Tears and the palace. Before Fergus ascended the throne, this area between the city Square and the dirty sea had been a hive of gambling and prostitution, swarming with thieves and cutpurses. It was worth a nobleman's life to come here unescorted by an armed guard.

Since Fergus, the sheriffmen under Padreg's direction had cleaned it up considerably. But even Padreg could not completely rid the Cauldron of its more unsavory elements. The brisk trade of the Cauldron merely became more subdued and circumspect.

Daryn obviously knew his way around. He led us down a twisting side street to a small inn built half on the waterfront embankment and half on the wooden planking of a derelict pier. The gate in the wall around the tiny courtyard hung drunkenly askew on rusted hinges.

"This place is safe," Daryn said as he dismounted in the tiny courtyard. "The innkeeper is a friend and no admirer of either my brother or Padreg. Gaerd is the man who hid Keagan from Fergus, and got him out of the city. We can trust him."

No stable boy came to assist us as we unsaddled the horses and closed them into stalls. I found some towelling to rub down the horses, and Daryn found some reasonably fresh hay. We carried armloads to the feeding troughs and made sure the horses had water.

The common room of the inn was nearly deserted. In a corner, four men sat at one table, mugs of ale before them, their heads bent over a gliss-board, completely absorbed in the slant and slide of the board pieces as the game progressed. All four studiously ignored us as we entered, our sheriffmen uniforms standing out like blood on snow. One of the serving girls appeared at the doorway to the kitchen, carrying a tray of ale mugs. She blanched as she saw us, then ducked back into the kitchen.

Moments later, the proprietor hurried out of the kitchen and across the room to meet us, his round belly wobbling beneath his stained, white apron. He wore a wide smile of welcome that was as patently false as the interest his patrons showed in the board game.

"How may I serve you gentlemen?" he asked.

"You can take us upstairs and find us a room," Daryn said. "Then you can bring us some food and let your customers get back to whatever debauchery they were practicing when we rode up."

"Debauchery, sir?" The proprietor's eyebrows rose in innocent shock. "I assure you—" He broke off and squinted at Daryn's face. "Ah. Of course. This way, please."

It wasn't until he had showed us to a small room under the eaves and closed the door behind himself that he spoke again. "I didn't expect to see you back again so soon, my lord Daryn," he said. "Is there trouble?"

"There will be soon, I fear." Daryn gestured toward Glyn and me. "These are friends, Gaerd. We're here seeking news of two women the sheriffmen or the Chief of Law may have brought to the city a few days ago."

"Maelgrun mac Durstan, curse his name." Gaerd spat into the cracked chamber pot by the door. "There's a truly black heart, that one."

"Have you heard anything?" Glyn asked.

"Nay, nothing about two women. But I can ask around. I may be able to unearth some news of them."

"They'd be either in the Tower or the palace dungeons, I think," Daryn said. "Try to find out which, if you can."

"For you, my lord Daryn, I'll do my best." With his hand on the latch, he said over his shoulder, "I'll send Anda up with supper for you all three."

An hour later, we slipped out the back way with Gaerd's promise to leave the small door hidden in the pantry unlocked for our return. We made our way through the narrow streets until the looming wall of the Tower seemed to lean out over us. The entrance, guarded by gates of iron-studded corewood and an outer gate of closely-spaced iron bars, faced the Square, directly opposite the balcony where Fergus had stood with Padreg beside him as he declared his only brother outlaw and wolfshead. On the crenellated walls, guards armed with crossbows paced in pairs, and as we passed the gates, a dog inside snarled alertly. We marched briskly past the gate and turned into another sidestreet leading off the Square.

"It's like a rabbit warren in there," Daryn said quietly. "And the rats are as big as rabbits, too. Half of it was tunnelled right into the rock. There are places where the corridors have collapsed, and water has come in. I doubt there's anyone living who knows all of it well enough not to get lost in there."

Glyn shuddered. "Let's hope Holly and Bronwyn aren't in there."

"Aye, well, the palace dungeons aren't much better," Daryn said. "Probably a little drier, but that's about all. We could do with some of your Feyish magic, Glyn."

"I wish I had some real magic," Glyn said. He tilted his head back to look at the walls. "Those could probably be scaled. There's hand- and footholds enough."

"The windows are too narrow to let a man through," I said. "We'd never get in that way."

"No one gets in without a pass personally signed by Fergus or Padreg," Daryn said. "There's another way in, though. Through the sewers, if we've the stomach for it."

Glyn glanced at him, a hint of a smile curling at the corner of his mouth. "More knowledge gleaned from a misspent youth?" he asked.

Daryn kept a straight face. "As a child, I was agile

and hated to spend the nights merely sleeping," he said gravely. "There were so many places forbidden to explore, and I was consumed by intense curiosity."

"And haven't grown out of yet," Glyn murmured. "Well, we'll use the sewers if we have to."

"If they're in there," I said. "I wonder if I can find them—"

Even as I began Casting, Glyn shouted, "Iain! No!"

The air around me popped and fizzed. The hair on the back of my neck and on my arms and legs rose, and the flesh of my back crept. A crushing weight slammed down on to me. All the breath in my body exploded out through my nose and mouth in an agonized burst. It felt as if my head were caught in a vice. My vision dimmed. I couldn't move. If Glyn hadn't caught me, I would have fallen to the cobbles.

"Iain, can you move?" His voice came from a vast distance, muffled as if he spoke through half a hundred layers of wool batting. I couldn't answer him. I couldn't even shake my head.

"We've got to get out of here." Daryn seized my left arm and thrust his shoulder under my armpit. Glyn got my other arm around his shoulder and they began running down the narrow street. I couldn't move my feet to help. The toes of my boots dragged along the rough cobblestones.

I was suffocating. The muscles of my chest had no strength to draw air into my lungs. Bright sparks danced before my eyes, but I couldn't even cry out. My head pounded with pain and I couldn't think. A curl of panic caught at my throat.

"Don't fight it," Glyn said. "Let yourself go limp. It will get better as soon as we're out of range."

I tried to stop struggling against the stricture of whatever gripped my chest and head. It went against every instinct I had. I forced myself to relax. Almost immediately I breathed more easily. But I still couldn't move; I still couldn't force my muscles to obey me.

Glyn and Daryn stopped running. Daryn began singing a bawdy song. A moment later, Glyn's voice joined his. Their voices were faint, nearly inaudible. Behind the thudding pain in my head, I understood what they were doing. To any bystander, I'd look merely like a man who'd consumed far more ale than was good for him being helped home by two companions who weren't in much better shape.

I have no idea how long the paralysis gripped me. But eventually, I was able to raise my head. My feet, clumsy as blocks of wood, tried to make walking movements against the uneven cobblestones. The pain my head and chest subsided and I drew in a deep, gasping breath.

"What was it?" I could barely form the words with lips and tongue that felt like they were made from stiffened leather, and my voice came out creaking like a rusty hinge.

"Wards against magic," Glyn said. "I thought I felt them when we entered the city, but I wasn't sure. I should have warned you. I thought you could feel them, too. Stupid of me."

"Wards?"

"Set by Padreg and his priests, I've no doubt," Glyn said grimly. "They weren't designed to kill someone who tried to use magic, I don't think. Just incapacitate him until whoever set them could come and collect him." He relaxed his grip on my arm a little. "Can you stand by yourself yet?"

I looked down at my boots. My vision was blurred, and it seemed a long way down to the cobbles. When I tried to take my weight on those distant feet, I thought my knees would bend backward.

Glyn and Daryn ducked into an alley and lowered me to the ground. I sat with my back propped against the side of a building, my legs splayed out before me. Glyn and Daryn crouched down to sit on their heels beside me.

My whole body tingled, like a foot coming back to life after the circulation had been cut off. I tried to move my hands, and nearly cried out with the sharp pain.

But my mind was working again. Without looking up, I said, "If they set wards against magic, they know we're here now."

"Well, they know someone tried to use magic," Glyn said. "But not who. I hope. I don't know if there's a way to actually identify the person who tried to use the magic. I've never heard of wards that can do that."

"But you've never run across real *chausey magic* before, either," Daryn said grimly. "How do you feel now, Iain?"

"Better," I said. I tried to clench my fist. It still hurt, but not as much as before. "I'm sorry. I've managed to alert every one of Padreg's priests who can read the wards, haven't I?"

"It wasn't your fault," Glyn said. "We'll count ourselves lucky they were set to stun, not to kill. No doubt there are some very puzzled priests back there right now wondering what set off the wards."

"Can they follow us?"

"I doubt it," Glyn said. "Or they'd be here by now. But those wards certainly mean it's going to be a lot more difficult getting Holly and Bronwyn out of here. Even if I had strength enough to use magic to cast an illusion to bring them out the way they brought Daryn out, I couldn't use it."

"Do the wards affect Communication?" Daryn asked.

Glyn's harsh grunt of laughter was bitter. "I'm not about to try it," he said. "If they reacted to Casting, I'd suspect they'd react to Communication."

"Pity, that," Daryn said. "We'll just have to find some other way of locating the women." He looked over his shoulder. Behind him, only the top of the Tower was visible above the roofs of the buildings surrounding us.

I remembered my own despair and fear, locked in the small cell in Caliburn, waiting for them to come with the morning to take me to Dundregan. I'd give my life to prevent that horror from overtaking Holly. And Bronwyn. I shuddered.

Presently, the itching and burning in my legs and feet faded to an unpleasant tingle. I could walk with reasonable assurance of keeping my feet under me. My head still pounded and throbbed, and my speech was slurred, but I was pretty sure that would eventually go away. Padreg's wards were a nasty piece of business. Remembering what Glyn had said, I counted myself lucky they had not been set to kill. I wondered if Padreg's balefire—his Wrath of Uthoni—was something he used on any miscreant or saved for other magic-users.

We made our way back to the inn, Daryn and Glyn half-supporting me between them, singing snatches of bawdy songs. My contribution was an occasional hiccup.

Two robed and cowled figures glided past in the nearly deserted street. One of them stopped and stared hard at us, standing with unnatural stillness, hands folded into his sleeves. His face was invisible, shadowed by the deep cowl over his head. I don't know if it was my imagination, or whether I really saw a glint of acid green beneath the enveloping cowl where his eyes should be. I *felt* his steady gaze boring into my back. Cold, it was, and sharp as a sword point.

Glyn stopped, swaying slightly, the tune on his lips dribbling off into silence. I stumbled, swinging Daryn around so that his back was to the priest as we caromed off each other. Glyn stood, listing slightly to starboard, and stared back at the priest. He offered the shadowy figure a wide, foolish smile.

For a moment, the priest didn't move. Then finally, when I thought my heart was about to tear itself right out of my chest, he turned and glided swiftly down the narrow street to catch up to his companion.

Glyn waited until they had turned the corner. "So, they can't tell who used the magic just by looking. Or by probing." He laughed softly. "Did you feel him, Iain?"

"I felt cold for a moment," I said. "While he was staring at us."

"*Chausey magic* version of Communication," Glyn said. "They don't have the same scruples we have about reading another person. They don't require permission. Apparently, it doesn't work as well as Communication does. A bit of luck for us, that."

"Let's get out of here," Daryn said. "I'll feel a lot better once we're back at Gaerd's inn. Those priests make my skin crawl."

We met no more priests on the street as we made our way as quickly as possible back to the inn. True to his word, Gaerd had left the pantry door unlatched for our return. He was waiting in the kitchen when we emerged from the pantry. He went pale as he looked at me.

"Is he all right?" he asked.

Daryn nodded. "He will be," he said. "Did you find out anything for us?"

Gaerd nodded toward the door to the common room. "The old man in the corner by the hearth," he said. "Works in the Tower, hauling out slops. I can't vouchsafe his truthfulness, but he's greedy as a suckling pig. Offer him some money now, more if his information proves right."

"Bring us four ales," Daryn said. "We'll oil his throat a bit and perhaps he'll talk more easily."

Gaerd laughed without humour. "Old Buzzard could drink more ale than the three of you put together—even you, my lord. You go ahead. I'll bring the ale."

There was only one man sitting near the hearth in the common room. Thin strands of sparse, white hair barely covered a blotchy pink scalp that gleamed in the light of the guttering lantern set on the mantle above him. He scarcely glanced up as Daryn and I sat down opposite him and Glyn slid onto the bench next to him. His bony fingers curled tighter around the tankard in front of him and he drew it closer to his chest in a protective gesture.

Daryn took two silver weyrins from his purse and placed them on the scarred table. "Your cup is nearly empty, friend," he said.

The old man stared avidly at the coins for a moment, then looked up at Daryn, his rheumy eyes blinking rapidly. "As empty as my purse."

Daryn placed his index and middle finger on the two coins and moved them in small circles before him. Gaerd came over carrying four tankards, two in each hand. He thumped them down on the table hard enough to slosh the foam onto the planks. Daryn flipped him another silver weyrin from his purse, and Gaerd dropped a small handful of coppers onto the table beside the two weryins.

Glyn reached for the tankards, pushing one toward me and another toward Daryn, drawing the third one in front of himself. Old Buzzard glanced at the last one, his toothless mouth drawn in on itself tensely. Glyn smiled and gestured for him to take the tankard.

Old Buzzard drained the last of his own tankard in one long swallow, then pulled the fourth to him, wiping the foam from his mouth with his hand. He smiled. His thin, caved-in mouth opened to reveal three blackened teeth, two in the bottom and one in the top. "Sheriffmen aren't usually this generous," he said. His *s*'s came out sounding like *sh*'s.

"You work in the Tower of Tears, do you?" Daryn played with the two silver weyrins before him again, moving them back and forth across the pitted wood of the table.

"Aye," the old man said, his attention riveted to the coins under Daryn's fingers. "Have for years." He took a long pull of the ale and glanced up. "What do you want?"

"Information. One of these weyrins now, and one more if your information proves right."

The old man's glance darted to the coins, then to Daryn's face. He smiled craftily. "Old Buzzard has plenty of information," he said. "But information about the Tower will cost you more than two silvers."

"You don't know what I want yet."

Old Buzzard cackled. "If it's about the Tower, it's not official information you're after. Three sheriffmen could get that without asking the likes of me."

Daryn cocked one eyebrow and inclined his head slightly in agreement. "Aye, very likely," he said. "And it could be that others would know more about what I need to know."

Old Buzzard eyed the coins, following the movement of Daryn's fingers carefully. "No one knows more than Old Buzzard about what goes on in that hellhole," he said. "I sees it all, I knows it all. And sometimes, I tells it all. For a good price."

Daryn took two more silver weyrins from his purse and placed them beside the others so that the coins made a neat square on the old planking of the table. "Two women," he said. "One about his age." He nodded in my direction. "The other older, the age his mother might be.

Red hair on the older woman. Black on the young one. Probably brought in half a fortnight ago."

Old Buzzard looked up, tearing his gaze from the coins with an obvious effort. He took another long pull at his ale. His grin gaped wide. "You'd be talking about Maelgrun mac Durstan's own ma, wouldn't ye?"

If Daryn was surprised Old Buzzard knew who Bronwyn was, it didn't show on his face. Or perhaps it did in the complete lack of change of expression.

The old man cackled again. "His own ma. Aye, our Chief of Law is a hard man." He reached out to snatch the coins, his hand quick as a striking snake.

Daryn was faster. His fist closed around the coins, whisking them off the table long seconds before the old man's hand slapped down where the coins had been.

"Not so fast, there," Daryn said easily. "I already knew the women were in the Tower. The silvers are yours if you tell me where in the Tower."

Old Buzzard chuckled, wheezing. He coughed for a moment, a loose, moist, nasty sound. "They're being kept in the royal apartment," he said when he caught his breath. "The same place they kept the prince before he disappeared right under Padreg's nose. With two guards in the cell with 'em and six outside the door so they won't get spirited away like the prince." He laughed again, then wiped his mouth on his filthy sleeve. "They're not taking any chances with them two."

Daryn pushed two of the coins across the table. The old man snatched them up and dropped them into a bag on a thong around his neck. The movement was almost too quick to follow.

"The other two will be with Gaerd tomorrow night if your information is correct," Daryn said. He gestured to Glyn and me. We got to our feet.

"Would you be wanting that?" Old Buzzard waved a

scrawny hand at the nearly full ale tankard Daryn left on the table.

Daryn smiled. "I don't imagine it will go to waste," he said.

The old man pulled it toward him, then reached out for Glyn's tankard. It was still half-full, and I hadn't touched mine. Old Buzzard arranged all four tankards in a semi-circle in front of him, then sat back to work his way methodically through all of them. We left him to his work and climbed the stairs to our tiny room under the eaves.

Daryn suggested we try to get some rest before we made the attempt to enter the prison. I lay down on the bed, grateful for the chance to shake off the effects of the wards. I didn't mean to sleep, but I did.

I dreamed of a red-breasted thrush, caught within the stone walls of a small room. Its wings beat frantically against the iron grilling of a window, but the grill was too fine for even its tiny body to pass through. It seemed I could feel the terrified beating of its heart in my own chest, a breathless pounding that drowned reason in mindless panic. Its fear and despair, dry as ashes, bitter as willow bark, clogged the back of my throat.

The tiny bird battered itself against the grill until all of its strength dissolved in fatigue and hopeless desperation, and it fell to the floor. It lay there, small beak open, frayed wings splayed on the stones of the floor. And when I looked closely at it, it stared back at me with Bronwyn's eyes. Demented eyes, passed beyond reason to madness.

Chapter Twenty

TWO HOURS BEFORE dawn, a thick, chill mist rolled in off the sea to blanket the city. Glyn and I stood shivering in a cluttered alley beneath the dripping stone walls of the prison. I could barely see him in the dark with the fog thick as treacle swirling around us. Debris from the crumbling walls of abandoned buildings choked the narrow passageway. Small rustling sounds rode clearly on the dense air as rats scurried back and forth in the alley, and the cobble stones beneath our feet were foul and slimy with their droppings and other refuse. The stench was enough to make me gag.

I wiped the moisture from my face and tried to peer through the mist for any sign of Daryn returning. It seemed a long time since he had left us here while he scouted for the breach in the wall of the prison where the sewer tunnel from the prison and the palace had fallen in years ago.

My belly churned with nervous strain, and there was no room to pace in the jumbled disorder of the alleyway. My fingers cramped against my palms. I made a conscious effort to relax my hands, but they wanted to ball themselves back into fists seconds later. I wanted Daryn to hurry and get back here, and I wanted to get *on* with it. This skulking in stinking alleys and waiting wasn't doing anything to get Holly and Bronwyn out of that accursed prison.

"Relax, Iain. That's not going to help." Glyn's voice sounded odd, preternaturally loud in the thick stillness of the alley, and muffled at the same time by the fog.

I turned on him. "That's easy for you to say," I snarled. "It's not your aunt and your betrothed in that hellhole."

"No," he said calmly. "It's not. But it's the woman who saved Ydonda's life and my own, and the woman who nursed me at great risk to herself."

The pent-up breath went out of me in an explosive puff, and I closed my eyes briefly. Some of the tension drained from my shoulders.

"I'm sorry," I said. "I apologize. I didn't mean to snap at you like that."

"We're both a bit overwrought right now, I think," he said.

Something clattered behind us, deeper in the alley, and a man's muffled curse carried clearly in the wet air. I whirled around to see Daryn materialize out of the fog.

"Keep your voices down," he whispered. "Come with me. I nearly got lost a few times, but I managed to find the place I was looking for. This thrice-cursed fog makes everything look different from what I remember."

He led us through a confusing warren of narrow streets and decaying buildings. This part of the waterfront had been falling to ruin even before Fergus and Padreg closed the Outport to the Out-ships. The ancient buildings were well beyond repair now, and left to the rats, both four-legged and two-legged, that scavenged the filth to eke out a meagre existence.

The smell told me we had reached the place Daryn had been searching for. The alley had been malodourous, but the stench coming from the hole in the crumbled wall was nearly overpowering. My belly clenched in nausea, and I had to swallow hard several times. Behind me, Glyn gagged audibly.

"Terrible, isn't it?" Daryn whispered, sounding almost cheerful. "It's even worse than I remember. But bad smells don't seem to bother small boys that much."

"Especially small boys out for adventure," Glyn said dryly. "I remember."

Daryn's teeth flashed white in a quick grin. Then he turned and disappeared into the hole. I took a deep breath and followed.

The street was dark, but some light reflected from the lanterns lining the thoroughfare leading up to the palace. The sewer tunnel was completely lightless. Blackness like the heart of a cave closed in around me. I could see nothing.

The stones beneath my feet were slippery and slimy. I didn't even want to think about what might be coating them. We seemed to be on a narrow ledge against the right side of the tunnel. When I reached out to put my hand against the wall to steady myself, I discovered the walls were slimy, too.

Behind me, I heard Glyn scrabble on the rocks, then a muffled splash and his exclamation of disgust.

"Are you all right?" Daryn asked from somewhere just ahead of me.

"I put my foot into that filth," Glyn said. "This boot is ruined."

My eyes were beginning to adjust. A greenish, patchy phosphorescence emanated from the rocks. The weak illumination gave barely enough light to see Daryn as a darker shadow against the dark walls. He was stretched up, fumbling in the rocks above his head.

He gave a small grunt of satisfaction and something scraped against stone as he drew his hands back. Moments later, I heard the scratch of flint on steel, then a flame burst to life. Daryn held a torch. The tiny flame guttered and smoked in the damp, pitch-soaked rags of the head. A rat squeaked in surprise and darted off deeper into the tunnel.

The feeble light gleamed off the thick, oily water flowing sluggishly a few inches below the ledge we stood on. I decided I could be happier about the smell if I wasn't able to see the filth and corruption floating by just inches from my feet.

"You used to crawl through this as a child?" Glyn glanced about in disgust.

"Quite often," Daryn said. "It didn't seem to smell so bad back then."

"Whatever did you do with the clothes you were wearing?" I asked. "Burn them when you got back home?"

Daryn chuckled. "I told them I'd been in the stables. They believed me."

"Even the worst stables I've ever seen smell better than this," Glyn said. "Well, we're here. Let's get on with it."

The torch made all the difference. By its wavering light, we were able to negotiate the tunnel with reasonable speed. Twenty minutes later, we came to another breach in the wall. The gap may have been wide enough to admit the small boy Daryn had once been, but it was a tight squeeze for grown men. I lost some skin off my shoulder and elbow following Daryn into the tiny cell.

The room was carved out of the rock of the promontory itself. It stank of mildew and must, but after the stench in the tunnel, the air in the cell was sweet and fresh by comparison. The walls and floor were damp, but didn't appear to be slimy.

A deep, rhythmic thrumming, almost below the threshold of hearing, throbbed around us, like the beating of a great heart. Fear flickered through me briefly until I realized it was the sound of the sea, alive and restless, pounding against the rocks of the shore not far away.

A heavy wooden door, banded by strips of badly rusted iron, hung drunkenly askew on its hinges on the far wall. In the corridor beyond it, no light showed. We were deep in the bowels of the old prison. Daryn mentioned this section had been out of use for well more than a century.

The corridor twisted and wound its way through the rock, honeycombed with cells. The only signs of life were the squeaks and scufflings of rats. Several times, we had to squeeze past a rockfall that partially blocked the passageway. Water splashed under our feet, lying in wide puddles in the uneven floor. Once, we waded through a place where the water came nearly to our knees. It smelled faintly of the sea.

"There's more water than I remember," Daryn whispered. "One of these days, the sea will come in and the whole prison will collapse."

"That won't be any too soon," Glyn said. "I can feel my bones rusting in this accursed damp."

We rounded a corner to find ourselves at the foot of a narrow, crumbling flight of steps carved in the rock.

"The main part of the prison is just up there," Daryn

said. "There's a door at the top of the steps that leads into the lower corridor of the deepest level still in use. I don't know if there are any prisoners in the cells. There weren't the last time I was in here, but that was quite a while ago. There might be lights up there. If there aren't, we should be able to find a lantern and use that. It would look a little less suspicious than this torch. Be careful of the steps. Some of them are broken. We don't want to kill ourselves here. That would be just too clumsy."

The rotten stone crumbled beneath my feet as I followed Daryn up the narrow stairs. The steps were deep enough only for the toes of my boots and I had to put my hand to the damp wall to keep my balance. Behind me, Glyn slipped, then swore. The echoes of the curse hissed through the twisting corridor around us.

At the top of the stairs, Daryn thrust the torch into the gravelly debris, dousing it. In the sudden dark, something scrabbled across my foot. My heart tried to choke me by leaping right out of my chest until I realized it was only a rat. Small stones pattered as the filthy rodent fled down the steps.

The screech of rusty metal sounded shriekingly loud. A crack of dim, flickering light outlined Daryn's figure as he pushed open the door. The crack widened to reveal another corridor, this time built of square building stones, not carved from the cliff. The light came from a single torch, guttering in a bracket on the wall of the corridor fifty feet from where we stood. Daryn slipped into the passage, then beckoned Glyn and me to follow.

Doors lined the corridor, each massive facade broken by a small, barred window. They were not more than six feet apart. I shuddered to think of the tiny, cramped cells. There was no sound but the muffled tread of our own boots on the wet stone floor. I hoped the cells were unoccupied.

We passed the torch in its rusty wall bracket, our

shadows skittering ahead of us. In the corridor beyond, something large moved, scrabbling like a huge rat in dry straw.

A face appeared at the tiny grill in a door to my left. Empty violet eyes stared uncomprehendingly out at us. I got the impression of white hair and a white beard flaring around a face pale enough to remind me of the faintly phosphorescent belly of a planefish.

A vision of Thon shanMetla flashed into my mind. But Thon shanMetla, although old, still had strength and character in his face. The face in the cell window was blank, the fire of intellect extinguished behind it.

"Feyi..." Glyn whispered, startled. He took a step toward the cell. An animal moan of fear came from the cell, and the face disappeared.

Daryn caught Glyn's arm. "No, Glyn," he said softly. "Leave him be."

"Feyish healers could make him well again," Glyn said. He sounded as sick as I felt.

"We can't help him right now," Daryn said grimly. "Not yet. My brother and Padreg have a lot to answer for, but at this moment, we have to find Lady Bronwyn and Mistress Holly."

Daryn led us through the labyrinthine corridors, through doors and up flights of stairs. Eventually, I became aware that the deep, dank chill had left the air, and I could no longer hear the heartbeat of the sea. I wondered if it meant we had climbed out of the bowels of the rock beneath the public square in front of the prison and the palace. I fancied I could feel all that weight lifting from my shoulders.

We marched along the corridor, Daryn leading, Glyn and I flanking him half a pace behind, as if we had a perfect right to be there. Daryn had the bearing of an officer, arrogant and sure of himself, to go with his stolen sheriffman's uniform. Glyn's footsteps exactly matched Daryn's in rhythm. Mine were a little less authoritative.

We came to a guard station and walked past without a word. The two guards hardly looked up as we went by. I dared not glance behind us as Daryn and Glyn wheeled in flawless unison and marched down another corridor.

The cells here were larger than in the levels below, and the prisoners in them more noisy. Some of the prisoners were women. They called out graphic insults as we passed the cells. Daryn and Glyn ignored them, but I found my face burning under the steel helm I wore.

Eventually, we came to a heavy, iron-studded door guarded by two men bearing swords and crossbows. They frowned at Daryn, obviously not recognizing him, but stepped aside at his imperious gesture. I sprang forward to open the door for Daryn, who swept past me without a sideways glance, trailing Glyn in his wake. The guards grinned in sympathy as I made a long-suffering grimace and trotted after Daryn and Glyn.

The stairway curved to follow the wall of the tower. At each landing, we met two stout doors. One opened to allow us access to a set of stairs leading to the next level of the tower; the other obviously opened into a cell. No sound came from behind the closed doors. I wondered if they were occupied, and if so, by whom.

We were well above the street now. I was breathing heavily by the time we reached the top of the last flight of steps. Two guards who had been lounging against the wall came to attention as we stepped out onto the landing. The door they guarded stood open.

"Nobody's allowed up here in the tower," said one of the guards, staring at the wall behind Daryn's left shoulder. "Sir," he added belatedly.

"Stand aside, man," Daryn said. "I come direct from King Fergus. I've orders from him to question these two prisoners."

The guards exchanged glances. One of them sniggered. "You wouldn't be meaning the two women, would you?" he said.

"It's none of your business who the King wishes questioned," Daryn said coldly.

The guard giggled nervously again. "Them two ain't here no more, sir," he said. "The Lord Padreg had 'em taken out yester evening. Mayhap he didn't bother informing the King of his plans?"

My breath caught in my throat. I pushed past the guards and stared around the cell. It was empty. No sign of either Holly or Bronwyn remained. It was swept clean. Hiding my fear, I fell back into place beside Glyn.

"It's true, sir," I said. "They're gone."

"You'll have to ask the Lord Padreg where they are," the first guard said, smirking. "I wouldn't doubt he had personal plans for them. The young woman was a tasty morsel, and it's said he's an eye for the ladies."

Daryn looked straight at the guard, one eyebrow raised in elegant disapproval. "Your insolence will land you in deep trouble without a doubt, if you aren't very careful," he said, his voice like silk over burnished steel. "Padreg had them taken out, you say? Where to?"

The guard straightened and stared over Daryn's shoulder again. "You'd have to ask him, sir," he said. "The Lord Padreg's not in the habit of informing us of his plans, either, you might say."

"It's said they was taken to the palace, sir," the other guard said. He shot a nervous glance at his companion. "At least, that's the rumour."

"Thank you," Daryn said. "I shall inform the King." He

turned on his heel and clattered off down the stairs. Glyn and I did a creditable about-face and followed.

We left the way we had come. Dawn made a pearly glow in the fog to the east, and the white stone walls of the palace gleamed softly in the growing light. We stood in the square, looking at the high walls. Daryn's face became thoughtful, his expression abstracted, as he watched the guards pacing the tops of the wall.

"I had hoped we wouldn't have to go in there," he said softly. He rubbed the new beard on his cheeks. "I know I've changed, but there might still be people in there who saw me growing up." He dropped his hand and shrugged. "We'll just have to hope I've changed enough."

Glyn abandoned his study of the walls and the gate, and looked at Daryn. "I suppose you know how to get in there without being seen, too," he said.

Daryn laughed. "I should hope so."

"A way that doesn't involve sewers?" I asked.

Daryn grinned at me. "There's a postern gate giving onto a cove behind the palace. If we're lucky, it's been completely forgotten by now. As far as I know, nobody had used it for years when I first found it. The gateway leads to a staircase that opens up into what used to be my grandfather's youngest brother's quarters. Apparently, with all his intrigues and womanizing, Great-Uncle Malcolm had need of secret ways of coming and going. The wing stood empty for twenty years after he died."

"We might as well try it now," Glyn said. "Waiting will do us no good. Nor will it help Holly and Bronwyn."

Daryn led us to a small cove behind the palace. The fog was thicker down on the shore and the cliff stood above us like a dark shadow. As I looked up at it towering above me, the image from my dream brushed against my mind again—a broken bird, mad with terror. And Bronwyn's eyes staring mindlessly out at me.

"They're in there," I said with conviction. "I can feel it. And they're hurt. Or Bronwyn is."

Glyn regarded me thoughtfully. "You're sure?"

"Aye. As sure as I'm standing here."

Daryn accepted my certainty with a nod. "The gate is up there," he said, pointing to the cliff face.

I looked up. I could see nothing that looked like a gate in the cliff wall, nor could I see any way of getting up there.

"This way," Daryn said. "There's a path of sorts."

The path was little more than a narrow ledge climbing steeply up the side of the cliff. We had to stand sideways in places, our backs to the rocks, to negotiate it. I was thankful for the fog. It made the sheer drop to the rocks and sand below look a little less dangerous, a little less immediate.

The gate itself was a small door, barely high enough for a man to enter without stooping. Daryn pushed on it. It refused to open. Glyn and I put our shoulders to it and shoved along with Daryn. The hinges screeched, and the door opened part way, then froze.

We squeezed through the narrow gap and found ourselves at the foot of a flight of steps carved into the rock. At the top of the steps stood another door, barely discernable in the wan light spilling through the opening behind us.

The steps were dusty and crumbling, but firm enough underfoot. At the top, Daryn put his ear to the door and listened carefully for a few moments. He pushed on the door, and it opened easily.

A pair of Kings Guardsmen stepped out of a small guard room just beyond the door.

"Oy, you three," one of them said. "Where do you think you're going?"

Chapter Twenty-One

IT WAS ALREADY far too late to turn back. I nearly stumbled, and my heart leapt mightily in my chest, as if it were a caged raptor trying to vault right through my ribs in a bid for freedom. But almost immediately, it settled into a rapid, pounding rhythm I thought the Guardsmen must surely hear. At the same time, my hand went of its own accord to the haft of my dagger. With an ice-cold clarity that surprised me, I noted there were only two of them, and three of us. Glyn's knuckles were white upon the hilt of his sword, but his face was as expressionless as I knew my own to be.

Daryn didn't hesitate, didn't miss a step. He ignored the Guardsmen and continued walking, intending to brush right past them. One of them stepped into the corridor, directly in his path. Daryn halted before he collided with him, one eyebrow raised in mild surprise and not-so-mild annoyance.

"Out of my way," he said abruptly, his tone that of a man who expects to be instantly obeyed. "I'm on special orders from the King."

The expression on the Guardsman's face landed half way between amazement and bewilderment. "The *King*?" he repeated. "Here?"

Daryn frowned at the Guardsman, the eyebrow still lifted in cool irritation. "Of course the King," he said. "Who else in the royal palace?"

The Guardsman refused to give ground. He bore up shakily under the fierce, Gael-blue gazes of both Daryn and Glyn. "We've orders from my lord Padreg that no one comes this way without express orders from him," he said. "I've received no such orders about you." He may have been wary of the officer's insignia on the shoulder of Daryn's uniform shoulder, but he was obviously terrified of how Padreg would regard violation of those *express orders*.

"My lord Padreg, is it now?" Daryn said softly, his tone quietly silky and infinitely dangerous. "Is the priest then countermanding the King's orders these days?"

The Guardsman went red, then white. But he didn't move. Some imperceptible signal must have passed between Daryn and Glyn. I almost didn't see Glyn's nod. He tensed and moved half a step to his left, away from me, giving his sword arm more space to maneuver within. The corners of Daryn's mouth flickered in a grim half-smile and his hand drifted toward the hilt of his sword.

But before he could draw his sword, the sound of a door opening echoed in the stairwell, and three more Guardsmen appeared around the corner from the upper chambers. An officer and two troopers, marching briskly.

The officer saw us and hesitated. I moved my hand toward the hilt of my dagger. We were well and truly outnumbered now, but if we were to die, I was going to die doing my own fighting and not let Glyn and Daryn fight for me.

The officer looked straight into my face and his eyes widened. He frowned. His glance flew to Daryn, then quickly to Glyn, and he paled slightly.

I knew him then. Alex mac Kyle. Holly's cousin. The man who had spirited Ydonda out of Celyddon and back to Lysandia. My heart thundering in my ears, I stayed my hand, but let it hover near my dagger. Just in case.

Alex's mind moved far more quickly than my own. Without pause, he stepped up to Daryn and saluted him. "You're expected, sir," he said. "I'm sorry I'm late in coming to escort you."

"We arrived earlier than originally planned, Unit Leader," Daryn said easily, with not a trace of noticeable hesitation or surprise. "Certainly you have nothing to apologize for."

Alex saluted again. "Let me conclude the change of the guard here, sir," he said. "Then I'll escort you to the palace."

"Directly to the King?" Glyn asked.

Alex had recognized him, too. He nodded. "Of course," he said. He didn't make the mistake of calling him *sir*. "I'll be but a moment with this."

Both Daryn and Glyn gave the outward appearance of relaxing. But I noticed neither of them let their sword hands stray far from their sword hilts, nor did the catlike balance of their bodies change much.

Moments later, the two Guardsmen who had accompanied Alex were established in the guard room, and the two who had accosted us sent on their way through a corridor leading off at a right angle from the foot of the stairs, presumably toward a barracks.

Alex rolled his shoulders and took a deep breath as he turned back to Daryn. "This way, please, sir," he said and led the way up the narrow staircase.

The stairway doubled back on itself twice. On the second landing, well out of earshot of the guards left in the guard room, Daryn reached out and put his hand on Alex's arm. Alex stopped, turned to peer at Daryn in the dim light of a torch thrust into a sconce on the wall.

"I see you recognized Glyn and Iain," Daryn said quietly. "Do you recognize me, then, Unit Leader?"

Alex studied his face carefully. He had regained most of his colour. But I could tell the instant he realized who Daryn was. He held his face expressionless, but paled again as he nodded. "You honour me, my lord," he said a little hoarsely. "Had you not said anything, I wouldn't have known you at all."

Daryn smiled grimly. "I believe I can trust you with the secret of my identity."

Alex stood a little taller. "We heard rumours you had returned, my lord."

"We?"

"Yes, my lord. The Cymry."

"Ah." As if that answered everything. It probably did. "But you must not call me *my lord* again."

"Of course. But why—?"

"Are we here?" I finished for him. "They've taken Holly, Alex. They've taken her and my aunt, the lady Bronwyn. Maelgrun and Padreg are holding them somewhere in the palace here."

His lips thinned as his mouth formed a grim, level line. "Holly? Here?"

"Aye. Here."

His pale face hardened into lines of outrage and anger. "Then we shall have to find her. Both her and the Lady Bronwyn, and we shall have to get them out of here. Please. If you would be so kind as to follow me."

The passageway decanted us into something that might have been a butler's pantry, or a service alcove. It was only a little wider than the span of both my arms, and about twice as long. The ceiling seemed incongruously high. A marble counter ran along one lengthwise wall, stacked with jars and bottles and silver trays filled with clear crystal goblets. The only light in the room came from a small oil lamp guttering softly on the counter. Two more doors opened off the other two walls. One of the doors, barely wide enough to admit a man, stood partly open. It led to an equally narrow set of stairs leading upward.

"To Uncle Malcolm's bedchamber, I believe," Daryn said wryly. "He needed ways of discreetly moving his nocturnal companions in and out of the palace. Padreg has probably taken over the secret passages as well as Malcolm's quarters, but it's unlikely he uses them for the same purpose. I would guess his bedchamber would not be a likely place to start looking."

Glyn raised one eyebrow in mild amusement. "With priests, one hardly knows sometimes," he said. "Where does the other door lead?" He stepped forward and pushed it open a crack. I caught a brief glimpse of a polished tile floor, and walls hung with thick, richly embroidered tapestries. A main corridor, from the look of it. Two men dressed in the robes of priests of Uthoni walked past, deep in conversation. Glyn closed the door quietly.

I turned to Alex. "Where might they keep two prisoners in the palace?"

He made a helpless gesture, raising one shoulder into it. "Two women? I don't know. If they were men, they'd probably be in the old cells below the kitchens. But two women, and one of them Maelgrun mac Durstan's own mother? I wouldn't know where to start looking for them."

I closed my eyes. Being very careful not to Cast, I merely opened myself to the sensations swirling in the air around me and let my mind float. Slowly, almost painfully, the image built again within my head—the small broken bird beating its wings futilely against the unyielding bars of a cage, its songs stilled, its heart beating frantically as its mind lost itself in the sheer terror of captivity and pain. The picture twisted in my gut like a knife, and my hands curled into fists of their own accord. Making an effort, I hastily thrust aside my own anger and outrage, as well as the disturbing and frenzied image of the little bird, and concentrated only on where the image might be coming from. I turned slowly, trying to sort out from which direction the sensations were the strongest. When I was sure, I opened my eyes. Glyn, Daryn and Alex stood watching me, none of them speaking.

"Up, I think," I said. "Not below. Somewhere up there."

The blue of Glyn's eyes flashed in the dim light. "You're not Casting," he said more in curiosity than alarm.

"No. I've always thought that Bronwyn has some of the Gift. I think she's sending without really knowing she's sending. But it's not strong enough to set off the wards Padreg placed against magic—the ones I walked straight into last time. I think I can pick it up when you can't because I know her so well. I know what patterns to listen for."

Glyn nodded. "That makes sense. Can you lead us to her?"

"I hope so."

"Right, then," Daryn said briskly. "Let's go and find her. And Mistress Holly, too. You had best go first, Alex."

We stepped out of the pantry into the brilliantly lit hall and fell into a precise formation. Alex moved to Daryn's left; Glyn and I shoulder to shoulder behind them. Two by two, in flawless step, we marched out into the corridor as if we had a perfect right to be there.

And it seemed to work. Nothing attracts attention more swiftly than men who move furtively. The natural inclination is to wonder what they're up to, what they have to hide, or hide from. Four men dressed in uniforms marching briskly down a corridor where men in uniform were as common as daisies on the verge of a road became nearly invisible.

The wide corridor teemed with people—members of the Royal Council, priests of Uthoni, Kings Guardsmen wearing the flash of the Holy Seal of Uthoni on their shoulders beneath the King's insignia, courtiers, and servants, all of them intent on their own errands. Very few of them spared us even a fleeting glance. Of all of them, the Guardsmen paid us the most attention. But even then, none of them seemed to look past the officer's pips on Alex's uniform, which they saluted automatically, then passed swiftly on their way.

The corridor ended at the foot of a staircase rising in a sweeping curve to the floor above. Alex glanced at me. I nodded slightly. The sense of Bronwyn's presence became perceptibly stronger as we ascended the stairs.

We were deeper into Padreg's territory now. We saw no more courtiers, no more members of the Royal Council. Several servants scurried past us, eyes downcast as they hastened along with their duties. They paid us no attention at all. Twice, we passed a pair of patrolling King's Guardsmen. They stared at us, but deferred to the officer's insignia on Alex's uniform.

A man in priests' robes stepped out of a room ahead

of us as we rounded a corner. He paused, staring at us in surprise. I caught a glimpse of acid green gleam in the man's eye as we marched past him. His voice came after us, cracking like a whip.

"One moment there, Unit Leader."

Glyn and I stood our ground as both Alex and Daryn turned to face the priest.

"Do you need something, Brother?" Alex asked mildly.

The priest stepped forward, his dark grey robes swirling about his feet. "Indeed, Unit Leader," he said. "I need to know what you and three Sheriffmen are doing here. Under whose authority do you come?"

Alex raised an eyebrow. "We have a message to deliver to His Eminence, the lord High Priest."

The priest was not listening. He stared intently at Daryn, a frown drawing the heavy eyebrows together above his nose. He drew in a quick, sharp breath. Glyn moved like a striking snake. His dagger was out of its sheath and deep into the priest's belly before I even realized the priest had been about to cry out.

Glyn managed to hold the priest on his feet. "Check out that room," he whispered.

Alex jumped forward and opened the door the priest had just come through. "Clear," he said, and together, they tumbled the body into the room. Daryn and I followed and closed the door firmly.

"He recognized you, Daryn," Glyn said. "I couldn't let him raise the alarm."

"I know," Daryn said. "I recognized him, too, unfortunately. We'd better hide him. Bodies are such messy things. If we leave him out where he can be seen, someone will surely be along here and raise the alarm immediately, and that will certainly do us no good at all."

The room was hardly bigger than a closet, and was

furnished as a study. A small worktable sat near the
deeply recessed window to take advantage of the natural
daylight streaming into the room. The only other
furnishings were a chair with a thinly padded seat and
a tall wooden cabinet. Beneath the mullioned glass of
the window, a plain, utilitarian window seat added more
storage space.

I raised the seat and glanced down. The storage space
was half-filled with sheaves of paper, but there was
more than enough room to hold the body. Glyn pulled
his dagger from the body, then he and Daryn picked the
priest up and heaved him unceremoniously into the
opening and I let the lid down quietly.

"Very neatly done," Alex said a bit breathlessly.
"There's not a trace of blood on the floor in here, or in
the corridor."

The corridor was empty as we slipped out of the study.
Another passageway branched off only a few paces
beyond where we stood. I hesitated for a moment. The
sense of Bronwyn's presence was much stronger down
the second hallway.

I stopped in front of a pair of ornately carved wooden
doors. "This is it. They're in there."

"You're sure?" Daryn asked. "The doors are unguarded."

"Nevertheless," I said. "I'm positive. They're in there.
Both of them."

Daryn made a wry face. "Padreg has a twisted sense
of humour," he said. "Uncle Malcolm used to house his
various and assorted mistresses in these rooms."

Glyn reached out to the door latch. "Locked," he said.
He glanced at Alex. "You wouldn't happen to have a key,
would you?"

Alex shook his head. "I'm afraid not."

Daryn stepped forward, his slender dagger in his hand.
"In my misspent youth," he said softly, "I made the

acquaintance of quite a variety of knaves and charlatans and other nefarious characters. They taught me all sorts of interesting and useful skills." He slipped the blade of the dagger into the narrow crack between the double doors. "Most of them were employed by my father in one capacity or another." He moved the dagger up, then twisted it slightly. "Not as thieves, you understand, but as—" Something inside the door made a soft click. "Ah, there we are," Daryn said and raised the latch. "That's done it." The doors swung open smoothly. We stepped into the room, and Daryn closed the doors swiftly behind us.

Holly sat in a chair beside the window, her back to the door, bent over Bronwyn who lay on the bed. Bronwyn's bright copper and silver hair splayed in a soft tumble about her head on a soiled pillow. Her eyes were closed and she had curled herself small, like a sleeping cat, on the crumpled bedspread. The wall hangings behind them had seen better days, but had once been opulently embroidered. Now, they would keep some of the drafts out of the room, but were too threadbare to be much good in the dead of winter.

As Daryn opened the door, Holly lurched to her feet and leapt to place herself between Bronwyn and us. She wore a plain gown made of undyed wool, crumpled and soiled, as if she'd worn it day and night since Maelgrun's men took her. Her face was pale as chalk, making her eyes look like bruises in her gaunted face. Rage drew her lips back over her teeth, and I had no doubts that she was ready to fight like a badgercat to protect Bronwyn.

"It's all right, Holly dear," Alex said gently. "We've come to take you both out of here."

She stared at him in disbelief, still holding herself stiffly ready.

Then I stepped forward, whispered: "Holly—"

Her whole body sagged in relief. For a moment, I

thought she might fall to the floor. But I had hardly taken one step toward her when she flew into my arms, making soft little noises that weren't sobs, but weren't coherent words, either.

"We've come to take you home," I said, my lips against her hair.

She pulled away from me and looked over her shoulder at Bronwyn, who had not moved. "She can't walk," she said. "Her feet...."

Glyn crossed the room quickly and lifted the hem of Bronwyn's gown. He made a soft, sick sound of horror and outrage, and turned away, his face white as milk. I was at the bedside in two quick steps. But when I looked down at Bronwyn's feet, my belly clenched with nausea and I had to swallow the bitter bile that threatened to choke me.

Bronwyn's feet were little more than grotesque, crushed masses of bloody flesh, the white of the fragile bones showing through.

"What happened to her?" I whispered in horrified awe.

Holly came across the room to bend over the bed. Bronwyn lifted a hand and made vague little gestures as if she would cover her feet again with the hem of her gown.

"Oh, Bronwyn, your hands," I said and reached for them. She glanced incuriously at me, and pulled away from me, dropping the hands with their broken, twisted fingers into her lap. I straightened and tried to control the blinding flood of fury that surged through me, abrasive as emery, hot as molten gold. "What happened?" I demanded again.

"Maelgrun took her away," Holly said. "When they brought her back, she was like this." She bent over the woman on the bed and murmured something soothing. She tucked Bronwyn's gown over her feet, and drew a tattered shawl tenderly across her hands. Bronwyn ducked her head back down onto the soiled pillow and tightly closed her eyes.

"Maelgrun did this?" Daryn asked in horror. "To his own *mother?*"

Holly straightened and turned to him. "The thing that Maelgrun has become did this," she said. "He murdered his father—"

"Durstan lived," I said quickly. "He found us and told us Maelgrun had taken you. That's why we're here."

Holly closed her eyes briefly, and I felt her thankful relief. She drew in a long breath, let it out slowly. "He took us out of the tower and brought us here. The next day, he took Bronwyn away, and when he had her brought back here, she was as you see her. She hasn't spoken since."

"Dear Mother of All," Glyn murmured. "But why?"

"For her blood and pain," Holly said, her voice breaking. "He said it would make him strong." She placed a hand on her belly. "He said he was saving me until he knew whether or not I was carrying Iain's child. He said—" Her voice caught in her throat. She steadied herself, then reached for my arm to help support herself. "He said that kin blood makes the strongest magic, and innocent kin blood—that of a child born or unborn—makes the strongest magic of all."

"*Chausey* sorcery," Daryn said softly. "So he has it, too."

Glyn sat down on the bed beside Bronwyn and placed a gentle hand on her forehead. She turned her head away from him, but otherwise made no movement. "Feyish Healers could Heal her hands and feet," he said. "I think they could Heal her mind, too. We'll have to get her out of here and to Lysandia."

"But how?" Holly asked. "She can't walk."

"No," Daryn agreed. "And because of Padreg's wards, we

can cast no Feyii illusion as they did the day they saved me from the tower."

Something struck me then. Something that should have been obvious a long time ago. "I wonder."

Glyn turned to me. "You wonder what?"

I studied him in the light streaming through the window. His eyes were a deep, intense blue—the blue eyes of a true Gael. But his eyes should have been gold-flecked violet. He had cast an illusion over them when we had left the Landholding, the illusion of Gaelish blue eyes as a disguise to hide his Feyish blood.

"Your eyes, Glyn," I said. "They're blue. Not violet. Blue. How can you be holding the illusion over them in the midst of Padreg's wards against magic?"

Chapter Twenty-Two

GLYN STARED AT me blankly for a moment, then put both hands to his temples beside his eyes. "Blue?" he repeated.

Both Daryn and I nodded.

"Ever since we arrived in Dundregan," Daryn said. "I remember now. It took me a long while to sort out what was so different about you. Of course it was the colour of your eyes."

"How very odd," Glyn said slowly. "I've been holding the illusion for so long, I stopped thinking about it and it became just automatic." He frowned for a moment, then quite suddenly his face cleared. "Of course. Yes, of course. That must be it."

"What must be it?" Alex asked, completely puzzled. "Wards against magic?"

"Padreg set wards all across the city against magic," Daryn said. "When Iain tried to Cast to locate Bronwyn and Holly, the wards nearly killed him. Yet Glyn's illusion of blue eyes to mask his Feyish violet eyes hasn't set off the wards."

"Because the illusion is all directed inward," Glyn said. "That has to be it. All the magic is directed inward, at my eyes. Not enough of it escapes to set off the wards. And it's not a very strong or potent magic to begin with."

"Can you do it so that it wraps all of us?" I asked.

He bit his lip. "Theoretically, I should be able to," he said. "It's the same magic, just spread over a larger space."

Daryn shook his head. "Not all of us, Glyn," he said quietly. "That would have to be a lot stronger magic. We can't take a chance of setting off the wards and alerting Padreg's people."

"Then just you and Bronwyn?" Holly asked. She glanced over to Bronwyn, who still lay curled like a kitten on the bed. "We have to get her out of here."

Glyn rubbed his hands together, then scrubbed them across his cheeks. "I'll have to try," he said. "If I set off the wards, the rest of you run. Take Bronwyn with you and run. You know the palace, Daryn. You should be able to find a corner to hide in until they get tired of looking for you."

"Leave you?" Daryn repeated. "Don't be ridiculous. But go ahead. See what happens. Might as well do it now as later." A brief smile flitted across his mouth. "When they took me out of the tower, all the guards saw was flickering shadows."

Glyn made a wry face at the sun pouring through the windows. "Shadows might be hard to accomplish in the blaze of noon," he said. "But let's see what I can come up with."

"If this doesn't work," Daryn said, "Alex, you take Mistress Holly with you. You know the palace as well as anyone. Take Holly to safety the best way you know how. Iain, you take the lady Bronwyn. I'll bring Glyn. Are we set?"

I nodded. So did Alex.

Glyn smiled grimly. He walked over to the bed and looked down at Bronwyn. The colour of his eyes flickered and the blue faded to violet as he let go of the illusion. He flexed his fingers, then bent down to pick up Bronwyn. He wrapped her in the bedspread and drew her up into his arms. She looked wonderingly into his face for a moment, but said nothing. Then a small, secret smile touched her mouth lightly and she settled against him, letting her head rest on his shoulder. He made sure of his grip on her, then took a deep breath.

Glyn and Bronwyn disappeared. In their place stood a heavy-set man dressed in the voluminous cloak and cowl of a priest of the Brotherhood of Uthoni.

For an endless moment, we all stood frozen. But nothing happened. Not so much as a glimmer or a quiver in the air. The wards were quiescent. I let out the breath I'd been holding. As the air rushed out of my body in relief, it felt as if all the strength went with it. I caught myself before I stumbled. I met Daryn's eyes and he gave me a weak, lopsided grin, indicating I wasn't the only one half-felled by relief.

"Well, that worked," Daryn said breathlessly. "I think."

Glyn's voice coming from deep within the cowl of the priest of Uthoni caused a shiver to crawl down my spine. "I couldn't feel anything to indicate a ward sounding the alarm."

"I'd suggest we all get out of here as quickly as we can,"

Alex said. He, too, sounded shaken, and I don't know whether he knew what the wards against magic could do. I'll admit, however, seeing a priest of the Brotherhood standing where we knew Glyn carrying Bronwyn should be was more than a little disconcerting.

The sound of a key turning in the lock on the door turned us all back into frozen statues. Daryn swore softly under his breath, his hand moving swiftly toward the sword on his left hip.

"No," Glyn said quietly, urgently. He turned to the bed. Bronwyn seemed to appear out of thin air as he laid her back down on the crumpled sheet. He straightened up, still in the guise of the priest. "Behind the wall hangings, all of you. Holly, sit in the chair. Quietly. Hurry."

I was less than half a step behind Daryn and Alex. There was a space less than the length of my forearm between the wall hanging and the stone wall behind it. The three of us pressed our backs up against the wall, breathing as shallowly as we could, just as the doors of the chamber swung open.

There was a small rent in the fabric of the tapestry in front of my face. I had only to move my head slightly to see out through it. Glyn's cloaked and cowled figure from the throat down, a corner of the bed and Holly's knee filled the small field of vision.

Two men in the uniform of King's Guards came into the room, their boot heels rapping sharply on the tiled floor. Glyn turned calmly, unhurriedly to face them.

"You interrupt me," he said in the coldly arrogant voice of a man accustomed to deference and instant obedience.

The two Guardsmen stopped suddenly. I saw only their booted legs from the knees down. But they had come to a halt well out of reach of either Glyn or Holly.

"Your pardon, Brother," one of them said. "We were

sent to check on the prisoners. There are intruders in the palace."

"Intruders? Surely that has nothing to do with my purpose here."

"A man has been killed, Brother," the other guard said. "One of the lay brothers assigned to the Scribery. The Captain of the Guard thought the intruders might be trying to rescue the prisoners."

Glyn made a sweeping gesture. "There is, as you can see, no one here but me. And I have been sent by the lord Maelgrun to make sure the women prisoners are fit for his—" He paused delicately. "—further attentions."

"Of course, Brother," the first soldier said. "But be on your guard as you leave. We believe there are four intruders. Be wary of any four men walking together."

Glyn inclined his head. "Of course," he said. "Thank you for warning me. You may leave now."

The two pairs of booted feet performed a smart about face, and marched out of my field of vision. The doors opened, then closed again with a firm thump.

"They're gone," Glyn said a moment later in his normal voice.

"That's torn it," Daryn said as he stepped out from behind the wall hanging. "If we go out of here together, they'll stop us and question us. Even with you wearing the guise of a priest. Now what do we do?"

Alex glanced at Daryn. "You and I are approximately the same build, my lord Prince," he said. "Change clothes with me. No one will stop a Unit Leader of the King's Guards who is escorting a prisoner to the lord Maelgrun. Glyn can take the lady Bronwyn out, disguised as he is as a priest of the Brotherhood. You take Holly out. You know the palace as well as I—or better. Iain and I will make our own way out. We'll be much less conspicuous as two Sheriffmen."

"Are you sure?" Glyn asked.

Alex made a wry face. "Believe me, my lord, Fergus and Padreg don't encourage men chosen to be palace guards to think for themselves. All they want from the Guardsmen is instant and unthinking obedience. No one will question my lord Daryn in this uniform. Not unless it's Fergus himself. Or Padreg. But I think it highly unlikely he'd run across either of them." He smiled faintly. "And no one will question a priest of the Brotherhood, either. Iain and I will meet you later."

"Change clothing with him, Daryn," Glyn said. "He's right." He turned to me. "Can you find your way back to Gaerd's tavern?"

"Yes," I said.

"Right, then. We'll meet back there."

It took only a few moments for Daryn and Alex to exchange uniforms. Glyn picked up Bronwyn again and settled her comfortably against his chest. She vanished into the faint shimmer that surrounded him, the only trace of the illusional magic he worked. Alex opened the doors, looked out to check the corridor, then nodded to Glyn. Glyn took a deep breath, then strode purposefully out into the passageway.

Daryn gave him five minutes, then nodded to Holly. She got to her feet, but came swiftly to my arms. I kissed her, stroked her hair back, and tried to smile down at her.

"Alex and I will be along shortly," I said. "We'll meet you at the tavern as soon as we can."

"Be careful," she murmured. She kissed me quickly again, then went to Daryn. "I'm ready."

He gripped her firmly just above the elbow, gave her a swift ghost of a wink. She smiled briefly, and they moved out into the passageway. Holly hung back, pulling against his grip, giving a more than creditable performance as a reluctant prisoner.

Alex sat down on the bed and wiped his sleeve across his forehead. "I don't mind telling you I'm a little nervous about this." He flashed me a grin. "But not as nervous as I was about traipsing the length of the land between Caliburn and Dundregan with an injured Feyish woman tucked into my baggage."

"That worked out well enough," I said.

"Aye, it did." He got to his feet. "Our turn, I think. Are you ready?"

I straightened my shoulders. "About as ready as I'll ever be. Let's go."

Alex led the way to the double doors. With his hand on the latch, he straightened his shoulders, stiffened his spine into the upright, erect carriage of an officer.

"Talley-ho," he whispered, then pulled open the doors.

Alex paused in the middle of what seemed like an endless series of corridors and swore softly.

"What is it?" I asked.

"I took a wrong turn somewhere," he said. "We're not where I thought we should be."

My heart made an odd little thud against my ribs. "Are we lost?" I asked.

He shook his head. "Not badly, I think," he said. He looked up the passageway, then back the way we had come. "There should be a set of stairs back there which will take us back down to the main floor."

We had been zigzagging our way through the palace since we left the room where Bronwyn and Holly had been kept prisoner. We had climbed and descended several sets of stairs. Alex said he was taking us out by a circuitous route to keep us out of the way of as many Guardsmen as possible. So far, it seemed to be working. We had passed no one but a few harried-looking servants scurrying along the corridors, intent on their duties. But in the process, I had completely lost myself. I had no idea where we were, and no clue how to find my way out and back into the streets.

Alex turned and led us back down the corridor. It was a narrow passageway but lushly carpeted. Doors led off it at regular intervals, and portraits in gilded frames of richly dressed men and women wearing expressions that ranged from severe to arrogant hung on the walls between the doors. Alex paused before one door and put up a hand to rub his chin.

"This one, I think," he said more to himself than me. He reached out and raised the latch.

A strange, tingling sensation washed over me. I caught Alex's arm. "No," I said. "Not there. That one." I pointed at a small, inconspicuous door half-way down the corridor. Something pulled me toward it. We *had* to go through that door. I couldn't have explained why to Alex if my life depended on it. I was at a loss to explain it to myself. I just knew it was imperative that we go there.

But we didn't step into a stairway. The door led into a small balcony that was probably a minstrel's gallery. Below lay a large room that should have been bright and airy with its bank of tall windows letting in the afternoon light. Deep shadows filled it now, the shutters on the windows tightly closed while the private audience chamber was not in use. At the opposite end from the gallery stood a raised dais holding an ornately carved chair, cushioned in embroidered purple velvet. Behind the throne, the royal banner hung beside the sigil of the Brotherhood of Uthoni.

Alex swore softly again and started to turn back to the door. Something moved in the dimness below. I caught

Alex's arm and held my finger to my lips. We moved carefully back into the deep shadows along the back of the gallery.

King Fergus strode into the audience chamber and looked around. He went to the dais, but didn't mount it to sit on the small throne. Instead, he paced impatiently back and forth on the carpet in front of the dais. A moment later, High Priest Padreg entered through the hanging banners. Obviously the banners concealed another door into the chamber. Fergus turned swiftly, the elaborately embroidered hem of his houserobe swirling around his ankles.

"You're late," he said abruptly.

Padreg folded his hands into the voluminous sleeves of his grey robe and inclined his head politely. "I have been busy with my duties, Majesty," he said. "I came as soon as I received your summons."

"You've been very busy lately, haven't you, Padreg?" Fergus said, his tone coldly acerbic.

Again, Padreg inclined his head. "I do my best, Majesty."

"You certainly do." Fergus whirled, his houserobe billowing about him, and paced the length of the dais. He turned on Padreg. "You had Margan mac Debnor executed this morning."

"He was a traitor, Majesty."

"I gave strict orders he was to be released," Fergus said, his voice grating. "He was my man—in my pay."

"He was a traitor," Padreg repeated, his voice smooth as silk. "I dealt with him as a traitor should be dealt with."

Fergus paused before replying. His stiff posture radiated outrage and fury the way a fire radiates heat. "You *burned* him," he shouted. "You burned him with that unholy fire of yours."

"That fire is the holy retribution of Uthoni," Padreg

said softly. "It is a sacred trust Uthoni bestows upon his chosen."

"It is from the Abyss, and you know it."

"You would do well to guard your tongue, Majesty. Uthoni hears all."

"It's you who hears more than is good for you," Fergus said darkly. "You had no right to execute Margan as you did. He was my man. You had no right—"

"Majesty, you had not told me he was your man."

Fergus turned and slammed his fist down onto the arm of the small throne. "Must I tell you everything?" he demanded. "You have countermanded my orders too many times of late." He made a visible effort to control himself. He took a deep breath, looked up at the ceiling, then calmly turned to face Padreg again. "You have been taking a lot onto yourself lately, Priest. Perhaps you forget that I, and not you, am king?"

Padreg straightened in a strangely jerky movement, and something dully green, like a flash from a faceted peridot, sparked within his cowl. "You are king, yes," he said in a low, dangerous tone. "But without me, you would be nothing. Without me, you would still be only the heir, and this land would be swamped in witchery and the unclean magic of the foreigners and strangers."

Fergus's head came up with a snap. "What do you mean, without you I would still be only the heir?" He took a step toward Padreg. "My father died of a wasting sickness placed upon him by the Feyii. Didn't he, Priest? Didn't he?"

Padreg said nothing. But the acid green glint within his cowl seemed to become brighter, stronger.

Fergus went very still. "You did it," he whispered. "You killed my father, didn't you? You and that band of cowled demons you call your Brotherhood."

"Majesty, you—"

Fergus spun around, took a few running steps toward the door. "Guards!" he shouted.

The virulent green spark flared to brilliance. At the same time, Padreg brought his hands out of his sleeves. The ball of scorching fire that formed in the air above his raised hands seared my eyes. It rose, expanding, into the air, a haze of acrid smoke and crackling air surrounding it.

The ball of *chausey* sorcery exploded into bolts of lightning. They caught Fergus well before he gained the door of the chamber. They engulfed him, turning him into a fiery pillar of actinic brilliance. Not so much as a whimper escaped from the writhing column of fire.

In seconds, the glare died. A tumble of scorched bones clattered onto the polished tile of the floor. Even as they fell, they began to flake away until nothing was left but a small pile of fine, grey, powder.

Alex made a soft sound of horror and turned away, sagging against the wall of the back of the gallery, his hands clamped over his mouth to prevent any sound from escaping his lips. Padreg's use of the *chausey* sorcery set my nerves shrieking under my skin. Nausea clenched my belly into a painful knot, but I couldn't look away from the drift of ash that only seconds ago had been a living man—the King of Celyddon. I swallowed, forcing the bitter, bitter bile down out of the back of my throat.

Something behind Fergus moved. He turned and looked up as another man entered the chamber through the door he himself had used. The other man walked over to the pile of ash and stirred it with his foot.

"That was a rather silly thing to do, my lord Padreg," the man said, his tone mild, almost disinterested. "Whatever are we going to do for a king now?"

"I shall rule," Padreg said harshly. "I shall declare myself Bishop of Celyddon, and rule in place of the king."

Ann Marston

"That would be interesting." The man laughed, and I recognized the sardonic ring of the laughter.

The man was my cousin, Maelgrun.

Chapter Twenty-Three

I STARED DOWN at the two figures caught in the shadows below me. Chaotic thoughts rioted through my head. Padreg had murdered Fergus; Daryn was now king. He wouldn't have to lead a rebellion against his brother. Only against a renegade and murderous High Priest who wished to declare himself ruling Bishop of Celyddon.

But there was still the *chausey magic* against us. Daryn needed to know about this.

Alex caught my arm. In the dim light, his face was pale, his expression stricken. He gestured toward the door, but I waved him back and shook my head. I couldn't leave yet. I had to know what Padreg and Maelgrun would do. Alex leaned back against the wall again, looking ill, still stunned, and anxious to get away, but obviously unwilling to leave me to my own devices. I dropped to my knees so I could watch through the carved columns supporting the polished banister of the gallery. This way, I could see more with less chance of being seen myself.

Below, Padreg thrust his hands back into his sleeves and stepped up onto the dais. He didn't sit in the small throne, but stood in front of it as if he were considering trying it for size. Maelgrun stirred the pile of ashes again with the toe of his boot. He laughed again, then dropped to one knee, bent forward and blew at the pile. It scattered, dissipating into a soft cloud like the fine dust it was. Maelgrun climbed to his feet and turned to face Padreg.

"Poof!" he said, amusement in his tone. "And no more trace of Fergus. What now, Padreg? Whatever are you going to tell the Royal Council? This might be very difficult to explain."

I couldn't see Padreg's expression beneath the cowl of his robe. But his voice came out sounding harsh and grating. "Uthoni decreed Fergus had to die for treason."

Maelgrun laughed again and shook his head. "Treason?" The sarcasm in his tone, his mockery of the situation, was obvious. "Treason? Oh, come now, Padreg. How can a king commit treason against himself."

Padreg sat, letting his robes drape around his feet and legs. He put his hands on the arms of the throne, fingers tight around the ornately carved ends. He leaned back and stared at Maelgrun. The green glint flashed beneath his cowl.

"Then he committed blasphemy against Uthoni," he said calmly. "The Wrath of Uthoni is swift in retribution."

Maelgrun glanced down at the floor, then at Padreg on Fergus's throne. "That is as may be. But what makes you think the Royal Council will let you appoint yourself Bishop of Celyddon, or let you rule in Fergus's place?"

"I am High Priest. I have the power—"

"Yes, a priest. And no priest has ever ruled Celyddon. The Council will want a king."

"I am a Priest of Uthoni. I would not be king."

Maelgrun paused before answering, as if he were carefully considering his words. "But I would," he said softly. "I would be king."

Behind me, Alex drew in his breath sharply, but made no other sound. He dropped down and crawled across the gallery to kneel beside me, peering through the gaps in the ornately carved balusters.

Padreg leaned forward on the throne, his cowl still obscuring his face. The knuckles of his hands were pale as he gripped the arms of the chair.

"You?" Danger lurked in his silky voice. "You would be king? How could it be that you might think you could claim a throne?" He ran is hands along the polished and carved arms of the chair. "This throne, specifically."

"And why not? Have I not been your faithful servant all these years? Have I not been privy to every secret you and Fergus plotted? I know as much about governing this Realm as you do, certainly."

Padreg sat back, his hands again gripping the arms of the throne. When he spoke, his voice was cold and flat. "You overstep yourself, Maelgrun mac Durstan clan Rothsey."

"I? I, who have been your faithful servant, as well as your most talented student?" He raised one hand and opened it, palm held flat. A ball of the virulent *chausey* sorcery hardly bigger than a plover's egg danced above his hand. "I overstep myself?"

Padreg surged to his feet. "It was I whom Uthoni led to the vault where the old scrolls were hidden," he cried. "It was I who studied them day and night until I knew what they said. It was I who revived all the old powers in the name of Uthoni. And it was I whom Uthoni commanded to rule this realm in his name. You—" He made a dismissive gesture. "You are nothing compared to me."

The glaring sphere in Maelgrun's hand grew brighter, searing my eyes. Then he closed his hand and it disappeared.

"Padreg, if you believe it's Uthoni who gives you this power, then you're a greater fool than I took you for."

"You dare—" Padreg cried. "You *dare* to call me a fool?"

Maelgrun approached the throne, each step measured and firm. He stopped well before the step up to the dais, though. "I call you a fool because you *are* a fool. I was the student and you were the master. But you never realized what was happening. You never so much as suspected how strong I was becoming. You still have no idea that *I* am now the master, and you—you are less than a student. No student could be such a fool as you."

"I warn you. You tread dangerous ground."

"No, Padreg." Maelgrun drew himself up to his full height. He seemed taller and broader than I remembered. "You're the one treading dangerous ground. I have more strength than you. I have taken my father's blood and pain and my mother's blood and terror, and traded it for power you never dreamed of. Kin-blood, Padreg. You're the one who told me kin-blood makes the most potent power of all."

Padreg screamed in rage. The cloud of *chausey* sorcery appeared fully formed above him. But Maelgrun had already formed his own sphere of the searing green fire. It met Padreg's only a few feet from Padreg's body.

For one shrieking moment, the whole room seemed to explode into brilliant soears of green lightning. The air boiled and bubbled, hissing and popping. Every hair on my body stood up straight. Had I not clapped both hands over my mouth, I would have sobbed aloud with the terror that shook me as a terrier shakes a rat. Beside me, Alex slumped, head down, shoulders heaving, his hands covering his face.

The combined sorceries writhed together for a moment, then slowly, inexorably moved toward Padreg. He howled in terror and tried to run. But he had forgotten about the throne behind him. He fell back into it. For a moment, he tried to ward off the hissing, bubbling bolts of *chausey* sorcery with his raised hands. They settled around him, twisting and writhing, wrapping his contorted body in that terrible glare.

It was over almost before it began. The flare subsided as quickly and completely as a candle blown by a gale. Padreg's crumbling bones clattered briefly on the carpet in front of the throne, then flaked into powder and vanished.

I was on my feet, dragging Alex with me toward the small door, even as the air currents in the audience chamber swirled Padreg's ashes into a smudge of grey. We came out into the empty corridor, both us choking and gagging.

"Stairway down," I gasped. "Which door?"

He took a deep breath, recovering his wits with an effort. He pointed to the next door down. "There," he said. "I only missed by one."

We were halfway down the staircase when Maelgrun found me. For a moment, I thought I had been shot in the head by a crossbow quarrel. I staggered, pain tearing through my skull. I had to catch myself with both hands against the wall to prevent myself from tumbling headfirst down the stairs. It seemed as if Maelgrun's face, eyes a malevolent, poisonous green, hung in the air before me.

"Well, well, well." His voice rang in my head. *"If it isn't Cousin Iain right here in the city."*

It was a moment before I realized that I was hearing

him the same way I heard Glyn when we Communicated. Maelgrun wasn't really there in front of me. He was still back in the audience chamber.

I put my hands up to my head and tried to clear away the pain. Then quickly, as I had shut Glyn out that night I thought Geordie had been killed, I shut Maelgrun out of my mind. But not before I saw in him his lack of knowledge of my exact location. And not before he took from me the fact that I knew what he had done.

As surely as I knew my own name, I knew that he would find me again. And he would be able to see through my own eyes to discover where I was. Even now, I could feel him Casting for me. His Searching flowed across my awareness like a sticky tide of rancid oil. I shut my mind tighter as Alex and I flew down the stairs.

Maelgrun stopped Casting. For a moment, I thought he had given up. Then I knew he merely stopped while he gathered a troop of Guardsmen. I couldn't keep my mind shut to him forever. I would tire, then he would find me, and lead the Guardsmen straight to me.

Before that happened, I had to tell Daryn what had happened, and make sure Bronwyn and Holly were well out of danger.

The door at the bottom of the stairway opened onto a narrow corridor. No hangings softened the stone walls, and the floor was uncarpeted tile. Alex shut the stairway door behind us and drew himself up, straightening the unfamiliar uniform. Then we strolled along the corridor, trying to look as innocuous as possible.

"Kitchens are that way," he said, pointing. "I didn't think anyone would look for us down here."

He was right. We passed casually through the kitchens. The servants there ignored us completely. They were fully occupied in preparing the evening meal. Alex knew the way. He turned right as we passed the scullery and led us out a small door into a small, neat kitchen garden.

The air smelled fresh, redolent of the nearby sea and the herbs in the garden. A small gate in the low stone wall at the bottom of the garden took us through to the stable-yard, then out onto the street at the side of the palace.

We rounded the corner, putting the palace out of sight behind us, and Alex let out a long, pent-up breath, nearly sagging in his relief. "I thought for sure we were two dead men there," he said. "I'm surprised to find myself alive."

"We might yet be dead men," I said. I got my bearings and turned toward the Cauldron and Gaerd's tavern. "We must hurry. Maelgrun will follow us if he can."

I held tightly to my concentration, blocking Maelgrun out of my mind. Even now, the foetid touch of his Searching slid over me like swamp mud. I hardly allowed myself to worry about Bronwyn and Holly. Alex and I had heard no uproar to indicate escaped prisoners had been seen. I contented myself with that small seed of comfort.

The narrow, crooked little streets of the Cauldron were closer to the palace than I remembered. I took one wrong turning, but found my way again. The sun had begun its slow slide to dive into the sea by the time I led Alex to Gaerd's tavern.

Gaerd met us at the door with an affable smile and expansive gestures. But his eyes were pinched small with worry and concern.

"Welcome, welcome, my lords," he said, bowing us into the common room. "Your friends are here already. Upstairs in their room. They asked that you join them as soon as you arrived."

Glyn opened the door to my knock. Relief made his

face go slack for an instant, then he grinned. "You're late," he said.

"We were unavoidably delayed," I said.

'We were worried. Padreg used his *chausey magic* again—"

"I know. I'll tell you about it in a minute."

Holly sat on the bed beside Bronwyn. She looked up as I entered. I crossed the room and sat beside her, taking her into my arms. She fit against me as if we had been made only for each other—two pieces of a matched set. We had no need of words. It was enough to be close to her, to know she was safe.

"How is Bronwyn?" I asked.

"No change," Holly said. "I've done what I can for her poor feet and her hands. But she'll need far more than I can give her."

"We'll get her to Lysandia," Glyn said. "Feyish Healers can help her. They'll Heal her flesh, then they'll help her heal her mind. I promise you, Holly. She'll be Bronwyn again." He glanced at me. "Iain, the wards are down. Can't you feel it?"

I hadn't. Not until he mentioned it. But it stood to reason. Padreg had raised the wards, and now Padreg was dead. The wards would fall when he did.

Alex made sure the door was locked, then turned to Daryn and went down on one knee. "My lord, I have dire news," he said. "Your brother Fergus is dead."

Daryn stiffened in shock. "Dead?" he repeated. "How can that be? What happened?"

"Padreg," Alex said. "He slew him using that accursed Wrath of Uthoni."

"I felt it," Glyn said softly. "I had hoped I was mistaken, but I thought he'd used it against you two. I felt it twice."

"The second time was Maelgrun, using it against

Padreg," I said. It was difficult to speak and hold my mind shut against Maelgrun. "He's very strong now. He would have himself declared king."

"Not while I live," Daryn said softly. He looked at Glyn, his eyes widening. "I'm king now," he said. "Or more correctly, Regent Prince. I rule Celyddon. And as ruler, I hereby make formal application to the Watch to deal with this Abyss-spawned *chausey magic*."

Glyn hesitated, then closed his eyes. I sensed his flash of Communication. "So noted and passed to Lysandia, Majesty," he said formally.

"We have to get Holly and Bronwyn out of here," I said. Maelgrun's Searching beat hard against me. Holding my mind shut to him was akin to holding window shutters closed against a spring gale.

"We've arranged a boat," Glyn said. "Gaerd has a trusted man who has a fisherboat. The captain will take us north to Borland's Foot to meet the Outship."

"Even now, Gaerd has a small boat beneath the tavern waiting to take us out to our rendezvous," Daryn said. "We were only waiting for you to return."

Pain thumped through my head hard enough to blur my vision. "I can't go with you," I said hoarsely.

Holly put her hand to my cheek. "What's the matter, Iain?" she demanded, alarmed. "You're pale as milk."

"It's Maelgrun," I said with an effort. "He's trying to find us. I can hold him out for a while longer, but if I go with you, he'll know where you are, and he'll send men to kill everyone. I'll have to lead him elsewhere while you get away."

Glyn frowned. "He's Searching, is he?" he asked.

I could not speak. I nodded.

"Right, then," Glyn said briskly. "Daryn, you and Alex take Bronwyn and Holly. Gaerd has the rowboat hidden under the tavern. He'll see you safely out to the fisherboat. You know where the Outship will be. They'll be expecting you."

Holly bent to wrap a blanket around Bronwyn's unresisting figure. She straightened up and turned to Glyn. "You take her, Glyn," she said quietly. "I'm going to stay with Iain."

"No, you won't," Glyn said. "You'll go with Daryn and Alex. Bronwyn needs a trained medician with her."

Holly started to protest, but Glyn cut her off. "No," he said again. "You go with Bronwyn. I'm going to stay with Iain." He gave me a crooked grin. "You didn't abandon me when I needed help. The Watch looks after its own."

Daryn carried Bronwyn down the stairs to the common room. The three men drinking ale in the corner by the hearth deliberately turned their backs to ignore us as we moved through into the kitchens. Gaerd, red of face and puffing like a wind-broken horse, pulled up a trap door in the floor. A short ladder led down to a small square of floating dock where a little unpainted dory lay bobbing on the oily water. The dory was barely big enough to hold four people. Alex unshipped the oars and fitted them into the oarlocks. The last rays of the sinking sun sent long, sinuous shadows flickering across the water.

"Remember," Gaerd said breathlessly. "The blue fisherboat with the white stripe at the plimsol line. It's anchored by itself to the north of the main pier."

"Blue fisherboat, white stripe," Daryn said. "I'll remember. Thank you, Gaerd. Your service won't be forgotten."

Holly settled onto the thwart in the stern. She held Bronwyn against her, bundled in the blanket andlooked up at me across Bronwyn's bright hair. "Be very careful, Iain," she said softly.

"We'll take the overland route to Eryndor north of

Borland's Foot," Glyn said with a confidence I couldn't share. "Good speed to you."

Alex nodded to us, then put his back into his rowing. With only the faintest splashing as the oars dipped into the oily water, the little dory slid smoothly out from under the tavern and disappeared into the gloom of twilight.

Glyn and I went to the stables. Gaerd's boy had already saddled our horses. We mounted and went swiftly through the streets of Dundregan until we had put the Cauldron far behind us. We paused in sight of the north City Gate. It was almost deserted. The guards had not yet closed the gate for the night, but were preparing to shut it.

"Will we need a pass to leave the City?" My lips felt stiff, my tongue like a stick of wood.

"I don't know," Glyn replied. "I propose that we don't stop to ask." He gathered his reins. "Ready?"

I nodded.

"Then let's go." Glyn put his heels to the flanks of his horse. It leapt forward, springing into a gallop. I was only seconds behind. We burst past the startled guards, and were through the gate and out onto the road leading north before they could so much as shout.

I relaxed and let my mind open to Maelgrun. I didn't have to pretend to be near exhaustion. Once again, a vision of his crimson-gleaming eyes hung in the air before my face. His triumph flooded through me.

"*Now I have you,*" he crowed. "*You're mine, Iain mac Drew. Mine.*"

Chapter Twenty-Four

WE RAN FOR the Crags, for the ridge of broken granite that reached down to join the rugged outcropping of basalt that was Borland's Foot. Great, soaring cliffs and spires rose to dizzying heights with hardly any transition between the rock and the gentle alluvial plain. Farmland stretched for three leagues from Dundregan, then abruptly became steeply rising rock.

By first light come morning, Glyn and I were well into the rise of the Crags a little more than ten leagues from Dundregan, when I looked behind to see a troop of sheriffmen riding hard in pursuit. I had been expecting them, but not quite so quickly. Maelgrun's Searching still rode my shoulder like a carrion crow, but I hadn't thought he could come after us so soon. Borland's Foot was still only a faint irregularity on the northern horizon, some three leagues distant.

"They've seen us," Glyn shouted over the pounding of the horses' hooves against the hard surface of the track.

Almost at the same time, I felt Maelgrun's presence recede, as if he, too, had caught sight of us and no longer had to cling to my mind like a leech. It was if a great weight had lifted from my shoulders. For the first time since leaving the palace, my head was clear. The pain was gone, and with it the clenched nausea.

We had been holding the horses to a slow canter to husband their strength. The troop of sheriffmen behind us showed no such restraint. We kicked our horses to a gallop and bent low over the pommel of our saddles. I didn't have to tell Glyn that we were too far from Borland's Foot. We were not going to gain the safety of the Eryndor border before the sheriffmen caught up with us. But we might gain another league....

Something zinged past my ear with a fluttering hiss. A crossbow quarrel. I swore and ducked closer to the neck of my horse. Whoever had loosed that quarrel was either a far better shot than he had any right to be, shooting from the back of a galloping horse, or he was the luckiest crossbow archer in Celyddon.

Beside me, Glyn rode bent as low as I, his face grim and set. The left shoulder of his shirt turned suddenly red with a bright spatter of blood. The quarrel missed his throat by no more than a mere finger's breadth. His horse staggered slightly as he flinched at the pain, but he kept his seat and the horse regained its smooth stride a length or two behind me.

I snatched a glance over my shoulder. The sheriffmen had gained several lengths on us. I couldn't see him, but I knew Maelgrun rode with them. His breathless excitement, his anger, his urgent need for vengeance, burned strongly in my mind.

That glance over my shoulder was a mistake, and I paid dearly for it. I should have been paying attention to where my horse was going. It put a foot wrong, stumbled, and nearly unseated me as it slowed to catch its footing. I brought it back into hand, but the stumble had given someone a clear shot at me. The quarrel caught me just above the hip bone and sank deeply into the soft tissues of my back. I went sprawling to the ground in agony.

Glyn didn't even check his horse's stride. As he passed, he bent down and scooped me off the ground. He tossed me in front of him on the saddle. He held me tightly, his hand gripping the fabric of my tunic near my upper arm, his fingers slippery with my blood, and his own from the wound in his shoulder.

"Hang on," he shouted. He turned his horse and spurred it for the shelter of a tumble of rock well off the side of the track. Broken rock littered the ground among clumps of thornbush. Dangerous ground to take horses over. Why Glyn's horse didn't break its leg, I'll never know. Behind us, the troop of sheriffmen slowed their horses cautiously.

A crossbow quarrel took the horse in the throat. Glyn kicked loose of his stirrups as the horse fell, taking me with it. I landed rolling. Sudden, unbelievable pain tore through me as the crossbow quarrel caught against the rough ground. I nearly lost consciousness.

Through the mist of pain, I saw Glyn land on his feet and stagger for balance He straightened then snatched me up as he ran. He got one of my arms around his shoulder, gripping tightly to my wrist. He snugged his other arm around my waist and half carried, half dragged me behind a low ridge of rock below the overhang of the cliff. I wasn't much help, still lost in the red mist of pain that threatened to stop both my breath and my heart.

The rock bulged above us, looking as if it were ready to tip forward and come crashing down at any moment.

It wasn't much protection, but it might be enough. The sheriffmen might not have seen exactly where we went.

Glyn sank to his knees in the dust behind the rocks and let me slide from his shoulder. We were trapped now, the sheer cliff against our back, the sheriffmen ahead.

Glyn knelt beside me in the gravel under the overhang of the crag. He ripped off his tunic and tore the fabric into wide strips. Working quickly and competently, he bound up the torn and ragged wound in my back, securing the bandage with firm knots.

"It would be handy if you had the Gift of Sorting," he muttered as he worked. "Then you could at least make sure the bleeding stopped."

"Is it bad?" I gasped. I could feel nothing now except nausea and a clammy chill on my face and chest. My back, my side and my leg to the knee were cold and numb. I began to shiver, a hard, juddering quiver in my belly and chest.

"Bad enough," he said. He finished tying off the bandage and sat back. "That fall you took from the horse ripped the quarrel loose, and I don't know what it tore up inside. That's the best I can do for now. I hope that stops the bleeding. If it doesn't, I'll have to try Holding, but that might knock you out."

"I can't feel a thing there," I said. "I can't tell if it's bleeding or not. It doesn't hurt now, though..." That could be a very bad sign. Men died of wounds they couldn't feel. I took a deep breath and got the shivering under control at last. I hoped he hadn't noticed it.

He grunted noncommittally. He had seen but chose not to mention it. "If we can get out of this, you'll mend well enough, I think."

"It would seem that we'll not get out of this one," I said, too dizzy to really care much. "Let me see your shoulder."

He shook his head, then pulled aside the collar of his shirt so he could look at his wound. "It's only a scratch. The skin is cut, but that's all. The quarrel only grazed me. It's already stopped bleeding. That sheriffman was a rotten shot."

"Not so bad," I said with an attempt at a smile. "He was shooting from a galloping horse. Could you do as well?"

He grinned ruefully but said nothing.

Beyond the low ridge of rock, the troop of sheriffmen milled irresolutely out of bowshot range. The sound of their horses' hooves on the rock swelled, then faded again as they pulled back. For a moment, I couldn't understand why they were pulling back, then realized they didn't know if we were armed. They were taking no unnecessary chances.

"What are they doing?" I asked.

Glyn snatched a quick glance over the rocks. "Just standing there, holding their crossbows," he said. "There are nearly a score of sheriffmen out there. Your cousin is with them."

"I know. Come for the kill. He wants my blood."

Glyn shuddered. "Filthy *chausey magic*," he murmured and shook his head. "I don't think they're sure where we are. They're deciding how to get us out." One of his hands clenched into a fist. "We could use a few crossbows ourselves."

"Where's the Out-ship?" I asked.

He glanced up and I sensed the swift, flashing thread of Communication between him and the Out-ship. "They're anchored just north of the Foot," he said. "Captain shanGreyl says he could have a patrol of the Watch here in a few hours. He's asking if we can hold on.

I've told him the point is highly debatable. I'm sorry I got you into all this in the first place, Iain."

"I believe I got you into this one," I said and managed a faint smile. "Am I still bleeding?"

"Just a little now, I think. Does it hurt much?"

"No. Just numb all across my back. What are the sheriffmen doing?"

He peered cautiously over the rocks again. "Getting ready to scour the place for us, I think," he said. "They look rather annoyed. Wait a moment. Your cousin has come forward." He paused, then swore vehemently. "*Chausey magic.* Dear Mother of All. He's going to use the *chausey magic.*"

I laughed breathlessly. "Can it come around corners?" I asked.

He glanced down at me. "Remember what it did to the Captain's Gig Ydonda and I tried to bring ashore," he said quietly.

I shivered. "All he'll have to do is hit the cliff above us," I said. "That should bring a hundred-foot cairn down on top of us. A fitting monument—"

"Iain, could you Still them from here?" he asked. "Have you any idea what your range might be?"

I raised myself painfully to glance over the top of the ridge. The sheriffmen stood in a cluster around Maelgrun. Maelgrun stood with his legs wide, feet planted firmly on the uneven rock. Above his raised hands glowed a bright, searing ball of poison green flame.

I triggered the Gift. Several of the sheriffmen in the front rank froze into immobility. But Maelgrun remained unaffected. I felt the Stilling impulse hit him, then I staggered as he repulsed it, sweeping it aside as if it were nothing more than a bothersome gnat.

"I can't do it," I muttered, my breath coming in gasps. "He's shielded against it or something."

He nodded. "I was afraid of that," he said. "But it would have been so handy if you could Still him."

He glanced to the right, north along the base of the cliff. The low ridge of rock we lay behind ran parallel to the rock face for nearly three hundred paces until it dissipated and flattened, then merged with the cliff itself. From there, it was only a matter of a pace or two to a fissure in the rock that could hide us more easily and safely.

"Iain," he said thoughtfully, "d'ye think you could make it up there if I helped you?"

I followed the direction of his gaze. "I don't know."

"It might be worth a try."

Maelgrun gestured at the globe of *chausey* sorcery. The very texture of the air shivered as the blinding shower of burning, raw lightning splashed against the rock wall about fifty feet up and a hundred paces beyond us to the left. It slagged the stone overhead. Shards of rock exploded out from the cliff and tumbled down into the narrow valley. Tons and tons of jagged, splintered boulders, some of them still glowing and half molten. They rebounded down the slope in a huge cloud of dust and steam that slowly drifted toward us. Clumps of grass caught fire and burned fiercely, sizzling and hissing and spitting sparks. Glyn made a startled exclamation and ducked back.

"The next one will have us," he said. He scrambled to his feet, crouching low. "Let's get out of here." He hoisted me to my feet. The movement caused a burst of pain to explode in my back, and I cried out.

Maelgrun loosed another cloud of balefire. The exploding bolts hit just about where the ridge and the base of the cliff merged, only thirty feet or so up the cliff. Part of the slag and molten rock splashed down into the gap between the ridge and the cliff, obliterating all traces of the narrow cleft. The rest of it boiled down into the valley itself. The loose scree shuddered under the new weight and gave way. The spill of rock sagged like wet clay and slumped forward to fill the northern end of the valley. Maelgrun couldn't have blocked our way of escape any more effectively than that.

"Now that's bluidy torn it," Glyn said. He dropped to his knees and eased me back down onto the ground.

The next eruption was close enough to rain small fragments of half-molten rock down on top of us. Several landed on my cheek and arm and I cried out with the searing pain. Glyn swore vehemently and colourfully, and slapped at the burning embers on his thigh.

That pain did something to me. It didn't burn. It was like the intense, absolute cold of the deepest sea, and it seeped into me like oil into a wick. It spread through me, filling me, then turned to icy rage. It built and grew, possessing me completely. I began to tremble in anger, at first only slightly, then violently until my whole body vibrated with it. I looked at Glyn, saw he was in Communication with the Out-ship.

"Stay in Communication," I shouted. Maelgrun conjoured another seething cloud of horror and let it burst. The rock above us exploded. I lunged for Glyn, grabbed him around the chest, and plunged deep into his mind, traced back along his line of Communication.

I could use my Talent to get him out of here. Shifting, he'd called it. I could Shift him to the Out-ship and at least he'd get out of this alive even if I didn't. But first, I had to know where the Out-ship was. Frantically, I tracked back along the slender silver thread of his Communication.

There.... There was the Out-ship. I knew its exact position. I felt Glyn's startled shock as the wall of rock above us began to tip. The shattered rock seemed to hesitate, wavering in the air for an endless instant, then burst straight out and away from us. It shot down the slope, rumbling like thunder, a flooding tide of half-molten rock and slag that poured down to engulf the knot of Stilled sheriffmen.

And Maelgrun, too. I heard his scream of terror. It rose shrilly into the quivering air, then cut of as sharply and suddenly as if it had been cut with a dagger.

I didn't realize I'd triggered that Shifting impulse. It must have been an instinctive reflex. All I cared about was that I'd found the Out-ship.

"Don't break Communication!" I shouted again. A glowing red rock the size of my head landed with a hissing crack only inches from my feet. The rest of the cliff was going to come down on our heads any second.

But I couldn't find the trigger to send Glyn out. Instead, I found that deeply buried Talent of his—found it and slammed into it with all my strength, all my concentration, all my intensity. It wasn't what I had intended to do, but I desperately hoped it would work.

I don't know what I did. All I know is that I did *something*. But one instant, we were there among the rocks, then there was a roaring in my ears and a great white sheet of flame exploded behind my eyes. The next instant, I was lying on the deck of the Out-ship, my arms still clutched tight around Glyn's chest, and a man wearing three thick gold stripes on the sleeve of his tunic was staring at us in complete astonishment.

The roaring in my ears grew louder. If Glyn said anything, or if the officer replied, I didn't hear it. I lost consciousness.

Much later, I awoke in a bed to find a Feyish woman wearing a lot of gold braid looking down at me. I was in no pain, but I felt as if I was no longer firmly attached to my body. It was an odd sensation, but I couldn't find the energy to be concerned about it.

The woman with the gold braid smiled at me. "How are you feeling, son?" she asked.

"I don't know," I answered truthfully.

She smiled again. "I'm Commander shielCarn," she said. "You're in a hospital in Lysandia. You're going to be just fine in a little while. There's no permanent damage."

"Glyn?"

"He's fine, too. You've got a highly unusual Talent, Iain. That's the first time I've ever heard of anyone Travelling and taking someone else with him. Do you remember how you did it?"

"I didn't do it. Glyn did it."

"Patroller shanBreyor did it?"

I tried to nod, but it hurt. "Yes. It was his Talent. He had it all the time, but it's a Deep Talent." I had taken the phrase from Glyn when we were in deep Communication. "All I did was trigger it. I didn't think I could go with him, but I did."

"How did you trigger it?"

"I don't know. I didn't even know I could do it until I did it." I was groggy with the drugs, but I picked the word out of her mind. *Enabler.* My second Talent. Rare, but not unique; Commander shielCarn possessed the same Talent herself.

She smiled at me. "Well, you'll remember in time. Once you do, you can tell us how you did it."

"Yes, ma'am."

"Get some rest now. We'll be talking again later when you're feeling more up to it."

As she turned to leave, I thought of something very important and called her back. "Ma'am?"

She turned back to me. "Yes?"

"Is there some way you can get a message to someone back in Celyddon?"

"It's a devious method, but we can do it."

"I need to let Holly know Glyn and I are all right," I said. "Things got a bit spectacular back there for a little while. She probably thinks we're under several tons of rock and slag."

She smiled. "Why don't you tell her yourself?" she asked.

She stepped out of the room, smiling, and held the door open. Holly came in.

Epilogue

I healed, and so did Glyn. The Watch sent him on another assignment, and sent me into training, where I began to understand the proper use of the Gifts and Talents I had been born with. It was a long and arduous training course, but for the first time in my life, I felt that I had found my place.

The Feyish Healers offered Holly the chance to work with Feyish Holders and Sorters as she finished her apprenticeship to be a fully qualified medician. I knew she wanted to return to Celyddon, but she simply could not turn down a chance like that—not after the tantalizing taste she had received working on Ydonda.

Bronwyn healed slowly under the care of the Feyish Healers. They mended her body, slowly rebuilding her crushed feet, her twisted and broken fingers. Mending her mind after the horror of what her own son had done to her took longer. Holly stayed as much to be with Bronwyn, I think, as to take advantage of the chance to work with Feyish Holders and Sorters.

As a wounded living body needs time to heal and cannot be mended in one day, so does a shattered realm need time to heal. Back in Celyddon, Daryn worked slowly and carefully to put his torn and bleeding Realm back together. With the help of the Watch, Daryn rooted out the last of the *chausey* sorcery. And to aid him with his Kingdom, he had the help of good men like Keagan mac Brys, and Bevan mac Clintlagh, and Durstan mac Lludd.

King Daryn walked a fine line to keep his kingdom intact and at the same time see that justice was done properly. He took great pains not to let those who cried for vengeance have their way, yet making sure the worst of the oppressors were punished suitably. If a civil war might set brother against brother, neighbour against neighbour, spilling bitterness that lasted a hundred years and more, so too could a rampage of revenge.

The day came when Bronwyn was pronounced fully healed. She was the same woman I had always known— or at least nearly so. A new sadness lurked in her eyes for the son she had lost, but the horror of it no longer haunted her dreams. I came to the Outport to see her off when she took ship to return to Dundregan to be at Durstan's side as he helped Daryn rebuild Celyddon.

That should have been the end of it. But there was a postscript. I returned from an assignment at sea to find orders waiting for me to report to Watch Headquarters. A junior page escorted me to Commander shielCarn's office.

She regarded me with a critical eye as I entered. "I have

a new assignment for you, Patroller mac Drew," she said. She picked up a parchment from her desk and scanned it quickly. "I've a request here for two or three Members for a ground-side assignment. I think it might suit you."

"I'd rather serve at sea," I said.

"I'm sure you would," she said and smiled.

I hesitated.

"But go and speak with the Patrol Commander about it," she went on. "You can let me know your decision later. He's waiting for you in the recreation hall."

My reflection kept pace with me as I walked quickly down the mirrored corridor to the recreation hall. I heard the click and whir of billiard balls as I entered. There was only one man there, bent over the green baize table, a cue stick in his hands. He made his stroke. The cue ball skittered and clicked against one of the coloured balls, which shot across the table, caromed off the sides twice, and dropped neatly into a corner pocket.

"Irrefutable evidence of a misspent youth," Glyn shanBreyor said in satisfaction. He turned and sat on the edge of the table, one leg swinging idly. He folded his arms across his chest and grinned at me. He wore the insignia of a Patrol Commander on the shoulder of his tunic, but the lazy smile had not changed at all.

"I'd say they've gone and made a creditable Member out of you, Iain," he said by way of greeting.

I laughed and stepped forward to grasp his outstretched hand. "They must have misfiled your record if they gave you a promotion," I said. "It's good to see you again, Glyn."

"Do you feel like helping me in a ground-side assignment?" he asked. "I think I can promise you it won't be as exciting as the last time we worked together."

"That gave me enough excitement to last more than a lifetime. What's the assignment?"

"Opening of a Watch office in a newly opened Outport. They want someone who's familiar with the language and the customs. It seems you and I are the only Celyddonians the Watch happens to have in captivity right now. Interested?"

"Back to Celyddon?" I repeated blankly.

"As ever was. And by way of inducement, I've already spoken with Holly. She says she can be packed in three days."

I smiled. It would be a fine thing to go back to Celyddon. There were people there I wanted to see again—needed to see again. As much as I loved the Outside and the Wildesea, Celyddon was home. With this assignment, I could have both. Oh, yes. A very fine thing, indeed.

Glyn and I walked together down the corridor toward Commander shielCarn's office. As we passed through the long mirrored wall outside the recreation hall, I caught a glimpse of myself and paused to look. The midnight blue and silver of the uniform suited me well enough, but it was my eyes that caught and held my attention.

Like Glyn's eyes—like my father's eyes—my own were now the vivid, intense eyes of the Outsider.

About the Author

Ann Marston has worked as a teacher, a flight instructor, an airline pilot, airport manager and literacy coordinator, and several other odd and assorted careers in between. While maintaining this weird schedule, she has also been writing most of her adult life.

Together with her friend Barb Galler-Smith, she teaches writing fantasy at Grant McEwan University in Edmonton, and mentors up-and-coming writers in a writers' group that grew out of the writing classes. She lives in Edmonton with her daughter and their floppy eared dog.

Books by Five Rivers

NON-FICTION

FICTION

CAT'S PAWN, BY Leslie Gadallah
GROWING UP BRONX, by H.A. Hargreaves
NORTH BY 2000+, a collection of short, speculative fiction, by H.A.
  Hargreaves
A SUBTLE THING, by Alicia Hendley
SID RAFFERTY THRILLERS, by Matt Hughes
  DOWNSHIFT
  OLD GROWTH
THE TATTOOED WITCH Trilogy, by Susan MacGregor
  THE TATTOOED WITCH
  THE TATTOOED SEER
  THE TATTOOED QUEEN
THE RUNE BLADES of Celi, by Ann Marston
  KINGMAKER'S SWORD, BOOK 1
  WESTERN KING, BOOK 2
  BROKEN BLADE, BOOK 3
  CLOUDBEARER'S SHADOW, BOOK 4
  KING OF SHADOWS, Book 5
  SWORD AND SHADOW, Book 6
A STILL AND Bitter Grave, by Ann Marston
INDIGO TIME, BY Sally McBride
WASPS AT THE Speed of Sound, by Derryl Murphy
A QUIET PLACE, by J.W. Schnarr
THINGS FALLING APART, by J.W. Schnarr
AND THE ANGELS Sang: a collection of short speculative fiction, by
  Lorina Stephens
FROM MOUNTAINS OF Ice, by Lorina Stephens
MEMORIES, MOTHER AND a Christmas Addiction, by Lorina Stephens
SHADOW SONG, BY Lorina Stephens
THE MERMAID'S TALE, by D. G. Valdron

YA FICTION

MY LIFE AS a Troll, by Susan Bohnet
EYE OF STRIFE, by Dave Duncan
IVOR OF GLENBROCH, by Dave Duncan
  THE RUNNER AND the Wizard
  THE RUNNER AND the Saint
  THE RUNNER AND the Kelpie
TYPE, BY ALICIA Hendley
TYPE 2, BY Alicia Hendley
TOWER IN THE Crooked Wood, by Paula Johanson
A TOUCH OF Poison, by Aaron Kite
THE GREAT SKY, by D.G. Laderoute

OUT OF TIME, by D.G. Laderoute
HAWK, BY MARIE Powell

YA NON-FICTION

THE PRIME MINISTERS of Canada Series:

SIR JOHN A. Macdonald
ALEXANDER MACKENZIE
SIR JOHN ABBOTT
SIR JOHN THOMPSON
SIR MACKENZIE BOWELL
SIR CHARLES TUPPER
SIR WILFRED LAURIER
SIR ROBERT BORDEN
ARTHUR MEIGHEN
WILLIAM LYON MACKENZIE King
R. B. BENNETT
LOUIS ST. LAURENT
JOHN DIEFENBAKER
LESTER B. PEARSON
PIERRE TRUDEAU
JOE CLARK
JOHN TURNER
BRIAN MULRONEY
KIM CAMPBELL
JEAN CHRETIEN
PAUL MARTIN

WWW.FIVERIVERSPUBLISHING.COM

THE GREAT SKY
D.G. LADEROUTE

The Great Sky
ISBN 9781927400999
eISBN 9781988274003
by D.G. Laderoute
Trade Paperback 6 x 9
August 1, 2016

**The first time Piper Preach died he was ten years old.
But the Anishnaabe spirits thought otherwise.**

Now, six year later, Piper struggles with the hard realities of life in a big city. The ancient ways of his people are a distant memory. But the spirits aren't done with him.

Pulled into their bizarre world, the place the Anishnaabe call The Great Sky, he's plunged into the middle of a brutal war raging just a step away from reality. And this time there may be no escaping death – or even worse.

The Adventures of Ivor
ISBN 9781927400890
eISBN 9781927400906
by Dave Duncan
Trade Paperback 6 x 9
June 1, 2015

The Adventures of Ivor brings together three of his young adult novellas into one convenient omnibus edition.

At sixteen, Ivor of Bracken is too young to be a swordsman like his nine older brothers, but he has strong legs and a fine memory, so he can serve his lord as a runner, carrying messages. That sounds safe enough, except that this is Dark Age Scotland. Dangerous outlaws and sinister old gods still roam the glens. Fortunately Ivor is a survivor—but sometimes only just!

Dave Duncan is the award-winning author of over 50 novels, and an inductee in the Canadian Science Fiction and Fantasy Hall of Fame.

Recommended a great story to immerse yourself in.

Goodreads

The writing is tight, the characters are believable, and the storyline is interesting.

LibraryThing

𝔗ype
ISBN 9781927400296
eISBN 9781927400302
by Alicia Hendley
Trade Paperback 6 x 9
June 1, 2013

After the fallout from the Social Media Era, when rates of divorce, crime, and mental illness were sky-rocketing, civilization was at its breaking point.

As a result, prominent psychologists from around the globe gathered together to try to regain social order through scientific means.

Their solution? Widespread implementation of Myers-Briggs personality typing, with each citizen assessed at the age of twelve and then sent to one of sixteen Home Schools in order to receive the appropriate education for their Type and aided in choosing a suitable occupation and life partner.

North American society becomes structured around the tenets of Typology, with governments replaced by The Association of Psychologists. With social order seemingly regained, what could go possibly wrong?

The writing is great, the pace is perfect and the book is addictive! I am anxious to read book #2 and I feel lucky to be given the chance to read and review it for free. If you liked Divergent you're gonna want to check this one out.

Goodreads

CPSIA information can be obtained
at www.ICGtesting.com
Printed in the USA
LVOW10s0831050517
532969LV00001B/1/P